THE WORLD IN THE EVENING
Christopher Isherwood

A subconsciously willed accident acts as a turning-point in Stephen Monk's life. A broken thigh dictates a ten-weeks' rest, but during this time his mind has no peace, and after a period of acute self-analysis he comes to realise the truth about his own motives and relationships.

CHRISTOPHER ISHERWOOD

The World
in the Evening

WHITE LION PUBLISHERS
London and New York

First published in the United Kingdom by
Methuen & Co. Ltd., 1954

This White Lion edition 1973

SBN 85617 484 X

Printed in Great Britain by
Biddles Ltd., Guildford, Surrey,
for White Lion Publishers,
138 Park Lane, London W1Y 3DD

TO
DODIE AND ALEC BEESLEY

Contents

PART ONE

AN END

ONE

THE party, that evening, was at the Novotnys'. They lived high up on the slopes of the Hollywood hills, in a ranch-style home complete with Early American maple, nautical brasswork and muslin curtains; just too cute for words. It looked as if it had been delivered, all ready equipped, from a store; and you could imagine how, if the payments weren't kept up, some men might arrive one day and take the whole place back there on a truck, along with Mrs. Novotny, the three children, the two cars and the cocker spaniel. Most of the houses Jane and I visited were like that.

It was quite late already and several people were drunk; not acting badly, just boastful and loud and thick-voiced. I was about halfway; which was the best way for me to be. As long as I was sober, I sulked. If I went on drinking, I was apt to turn nasty and say something embarrassing, or else fall asleep and snore. Jane was always worried about that, and yet she never could tear herself away until the end. 'Why in hell don't you go on back home, if you're so bored,' she sometimes whispered to me furiously, 'instead of drooping around like a Goddam martyr? What's the matter? Afraid I might do something *you* wouldn't do?' I used to grin at her without answering. That was exactly how I wanted her to feel: unsure of me and uneasy and guiltily aggressive. It was the only way I knew of hitting back at her.

I was alone, now, at the uncrowded end of the living-room. A mirror on the opposite wall showed me how I appeared to the outside world: a tall blond youngish-oldish man with a weakly good-looking, anxious face and dark, over-expressive eyes, standing in a corner between a cobbler's table and a fake spinning-wheel, holding a highball glass in my hand. A miniature brass ship with a fern growing out of it was fastened to the wall beside my cheek. I looked as if I were trying to melt into the scenery and become invisible, like a giraffe standing motionless among sunlit leaves.

I was wearing my usual crazy costume, the symbol of my protest against this life I was leading: a white tuxedo jacket, with a crimson bow tie and carnation to match my moiré cummerbund. Elizabeth, if she could have seen me, would have said: 'Darling, what on *earth* are you supposed to be? No—don't tell me. Let me guess——' In a way, I think I did dress like this just because it would have amused Elizabeth. Certainly, no one here saw the joke, not even Jane; my masquerade as a musical-comedy-Hollywood character passed entirely unnoticed. And why, after all, should any of these people notice it? This was the only way they knew me—as I appeared, night after night, at Jane's side, in the doorways of their homes. (We never stayed home alone together in the evenings, any more; it would have been unthinkable.)

If you had asked who I was, almost every one of them would have answered 'Jane Monk's husband', and let it go at that. It had been the same right from the start, when we'd first arrived in California, the previous year. Even the society columnists decided I was no fun and had better be ignored. They never mentioned me directly if they could avoid it, though they bubbled with items like: 'Saw Jane (Mrs. Stephen) Monk looking gorgeous (as usual) in white satin with some stunning antique Brussels lace. They're here from New York, via Nassau. Plan to settle for a while. Jane tells me——' etc, etc. Jane loved it. She never seemed to get tired of being talked about, no matter how bitchily. She even told me once—taking it as a huge joke—how a man at Chasen's had been overheard saying: 'Well, he may be a Monk—but, brother, she's no nun.' That was one of the things about her I still found charmingly innocent and touching.

'Out here on the Coast,' someone declared, in the group nearest to me, 'you just don't know what the score is. Why, back East, we're practically in the war already.' Someone else agreed that F.D.R. would get us in as soon as he could find an excuse. There was talk about the London Blitz, and Rommel and the fighting in Africa (this was April, 1941), but you could tell that none of them cared very much. Their fears and their interests were elsewhere. Sid Novotny was a screen writer, and this party was just in case the studio might be hesitating to take up his option. Alice Faye, who was to have been the guest of honour, hadn't shown up. However, several of the front office executives were present, a couple of second-magnitude stars, and a lot of young actresses and actors. Such as Roy Griffin, for instance.

A man disengaged himself from the conversation and came over to me. I'd been watching him preparing to do this for several minutes. We'd been introduced to each other earlier in the evening; I knew he was a producer, though I'd forgotten his name. He had a crew-cut, clean hairy hands, inquisitive eyes and a very sincere manner.

'Say, Mr. Monk, you know I've been wanting to get together with you ever since I heard you were out here? It was quite a thrill, meeting you tonight. It really was. Believe it or not, I'm one of the old original Rydal fans. Yes, I'll bet I was one of the very first in this country.'

I made a suitable noise.

'*The World in the Evening*: Jesus—that's a great book! One of the truly great books written in our time.' The producer lowered his voice, as though we were just entering a church. 'You know something?' He glanced quickly at the group he had left, afraid, apparently, that they might be listening. 'Somewhere in that book, there's a great movie. *One hell* of a movie. Most people wouldn't be able to see that. But I can. I can give you my word that it's there. . . . Did anyone ever buy the rights?'

'I don't think so.' I was looking over the crowd at the other end of the room. I had just noticed that Jane wasn't there. 'I could find out, if you're interested.' Roy Griffin wasn't there, either.

'I'm definitely interested. Definitely. . . . Say, supposing we manage to work something out, would you possibly consider helping us on the screen-play?'

'I'm not a writer, you know.' Jane might be in the bar, of course. Or with Mrs. Novotny, admiring some new clothes. Maybe she wasn't with Roy at all.

'Not a writer, Mr. Monk? Come now—let's not be so darned modest! What about that introduction you did to the *Collected Stories*? I read that over and over. You did a beautiful job. Fine. Sensitive. No one but yourself could have written that way. No one else was in a position to know her as you did.'

'Well—I'm glad you liked it, but——'

'And it's not a question of movie experience. Let me put it this way—we'd need you as a sort of a, well, an artistic conscience. Someone to tell us when we're getting off the beam. You're the only man who could tell us that. And we've got to watch our step clear through, from start to finish. Got to watch every darned little nuance, or we're sunk. Every word Elizabeth Rydal wrote is sacred to me. Sacred. I'm not kidding. I'd want to make this picture just as she'd have wished it—catch that wonderful delicate style and preserve it in celluloid, if you get what I mean——'

I've got to find them, I said to myself. Now, at once. I can't stand any more of this. This time, I've got to be absolutely sure.

The producer's voice faded in again: '. . . say, how about lunch, some time? Say, why don't I call you around the first of the week?'

'All right.' I tore a leaf from my notebook and scribbled the telephone number, substituting one wrong digit; a favourite

trick of mine. If they finally track you down you can always
pretend it was a slip.

'And Mrs. Monk too, of course. If she'd care to join us.'

'I'll ask her.' I thrust the paper into his hand and walked away
before he could say another word.

At the entrance to the bar I ran into Mrs. Novotny, dainty
and haggardly bright, in a dirndl costume with slave bangles.

'Getting yourself a drink? Good!' She smiled brilliantly,
squeezing the crow's feet around her eyes. 'I like a man who
knows how to look out for himself.'

I grinned at her numbly. ('Your dying-Jesus grin,' Jane called
it, when she was mad at me.)

'Sid and I were both so glad you could come, this evening.
Jane's such a lot of fun. She enjoys herself so. She always gets a
party going. She's such a *happy* person——'

'Yes,' I said.

'Excuse me——' She gave me another smile, touched my arm
lightly and headed eagerly back into the crowd. I'd been getting
ready to ask her if she knew where Jane was. It was so hard to
hit on exactly the right tone of voice; casual, but not too casual.
Now I felt glad that I hadn't tried.

The bar was three steps down from the living-room. Here,
the duelling-pistols and the ships' compasses, the Toby jugs, the
clay pipes and the Currier and Ives prints clustered around a gay
altar of coloured bottles, and the air was thick with smoke and
chatter. I stood on the top step, looking down. A couple of men
recognized me and nodded, and I nodded back; but I knew very
well that none of them really wanted me to join them. A cold,
bored, boring highbrow: that was how I seemed to them, no
doubt. Or else a snooty, half-Europeanized playboy with a
Limey accent and a Riviera background, who knew Italian
princesses and French counts. An alien, in any case, who didn't
belong to their worried movie world, where you lived six
months ahead of your salary and had to keep right on spending

lest anyone should suspect that your credit wasn't good. I had no part in their ulcers and anxieties, their mortgages and their options. I had never sweated it out at a sneak preview or a projection-room post mortem. And so, when these people thought of me, they certainly envied me my unearned money but probably also despised me for my irresponsible, unmanly freedom.

I came near to startling them all, at that moment, with a great bellow of despair, like an animal trapped in a swamp. Somehow or other, I'd wandered into this gibbering jungle of phonies and now here I was, floundering stupidly in the mud of my jealous misery and sinking deeper with every movement. I hadn't even the consolation of being able to feel sorry for myself. I wasn't in the least tragic or pitiable; no, merely squalid and ridiculous. I knew that, and yet I couldn't help myself. I couldn't get out of the swamp. I tried to think of Elizabeth and what she would have said; but it was no good. Elizabeth wasn't here. I was all alone. I should go on struggling and sinking. I had no control, any more, over what was going to happen.

Jane wasn't in the bar. Neither was Roy Griffin.

Turning from the steps, I walked quickly along a short passage, opened a glass door and stepped out into the garden. It was cut from the steep hillside in two terraces; a dichondra lawn above, and, below, a small kidney-shaped swimming-pool. The water of the pool must have been heated for it steamed gently in the beams of submerged lamps, its green-lit fumes rising theatrically against the enormous cheap-gaudy nightscape of Los Angeles which sparkled away out to the horizon like a million cut-rate engagement-rings.

There was nobody in the garden.

I came to a halt at the edge of the pool. It was brilliantly clean; not one leaf floating on its surface, not one speck of dirt on its tiled floor. God curse this antiseptic, heartless, hateful neon-mirage of a city! May its swimming-pools be dried up. May all its lights go out for ever. I drew a deep dizzying breath in which the perfume of star jasmine was mixed with chlorine.

So this time was going to be like all the other times. I wasn't going to find her. I wasn't going to know for certain. Later, she'd walk into the living-room quite casually, smiling as she said: 'We took a ride. I felt like I needed some fresh air.' Or else simply smiling and not bothering to explain at all. And Roy would either be casual too, as some of the others had been, or else embarrassed and in need of a stiff drink, avoiding my eyes. And I'd look at Jane and she'd look right back at me; and there would be nothing to say about it because I could prove nothing.

She and Roy had probably driven off into the hills together, the way the high-school kids did. The other day, at another party, a man had told us how he'd had a flat tyre on Mulholland Drive, and how he'd gone over to a car parked nearby, after suitable warning coughs, to borrow a jack, and surprised a couple of them—the boy around sixteen, the girl maybe less—stark naked. 'Holy smoke,' the boy had said, 'for a minute I thought you were a cop!' They hadn't seemed the least ashamed of themselves. . . . Jane's comment on this story had been: 'Well, good for *them*!'

I became suddenly aware of my hand, and the glass in it flashing green with the magic light of the water. The glass was empty, asking to be filled. I would have to go back into the house to fill it. I'd fix myself a huge drink and then sit down somewhere and figure out a very clever way to trap her once and for all, and be sure.

Wait, though. What was that?

Not the distant noises from the house. Not the crickets, which were chirping all over the hillside. Not the beating of my own heart.

There it was again. Quite close.

But—of course! I had entirely forgotten about the doll's house.

It was a playhouse, actually; fixed up to look like the Witch's candy cottage in *Hansel and Gretel*, with curly pillars that were supposed to be sugar-sticks and shingles painted the colour of toffee. The three Novotny children were still just small enough to squeeze into it together; Mrs. Novotny thought it was cute to make them demonstrate this to her guests, on Sunday afternoons. All you could see of it now was a black outline, standing back among the shadows of the oleanders around the pool.

I set my glass down very gently on the paving and tiptoed across to it, holding my breath.

Small but unmistakable sounds. Out of the darkness, right at my feet.

And then Jane's voice in a faint gasping whisper: 'Roy——!'

I stood there, death-still, clenching my fists. But I was grinning.

For now, suddenly—now that there was never again to be any more doubting, dreading, suspecting—here, right in the brute presence of the simple unbelievable fact—I felt what I had never guessed I would feel; a great, almost agonizing upsurge of glee, of gleeful relief.

Caught. Caught her at last.

At my first boarding-school in England, on winter evenings, we had played hide-and-seek sometimes, turning out the lights and hiding all over the big house. When you were He, you tiptoed around holding your breath and listening, until your ears grew so keen it seemed you could hear every sound within miles. I had always hated being He, but it was worth bearing the tense, spooky loneliness just for the sake of that one intoxicating, gleeful instant when you knew you'd caught them, those whisperers lurking and mocking you in the darkness.

A funny thought flashed through my head: I've been He for nearly four years. What a long game——

Right at my feet, Jane giggled: 'Roy—you sonofabitch——'

And, as if this were the signal they had been waiting for, my clenched fists jumped from my sides and pounded thundering on the doll's house roof.

Then, light and quick as a murderer, I turned and ran laughing up the steps from the pool, jumped a flower-bed, burst through a line of bushes and was out on the driveway. Luckily, my car was parked some distance from the front door of the house. I fumbled frantically for the key, started the engine, backed out like a rocket, smashed into another car—crumpling the fenders, probably—bounced off it, whirled the steering-wheel around, and was away.

After that, everything came unstuck. The car bolted headlong with me down the road, squealing and skidding around the curves. My left hand wanted to swing it over the edge and plunge it to a blazing wreck in a gully; but my right hand refused, and was stronger. My voice was yelling dirty insane words about the things it would do to Jane. My mind sat away off somewhere, calm and strangely detached, disclaiming all responsibility for this noisy madman, just watching, listening and waiting for what would happen next.

And then I was up in the bedroom of our house. I had found one of her lipsticks and scribbled the mirror and the walls with the words I had been shouting, in big scarlet letters. Now I was throwing stuff into a suitcase as if the place were on fire. Reaching into the closet for clothes, my hands touched an evening gown, gripped and crumpled it and dragged it out, and it was Jane I was going to kill. 'Rip her up. Rip her wide open,' I muttered, hunting for a razor-blade in my shaving-kit. The blade was double-edged, awkward to hold. I cut my thumb deeply as I slashed with obstinate rage at the dress; the silk was amazingly tough. But it was done at last. Sobbing, I flung the poor beautiful harmless thing into a corner, all gashed and bloodied and spoiled. How horrible! I was going to vomit. I stumbled into the bathroom with my bleeding thumb in my mouth and reached the toilet bowl only just in time.

When I had washed myself, I came back into the bedroom for

my suitcase, feeling weak and shaken and nearly sober. It was then that I remembered Elizabeth's letters. They were in a file, standing on the desk in the room I called my study but never used; I hadn't looked at them in months. I couldn't leave them, alone with Jane. She might burn them. She might even read them. I should have to take them along with me—wherever it was that I was going.

At the front door I paused and turned for a last look at our little hate-nest. Perhaps I had never seen it properly until this moment; my feelings about Jane had reduced it to a sort of flat, colourless backdrop. Actually, it had considerable comic possibilities. The hall was Hollywood-Spanish, with decorated beams and a staircase of curlicue ironwork and tiled steps gaily painted with birds and flowers. High up the wall, which had a surface like very expensive cream notepaper, there was a balcony draped with an Indian blanket. 'Romeo and Juliet,' I said aloud. Then I noticed a bottle of whisky standing unopened in a paper bag on the carved Italian dower-chest. I picked it up and ran down the crazy-pavement to the car, leaving the door ajar and all the lights burning.

In the darkened hotel lobby, only the reception-desk was illuminated. It was quiet here and calm like a chapel, with the desk clerk keeping his vigil amidst the shadows of big sleepy indoor leaves. I signed the guest-card, saying to myself as I often did: After all, I suppose I do actually exist. Anyhow, I seem to have a name, just like anybody else.

'Stopping with us long, Mr. . . . Monk?' the desk-clerk asked, with an instant's glance at my signature. His manner was perfect; correct yet discreetly understanding. It was as if he knew just what I was thinking. You can trust us, his reassuring smile seemed to say. We shall accept you for what you tell us you are. We shall assume that you are a real person. All our guests, by definition, are real people.

'I'm not sure about my plans, yet.' (But, even as I said this, I knew suddenly what I was going to do.)

The clerk nodded pleasantly and wrote something in a book. He was dressed for this death-watch job as if for a lively party; his suit, shirt, tie and teeth were immaculate, and his handsome sunburned young face showed not the least sign of fatigue. How is it, I wanted to ask him, that you can sit there, hour after hour, so calm and alone? What's your secret? How did you learn to inhabit the Night? I would have liked to stay and talk to the young man, telling him everything exactly as it had happened, without shame or excuse, as you might tell a doctor or a priest. But already the porter stood behind me with my suitcase; and the clerk was saying: 'Four Sixty-two, Sir. I hope you'll be comfortable.'

'Will you put a call through for me, please?' I said. 'Long-distance to Dolgelly, Pennsylvania. You'll have to get the number from Information. It'll be listed under Pennington; Miss Sarah Pennington. The house is called Tawelfan. T-a-w-e-l-f-a-n. It's on Boundary Lane.'

'Surely.' The clerk was scribbling this down. 'Goodnight, Mr. Monk.'

The call came through very quickly; only a few minutes after the porter had left me alone in my room.

'Go ahead, Los Angeles. Your party's on the line.'

'Hello——'

'Yes——?' Sarah's voice sounded faint and anxious and old. I could picture her—with her hair in pigtails, probably—startled from sleep in the grey of dawn and fearing news of some disaster.

'Aunt Sarah, it's me, Stephen. . . . I woke you, didn't I? I'm so sorry, but I had to tell you this at once. I——'

'*Stephen!* It's *you*! Where are you?'

'Still here. In California. But listen——'

'I'm sorry, Stephen dear. I can't hear you——'

'What I want to know is—could you possibly have me at Tawelfan? I mean, right away?'

'*Stephen!* You mean to *stay*? To *live* here?'

'Well—it might be only for a day or two. Or maybe longer. I'm not sure, yet. . . . But are you quite certain it won't be inconvenient?'

'Inconvenient! Listen to the man! He expects *me* to tell *him* that it's inconvenient to have him *here*. . . . Oh, Stephen dear, I'm so excited I can hardly believe it! When do you suppose you'll be coming?'

'I ought to be with you tomorrow. That is, if I can get on a plane sometime later today. I'll send you a telegram when I know for sure.'

'Oh, how wonderful. . . . Stephen, I'm not dreaming, am I? You really *are* coming?'

'Of course I'm coming, Aunt Sarah. Now you go right back to bed and finish your sleep.'

'Oh, I shan't sleep another wink. Besides, it's getting light already. I must be up and doing. Goodnight, Stephen, my dearest. I suppose it *is* still night, with you? How odd that seems! God bless you.'

'Goodnight, Aunt Sarah.'

I hung up with a sigh of pain and relief. Her joy made me feel sad and guilty, as though I had somehow cheated her. But what a relief to know that it was done, now; I had taken the single, necessary irrevocable step. And now I knew what I hadn't realized or admitted to myself until this moment—that I'd taken it only just in time. The least delay in getting that phone-call through, and perhaps—no, it was certain; I'd have gone back to the house. Back to Jane, on her own terms, any terms. That was the simple, miserable truth.

'But it's done now,' I repeated aloud. I opened my suitcase and took out the whisky-bottle. First I would get into bed, then drink until I slept. Very soon it would be morning. Things would start to happen of themselves, and Life would begin to carry me slowly, slowly away from the wreck.

But the whisky nauseated me. I couldn't touch it. Instead, I lay there staring at the ceiling and was shaken by another trembling-fit of hate. Grinning savagely, I thought of Roy Griffin, that film-fairy, that pansy male-impersonator who fooled nobody but himself, stuck with a very expensive nymphomaniac. Stuck with her, and not knowing how to wriggle out of it, and scared silly because of his career. Maybe he'd even have to marry her. Ha-ha, what a laugh! The poor miserable little pansy bastard, married to a bitch who's been accustomed to spend more on herself in one week than he earns in six months. Or did he think he was going to live on alimony? Well, if he did, he certainly had another guess coming. Not one cent would that whore get. Not one single cent. Not even if she took the case to the Supreme Court. I'd go to jail, first.

But I got hot, then, thinking of them together; two mating giants filling the dwarf world of the doll's house, and nearly bursting it apart with their heavings and writhings. I played the scene over and over to myself, elaborating every detail, until it left me sick with disgust and exhaustion. And so, toward dawn, I fell asleep.

TWO

WHAT are you doing now, Jane? What are you thinking? Aren't you wondering where I am? Aren't you amazed? Aren't you angry? Aren't you sorry? Aren't you a bit scared? Oh, Jane, why did you make me do this to you? I hate you for that. I hate you for making me hate you.

I hate you for going your own way always, and not giving a damn. I used to lay plots and set traps; but you never worried and you always won. I hate you because I couldn't hurt you.

I hate you for what you made me do to Elizabeth. It meant nothing to you. It merely tickled your vanity. You never understood how I felt about all that. I hate you for making me hate myself.

You've never known me, really. There's such a lot you just couldn't be bothered to explore. Sarah and Tawelfan are part of what you don't know. Elizabeth is another part. I never could tell you properly about any of that, because you were never really interested. At first, I used to make all sorts of little tests to find out if you wanted to share any of it with me. And you didn't. You didn't even realize what I was doing. You were much too tightly wrapped up in your own cocoon. Watch out, though; it's getting thicker all the time—as you'll discover one day, when you try to break out of it and find you can't.

I minded then. It hurt me more than I'd admit to myself, that you didn't care. But now I'm glad. Christ, I'm thankful I've got something of my own to take away with me, that hasn't anything to do with you. Something you haven't touched and made cheap and stupid and rotten.

Look, Janey—it doesn't really matter any more—but now

that this business is all over, there's just one thing I would like you to understand, and that's——

Stop it.

Stop talking to her. Stop thinking about her. You only give her power. You're making her stronger and stronger.

What's the matter with you, for Christ's sake? No wonder she despises you. You make me sick.

Come on, relax. Unclench your fists. Lean back in your seat. Breathe in deeply. Breathe out.

That's better.

Let's see if you can't forget all about her for a whole minute. Think about nothing but Now. Look out the window.

Our plane was over the desert, somewhere near the Arizona state-line, and the sun was setting directly behind us, making every tiniest crumb of rock on the littered floor of the wilderness stand out black against the last blinding beams of level light. The hills, which at midday look like pale crumpled sandpaper, now showed the most unearthly mineral tints of violet and green and orange, with deep-scooped crimson shadows. It was the sort of super-spectacle which makes some people think of God or Michelangelo, and which others find merely disgusting and dull because it seems to exclude their egos so completely. Jane had reacted to the desert like that, on our trip out to the Coast; she had buried her nose sulkily in *Vogue* and told me to tell her when we sighted civilization again. And I knew just how she was feeling.

But now, the aloofness, the absolute otherness of this country made me almost happy. These are real badlands, ruthlessly untidy and austerely useless. A world fit only for hermits, reptiles and military manœuvres; prehistoric, posthistoric, timeless, strictly neutral; proving nothing, disproving nothing. A simple geographical demonstration of Jane's total absence.

I should have remembered this more often, I said to myself, looking down. I should have remembered that it is out here, always, beyond their dirty coast of movies and oil-wells and advertisements and unreal estate. Beyond their swimming-pools and their doll's houses. This would have been a place to come to, in my mind. She couldn't have followed me here.

And now the lights snapped on, making the long tubular upholstered cabin seem falsely snug, as we climbed toward the sierras and the night. Closing my eyes, I could see the crumbling whirl of a snowstorm, feel the air grow deathly cold, hear the sputter of a failing engine, as we buckled our safety-belts and the plane nosed down into white nothingness, tiny and lost. Then, at the very last instant, right ahead, the terrible, declared face of the precipice. . . . Days later, the search-party would reach the wreckage and the scattered bodies. Myself, of course, lying unscarred, relaxed, beautifully dead, faintly sneering. The Picture of the Week in *Life* magazine. Jane would keep a copy of it beside her bed. She would see it in her nightmares and wake screaming. 'It was all my fault. I failed him. I sent him to his death. I shall be punished as long as I live.'

But there was no snowstorm. The engines were running smoothly. The night was going to be clear and full of stars. And there was no Jane. Only the cute little hostess emerging brightly from the Charm Room (as they call it) and smoothing her uniform as she advanced along the gangway. Bending over each chair in turn, smiling her Big Sister smile, she murmured to her charges: 'I bet you're hungry? Sure, of course you are! Well, now I'm going to fix your supper right away.'

This is what you always expected, isn't it, Elizabeth?

(It was very late, now; maybe over Kansas. I was falling slowly asleep, somewhere away high up in the thin cold air. So high, so far. In the nowhere of space and night. I felt almost disembodied.)

Oh sure, you'd have warned me. You were always warning me against something. And you were always right. But why couldn't you ever let me make my own mistakes? Then I wouldn't be so helpless. Then I wouldn't ever have gotten into this mess.

Well, now that it's happened, I hope you're satisfied.

Naturally, you hate Jane. I don't blame you for that. You couldn't help it. She gave me the one thing you never could give me; the thing you talked all around and were so brilliant and wonderful and funny about, and didn't have. I realize now how you must have hated the others, too. Only you were much too clever to show it.

Is that what you want—that I'll be alone, always, from now on? Always looking for someone and always having to admit that there's nobody, anywhere, to take your place? Can you really be so vain and cruel? What do you expect me to do? Go into a monastery? Or spend the rest of my life keeping up your precious cult—editing and annotating and explaining you, until people get sick of the sound of your name?

Yes, I admit it, you invented me. Until you'd told me who I was, I didn't begin to exist. I was the most lifelike of all your characters. People admired me, and that pleased you. But I don't believe you ever cared for me at all.

No, Elizabeth. No, forgive me; I didn't mean that. It wasn't your fault; it was my own selfishness. It was I who used you. I clung to your strength. I insisted on your being perfect, and got scared and angry when you weren't. I never considered how you must be feeling. I never helped you through your bad times. But you didn't complain, not even at the end. Even then, you were helping me. You were the bravest person I'll ever know.

Now I'm going to need you more than ever. I hope you know how much I need you and love you. Without you, I'm lost. I'm nothing.

Goodnight, Elizabeth. Help me to feel that you're with me. Help me to remember.

On Broad Street Station, Philadelphia, next afternoon, there were a lot of uniforms among the crowd. Here already—faintly still, but unmistakably—you could smell the War. Every man and woman in that crowd could smell it; and you could see how it scared and yet excited them. Through the weeks and the months ahead they would run sniffing alertly after it, muttering: 'How dreadful! How dreadful! We'll be in it soon! We'll be in it soon!' They wouldn't rest, now, until they found it, or it found them.

The War smelled of blood and dirt and sweaty bodies and the fumes of engines and explosives. It was filthy and evil, but at least it had nothing whatsoever to do with feelings about Jane. It would accept everyone, like a brutally dogmatic but completely reassuring religion which imposed terrible penances but guaranteed, at the same time, to take away your guilt; the guilt of having dared to indulge in private misery in an exclusive Beverly Hills home, rented at four hundred dollars a month.

All through this last year, the War had existed merely as a loud, ugly appropriate background music for my expensive private hell. Why shouldn't London blaze, why shouldn't Jews be tortured, why shouldn't all Europe be enslaved, as long as the great tyrant Me was suffering? It had seemed no more than natural.

I suppose that's exactly the way people in madhouses feel. I must have been very near to going insane, I thought. Maybe I *was* insane for a while. But here, amidst the hurrying afternoon crowd, the word was just a word. It didn't frighten me. I would be all right, now; I knew it. Even though it was tainted by the war-smell, the outside everyday air was deliciously refreshing. I breathed it in, inhaling deeply, like a convalescent.

And then the local electric train arrived, to carry me out of the city into the smugly pretty, vivid green country of the Main Line. Little towns, golf-courses, gardens, discreet prosperity adequately insured. A landscape without secrets, inhabited by people whose every word, thought and action would bear thorough investigation by the F.B.I. I didn't exactly remember any of it, but the feeling it gave me was familiar.

I looked my fellow-passengers over, trying to pick out the Quakers amongst them. I thought that I could. Their men are tall, bony, big-shouldered, deliberate and healthily pale. They speak slowly and prudently, selecting their words. They seem quietly harassed. Their women are energetic and bright. They comb their hair back and twist it into a knot. They use no make-up. They wear flat heels, cheap sensible dresses, and, in summer, straw hats which somehow resemble sunbonnets. Everybody knows everybody. Everybody is married.

If War has a smell, the Quakers remind you of a taste; the taste of plain home-made bread. It is always obtainable and ordinarily you take it for granted, crumbling it wastefully in your fingers and eating a little of it between mouthfuls of Lobster Newburg and sips of Liebfraumilch, hardly thinking of what you are doing. But sometimes, after a long illness, when the tired stomach recoils from every kind of sauce, spice or sweetness, you ask for that bread and you munch it humbly and gratefully, admitting sadly to yourself that this is your sane and proper diet, that all those fancy dishes were unwholesome and that you had better eat more wisely in the future. Well, here I was, at the beginning of my convalescence from Jane; and the Quakers and Aunt Sarah and Dolgelly were going to be my diet, maybe for months to come. So I had better make up my mind to it and swallow it down somehow. It was certainly wholesome. It was so wonderfully horribly drearily wholesome that the mere prospect of it made me want to weep.

Dolgelly Station came sooner than I'd expected. I started out of my thoughts to find that I was staring at its signboard, and I had to hurry to get myself off the train, which only stopped two minutes. The station was just like several of the other stations we had passed, and the drug-store opposite to it was shiny and new. Nothing to recognize there. A taxi was standing at the bottom of the station steps. I asked the driver if he knew Tawelfan. When he said that he did, I felt surprised. It was as if I hadn't quite believed, until this moment, that the place really still existed.

When we turned into Boundary Lane, I did start very dimly remembering. It was a proper lane, like the lanes of southern England, with high-banked hedgerows and overarching trees. The fresh foliage was thick already; and, by full summer, the houses along it would be mostly hidden. Tawelfan, I knew, was at the top of the hill, standing far back from the road at the end of a driveway with a long white gate. Sarah had often told me about that gate, and how I'd loved to ride on it, and how I'd been forbidden to because it was set rather crooked and swung violently open by its own momentum, banging against the gatestone hard enough to throw you if you didn't hang on tight. Finally, it seems that I was thrown off and landed on my head. I didn't remember the accident, but I still carried a faint scar on the right temple, where they had put in the stitches.

However, the gate had gone now, and the driveway was shorter than I'd expected. There was no time to register a clear total impression, a real image I could superimpose on my memories of the yellowed photographs in Sarah's album. But, as far as I could judge, everything seemed to be more or less in place: the tall maple on the lawn, the dark firwood to the left, the great barn to the right and, in the centre, the whitewashed, lopsided stone house. Tawelfan was actually two houses of different ages and sizes, joined together. The smaller and older building, a severely plain little early-nineteenth-century farmhouse, had a porch and a high brick chimney; the larger and newer was a pretentious copy with slightly bogus additions

—shutters that were too fancy, dormer windows that were overly picturesque. As was only natural, there were two front doors.

The newer front door was standing half open, and a little one-eyed dog, a Boston Bull, dashed out barking, as the taxi stopped. He barked around my ankles while I paid the driver, and meanwhile Sarah herself appeared in the doorway; a small compact resolute figure, eager and girlish, despite her white untidy hair. Sarah's hair had always been untidy; and it seemed to me that the only thing about her that had changed was its colour, in all the years I'd known her. Her eyes and spectacles shone with excitement. 'Stephen,' she cried, 'welcome home!'

I bent my knees slightly and she threw her arms around my neck, pressing my face against her soft wrinkled cheek. She smelled very clean. I just stopped myself in the act of patting her bottom—a conditioned reflex.

'Stephen, my dearest boy! How was the journey? Not bad, I hope? I was getting anxious. I expected you hours ago.'

'We had to wait a while in Chicago. There was a storm some-where around.'

'Well, let me look at you. My, but you're so *thin*! I'm sure that isn't Jane's fault. Too many late nights, I expect? Tell me the truth, now! I've heard all about those Hollywood parties.'

'Why, Aunt Sarah! You've been reading those mean old gossip columnists. They all exaggerate.'

'And look—you cut yourself! What were you doing? Fixing yourself a midnight snack, I'll be bound? That's what comes of letting a man inside the kitchen.'

'Oh—that?' I looked down, somewhat disconcerted, at the sticking plaster around my thumb. Sarah had eyes like a hawk. 'That's nothing. I scarcely felt it.'

We got ourselves into the house; not without difficulty, for Sarah tried to help me with my bag, and the Boston Bull was jumping and snapping underfoot.

'Thee doesn't know thy Uncle Stephen, does thee, Saul?'

'Hello, Saul.' I stooped down and held out my hand. But the dog backed away from me, growling. That was a strange thing about Sarah's pets; they were nearly always ill-natured. She seemed to be drawn instinctively to problem-animals.

'Saul and I found each other last year, in New York. That was a terribly hot summer, you know, and I working up in Harlem, at the Friends' Centre. Well, one night I came back to my room —I was so weary that I was walking in my sleep, almost—and he followed me. At first, I tried to shut him out, thinking he must belong to someone in the house. But he stood before my door and barked and barked. And then—well, I'm afraid I said something dreadfully profane——'

'What was that?'

'I said: "Saul, Saul, why persecutest thou me?" I just cannot imagine what brought the words into my mouth; but that's how he got his name. . . . Of course, I don't tell that story to everybody——'

'I should hope not! They'd put you out of Meeting.'

Sarah giggled: 'Why, Stephen! You wouldn't tell on me? I can trust *you*, surely?'

'I'll have to think it over. At any rate, I've got something on you, now.'

It was like talking a foreign language again after a long time, a language you thought you'd forgotten. The Sarah-Stephen language had its limitations; there were many things you couldn't say in it, at all. But how comforting and safe it was, just for that very reason! Once started, the sentences came to me fluently enough, even though they did sound rather like quotations from a phrase-book.

Meanwhile, I was looking around the living-room for something I could recognize. There was nothing. But this was hardly surprising; for, as I now remembered, the whole place had been redecorated by my arty Uncle George, who had lived here until his death, five years ago. In trying to catch the authentic farm-parlour atmosphere, he had merely succeeded in assembling a self-conscious museum. There were huge mahogany cabinets with glass doors curved like bay windows, and Victorian Gothic wall-brackets, and black Pennsylvania Dutch chests decorated with twin hearts in gold and red. A gasolier wired for electricity hung from the ceiling, which was covered with embossed sheet-metal.

'Well,' Sarah asked, beaming at me, 'how does it feel to be back?'

'Wonderful!' I made it sound as enthusiastic as I could. She was watching every movement of my face.

'Oh, Stephen, you don't know—you can't possibly know—how happy I am that you're here! If only your darling Mother could see us! We're going to have some great times together, aren't we, you and I?'

How small and frail she was! How vulnerable, yet throbbing with an intense life, like a bird. I noticed that the frame of her spectacles had been mended with wire, very awkwardly; most likely, she had done it herself.

'Sure we are.'

Jane, Jane, Jane, Jane. Suddenly it had started up inside me again, like a toothache. Jane, where are you now? Aren't you thinking about me? Don't you want me back? Don't you even care if I hate you? Don't you care for me at all? What am I doing here, three thousand miles away from you, talking to this old woman? I have no business to be in this house, infecting it with my nasty boring misery. I ought never to have come here at all.

'I haven't asked you yet how Jane is.'

'Jane's fine,' I said, instantly on guard; I had forgotten about Sarah's dangerous powers of telepathy.

'Is she coming East, too?'

'I don't know. . . . Not right now.'

•

'I suppose she finds a great deal to occupy her, out there?'

'Yes—she does.'

'I must write to her, bless her heart. I want to thank her for letting you visit with me.'

'You don't have to do that.'

'Oh, but I'd like to. Though I'm sure she knows just how I feel. She must be missing you already, and sorry she ever let you go. That's the worst of having such a popular husband! But she'll never complain, will she? Jane's a very brave little person.'

'Sure. It takes a real heroine to do without me.' I forced a grin, to cover my irritation. That was so exactly like Sarah. She scarcely knew Jane at all—they had met only a couple of times, when we were in New York, last year—and here she was, claiming full possession of her. Sarah used to do that in the old days, with the friends I brought back from school. Within an hour, she would know far more than I did about their homes and families, and be taking a positively vampirish interest in their hobbies, batting averages and school-work. And she never could understand why this made me so mad at her.

'Why, Stephen Monk, I do declare you haven't changed one particle! Always teasing your poor old Auntie. And you know she just loves it!' Sarah squeezed my arm. Then her glance fell on the sun-and-moon face of a grandfather clock which stood in the corner. 'My lands—is it *that* late? I must be about my business. Let's see if everything's to rights in your room.'

There was a doorway in the wall that separated the two houses. You went down three steps into the low-ceilinged dining-room which must once have been the parlour of the original farmhouse. Sarah led the way across it to what looked like the door of a closet, and was actually the entrance to a very steep, narrow staircase completely boxed in between white-painted boards and lighted only by one small stained-glass window. Whenever I'd thought about Tawelfan, I'd always remembered this window. It had a design of blue grapes and yellow leaves against a diamond of red. I must have spent hours at it, as a kid, peering out at the garden through the different colours of the glass; changing the scene, at will, from colour-mood to colour-mood and experiencing the pure pleasure of sensations which need no analysis. ('That's my idea of heaven,' Elizabeth said once, when I'd told her about the window: 'A place where you don't have to describe *anything*.') How had red felt, at the age of four? What had blue meant? Why was yellow? Perhaps, if I could somehow know that, now, I should understand everything else that had happened to me in the interval. But I never should know. The whole organ of cognition had changed, and I had nothing left to know with. If I looked through that window now, I should see nothing but a lot of adjectives.

'The house isn't looking at all the way it should,' said Sarah, who was climbing the stairs ahead of me. 'I'm afraid the last tenants were far from considerate. And then there's such a terrible lot to clean.'

'Why don't we throw this junk out, then; and put in some of that modern French furniture? You know—all glass and aluminium and string. You could wash it down with the garden hose.'

Sarah chuckled, after first turning and glancing quickly back at my face to make sure I wasn't serious. No doubt she thought me quite capable of any extravagance, like some mad nineteenth-century German prince.

As we reached the top of the staircase, Saul, who had squeezed himself past us, came scampering out through a half-open doorway on to the corridor.

'Saul's been getting your room ready for you,' Sarah said.

'Thanks, Saul. I certainly appreciate it.' Saul's eyes met mine with a look of most undoglike contempt. I had the feeling that he and I understood each other, by virtue of our mutual antipathy, far more profoundly than Sarah, in her innocence, would ever guess.

'I hope I haven't forgotten anything,' she murmured to herself, as she led the way into the bedroom: 'Soap, towels, an ashtray—you do still smoke, don't you, Stephen?'

'I'm afraid so, Aunt Sarah. But while I'm here we're going to lick this thing together. I'm counting on you to help me wrestle with the Demon Nicotine.'

Sarah spluttered with amusement. She loved that kind of talk.

'Oh, Stephen, you dreadful boy! As if *I* could ever help you, when you know it's always *you* that leads me astray! What about that Martini you gave me at the Barbizon Plaza?'

'Well, I never said to drink it. I just wanted you to know how they smelled, in case you ever led a temperance crusade.'

'If I live to be a hundred, never shall I forget that horrible taste.'

'Listen—you liked it fine. And don't you deny it. You were pretty happy afterward, when we walked in the Park. I seem to remember you singing—what was it? Jeepers, creepers, where'd ya get those peepers——'

'Why, of all the wicked untruths! I never even heard of such a song! You *know* I didn't!'

'Well, of course, if you deny it there's no more to be said.' I was suddenly tired of the Martini episode; it threatened to grow into one of Sarah's many sagas. I dumped my suitcase on the bed, opened it and was starting to unpack when I remembered the file of Elizabeth's letters, which lay inside, wrapped in my pyjamas. If Sarah saw it, there would be more questions. I pretended to feel a need for a cigarette and stopped to take out my case and light one.

Sarah watched me, dabbing two small tears of laughter from her eyes with the corner of her handkerchief. 'Where's the rest of your baggage?' she wanted to know.

'Oh——' I became very vague, 'that'll be coming along later, I guess.' And I thought how I would have to sneak out and buy some more clothes, as soon as Sarah had had time to forget about it.

'And now you'll be wanting to wash up. You'd like to eat early, I expect? I'll have supper ready in half an hour.'

'I'll be right down to help you.'

'Fiddlesticks! We don't allow the men to work, around here. Besides, there's really nothing to do. Gerda fixed most of it, before she went out——' Sarah checked herself, putting her hand over her mouth with an archly theatrical gesture: 'Mercy, what an old chatterbox I am! And I'd meant it for a surprise! Well, the mischief's done now, so I may as well tell you. She's here already! She arrived the day before yesterday.'

'Oh—good.'

I must have looked slightly blank, for Sarah exclaimed reproachfully: 'Why, Stephen—don't tell me you've forgotten? Gerda—Gerda Mannheim. You know—the girl I wrote you all about.'

'Yes—oh sure, of course.' I hadn't the faintest idea whom Sarah meant; but that was hardly surprising, because I seldom read her letters beyond the first couple of paragraphs. They were so terribly long and incoherent, and she wrote them (being constantly anxious not to waste anything) in a microscopic hand on various odd scraps of paper, such as grocery bills and the covers of Quaker pamphlets about peace. 'Gerda Mannheim,' I repeated, trying to fix the name in my mind.

'The formalities were settled even sooner than I'd hoped. I went to see the District Attorney myself; and, I must admit, he was very co-operative.'

'That's swell.' I decided that this Mannheim girl must be one of Sarah's criminals—quite possibly a murderess—who was being released from the State Penitentiary on parole. Sarah had a passion for criminals. She had made herself responsible for several such cases, already. And they had found admirable jobs and married and settled down—all except one, who had strangled her nearly to death and set fire to the house and was now in an insane asylum.

'Gerda's a very lovely person. So thoroughly straight. You two are going to be the greatest friends, I'm sure.'

'She must have had a pretty rough deal,' I said, angling for further information.

'Oh, Stephen—when you hear the rest of her story! Such heartbreak! Such dreadful insecurity and fear! And now she comes to us, asking for a new life, something to believe in and hope for. We must try hard to give it to her, mustn't we?'

'Yes, we must.'

'She's gone into Philadelphia, now, to visit friends—some of her own people. So I'm afraid you won't see her until tomorrow morning.'

'That's too bad.' I felt greatly relieved. I was beginning to be deathly tired; in no mood to face any stranger—least of all a reformed murderess with a lovely disposition and a demand for faith and hope. Sarah must have sensed this, for she said briskly: 'Come, Saul, we'll leave Uncle Stephen in peace.'

When the door had closed behind them, I walked across to the window and stood there, looking out. The faded crimson barn showed all its cracks and weatherstains in the clear rainy light. Below me, was the orchard, and the spring-house standing among dogwood trees that would very soon be in flower. And away beyond them, down at the bottom of the shallow valley, you could see the roofs of Dolgelly village against a background of low wooded hills. Those woods seemed wilder and more tangled than the woods of England, and they reminded you that this country was only so recently snug and suburban; that this used to be an outpost of a world, a front-line of fanatically humourless, drably heroic men and women, entrenched behind their Bibles and prejudices, their dark stuffy clothes and their stone farmhouse walls, grimly confronting the pagan wilderness.

Turning from the window, I inspected the room. A brass bedstead. Two hand-coloured Audubon etchings; an American Flamingo and a Snowy Heron. A marble-topped bureau. A washstand with bowl and pitcher; for decoration only, since there was also a modern built-in washbowl with running water. Striped blue wallpaper with golden flowers. All unfamiliar. Nothing whatsoever to prompt me to the sensations you are supposed to have on returning to the first room you ever saw in your life.

Yes, I had been born here; probably in this very bed. It didn't signify anything. Jane had never slept with me here; Elizabeth had never looked out of this window, never seen those woods. This was really a fresh start; or, at worst, a dead end. After thirty-two years, I had come back to the room I was born in, bringing nobody with me, nothing except a suitcase. Now at last, I told myself with apprehension and excitement, I've actually done it. I've cut all the life-lines, kicked away all the props. From here on in, whatever happens, I'll be entirely on my own.

THREE

SARAH was explaining that Tawelfan means in Welsh 'The Quiet Place', that Dolgelly, also, is a Welsh name, and that the village, like several others in this neighbourhood, had been founded by Welsh settlers during the eighteenth century. From force of habit, she had assumed the consciously informal attitude in which she would have addressed a Friends' Meeting for business; leaning forward a little in her chair with her hands resting on the table, loosely clasped. She spoke slowly, loudly and very distinctly, so that Gerda Mannheim should understand.

This was the next morning, and the three of us were in the dining-room, eating breakfast. Gerda Mannheim sat opposite to me. She was a sturdily built young woman in her late twenties, with thickish legs, an otherwise good figure, and quietly watchful brown eyes; attractive rather than pretty. Her hair was chestnut and glossy; she wore it braided around the back of her head in German peasant style. She had a frank warm smile, good teeth, and a mouth and chin that were firm without being severe. Sarah had talked more about her at supper, and I now knew that she wasn't a criminal, after all, but a refugee from Nazi Germany. I liked her, I thought. Or rather, I thought that I could like her if I ever again found myself able to take an interest in anyone except Jane, Jane, Jane, Jane.

'But the Monks aren't Welsh, of course,' Sarah added. 'They came originally from the east of England—Suffolk, wasn't it, Stephen?'

'Yes.' I answered rather curtly because Sarah's question irritated me. She knew where the Monks came from as well, or better, than I did, and her appeal to me for confirmation was merely part of a would-be-cute family act, put on for Gerda's benefit.

Involuntarily, I glanced up at the big oil-painting which now hung above the Dutch-tiled fireplace. This was another of the surprises that Sarah had prepared for me. She had had it sent out from the boardroom of the Philadelphia office of our family firm, as soon as she knew that I was coming to Tawelfan— because, as she put it, 'it seemed only natural and fitting that he should be here to greet you'. Part of the surprise had gone wrong, however. For the painting hadn't been there to greet me; it had arrived late (actually a few minutes after I had, yesterday, while I was still upstairs in my room) and with its wire broken. So Sarah had had to hide it from me in the barn and phone Gerda to bring some more wire back with her from town; and the two of them had had to rise extra early this morning in order to get it up on the wall before I came down to breakfast. And now here it was, staring me gravely in the eye. I felt touched and embarrassed by its presence; touched because of all the trouble Sarah had taken, embarrassed because I still mildly disliked my Father, or rather, his legend—there had been a time when I'd hated it passionately—and was certainly in no mood to be reminded of him right now, when I'd done just about everything he could possibly have disapproved of.

The portrait, which was a slightly better-than-average school-of-Sargent product, showed him as a handsome, conscientious-looking man in his late forties, every inch a company president. It wasn't altogether a Quaker face; for impatience appeared in the nervous lines around the mouth, and perhaps, behind the straightness of the thick eyebrows, doubt.

'Don't you think Stephen's like his Father, Gerda?'

Gerda looked at me, looked at the portrait, looked back at me, and smiled. 'No,' she said, quietly but decidedly, 'No, I do not think so at all.' Her voice was low, with a slight, agreeable accent. I grinned at her, pleased.

Sarah was not so pleased. Gerda had committed heresy, for the likeness was an important dogma of the family creed. 'No, I suppose you wouldn't, my dear,' she conceded, with bright impartiality. 'Unless you'd actually known them both, you could hardly be expected to see what I mean. Now, *I* find many, many resemblances. And not only physical ones, either. Stephen has his Father's lovely whimsical sense of humour——'

'Aunt Sarah,' I interrupted, blushing in spite of myself, 'I'm sure Gerda isn't interested in any of this——'

'And then, of course,' Sarah continued imperturbably, 'they had deep spiritual values in common, too.'

My stomach gave a big squirm. But I wasn't going to let Sarah get me down. 'Look, is that a hint that I'm to come with you to Meeting, this morning?'

'Stephen, you *know* I never beat around the bush! You're old enough to make your own decisions, I should hope. . . . Though I'm sure everybody would be very happy to see you there——'

'You know quite well there's no one who could possibly remember me.'

'Dolgelly has a long memory, you'll find.'

'Oh—you mean you've been spreading the good news?'

It was Sarah's turn to be embarrassed. 'Well, no—I only just happened to mention to Martha Chance—oh yes, and to Dr. Harper over at the College—that you were returning here——'

'They must have been thrilled.'

'Well, naturally they were interested. After all, they knew the Family. . . . Stephen dear, I didn't do wrong, did I? You aren't displeased?'

'No, of course not.'

'I certainly never even hinted that you'd come to Meeting. Or that they'd see you at all, for that matter. I'm sure everybody here will respect your privacy——'

'Okay, okay. I'll come. . . . That is, provided Gerda comes too.'

'Naturally I come,' said Gerda quietly, with a smile at Sarah.
'Well, that's splendid, then.' Sarah beamed at both of us. 'I
think we should start about twenty minutes of eleven. I never
like to have to hurry to Meeting. You get there all in a fluster,
and then it's so hard to still yourself. At least, that's what I find.
But then, I'm afraid my mind is just naturally restless.'

When it was time for us to leave the house, Saul made such a
commotion that Sarah was obliged to lock him in her room.
'I hate to have to do that,' she said. 'It's so dreadfully humiliating
for both of us. I always wish I could take him with me to Meeting. Saul has every right to share in the silence. He understands
it perfectly, in his own way—and I'm sure he needs it just as
much as any of us. He's such a searching, unquiet little person.'

And then the telephone rang. 'That was Emily Bradbury,'
Sarah told us, when she had finished speaking. 'You'd both enjoy
her, I know. She has such a beautifully clear, dedicated mind. . . .
Well, Emily has a deep concern about the plans for our new
community centre. We've been working on them together, you
see, and they have to be laid before the committee to-morrow,
so there's very little time. She's coming by for me in her car,
so she and I can talk on the way. . . . I don't imagine you young
people will mind sharing each other's company? I'm sure you'll
find plenty to talk about.'

'You aren't a Quaker, are you?' I asked Gerda, as we started
out.

'I? Oh, no. I do not believe anything, I think. At least, not
formally. But I can respect that you and Miss Pennington believe
—very, very much.'

'I'm not a proper Quaker. In fact, I'm not one at all, any
more. I was just raised that way, because my Father and Mother
were. I'm only coming along this morning to please Sarah.'

'I also. Still—it is very good sometimes to be quite quiet.'

I thought perhaps this meant that she didn't want to talk. But,
when we turned out of the driveway into the lane, she drew in

a deep breath of pleasure and exclaimed: 'Oh, it is so good to
be here!'

'You think you're going to like America?' It was the sort of
inane question you ask with a sixteenth of your mind, when
your thoughts are miles away.

'I did not mean America. I mean the green trees. To be in the
country again.'

I glanced down at her, walking beside me with relaxed, easy
movements. All women pretend to like the country; it's part
of their act. But she meant it. She seemed really to belong here.
Jane had never belonged. Jane, as soon as she got outdoors,
needed all kinds of equipment, like blankets and cushions and
umbrellas and deck-chairs. I caught a brutally vivid, split-second
glimpse of her, oiled and brown and stark naked, on the terrace
of the villa at St. Luc; and the pang of lust was so painful that
I almost gasped out loud.

'In the camp,' Gerda was saying, 'there were no trees. Nothing
grew there at all.'

'You mean, in the——' (I felt a sort of respectful hesitation in
uttering the words) 'the concentration-camp?'

'Oh no! Not so bad as that, thank Heavens! The internment-
camp. In France. You see, my Husband and I, we were living
already in Paris when the War started. So he enlists in the
French Army. And I am interned.'

'That was a pretty rotten thing to do to you.'

'It was the same for all German civilians. The French had to
be careful. There were some Nazis amongst us, also.'

'Was it very bad in there?'

'Bad for those who were sick or old. For the rest of us, it was
only the problem not to be too bored. I had always my routine.
Most important was to wash.'

'That doesn't sound very exciting.'

Gerda laughed. 'You think I am joking? No. If you are dirty,
you become sad. And it was so easy to be dirty. We had not

enough washing-place for all of us. So I would wait and wash myself at night, when everybody was asleep. Also I would make callisthenics. One hour. And study the English language. So I was quite busy, you see.'

'And then they let you out again?'

'When the Nazis invaded, yes.'

'And you got away to Portugal?'

'Not immediately. First Marseille. Then North Africa. . . . It was rather difficult to arrange. Why are you smiling?'

'Because you make it all sound so matter-of-fact.'

'Do I? Well, I think I was more lucky than most.'

'Maybe that's just your way of looking at it. Sarah's been telling me some things. How you were all crowded on to that leaky old freighter. And then the storm, when you nearly sank. And then the mixup in New York.'

'Oh, that was worst of all! Though to think of now, it seems rather funny. We thought we shall be sent back to Europe. Suddenly, at the Immigration, they tell us that the Society which has guaranteed for us cannot longer give the money. They do not know what to do with us. We have no right to be here, We do not legally exist. And then Miss Pennington comes and she saves our lives. . . . Does she do such things often?'

'Yes, all the time. Sarah's incredible. Once, it was a party of Letts who'd arrived here in a sailboat without any passports. And then there was a Negro who'd escaped from the chain-gang; they were trying to extradite him to Georgia. And I don't know how many others. . . . If she sees someone in a jam, she doesn't even stop to think. She rushes right into the middle of it—like the kind of sailor who gets into fights in bars without even knowing what they're all about. And if she can't find any humans who need help, she picks up stray dogs and cats.'

'And you? You are not like that, I suppose?'

'What do you mean?'

'Miss Pennington told us all what you have done for us. You

sign our affidavits. You pay for food, clothes, everything we have. And to me you give a home in your house.'

'But, Gerda, you don't understand. I simply have an arrangement with my lawyer that Sarah can go to him and ask him for whatever she wants. The lawyer sends me papers. I sign them. Half the time, I don't even read them properly. Why, until yesterday evening, I didn't realize you existed—let alone those six others who were with you on the boat. And I don't suppose I'll ever meet them. . . . As for this house, it was standing empty anyway. I just told Sarah she could use it and invite who she liked. . . . Don't you see? All this has really nothing to do with me——'

'Nothing? I believe you! To me it is not nothing.'

'Besides which, I happen to be filthily rich.'

'Others are rich too. They do not give.'

'Now listen here, Gerda—I suppose Sarah's been building me up into a little plaster saint? She does that whenever she gets a chance, because she hates it when people thank *her*. You don't know anything about me yet, not really; and there's lots of things I hope you never find out. You wouldn't like them at all. . . . If I'm expected to walk around wearing a halo—well, I just can't take it. So will you do me a favour? Let's not ever talk about this business again.'

'Very well, Stephen. I am glad you say this, because I do not like plaster saints either——' Gerda smiled up at me: 'Even when they are not so little.'

We walked on for a while in silence, downhill. Just beyond Tawelfan, the lane dipped steeply into a hollow, skirting the big pasture or town common, which looked like an oversized English village green. Dolgelly is one of the very few places in America where cricket is played; not by villagers, however, but by the College boys, as a kind of sophisticated traditional joke.

Gerda asked suddenly: 'You are married?'

'Yes. I'm married.'

'She is an American girl?'

'Yes.'

'But you are not American?'

'Technically I am. My Father was American, and I was born here. But I went to England when I was five years old. You see my Mother was English, and after my Father died, she preferred to go back there.'

'Miss Pennington is her sister?'

'Oh, no. I just call Sarah 'Aunt' because she's such an old friend of the Family. She came along with us to England. In fact, she more or less raised me. You see, my Mother died too, while I was still quite young. Sarah and I lived together until I left college. Then I started to travel around; I was hardly ever in England after that. I came back here once—only on a short visit, though. Mostly, I was on the Continent: Austria, Germany, France, Italy, Spain, Greece—all over the place. . . . So now, I don't really belong anywhere.'

'That must be strange. I feel so very German. Never to be homesick—I cannot imagine it.'

'I get homesick for people, I guess, instead of countries.'

Gerda looked quickly at me, her eyes shining. I saw that what I'd said had somehow moved her deeply. 'Oh, how I know what you mean! There are some people, they are *like* countries. When you are with them, that is your country and you speak its language. And then it does not matter where you are together, you are at home. . . . You have known such people, Stephen? They are not many.'

'Three or four, perhaps. But one especially.'

'Who was that?'

'An English writer named Elizabeth Rydal. Maybe you've heard of her? She's quite famous.'

'Rydal? No—I do not think. . . . What has she written?'

'Stories. Novels. The best-known one is called *The World in the Evening*.'

'*The World in the Evening*? *Die Welt am Abend*. . . . Funny— that was also the name of a Communist newspaper in Berlin. Before Hitler came.'

'Really? Well, this book hasn't anything to do with politics. It's about some people spending a weekend at an old house in the country. They all talk, and gradually you begin to discover that three of them—no, I'll only spoil it for you if I try to describe it. . . . I wish I had a copy with me. Maybe Sarah has one. You ought to read it.'

'I shall read it. But tell me more things. This Elizabeth—you know her already a long time?'

'I married her when I was twentytwo.'

'Married? Oh, but I thought——'

'This is my second marriage. Elizabeth died, six years ago.'

'I am sorry——'

'No. I love talking about her. And it's been quite a while since I had anyone I could tell. . . . I wish you could have met her, Gerda. I wish everybody I know could have met her. . . . Only, I want you to read this book first. It'll give us something to start on.'

At the far corner of the common, there was a bridge over a creek. Button Creek—the name came suddenly back to me. Then the lane began to climb again, over gently rising ground, through a ramshackle district of shabby frame houses in gay, untidy gardens, lively with children and dogs. Negroes lived there. They were sitting out on their porches in the sunshine; laughing and calling across to each other. Far ahead, at the turn of the road, you could see the Meeting House; a long low building, showing grey amongst the trees.

Looking down at Gerda, I saw that she was smiling to herself.

'What are you thinking?' I asked.

'Only that what you say makes me very happy. You see, I also—there is someone I wish to talk about——'

'Someone who's like a country?'

'Peter, my Husband.'

'I was wanting to ask you about him. Where is he now?'

'I do not know. He was taken a prisoner—it must have been near Abbeville—just before the fighting ended. We have heard that he with many others are sent into Germany, to work in the factories. But this is not sure.'

'Is there no way of finding out?'

'There are ways. But I am afraid to try too much. You see, Peter must pretend to the Nazis that he is French. He will have a false name—papers too, I hope. He speaks French well. It may be possible, if his comrades will help him. He is very clever at such things. But if the Nazis discover who he is, that will be bad.'

'Yes, I can see that. He fought against them.'

'Not only this. His name is on a special list. You see, he worked against them always. From the beginning. In Hamburg, before Hitler became Chancellor and there was still time, he made speeches openly and wrote, to try to warn people. Then, when that was no longer possible, in thirtythree, he began to print an illegal newspaper. And to hide those who are running from the Police.'

'You did that, too?'

'Yes, naturally.'

'Were there many of you?'

'Many at first. But the organization was not good. So, one by one, we get caught.'

'They didn't catch you?'

'No. We got the warning in time, and so we could escape into Denmark. But the Nazis know all what we did. They printed our pictures with a reward. So it can be that now someone will recognize Peter. It can be that he is already dead.'

'Gerda—you don't really believe that, do you?'

'No. I do not believe it. Until I know for certain, I will never believe it. But it can be. One day, I shall know.'

Then, after a long pause, Gerda said quietly 'Elizabeth and Peter,' as if she were thinking aloud.

The grave white walls of the Meeting House, the hard plain old benches, the Elders seated on the low facing gallery, the bowed heads and the Sunday hats. Latecomers found places hastily at the back and settled themselves, like chickens getting ready to roost. We had found Sarah waiting for us at the door, and had come in with her. Nobody looked at us directly, but it seemed to me that everyone was aware of our arrival.

I was sitting between Sarah and Gerda. Sarah sat very erect, with gloved hands folded in her lap and eyes closed. Her un-seeing face was beautiful in its innocent openness. Speak, Lord, she seemed to be saying, for Thy servant heareth. For her, that wouldn't be just Bible-talk; it was actually how she lived her life—poor as a mouse, eager, busy, happy. How can you look like that and really *be* like that, I thought with affectionate exasperation, and yet be such a melodramatic, bossy old fuss-budget? How can you be so fearless and silly and strong? What right have you to love me and misunderstand me and make me feel so dirty? Why won't you leave me alone? What am I to you, anyway? Still poor darling Gertrude's baby, little Stevie in short pants? Are you praying for me, now? Are you giving thanks that the Prodigal Nephew returned? Or reckoning up the household accounts and wondering if I'll think you've been extravagant when you insist on showing me the bills?

Gerda had closed her eyes, too, but she didn't look withdrawn. I felt sure she was acutely conscious of her surroundings. I tried to imagine how they would seem to her. What do you think of these silent people, my mind asked hers; do you envy them for being at home in this comfortable country, so settled and cosy and safe? Or do you despise them a little, because they never lay awake in the dead of night, afraid and listening for heavy boots on the staircase and fists banging on the door? How can this place

possibly be real to you? Isn't it more like a slightly ridiculous
dream which began as a nightmare? Don't you half-expect to
be kicked and shaken out of it, to find yourself on the floor in
an S.A. barracks, with the guards telling you that you're next?

Nevertheless, the Silence, in its odd way, was coming to life.
Was steadily filling up the bare white room, like water rising in a
tank. Every one of us contributed to it, simply by being present.
Togetherness grew and tightly enclosed us, until it seemed that
we must all be breathing in unison and keeping time with our
heart-beats. It was massively alive and, somehow, unimaginably
ancient, like the togetherness of Man in the primeval caves.
The Sunday hats couldn't disturb it; nor could the tap-tapping
of leaves against the big windows overlooking the College
campus. And, after all these years, the sense, the mere animal
feel of it, was as familiar to me as ever. Only now, I thought,
I'm a little afraid of it. Part of me fears and resists and hates it.

Elizabeth, I pleaded, don't stand outside. I know this has
nothing to do with you. You had your different way of understanding. Your strength came from another source. But come
into this with me and explain it for me. What am I doing here?
What's going to happen to me? What is it that I'm afraid of?
Elizabeth, please, help me to understand.

In order to hear what Elizabeth would say, I had to make her
appear. There was a way of doing this which I had discovered
after many experiments; it nearly always worked. Closing my
eyes now, I willed myself to see the tiny slant-ceilinged upstair
room of our house on the Schwarzsee. I stood in the doorway—
you had to duck as you entered—and saw her high shoulders
and the back of her head with its long slender neck bent slightly
over the school copybook in which she was writing, framed in
the window against the cold morning blue of the lake. Before
her, on the table, were the inkpot and the dictionary and the
flowers in the jam-jar, the lump of fool's gold from Utah, the
sharp-nosed Aztec idol which Lawrence had given her, and the

snapshot of her with Mary Scriven on Brighton pier, wearing the funny sacklike garments which had seemed so ordinary in the Middle Twenties.

Standing there behind Elizabeth, applying my will very gently and carefully so as not to break the contact, I made her turn slowly round toward me until I could see her face. Hello, darling, she said. She was smiling. She never minded being disturbed.

Elizabeth, tell me, was I crazy to come here? What am I getting myself into?

Don't worry, darling. Just be patient. You'll find out.

But I can't be patient. These people—oh, I know it's my own fault—I don't think I can stand it much longer.

Stephen, what nonsense! Don't be so melodramatic. *I* think they're simply fascinating.

You do? Well—yes, I suppose they are—in a way. If only I could see them the way you see them.

But you can. That's what I'm here for.

I know. Only—oh, it's too difficult. I always forget. I let myself get rattled. And then everything's confused and I do something idiotic. Some day soon, I'm afraid I'll suddenly walk out.

Well, let's suppose you do. What then?

I wouldn't go back to Jane—if that's what you think.

Are you sure?

She wouldn't take me back, anyhow.

Yes, she would.

Don't say that!

Then don't ask me. You know I can only tell you the truth.

Anyhow, I wouldn't go. That's final.

Then where would you go?

New York, first. Then maybe up to Canada. There must be some kind of an outfit I could join.

And then?

Well—then I'd be doing something. I wouldn't have to think

for myself. I wouldn't have to make any more decisions. I'd be in the War.

And then?

I might get killed.

Oh, if that's all you want, darling, why not get some more of those sleeping tablets you had in California? You only need fifteen to do it. And it wouldn't hurt a bit. Of course, if you do it in a hotel, it's rather selfish; you make a lot of trouble for the staff. But you could always take an apartment——

Elizabeth! You never talked to me like this before.

I'm trying to startle some sense into you.

Of course, there's Sarah. . . . I have to think of her. She's counting on me. I can't let her down.

Stephen, at least be honest. You're not thinking of Sarah. You're not thinking of anyone but yourself. You can't be expected to, poor darling, as long as you're in this mess. But isn't it about time you stopped running away from it?

What's the matter with me? Why do I feel so guilty? What makes me act like this?

Do you really and honestly want me to tell you?

Yes—no—no, not now. I don't want to think about all that. Not yet. It'll only make me feel worse than ever. . . . Oh, Elizabeth, I'm so terribly unhappy.

You needn't be, darling. Nobody need be.

I know—that's what you used to say. And I remember all the things you told me. Only—you've got to help me. Don't let me ever forget them. Not for a moment. Promise you won't ever leave me.

I can't leave you, Stephen. Don't you realize that? Even if I wanted to, I couldn't leave you as long as you still needed me. We're not separate people, any more.

I'll always need you.

I hope not, darling. Not in the way you do now.

But, Elizabeth——

Too late. The contact was broken. She had gone. Opening my eyes, I saw that an old gentleman was rising from his seat on the facing gallery. As he did so, you felt rather than heard the faintest possible sigh escape from the Meeting. The Silence was about to speak.

'When I was a boy in Kansas, on my Father's farm, and one of us had to go out at night, he used to take a storm-lantern. Now these storm-lanterns didn't amount to much. One of those lanterns couldn't give no more than a flicker of light. There was a great darkness all around. But sometimes, when there was some particular work to be done, half a dozen of us would gather together, each with his own lantern, and the whole lot of us together, why, we'd give forth a powerful amount of light, and the darkness would be driven back. . . . Friends, isn't it the same thing when we come together in this Meeting——?'

When the old man had finished developing his theme, he sat down with a suddenness which seemed strangely unemphatic. Subconsciously, you were waiting for the applause which didn't follow. Then, one after another, other voices spoke. A woman's voice, flat and quiet, with a faint nasal twang: 'My self-will comes between me and the Light that is within me. I know that. So then I think: I wish I could put my hand into my heart and pull out my will by the roots. I hate my will, and I want to tear it out like a weed. But that's wrong, too. Because my will doesn't *have* to be self-will. My will is a necessary part of me. I need it. And God needs my will, to draw me to Him.' A man's voice, more cultured (probably belonging to one of the College professors), quoting from Meister Eckhart and George Fox. In the pauses between the voices, the Silence was gradually draining away, as they used up what it had contained. I barely listened to them. Troubled and suddenly tired after the effort of my talk with Elizabeth, I waited impatiently for the end.

At last, one of the Elders turned to his neighbour and shook hands with him. And then the general handshaking started, all

over the room. Sarah gave my hand a warm squeeze, and
whispered, 'Thank Thee.' (Just what did she mean?) As she
turned from me to a woman who was sitting on the other side
of her, Gerda and I shook hands with a kind of mock-formality.
'Well?' I asked. 'What did you think of it all?' But she merely
smiled and said politely, 'Very interesting,' as though we were
in a theatre, at the end of a play which I'd written.

The next moment, the Meeting had dissolved into greetings
and conversation. And the Meeting House contained nothing
whatsoever, now, but a lot of pleasant individuals in their best
clothes, all looking forward to Sunday dinner.

Back at Tawelfan, about three-quarters of an hour later, I sat
alone at the table in the dining-room, writing a note to the Los
Angeles lawyer.

'Dear Mr. Frosch——'

From the kitchen came sounds and smells of cooking. Sarah
and Gerda were in there, getting the meal ready. Despite what
she had said at breakfast about respecting my privacy, Sarah
had invited Dr. and Mrs. Harper and Martha Chance to join
us. It was no use getting mad at her. She was always like that.
She simply couldn't resist any opportunity of feeding people.
The Harpers had refused, having guests of their own; but they
were coming to tea. Martha Chance had accepted, eagerly.

'Dear Mr. Frosch,

'Will you please call my Wife and find out if there is
anything she needs? Transfer some more money to her account,
if necessary. And, of course, she can keep the house on for as
long as she cares to. My own plans are rather indefinite——'

I looked up from the paper to the portrait over the fireplace.
We stared each other straight in the eyes. Cheer up, Father, I

told it. You don't understand any of this, do you? Well, you don't have to. Just relax. Your son is nuts.

'If she asks you where I am,' I continued writing, 'you can tell her that I——' I stopped, crossed this sentence through with great care that it should be quite illegible, signed my name and addressed the envelope.

'Aunt Sarah,' I called, through the open doorway, 'I'm just going out to mail a letter.'

'Don't be long, then, Stephen dear. We'll be ready in half an hour.'

Out in the lane, my footsteps began to quicken at once, until I was striding downhill, almost running. No, I was saying to myself. No. No. Dr. Harper. No. Mrs. Harper. No. Martha Chance. No. And all those other people Sarah had introduced me to, after the Meeting. I couldn't remember a single name, or a face. Well, yes, there was one—a skinny red-haired boy, who looked as if he might just possibly be human. But the others— no. Good, kind, worthy, wonderful, no doubt. But as remote from me as Martians. They breathed a different air.

The red-haired boy had grinned and said nothing. Dr. Harper had quoted Emerson. Mrs. Harper had described the cabbages she was raising. Martha Chance had declared she just couldn't wait to have a real long talk with me, because she'd known my Father and my Mother, not to mention my Uncle George.

Well, she would have to wait. For the rest of her life, probably.

Because I was never going back to that house. I was crazy to have imagined, even for an instant, that I could live there. I only dared admit this to myself now, for the first time. I must have known it, subconsciously, ever since my talk with Elizabeth at the Meeting; but I could never have walked out just now if I hadn't pretended to myself that I didn't know what I was going to do—if I hadn't left everything behind me; my suitcase, my toothbrush, Elizabeth's letters. (I could rely on Sarah to take care of them.)

But what about Sarah herself? Oh, she'd be all right. She had Gerda to look after her. Just the same, she was going to be terribly hurt and bewildered when she found out—— (I censored that thought, hastily.) Call her later. Send a telegram. Invent some excuse. Make her understand, anyhow, that this has nothing to do with her. It isn't her fault. (Elizabeth tried to tell me something, at this point. I censored her, too.)

At the drugstore corner opposite the station, I dropped my letter into the mailbox. Mr. Frosch ought to get it the day after tomorrow, at latest. And then he'd call Jane, and then—— Don't think about that. Everything was perfectly simple as long as I didn't think.

There was a train to Philadelphia every twenty minutes. All I had to do was to cross the road to the station. Road to station. Station to train. Train to Philadelphia. Philadelphia to——? Never mind, yet. Just cross the road.

I suppose the truck must have appeared about this time, at the very edge of my consciousness, coming down the hill, not especially fast. A green truck. Plenty of time to cross, however. I stepped off the sidewalk on to the road. Road to station to train. It was really so simple. But my feet seemed enormously heavy and unwilling, as they sometimes are in dreams.

And then it was as if my nose suddenly caught a whiff of Sarah's dinner, a concentration of all the dinners she had ever cooked for me. It was an intolerable, infuriating smell. It was the smell of Sarah's love. And I was rejecting it, leaving it to get cold. That would be the cruellest thing I had ever done in my life. No, it was impossible. I couldn't. . . . I turned back toward the sidewalk. Hesitated again. The green truck, that entirely irrelevant object, was nearer. Much nearer. It was actually going to intrude on the situation. I had to give it my attention. Quick. Somehow or other, my feet got entangled. I slipped—though the roadway was quite dry—and fell on my hands and knees. For one immensely long moment, I gazed stupidly and passively at the truck.

What happened next was completely impossible. It belonged to the order of things which happen to other people, and only in the newspapers. It happened very slowly, with a lot of noise, but I don't think it hurt, at all.

PART TWO

LETTERS AND LIFE

ONE

'IT is finished?' Gerda asked. She had come back into the room without knocking.

'Quite finished, thanks.'

'And successful?'

'Very successful.'

'Oh, I am glad! You will be a good patient, I see already.'

'No patient is better than his nurse.'

'And I am not so good, you find?'

'That's not what I said.'

'But you are right. I am not good. I forget all what I have learned. You know, many years ago, when we are first married, Peter and I made studies for the first aid?'

'Why did you do that?'

'Peter said all people should know such things. To be prepared for the worse.'

'Boy! What a pessimist!'

'How can you say! Peter is optimist, always. A pessimist does not prepare. He thinks all is hopeless, so he sits sadly and waits——' Gerda came over to my bed as she spoke, and reached under the sheet for the bedpan. I bore down on it with my whole weight, so that it wouldn't move. She put her hand on my cast, to get more leverage.

'I do not hurt you when I do that?'

'Can't feel a thing. Pull harder.'

As she gave a violent tug, I gripped the side of the bed, made a tremendous effort, and rolled suddenly over on to my hip. She staggered backward, bedpan in hand, and very nearly sat down on the floor.

'Um Gotteswillen!' she gasped. 'I almost drop it!'

'My! Aren't you clumsy!'

'You! You made so I should do that! You did!'

'You looked so funny!'

When we had finished laughing, Gerda examined the contents of the bedpan with a critical eye. 'Good,' she said. 'Very good.'

'Gerda!'

'What is?'

'You aren't supposed to say such things.'

'And why not? I only congratulate you. Should I not?'

'You shouldn't even look at it. Not in the sickroom. Throw a towel over it and carry it away with your eyes lowered, as if it was something sacred. That's what the nurses did at the Hospital.'

'Those nurses! They must be very hypocrite.'

'Not at all. They're just nice girls.'

'And I am not nice? Because I do not pretend to be shocked? Why should I? It is Nature.'

'Aren't you ever shocked?'

'Not if it is Nature. No. Never.'

'Are you sure?'

'I am sure, absolutely.'

'Okay—then I'll tell you a story.'

'A shocking story? But they are always so stupid, I find.'

'No, this is a natural story.'

'Good.' Gerda sat down, putting the bedpan on the floor beside her chair. 'I listen.'

'Well—it happened sixteen or seventeen years ago, while I was still living in England, with Sarah. In fact, I was still up at Cambridge; only this was in the Long Vac, the holidays, in summer. We had a small house on the Thames, not far from London. And Sarah had a cat, named Seraphina. And, in due course, Seraphina had kittens——'

'Oh dear, I am so shocked!'

'No, wait. . . . You see, this Seraphina was a very good mother, so she used to catch mice for her kittens. There were an awful lot of mice around the place. She caught dozens. She used to eat half of each mouse herself—she had a terrific appetite—and leave the kittens the other half. . . . Well, one night, I got home late, I'd been up to town, and I wanted to fix myself a sandwich. I'd had a few drinks, so I may have been kind of careless, and besides there wasn't much light in the kitchen; we had no electricity, only lamps and candles. Anyhow, I went to the icebox and took what I thought were chicken livers. But when I bit into them, they tasted disgusting. . . . You know how Sarah hates to waste anything? Well, she'd seen all these half-mice lying around, so she'd put them in the icebox to keep fresh until the kittens got hungry again. . . . When I looked closely at my sandwich, there was a tiny little tail sticking out of it——'

'Pfui!' Gerda exclaimed, making a face as though she were spitting out something filthy.

'What's the matter? That's Nature.'

'You call it Nature? A mouse sandwich! Even the Nazis would not invent such a thing. . . . And what did Sarah say?'

'I never told her. She'd have thought she was to blame. She takes those kind of things so seriously.'

'Tell me, Stephen—when you were young, if you got ill, it was Sarah who looked after you?'

'Yes, of course. Why?'

'Because this morning she said to me: "I do not think Stephen likes me to come into his bedroom".'

'But that's ridiculous! However did she get that idea?'

'I think you give it to her.'

'Me? Are you kidding?'

'When they brought you back from the Hospital, day before yesterday, and she wanted to help with the bed, you said: "No. Gerda shall do it." I think you hurt her feeling.'

'But it wasn't that, at all. I was only thinking of Sarah. I mean, she's not so strong any more; and there's some things you have to do for me——'

'Like lifting this?' Gerda nodded ironically toward the bedpan. 'You find me such a Hercules?'

'No—but——'

'No buts. I do not think you give the true reason.'

'You don't? Well, I guess you're right. . . . You see, Gerda— I don't know if you'll understand this—when Sarah starts being motherly—or auntly, I should say—I get so embarrassed I don't know where to put myself. It brings back the time when I was a kid. Such a lot has happened since then, and——'

'And yet,' Gerda smiled, 'some part of you is still a kid. You know this, but you do not like to be remembered of it. Am I right?'

'Yes. More or less.'

'Perhaps I begin to understand you. More than you think.'

'I'm afraid you do, damn you.'

'Oh, it is nothing to be afraid. This kid I can see in you I like, very much. Only, Stephen, you know, children can be cruel sometimes, by not thinking. You must not be cruel to Sarah. She loves you. You love her, too. But you must show her this.'

'You think I ought to let her nurse me?'

'No. That is not necessary. Beside, I want to nurse you myself.'

'You do? Honestly?'

'Yes. I am very content that I have this work. Just now, it is good for my mental condition——' Gerda checked herself, as if she had been about to say more than she wished. Then she added: 'But be very nice to Sarah.'

'I'll try.'

Outside, there was a sound of footsteps, much heavier than Sarah's, rapidly mounting the staircase and coming along the corridor.

'Terrible!' exclaimed Gerda, jumping to her feet. 'That must already be Dr. Kennedy——' She whipped a towel from the rail and threw it over the bedpan. There was a very gentle tap on the door; so gentle that it was obviously meant to be comic. Then the door opened a little, and Charles Kennedy's head appeared, thrust forward into the room and peeking around cautiously, like a conspirator.

'Hello,' he said to Gerda, in a hoarse stage-whisper. 'Is he still breathing?'

'Oh, very much!'

'You're quite certain?'

'But of course I am certain!' Gerda started to giggle. She loved being teased by Kennedy.

'Just the same, I think I'll take a look at him, myself. With the kind of patients I have, it's very hard to tell.'

Kennedy came into the room as he spoke. He was a huge man, powerfully built. He wore rimless glasses, which slightly magnified his dark lively eyes. His clothes were so severely plain that they looked like a uniform: a dark blue suit, a white shirt, black tie, shoes and socks. Though he was probably a few years younger than me, he was nearly bald; and the remains of his black hair were shaved so close that they gave the appearance of a mere shadow over the top of his skull. His baldness emphasized the tense, firmly modelled muscularity of his head; compact with nervous energy, it reminded you of a clenched fist. He was handsome, in a brooding, archaic way, like a face from early Asiatic temple sculpture. I supposed he might be Jewish.

'Sleep all right?' he asked me, in his rapid, nervous, staccato voice.

'Fine.'

'Any pain?'

'No. Not now.'

'How are the bowels?'

'Ask Gerda. That's her department.'

'They are excellent,' Gerda told him. She went out of the room with the bedpan, laughing.

Kennedy brought a chair over and sat down by the bed, taking my wrist in his big hand. His eyes focussed intently on my face, with a delighted amusement, as though my broken thigh in its clumsy cast were a private joke between the two of us. I began to feel pleasantly passive and cosy and safe. His mere presence was almost hypnotically protective; it made you want to go to sleep. If there was any worrying to be done, I felt, he would take care of it all. I imagined him as a passionate worrier over everyone he met; but only with the upper surface of his mind. He thrived on it. Underneath, he was quite relaxed.

'I've brought your second lot of X-ray pictures,' he told me. 'They're downstairs in the car. Do you want to see them?'

'Should I?'

'I can't imagine why.'

'Then I don't want to.'

'Good. Most patients love them. . . . Look, the point is, you were lucky. You got a spiral break; that's as if you were to twist a piece of chalk. When the fracture's reduced, the bone-ends fit together again. Much better than if the bones had been sheared off directly. When the cast is put on, there's always a danger of angulation—that's when the pull of the muscles gets the bone-ends out of alignment, so that they aren't accurately opposed. That's why we take more X-ray pictures, to see. Your alignment's good.'

'So everything's all right?'

'Yes—so far. We'll take another X-ray at the end of six weeks, to see if it's continuing to knit well. By that time, there ought to be callous formation around the site of the fracture. That's what holds things together. Under the X-ray, it looks hazy at first; then there's increasing density. . . . Anything else you want to know?'

'When'll I get out of here?'

'Oh, ten weeks.'

'My God, that long!'

'I can't promise. But that's average. We should be able to take the cast off, then. Make you a splint. Then you'll be able to walk, with crutches.'

'I see. . . . But you don't think—it won't be anything permanent, will it?'

'No. Of course not.' As if suddenly bored by the whole subject, Kennedy let go my hand and stood up, looking out of the window. Then he asked abruptly: 'Do you want to tell me what really happened?'

'What do you mean?'

'I mean, just what do you think you were doing under that truck?'

'I don't understand——'

'You don't have to tell me if you don't want to.'

'But what is there to tell? I slipped.'

'The girl who works at the drugstore saw it all through the window. She thought you must be drunk.'

'I most certainly wasn't.'

'I know that. But she can't understand why you didn't get out of the way. She says you had plenty of time to.'

'It didn't seem so to me.'

'Another thing——' Kennedy smiled at me with the blandness of an inquisitor: 'They just told me over at the Hospital that you signed some kind of a document for a representative of the trucking company. If I'd known, I'd have advised you not to do that. You ought to have talked to a lawyer first. I suppose you agreed to accept their offer of compensation? Don't you realize they'll usually offer the absolute minimum—much less than they expect to have to pay?'

'If they did, they must have gotten a big surprise. I waived all claim to damages.'

'You did *what?*'

Kennedy's expression of horror, part genuine, part clowning, was so funny that I started to laugh. 'I told them I didn't want a single cent.'

'But *why?*'

'It was all my own fault.'

'That's no reason. Very often, it's the pedestrian's fault. He collects, just the same.'

'But I don't really need the money. And if I'd taken it, they'd be more likely to fire the driver. . . . Besides, this wasn't an ordinary case of carelessness——'

'Oh? You admit that?'

'Sure, I do.'

'You mean, you did it on purpose?'

'Not exactly. It wasn't a suicide attempt—if that's what you're getting at.'

'Not even a subconscious one?'

'No.' I was even a little surprised at my own certainty about this. 'I'm positive it wasn't.'

'I had a hunch it wasn't, myself. That's exactly why I'm interested in this business.'

'But, honestly, Doctor——'

'Charles,' Kennedy corrected me, with a quick nervous frown.

'Honestly, Charles—I can't tell you any more than I have. I simply don't know.'

'You refuse to know, you mean.'

'Maybe.'

We grinned at each other, like poker players. 'All right,' said Charles. 'I won't ask any more questions. Only, some time, you must figure this out for yourself, you know. Thank God, I'm not a psychiatrist!' He strode abruptly over to the door, opened it, and called: 'Sarah! You can come up, now.' Turning back toward my bed, he told me: 'When you get to know me

better, Stephen, you'll find I'm the most inquisitive bastard you
ever met in your life.'

'That suits me,' I said. 'When people aren't inquisitive, it
usually only means they aren't interested in you at all.'

'Do you know, that's absolutely right?' (I'd already noticed,
during our brief talks at the Hospital, that Charles had a way of
pouncing on any idea, however trivial, with intense, exagger-
ated eagerness.) 'Your friends *ought* to be inquisitive. That's just
what makes them different from other people. Other people are
merely nosy.'

At this point, Sarah came into the room, with Saul at her heels.
They were followed by a young man wearing jeans and a leather
jacket, who walked slouchingly, his hands in his pockets. I
recognized him at once.

'Well?' Sarah asked Charles. 'How is he?'

'Oh, he'll live. But I'm afraid he'll still be hopelessly insane.'

'Why, Charles Kennedy! Is that the way you talk about your
patients? I wonder you have any left!'

'Stephen,' said Charles, in his nervous staccato, 'this is Bob
Wood.'

'Yes,' I said. 'We met already. Only last Sunday—though my
Goodness, it seems like weeks ago!'

Bob Wood grinned at me. His hair was even more aggressively
red than I'd remembered. He was really quite nice-looking,
except for the swarming freckles which covered his finely drawn,
sensitive features.

'Bob came to Meeting,' Sarah put in, smiling at him as though
she was proud of him.

'To *Meeting*?' Charles regarded Bob with an air of astounded
curiosity. He was smiling, too; but I didn't think he was altogether pleased. 'You never told me that.'

Bob looked down at his shoes and said nothing. He had
coloured noticeably.

'You said you were going out to play tennis.'

'Well, I changed my mind.' Bob had an unexpectedly deep gruff voice which contradicted the delicacy of his face but went with his broad strong shoulders. They seemed over-heavy for his slim-hipped, skinny body.

'We were so happy to have Bob with us again, after all this while,' Sarah continued brightly. 'Now, Bob, I hope this is going to become a regular practice?'

Bob, who had squatted on his heels to pet Saul, muttered something inaudible.

'Listen to him growling!' Charles exclaimed delightedly. 'What's he saying, Saul? You know, Stephen, Bob's one of the Dog People. Even when he talks English, he has a thick Airedale accent. Sometimes, he does nothing but growl for days on end.'

'Yeah,' said Bob, grinning. 'When Charles and I met, I bit him and he got rabies. He's been crazy like this ever since.'

'I'm sure I wish you'd bite *me*, Bob,' said Sarah, 'if only it would make me as clever as Charles. . . . Oh, and that reminds me—though I really don't quite know why it should—Dr. Harper was speaking of your paintings, the other day. He said he was sure they *meant* something, but he couldn't understand them at all. Let me see, what did he call you? An impressionist? Or a futurist? Or was it a surrealist? I'm afraid I'm dreadfully ignorant about these matters. There, Charles—you're laughing at me! Have I said something very foolish?'

'Of course not, Sarah. I'm only amused by Dr. Harper's ignorance. A surrealist, indeed! Doesn't he know a primitive when he sees one? Bob's a dog primitive.'

'I paint with my paw,' said Bob, 'in various styles. I'm the canine Cézanne, the pooch Picasso, the mongrel Matisse——'

'Sure, you are.' Charles patted Bob's shoulder, as though he were trying to soothe an hysterical patient. '*And* the tyke Toulouse-Lautrec. . . . Don't be scared of him, Stephen. He gets these attacks quite often, especially when he's in company. I see I shall have to take him home now, and muzzle him. Then he'll sleep it off in his kennel. He's really perfectly harmless.'

'Don't worry, Steve.' Bob had started to laugh idiotically. 'Want to know something? My Braque's worse than my bite.'

Charles rolled his eyes upward in mock despair. 'I'm terribly sorry, Sarah. I do apologize for this painful scene. . . . Goodbye, Stephen. I'll look in again, early next week.' He put his hand on Bob's shoulder as they moved toward the door.

'So long, Steve,' said Bob.

'I'm looking forward to seeing your work,' I told him. 'As soon as I'm able to get around again.'

'As your doctor,' said Charles, 'I forbid it, for at least a year. The emotional shock could easily be fatal.'

'Oh dear!' Sarah exclaimed, when they had gone. 'Those two boys! They're so comical, when they're together, I could laugh myself into a fit! Though, half the time, I really haven't the least idea what they're talking about. . . . You know, Charles Kennedy was so wonderfully kind and helpful to us when I had poor dear old Anna Partland laid up here last winter, with her pleurisy and the three great-grandchildren. A regular tower of strength. But I wrote you all about that, didn't I?'

'Oh, yes,' I said hastily; 'everything.'

'He's such a brilliant man. They think the world of him, at the Hospital. I'm sure you couldn't be in more capable hands.'

'And who's this Bob Wood?'

'Oh, he's Luke and Esther Wood's son, from over at New Faith. They were both birthright Friends, such splendid people. Esther was clerk of the Monthly Meeting for many years. They've both passed away, now. . . . Oh, you're just going to love Bob! Such a fine, clean boy. So thoroughly wholesome.'

'Does he do anything else—I mean, as well as paint?'

'Well—not exactly. Though he's very useful about the house. He fixed the electric toaster for me, one time, when it kept giving me shocks. And he mended all the screens. He knows a lot about gardens, too. I think he's sort of finding his feet. He was in the Navy, you know. That always seems to unsettle people. And I hear he may be called back again, before long. Oh, this terrible War! I'm sure I don't know what Charles would do without him! Bob's been like a younger brother to him.'

'They live together?'

'Yes—ever since Charles moved here from Baltimore, three years ago. You should see their house! They've made it so charming, in an informal, masculine way. I always think it's so nice when two men get along together, like that. Men seem to manage it so much better than women, as a rule. Of course, your darling Mother and I—we were an exception——'

Sarah had moved slowly across the room as she told me all this, pausing to set various objects in order and slightly alter the positions of the chairs. By now, she had reached my bed.

'Stephen dearest,' she exclaimed reproachfully, 'you *can't* be comfortable like that!'

'But I am. It may look uncomfortable, but it isn't, in the least.' (The cast enclosed not only the whole of my left leg and the upper part of my right, but also the middle of my body as high as the ribs; so that it was impossible for me to sit upright.)

'You need at least two more pillows.'

'Do I?'

'Of course you do! Why didn't Gerda notice it?'

'Well, you know, Aunt Sarah, she isn't accustomed to nursing. She quite admits that, herself.'

'This has nothing to do with nursing. It's a matter of common sense. Anyway, I don't see why you should be used as a guinea-pig.'

'Oh, I don't mind. She'll soon learn.' I tried to make this sound like the tone of a cheerful, smiling little martyr. 'You see, it's so good for Gerda to have something to occupy her. It takes her mind off worrying about Peter.'

'Yes, that's true. Poor child——'

'We've got to help her, Aunt Sarah. Both of us. Of course,

I'd be a lot more comfortable if you were taking care of me. You know that. But it might hurt her. She'd feel excluded. I'm sure she'd appreciate it, though, if you'd give her a few hints. She's so eager to learn. Only, be tactful about it, won't you? Remember, she's in a strange country, and she doesn't know our ways——'

'Oh, I will, Stephen dear.' Sarah took this so earnestly that I felt rather ashamed of myself. 'Thank you so much for telling me this. I'm afraid I've been terribly selfish. I've only thought how much I wanted to be near you and help you in this trouble. I should have realized how Gerda would be feeling. You're such an example to me. Always so thoughtful of others, even when you're suffering.'

'Nonsense,' I said, grinning at my own slyness.

'Still—though I do quite understand, now, why you wanted her to nurse you—I would be so glad if there was something I could do for you.'

'But there is. There's lots of things.'

'Oh—do tell me!'

'Well, for example——' I was thinking fast: 'If you have the time, that is, you could read to me. You know, the newspaper, or a book. Something very long, and classical; that we both ought to have read before, and haven't.'

'Oh, I'd love that! When shall we start? Today? This afternoon?'

'Fine.'

'Stephen, how very nice! Do you remember how I used to read to you every night in bed, when you were little?'

'Of course I do.'

'This'll be like the old times, won't it?'

'Sure. Just like the old times.'

When Sarah had fetched me the extra pillows and left me alone, I lay quietly, smiling to myself for no particular reason.

The bedroom no longer seemed strange to me, as it had seemed, a week ago. It was my room, now, and I was going to stay in it for a long while. I felt as if I had been here for years, already. The Heron and the Flamingo, the washstand and the blue wallpaper had become completely reassuring and familiar. I liked them. My bed had been moved over near to the window, so that I could look out. That view—the barn, the orchard, the spring-house and the distant hills—was all of the external world that I was going to see, for the next ten weeks. And it was quite sufficient. I suppose I must be happy, I thought. And I remembered a favourable phrase of Jane's when she was referring to drunks: 'he was feeling no pain'.

When I recovered consciousness at the Hospital—a bump on the head, not very serious, had put me out for, maybe, twenty minutes—I had had, thank Goodness, the presence of mind to realize that they might try to get in touch with Jane. And so, by the time Sarah arrived, I had a speech all ready prepared. Jane mustn't on any account be told of this, I warned Sarah, or she would come running back here at once. (Would she have? Yes, I had to admit that she almost certainly would.) If Jane came, I hinted, she would want to take me away with her some place and nurse me herself. (This was untrue. Jane hated all kinds of illness, and had an instinctive resentment against sick people, of which she was scarcely even aware. She couldn't bear to be around them for any length of time. They somehow scared her.) My threat had overcome Sarah's scruples. She had promised faithfully not to tell Jane—in fact, not to write her at all.

But the amazing discovery, the miraculous relief of those first forty-eight hours after the accident was that I had very nearly stopped caring about the Jane-situation. Jane had lost her power. She could only get at me through emotions, and my emotions had ceased to function. They had turned themselves into physical sensations. Jealousy was now merely a bad headache; rage was the throbbing of my broken thigh; self-pity was distributed among my various bruises. I had no energy to spare for anything else.

And even now that my body had almost ceased to hurt at all —even now, I felt differently. Yes, the Jane-situation still existed, and would continue to exist, probably, for a long time. But I could keep it in its place. It wasn't going to monopolize my attention. There were other situations, other people, in my world. Something basic, I now realized, had happened. The axis of my world had shifted. And it was because of the accident. The accident had had nothing to do with Jane.

I had lied to Charles Kennedy. Naturally. It was no business of his. But I was grateful to him for asking me those questions, because they had made everything much clearer to me. Now I knew exactly what the accident was all about.

I knew, now, what Elizabeth had wanted.

Very well, I told her. You finally succeeded. You stopped me from running any further. It was rough, but I guess you couldn't have done it any other way, because I refused to listen. But now you've got me, and I'm glad you have. I'll listen to you, now. I'll try and face up to whatever it is you want me to know. I'm at your disposal. Just tell me what I'm to do next.

But I knew that, too.

When Gerda came in with my lunch-tray, I asked her to open my suitcase and give me the file of Elizabeth's letters.

Soon after Elizabeth's death, I had begun writing around and collecting her letters from her various correspondents. I had done this because it was one of the routine things you are supposed to do, in such a situation, and because I found it unbearable not to be occupied. When the letters arrived, I began to sort them, arrange them in chronological order and make notes of the cuts which would have to be made when they were published. I kept on at this work, by fits and starts, during the next three years; rather furtively, toward the end, because Jane didn't like hearing about it. By the time we reached New

York, I had sorted two whole files which covered Elizabeth's childhood and early life, and I left them there, in a safe-deposit box at my bank.

These were the remainder; they dated from 1926 to 1935, the year of Elizabeth's death. I had kept meaning to get to work on them; I had tried, over and over again, to make a start in California, but I was never in the mood to do it. I was paralysed by the laziness of my misery.

Elizabeth had written fewer letters as she got older, and most of them were short. She always wrote them by hand, in her small, clear, rather backward-leaning writing which would climb up the page in sudden spurts of optimism and then falter downward, as if overcome by doubt or fatigue. She often wrote on pages torn from her notebooks, because she had the habit of starting a letter when she found that she was stuck in her work. It was characteristic of her that she never kept to the ruled lines.

Now, lying with the file resting on my stomach, I drew one of the letters out of it at random. Elizabeth very seldom put a month-date on her letters, much less a year. The most she would write would be 'Thursday' or 'nearly two weeks since our arrival'. I couldn't date this one, at all, for the moment, but I knew from experience that I should almost certainly be able to place it in its proper chronological order, later—that kind of detective-work was one of my greatest pleasures. It was a very brief note, headed 'Van Gogh's Birthday'. (I would have to look that up.)

'We were both wrong about the Donne quotation. It's:

> Thou art the Proclamation; and I am
> The Trumpet, at whose voice the people came.

Wouldn't that be the *perfect* inscription for a great actress to write on the photograph of herself she was sending to the author of her play? Bernhardt should have quoted it to Rostand, after the first night of *L'Aiglon*. Oh dear, why didn't she? Let's make an anthology, shall we, of the things people *ought* to have said on famous occasions?'

I put the letter back and dipped into the file for another. But no—I wouldn't read any more, now. Sarah would be coming up, soon. And besides, I wanted to anticipate my enjoyment a little, before I began.

Let's wait, I told Elizabeth. We've got lots of time. We don't want to spoil it by hurrying. Tomorrow morning, we'll start.

TWO

THE earliest letter in the file was written from London, to Elizabeth's sister, Cecilia de Limbour. Cecilia, who had married a French consular official, spent most of her life in distant parts of the world. Just then, she was in Uruguay. I didn't meet her, myself, until several years later, when the Limbours were back in Paris on leave, and then I took an immediate dislike to her. Cecilia was younger than Elizabeth but seemed much older; a bitterly intelligent, plaintive, dried-up little woman whom I suspected of nursing a permanent grudge against Elizabeth's talent. But Elizabeth was devoted to her. Though they saw each other so seldom, Cecilia was one of the very few people to whom she would talk in detail about her work. This certainly wasn't because Cecilia was particularly responsive or interested; her answering letters were chiefly about the inconveniences and high prices of whatever country she happened to be living in. Elizabeth appeared not to mind that. I think her letters to Cecilia, and to three or four other regular correspondents, really took the place of a journal; they demanded no comment. I was surprised, later, to find that Cecilia had even bothered to keep them. I suppose she was proud of Elizabeth, in her own envious-snobbish way.

'Do forgive me, darling, for this long silence. It's weeks, now, since I wrote to anyone. This wretched novel—I'm so *heavy* with it, I feel sometimes as if I could scarcely drag myself upstairs.

I didn't want to write, anyhow, until I had something more to report than the usual dullness, frustrations, doubts. Well

now at last—though I scarcely dare say it—I think I have.
It happened four days ago, and I'm still trembling with
excitement.

I'd picked up that fat ugly Shakespeare—the one from
Father's library—and was sitting with it, not actually reading,
just turning the pages like a prayer-wheel, in a kind of trance.
Suddenly, I found I'd stopped at that scene in the fourth act of
Macbeth (such a noisy play; it's never been one of my favourites)
where Lady Macduff is talking to her little son, just before
they're both murdered. You remember?

> Sirrah, your father's dead:
> And what will you do now? How will you live?
> As birds do, mother.
> What, with worms and flies?
> With what I get, I mean; and so do they.

Cecilia, I can't possibly describe to you the extraordinary
shock of revelation I had, at that moment. I must have read those
lines dozens of times before, and I've seen the play on the stage,
twice. But now they seemed completely new—a personal
message, telling me what my story is essentially *about*. Everything
has to be related to these two central figures, the mother and the
boy. The mother, so utterly, angrily alone with her tragedy—
nobody else understands it, and it cuts her off, even, from her
own son. She sits watching him, sadly, quite objectively, almost
with a kind of mocking hostility. She longs to break down the
barrier between them, to get through to him and make him share
what she feels, somehow, even if she has to hurt him. And the
boy, absorbed in his play, answers her probing, teasing questions
with that strange obstinate inner certainty that children sometimes have. You try to warn them about life, all its pain, its
cruelty—and they simply won't believe you. They refuse to be
intimidated. They're so absurdly, idiotically, heartbreakingly
confident. You're sure they're wrong—they must be—and yet,

you wonder uneasily, *are* they? Can they conceivably *know* something you don't? It baffles you.

As Birds Do, Mother. That's to be my title. Try repeating it over to yourself. At first, you won't like it. I didn't. But it has forced itself upon me. Because it says *exactly* what I want this book of mine to say. The older generation still sitting under the shadow of the past war—disillusioned, bereaved, resentful— and watching this new generation at play. Trying, desperately, to warn it of its doom, the doom of its dead fathers, and being answered with this absurd heartbreaking innocent-cynical confidence of the young people today. Jazz, Dadaism, flappers, cocktails, night-clubs—that's what they all mean. "I can look after myself. As birds do, mother. I'll be all right. Why can't you leave me alone? Je m'en fiche. What do I care what happens to me, anyway?" That's the tone of voice I have to catch. That's what my character, the young man Adrian, has to feel, and *be*.

As you see, I'm making the Macbeth scene mean something it actually doesn't. (One always seems to do that, with Shakespeare.) Macduff, of course, *isn't* really dead; but that's beside the point, for my purposes. Adrian's father *is* dead. Adrian isn't denying that, but he revolts nevertheless against his mother's cult of her grief. What he says to her in effect, is: "Stop torturing me with these terrible lamentations. Either die with him or live without him, but don't keep trying to drag me into your wretched half-world of mourning. I won't share it with you. I have my own life. If I make a mess of it, it shall be *my* mess. I reject all your warnings, prophecies and omens of doom. I refuse to be intimidated by the past. The past proves nothing. Put it in a glass case and treasure it, if you like. It doesn't concern me."

Enough of this, for the moment. I must do a lot more thinking before I can go into details——

I'm really very glad I left Italy, very content to be back here, in this flat. The bedroom's no more than a cupboard, and the water-heater for the bath is a monster of violence and caprice; but I love my sitting-room. It looks out over Regent's Park; such a beautiful, calm, classically autumnal view, lit by pale lemon-yellow sunshine. London is the perfect autumn city. You feel no sadness, here, that the year is passing. And the winter will be mild and snug, one long teatime, as it were, in front of the toast-making, story-telling fire. Only, I hope there'll be no wind—my chimney smokes!

A most charming person has moved into the downstairs flat. A middle-fortyish little woman, brisk and bright, and so *good*. Yesterday was frosty, and she said: "This weather should encourage us to be very active." *She* certainly is. She darts about like a bright-eyed mouse, feeding the poor and attending welfare committees; a regular mouse-saint. She's an American Quaker—very *Early* American. You imagine her hurrying eagerly ashore off the Mayflower and kneeling at once on the beach to give thanks for having been led safely "through the watery maze". We became acquainted over the problem of the milkman's unpunctuality, and now I see her nearly every day. She abounds in recipes and household hints, and she talks and talks —chiefly about a young man whom she calls her nephew; though they aren't really related, she's careful to explain. He seems to be such a paragon of every known virtue that I quite dread his arrival here from abroad, next Wednesday.'

At the time of this letter—the first week of November 1926 —I was still over in Germany. About a month earlier, I had written to Sarah, telling her I was planning to return home and asking her to find us a place to live, in London. This was why Sarah had rented the flat.

Sarah had begun writing me at once about her upstair neigh-bour, whom, at first, she called 'Miss Wrydale'; how kind she was, how helpful with the milkman, and how much she was looking forward to meeting me. When I learned that this was the Elizabeth Rydal whose stories I'd read in the *London Mercury*,

I was interested, but not unduly excited. Sarah's letters gave me the impression that Elizabeth was quite elderly and a great chatterbox. I pictured her in loose garments, with coils of unhealthy dull grey hair and arty beads. Sarah described her as 'sophisticated'; which would merely mean, I scornfully decided, that she smoked. Perfumed Turkish cigarettes, no doubt; in a long jade holder.

I was in a thoroughly scornful mood, at that time, because I was convinced that I'd seen through everything. I'd investigated every kind of pleasure, vice, shame and mental anguish, and found them all greatly overrated. The poets—except for T. S. Eliot —had lied: they pretended life was exciting. I now knew that it wasn't. The only valid emotion was boredom (or *ennui*, as I preferred to call it). I was twentytwo years old; and I had made this discovery during the five months—they seemed like five centuries—since I left Cambridge.

In the first term of my last year up at the University, I'd made friends with a young American named Warren Geiger, who was a post-graduate student from Yale. I was drawn to him at once, by his brash cocky manner and boundless self-confidence, so different from the prim British caution of the intellectuals I'd been going around with. I don't know why Warren liked me; perhaps simply because I was so shy and shockable, and so ready to believe every word he told me. Also, of course, I had plenty of money and was always eagerly ready to stand drinks. It was only after I'd met Warren that I began drinking regularly; before that, I'd been almost teetotal, except at college feasts and old boys' suppers, when I invariably got sick. But my stomach soon strengthened with practice.

Warren was an inexhaustible storyteller. He told me stories of New York and Chicago, full of gangsters, bootleggers, speakeasies, show-girls and petting-parties, and I could never hear enough of them. They made me feel a sort of second-hand homesickness for my nearly-forgotten native land. If Warren had wanted to return to the States after leaving Cambridge, I would certainly have gone with him.

But Warren yearned to get back to Paris, which he regarded reverently as the erotic capital of the world. (I found out, later, that he'd only been there once, for less than a week.) 'Till you've laid a French girl,' he told me solemnly, 'you're just plain ignorant, that's all. These English dames, they can't *teach* a fellow anything. They don't have any temperament.' I would nod wisely, but with an uneasy feeling that English dames were quite as much as I could handle, for the present. I had an awful long way to catch up. I wasn't nearly ready to graduate yet.

Until Warren had undertaken my education, I'd had very little sex-experience of any kind. There had been a couple of scared, hasty acts with other boys at school. There was a girl from Girton I used to invite to tea in my rooms, whom I managed to kiss a few times while our chaperone was busy next door, boiling the kettle. And then there were the town girls you took out on summer nights, in punts on the Cam. They giggled and screamed and were so silly they seemed half-witted. Until you touched them. Then they turned suddenly shrewd and grudging and ladylike. There were some men who could deal with this (or so they claimed) by extreme firmness. But I lacked the necessary conviction.

Warren was contemptuous of Cambridge as a hunting-ground; instead, he used to take me up to London. This was better, certainly; you could be sure of results. But Jermyn Street on a wet night was dreary and sinister, and so were the dirty little hotels near Charing Cross where we went with the girls. I always felt like a criminal with the police hot on my trail, and it was only Warren's encouragement that kept me going. According to him, the girl he was with invariably preferred me. (Mine obviously didn't.) 'You know something?' he'd tell me, as we were returning to Cambridge on the train next morning. 'That cute little brunette said she thought you must be an artist, you had such beautiful hands. Jesus! Can you beat that? Honestly, Steve, you've got what it takes. Trust Uncle Warren. Believe me, kid, I'm going to raise you to be a regular Don Ju-ann.'

Though I thought about nothing but Sex, at that time, from morning to night, I got very little pleasure from the act itself. After so much anticipation, it came as an anticlimax, accompanied by impotence-fears, compulsive strain, and nausea. The smell of those hotel bedrooms was as nauseating to me as the smell of the operating-theatre to a patient going into surgery. I was literally sick with excitement. The only pleasant moment was right after the orgasm, when all the strain was over and I felt a huge relief.

But the relief didn't last more than a few minutes. It was followed by panic and guilt. I was terrified of venereal disease. If I caught it—as I was sure I should, sooner or later—I supposed I'd have to commit suicide. My whole life would be ruined. Morally, I was ruined anyhow, already. I'd betrayed Sarah and everything she stood for. Sarah had never taught me sexual puritanism—her mind was incapable of such dirtiness—but the possibility of her finding out what I'd been doing was too humiliating even to imagine. As for the Friends, I began to hate them and all their works. They were responsible for making me feel such an outcast. I tried to pose to myself as an honest rebel against their hypocritical smugness: they were secretly longing to behave just as I did, I told myself, only they hadn't the nerve. I couldn't hate Sarah—I still loved her very much—but I felt completely alienated from her. When my visits to London took place during a vacation, they were extra painful, because I had to come home from them to face Sarah in person. If she had even the faintest notion of what was happening to me, she never gave any hint of it; she was the same to me as always. Sometimes I longed to be able to confess everything to her; but, of course, that was unthinkable. I couldn't even bring myself to tell Warren how I was feeling.

All through that winter, Warren had kept promising me

Paris. And then, in the spring, he suddenly got engaged to be married—to an English girl! Such disloyalty to his own principles was too fantastic to get angry about. I merely gaped at him, bewildered, when he told me the news, which he did with sheepish embarrassment. There was nothing much to be said, on either side. In due course, I bought him an unnecessarily showy wedding-present, a whole cabinet of table-silver. This embarrassed him even more, as I had subconsciously intended that it should. It was a kind of revenge.

Warren had left me flat, without a mentor, in the middle of my initiation. But, Warren or no Warren, I knew I'd have to go to Paris. It was my only possible next move, the one door by which I could enter the future. I couldn't stay in England and continue the old life with Sarah. It was nothing but a pretence, now. Everything had changed. If I went on pretending, I'd feel more and more guilty and ruin what was left of our relationship. So for Sarah's sake as well as mine, I argued, I must go.

I left England early in July, telling her vaguely that I wanted to improve my French. Sarah accepted this, as she accepted all my decisions. She seemed to have no anxiety whatsoever about my future; and had actually urged me, on several occasions, not to be in too much of a hurry to make up my mind what I wanted to do. What did she privately hope? That I'd go back to Philadelphia, enter the family business, get married, have children, become a Weighty Friend? I didn't know. She who interfered with everybody else, and could scarcely watch anyone boil an egg without giving advice, never interfered with me.

I said Goodbye to her tenderly, sick with misgivings, as though I were leaving for a war. Without knowing just what I expected to happen, I felt almost as if we'd never see each other again.

Within two weeks, all these apprehensions had begun to seem as silly and unreal as the terrors of a past nightmare. Had

I ever really thought of Paris as an initiation-symbol, a dreaded test of my manhood? I could hardly believe it. For now Paris was just Paris, a beautiful but completely matter-of-fact summer city, full of fascinating things to see and delicious things to eat, where people were delighted to help you spend your money. I felt as free as a bird. I could come and go as I wished. Nobody was watching, much less condemning me. In this town, you were allowed to enjoy yourself.

Something strange had happened to me. It was as if I'd turned into another version of myself: Stephen-in-France. I'd never realized before that my inhibitions were so tightly identified with the words of the English language. This new Stephen chattered away without restraint—not the least ashamed of his accent and his bad grammar—and never hesitated to ask for anything he wanted.

Stephen-in-France didn't waste any time with shy furtive glances; he didn't blush and mutter: 'I wonder if—I mean— that is—would you care to——?' He asked right out for Sex; and got it immediately. On my second evening in Paris, I picked up—or rather, was picked up by—a blonde, half-Polish girl named Marie. Marie was a sweet, good-natured person, whose attitude toward me was realistic but not particularly mercenary. That I got her, and not one of the other girls I met later, was a big piece of beginner's luck.

Marie didn't care to drink much, or sit up late in bars. She liked steamer trips on the Seine, excursions to Fontainebleau, movies and huge meals. And she really loved going to bed. In her arms, I slowly relaxed and stopped worrying about myself. 'Don't kiss so quick,' she used to tell me. 'You kiss like a little bird; peck, peck, peck. Slowly, now. You see? Isn't that much better? No—not yet. Don't be in such a hurry. You wish to catch a train? Stupid, we have the whole night.' And so, for the first time in my life, I began to enjoy the physical act. I actually cried with pleasure, sometimes, because it was so beautiful, so natural, so warm, so kind, so silly. In the middle of it, we would laugh together like children. Warren, despite all his lectures, had somehow never gotten it through my head that Sex was meant to be fun.

From the first, Marie had made it clear to me that she had other men friends beside myself. She wasn't coy or bitchy, and she never discussed them in a way that would make me jealous; it was just that she didn't want me to get any wrong ideas about our relationship. I understood this and was grateful for her tact; otherwise I might quite easily have fallen in love with her.

Even as it was, I got a nasty jolt when, toward the end of August, Marie told me she was leaving Paris. Now, for the first time, she explained that she had a lover, a real lover, who was 'serious' and would marry her. The lover was captain of a merchant ship, a good bit older than herself; they had been going together for several years. He had always known about the life she was leading, and didn't object, as long as he was obliged to be at sea. But now he could afford to retire and buy a farm, and he was sending for her.

The news made me sentimental. Marie and I spent a farewell night together, and I wished her happiness with tears in my eyes. 'You ought to marry too,' she told me, 'Don't wait too long. You're a sweet boy. You'll make a good husband. The woman who gets you will be lucky.'

'No, Marie,' I answered, feeling sorry for myself and somehow rather noble, 'You only say that because *you're* so good. I'm not. You don't really know me. I don't think I'll ever marry.' I kissed her on the forehead as though she were already the captain's wife, and pressed an envelope into her hand. 'Don't open this till you get on the train'. The envelope contained a wad of thousand-franc bills. Another wedding-present!

Marie left me with many solicitous parting instructions: how much I ought to pay my girls, which bars to avoid, how to deal with various kinds of confidence-trick and blackmail, which places were safest for hiding my money. She even nominated her successor, a friend of hers named Annette, whom she guaranteed to be honest.

Annette was honest, all right, but she was dull and not my type. I'd soon stopped seeing her and tried a whole series of other girls, seldom sleeping with anybody more than two or three times. I grew bored and restless. It wasn't often that I found a girl amusing enough to spend even one day with, and I had no other friends. I took to sitting for hours in big cafés like the Dôme and the Rotonde, sipping pernod and trying to look interesting and habituated, in the hope that some writer or artist would come up and talk to me. I longed to be invited to enter the real Parisian bohemia, which I vaguely imagined as a kind of aesthetic paradise where Joyce and Gertrude Stein were eternally united in communion with Picasso, Stravinsky and Cocteau, and encircled by the legendary creatures of the Russian Ballet. But nothing of the kind happened. Partly, no doubt, because I looked sulky rather than interesting; partly because nearly all of the artists and writers had gone south for the summer. The city belonged to the foreign visitors; and the only people who spoke to me were touts selling dope or dirty pictures.

Boredom made me careless. I forgot all Marie's instructions, visited the bars she'd warned me against, and carried far too much money in my pockets. One evening in September, at a place near the Place Pigalle, I was given a Mickey Finn. I woke up next morning in the Police Station without a centime. I had a splitting headache and I must have been dumped in some gutter, for my clothes were filthy. This adventure made me unreasonably indignant. Paris had betrayed me, I felt. It had treated me like a common tourist. The city wasn't friendly, as I'd imagined. It was a nest of cheap cold-blooded crooks. I suddenly hated it. Two days later, I'd left for Germany.

Berlin was a complete contrast. Outwardly, it was graver,

stiffer and more formal; inwardly, it was far more lurid and depraved. For a runaway Puritan, it was a more congenial refuge than Paris, because it recognized Vice, and cultivated it in all its forms with humourless Prussian thoroughness. In Berlin, it wasn't enough merely to want Sex; you were expected to specialize, to ask for a teen-age virgin, a seventy-year-old woman, a girl with a whip and high boots, a transvestite, a policeman, a pageboy or a dog. There were various kinds of brothels and bars to supply your needs. And, in case you couldn't make up your mind what you wanted, there was a Museum of Sexual Science where you could study photographs of herm-aphrodites, sadists' torture-instruments, fantasy-drawings by nymphomaniacs, female underwear worn by officers beneath their uniform, and many other marvels. The Director of the Museum, a highly respectable and strictly scientific old pro-fessor, seemed a little disappointed that I had no 'special tastes'. He regarded me reproachfully through his pebble glasses, ran his fingers through his untidy white hair, and finally diagnosed my case as 'infantilism'.

I had tried conscientiously to get into the spirit of the Berlin night-life, which, at that time, still had some of the lunatic public shamelessness of the inflation-period. At first, I'd been shocked, disgusted, and rather intrigued; these self-consciously perverse antics were certainly a change from my simple pleasures with Marie. But they soon got very tiresome. I could never quite believe that anybody really enjoyed them; except, perhaps, a few exhausted old men whose appetites needed a drastic whetting. To me, these bars were like the Sex Museum; you only had to visit them once. At the end of the tour, you had seen every-thing, and that was that. There was nothing more they could teach you.

Nevertheless, it was a Berlin girl named Trude who had completed my initiation, by giving me gonorrhœa. The moment when I woke up, one morning, and discovered what was the

matter with me wasn't at all as I had pictured it in my imagination; it wasn't in the least horrifying; it was even quite comic.
Trude, who was lying in bed with me, laughed and said we had
the *Kinderkrankheit*, the Children's Disease. She didn't apologize, but she took me at once to a doctor. It was as if we had
been going off to get married. For the first time, we had a genuine relationship, we were in this together, and I felt warmly
toward her in a way I'd never felt before. At the doctor's office
we were separated, however, and put, respectively, into a male
and a female waiting-room. (Trude explained to me that this
was done for the sake of propriety, because the doctor only
handled V.D. patients.) My waiting-room was full of people:
plump middle-aged men who might be shopkeepers or government officials, factory operatives in their working-clothes,
picturesque individuals who were probably actors, boys of
college age. Some looked gloomy, some cheerful, some prim
and severe, some easy-going and dissolute, some innocent and
pure and even saintly. It amused me to think that this was the
one thing we all had in common.

The treatment itself certainly wasn't amusing: the disinfectant
burned so much, the first time, that I yelled. But it was quite
successful. And, at the end of two weeks, I was cured not only
of the infection but of the last of my fears. This, after all, was an
ailment like any other. Millions of people had had it, would
have it; it was part of the human condition. Instead of becoming
an outcast, I'd shared a common experience. I wasn't branded
with the mark of Cain. I wouldn't have to commit suicide. I
could go back home.

Back to what? I didn't know. My attitude toward the future
was quite passive. I supposed vaguely that it would present me,
sooner or later, with an occupation. Perhaps I'd write something
or try translating. Perhaps I'd join an expedition to South
America or the Arctic, or get myself psycho-analysed. I didn't
really care. If anybody or anything could manage to interest

me—which I privately doubted—then I was ready to be interested.

Standing alone at the rail, as the boat crossed the Channel toward England, I felt wonderfully old; wearily mature, calmly disillusioned. I decided that I must be very kind to Sarah, and to everyone else I met. Very kind and patient and understanding. Because, after all, it wasn't other people's fault that they hadn't had my experiences. How could they be expected to know, even dimly, what it was like to be me?

A few days after my arrival in London, Elizabeth wrote again to Cecilia:

'This isn't really another letter; just a postscript to my last. There's something I must put down, and fix for myself, while the first impressions are sharp.

Since I wrote to you last week, Adrian has, almost literally, come to life!

It's uncanny. Let me describe him.

He's very slender and quite tall (I used to imagine him rather small, but I see now that that was absurdly wrong) with a heavy fringe of fair hair, and dark eyes. He has a fresh complexion and the appearance of being delicate; but he isn't. He's surprisingly strong. You can picture him controlling an enormous frantic horse. At the same time, there's a kind of magic air of vagueness about him; he's like a child lost in a fairy-story forest. In repose, his face looks lost and sad, so that people long to help him in some way. That's his charm, and that's what makes him dangerous; because you couldn't. You could no more help him (psychologically, I mean) than you could help an animal. If you tried, you'd probably get bitten. Oh yes, he's very much on his guard.

I'll put it in another way. Adrian's like the young man you sometimes see in a bookshop, wandering about aimlessly but with a kind of repressed excitement. If the shop-assistant asks what he wants, he starts guiltily and mutters: "Oh, nothing, thanks. I'm just looking round." And yet, all the while, he's searching—unconsciously, almost. If only one could guess what the *right* book was, and put it where he'd find it for himself! If you *did* guess, and offered it to him directly, he'd be furious. He'd turn and run out of the shop.

Adrian affects a bored, languid tone, especially when he's talking to his elders. But his eyes give him away. They fairly burn with eagerness; and he knows this, he's ashamed of it and keeps looking down at the carpet to hide them. He says languidly: "Of course, one can't possibly read Meredith nowadays." And, really, he's imploring you to contradict him; to make some tremendous, definite statement. To utter the final, wonderful Word about Life and Art. And one does so wish one could! That's how the Young seduce us, always. You're seduced by your own vanity into playing the prophet. Then they see through you, and they never forgive you. And, after all, why should they?

Where I've been wrong about Adrian is that I'd imagined him very lively on the surface—lots of noise and jazz and wildness— and inside, empty, lost, despairing. No, no—that's the conventional stock character: the Orphan of the Saxophone Age. *My* Adrian's far more interesting. On the surface, this polite, guarded boredom; this self-protective vagueness. And inside— flashing out of him at moments—a really startling joy, a marvellous, pure silliness and fun. I want to do a scene where he and the girl go to the Zoo together, to talk over their problems, very serious and adult. And, suddenly, he's a little boy. He jumps about, he shouts, he pulls faces at the monkeys. It's incredible!

I don't imagine any of this will make much sense to you, Cecilia darling. I'm still rather incoherent, I'm afraid, when I think about Adrian. But it has helped me, enormously, to write this down.

That's one of the worst problems of this tantalizing occupation. You think out a character, quite coldly and objectively,
with the top of your mind. He's just a dummy, so then you
pray for him to come to life. But if, by some miracle, he does,
you find yourself losing all control of him. You're infatuated,
possessed. You have to struggle to get out of his clutches; to
stand back and take a good calm look at him.

I can see I shall have to be *very* objective about Adrian. And
I'd better start at once, before it's too late!'

Is that really the way you saw me, Elizabeth? How absurd,
how wonderful of you. Oh, if only we could be reading this
now, together! I can just hear you laughing over it.

How I wish I'd written down my first impressions of *you*!
What can I remember?

Sarah took me upstairs to your flat right away, as soon as I'd
arrived. I was tired and I didn't particularly want to meet you
just then, but she insisted. When you called to us to come in,
she opened the door with a dramatic sweep and announced
'Here he is!' I was terribly embarrassed. I was sure we were
interrupting you in the middle of your work. But you were
charming. You offered us sherry. You said, 'I don't suppose I
can tempt you, Sarah?' And Sarah said, 'Oh, but you most
certainly can! This is a great occasion!'

Sarah rattled on about me, and the things I'd said and done
when I was a kid. You'd probably heard them all before, but
you smiled and seemed to listen very attentively. I just stared at
you. You were so utterly different from what I'd expected. How
could I have expected you, anyway? I'd never met anyone in
the least like you.

Your rather long, amused mouth, and your grey eyes with
that marvellous light in them, so alive, so aware of everything
around you. Your clear thoughtful voice, that gave special
shades of meaning and second meaning to even the most ordinary

words. And the way you moved, making everything you did seem exactly right, as if it couldn't be done otherwise. I thought you must be a very happy person. It made me happy, simply being in the room with you. I knew you must be about ten years older than me—in your thirties, certainly—but that wasn't important; you could have been sixty, and I'd have felt the same. If I'd had to describe you, then, I'd have just said, 'She's beautiful.'

I remember our second meeting much more clearly. It was later that same evening. I felt as if I couldn't possibly sleep until I'd talked to you again, alone. So, after Sarah had gone to bed, I went up and knocked on your door, all ready prepared with an excuse that I wanted to borrow a book I'd noticed on your shelf. It was Cocteau's *Rappel à l'Ordre*. I had a copy of it downstairs in my suitcase, but I chose it because I thought it would start an interesting discussion and because it would show you I could read French. And then you opened the door and seemed delighted, and exclaimed, 'But this is positively telephathic! I was just wondering if I dared come down and disturb you——' For a moment, I was struck breathless with joy and excitement. I don't know exactly what I thought you were going to say. I suppose I expected some amazing declaration that you liked me, thought me interesting, wanted us to be friends. Or, maybe, even more than that. In the crazy state of mind I was in, nothing seemed impossible. But then you went right on to explain that you'd suddenly decided it would be better to have the sofa in front of the fireplace, instead of over by the window, and that you couldn't move it by yourself. 'But please don't imagine you're going to be victimized regularly,' you said, 'just because we have a man in the house. I hate helpless females. And it'll do quite as well in the morning. It's late, and you must be exhausted.' I grabbed the sofa at once, before you'd even finished speaking, and staggered right across the room with it. Is that why you write that I was 'surprisingly strong'? I'd have done anything to show off to you. I'd even have tried controlling that 'enormous frantic horse'!

Then you suggested making some tea, and of course I stayed. I felt I'd got to make you realize, somehow or other, right away that I wasn't just Sarah's Nephew, that I was utterly different from the good little boy she'd been telling you about. I was meanly jealous of Sarah, at that moment, because you seemed to take her so seriously. I refused to believe that you really did, because that lowered my own value. I wanted you to be mercilessly penetrating in your judgment of other people, terribly fastidious in your choice of friends—and, at the same time, to choose me!

So I started to apologize for Sarah. It was clumsy and horrible, but I couldn't stop myself. 'I'm afraid you must have been bored to death,' I said. 'When she gets on the subject of me, she'll go on for ever. She has absolutely no consideration. It never occurs to her that you aren't interested. The only thing to do is to snub her.'

You burst out laughing: 'I never heard such nonsense! Come now, you don't *really* think you're such a boring subject, do you, Stephen?'

I blushed violently. It was the first time you'd called me by my Christian name. 'Actually,' I said, 'she doesn't understand me at all.'

'Oh, I don't agree with you there. I think she understands *her* part of you very well. Only I'm sure there's a great deal more of you. That's what I want you to tell me about.'

So then I was happy and flattered, and I begged you to ask me anything you wanted to know. 'Anything,' I repeated, very significantly.

'Well, first of all, tell me about the Quakers.'

And, of course, I started in to attack them: they knew nothing about Life, I said; they were self-righteous smug hypocrites, intolerant and stupid and dull, and crazy about money for all their so-called plainness. I could see at once from your face that

I was saying the wrong things; you looked disappointed and puzzled. But I'd committed myself, and I had to go on.

'But, Stephen——' you finally interrupted me. 'What about Sarah?'

That stopped me dead. 'Oh, she's different,' I said, feeling very small. 'She's how they ought to be, and aren't.'

'So you don't belong to them any more?'

'Oh no,' I said, rather grandly, 'I broke with them, ages ago. I'm afraid I think their whole position is a little childish.'

This sounded so idiotic that I was sure you'd laugh at me. But you didn't. You said, simply, 'I'm sorry, because I was hoping you'd be able to explain to me how they *feel*. Sarah's told me what they *believe*, and I've tried to feel it but I can't. I do so wish I could. I think it would be wonderful to have that kind of faith, but it seems to have been left out of me. I just can't trust this Inner Light—in myself, I mean. I keep suspecting it's only me, pretending to be Her Master's Voice. . . . But, of course, when you're all together at the Meeting, there *is* something. Even I could feel that.'

'Do you mean to say,' I asked in amazement, 'that you've actually been to *Meeting*, Elizabeth?'

'Oh yes. Twice.'

'But—why?'

'Well, Sarah rather hinted that she'd like me to. And then, when I did go, I was simply fascinated. I'd have kept on going, but I was afraid Sarah would think I was getting converted, and that wouldn't have been fair to her, would it?'

'No, I suppose not.'

'Stephen, you look almost shocked,' you said, smiling. 'Do you think it was wrong of me to go, as an unbeliever?'

'No—no, of course not. It's only that I just can't imagine you there, somehow.'

You laughed at that. 'How *do* you imagine me, Stephen? Oh, please tell me!'

I couldn't answer that; I blushed and stammered.

You went on gaily: 'Now I *know* it must be something awful! Let me try and guess. . . . Oh dear, I can see an exquisitely cultured, aloof female, lying on a Chinese couch and reading Mallarmé. And I'm sure she's smoking cigarettes through a long ivory holder.'

So then I had to confess that you'd been right about the holder; and we both laughed a lot. You were so amused that you clapped your hands, as you sometimes did. 'But go on with what you were saying,' you finally asked, 'about the Quakers' position being childish. In what way, do you mean?'

'I didn't mean anything,' I said, feeling quite relaxed, now, and able to be frank. 'I was just trying to sound impressive.'

'Oh, Stephen, how sweet of you to want to impress me! I'm like that, too, sometimes. Isn't it absurd? I expect we all are—except people like Sarah.'

That was wonderful, and it seemed we were getting along splendidly. But I spoiled things again, just as we were saying Goodnight, by making a pompous, insincere little speech about your stories. I said, 'They're some of the most significant work anyone's done since the War.' And you looked suddenly weary and pained and somehow lonely, as if I'd locked you up in a room all by yourself. 'Oh no, Stephen,' you said. 'They aren't any good, really. They aren't in the least what I wanted them to be. Please don't let's talk about them.' So I went downstairs feeling dissatisfied, and I kept waking in the night to think of all the brilliant, intimate, intuitive things I ought to have said to you.

From then on, we were together a lot; soon, it got to be almost every day. At first, I was afraid of bothering you. I even made excuses, sometimes, when you suggested our meeting and I had nothing whatever to do. But then I came to realize that you never saw me out of mere politeness, or when you were busy. You always worked in the mornings; and I thought

I could tell how the novel was going by your manner, although you didn't care to talk about it much. You never liked talking about your work, although you'd write about it to Cecilia and others. 'I'm always afraid I'll talk myself right out of it,' you explained to me, once. 'One can, you know. In letters, it's different; you can be careful what you tell. But somewhere, deep down inside, there's the bud of the interest itself. If you pluck that out and show it to other people, then it'll never unfold. It dies, and you simply don't care to go on.'

Sometimes, everything was perfect. Sometimes, I felt I was ruining our whole friendship. In spite of myself, I kept trying to show off. I made remarks like the one about not being able to read Meredith, and you always took them literally, so that I ended by having to confess I didn't mean them. 'You must say exactly what you mean,' you told me, 'when you're with me. Because I'm really a very stupid person. No—that's not mock-humility. I think it's even a kind of saving fault. It's my way of getting to the bottom of things.' I tried hard to be as you wanted me to be. And, now and then, I didn't try and was perfectly natural. Those were the best times—like the visit to the Zoo you mention. Only, it was you who started making faces at the monkeys. You were always the one who got us into that mood. Your silliness was much more spontaneous than mine.

One day, I started telling you about my adventures in Paris and Berlin. I rather hoped I'd shock you, a little; I was still busy proving I wasn't Sarah's little boy. So I referred archly to the bars and the whorehouses and the Sex Museum, and hinted at my knowledge of weird perversions. I was vulgar and nasty; and you weren't in the least shocked. You just smiled and looked indulgent and abstracted, like a mother who listens to her child telling her about the dog having puppies. But when I mentioned Marie and Annette and Trude, you were interested at once. You wanted to know all about them. You asked me dozens of questions: how they dressed, how they talked, what they thought about. I could see you were projecting yourself into their lives. You always did that. You translated everything into terms of individual human beings. You taught me so much, in those days, and so simply. I'm sure you weren't even aware that you were doing it.

I assumed, of course, that you'd had a glamorous love-life of your own. But you never spoke of it at that time—not until much later—and your silence made me feel petty and indiscreet. Sometimes, though, you talked about Love in a way that showed me you were remembering a personal experience. I can see you now, in the twilight of a winter afternoon, sitting with your finger-tips stretched toward the fire, looking deeply into it, and saying, 'No, Stephen; that's not how it begins—not by two people feeling drawn together. It's the moment when they suddenly know they're different from each other. Utterly, utterly different; so that it's horribly painful—unbearable, almost. You're like the North and South Poles. You couldn't possibly be farther apart. And yet, at the same time, you're more connected than any other two points on the surface of the earth. Because there's this axis between you. And everything else turns round it.' When you said that, I thought it was so beautiful that my eyes filled with tears. Several months later, when I read it, repeated almost word for word, in the manuscript of *As Birds Do*, *Mother*, I was somehow a bit shocked. That was very naïve of me. I suppose I wanted my private Elizabeth to be an entirely separate person from the Elizabeth who wrote your novels.

Always, in the background of our talks, there was that question I longed to ask you and never quite dared. 'Why do you like me?' What makes you spend so much time with me? How can I possibly be of any interest to you?' I dreaded your answer, because I felt I knew what it would be. I was afraid Sarah had predicted it only too well when she said to me innocently: 'I'm so very glad you and Elizabeth Rydal have become such friends,

Stephen dear. And I'm sure she is, too. She probably gets tired of all those grand intellectual friends of hers, and needs someone young and lively. Someone who'll take her mind off her work.'

Those 'grand intellectual friends'! I was acutely conscious of their presence, around you, all the time; even though you seldom referred to them, and then only in the most casual way. Occasionally, you'd suggest taking me to see Virginia Woolf or Ethel Mayne, or ask me to come up to the flat when you were having them to tea. But I always refused. I regarded these people as my natural enemies. I imagined them looking through and through me, judging me, dismissing me; and then, when I'd gone, making some clever, sneering remark about me to you which would work in your mind like slow poison until you began to agree with them, to see me as they did; and stopped having anything to do with me. I met Hugh Walpole once, on the stairs, on his way up to visit you. He stopped and introduced himself, saying that he'd heard so much about me from you. His apple-cheeks shone with geniality and he was kind and chatty; doing everything to put me at my ease. But I refused to relax. I didn't dare let myself trust him.

There was one friend of yours I actually hated: Alexander Strines. Poor Strines! How incredible that seems, now, when I think of him as I last saw him in 1936, crippled with arthritis and prematurely old—a miserable, plaintive creature who claimed that all his friends had betrayed him! But, in 1926, he was still very goodlooking in a rather cold eighteenth-century style, with his hair getting becomingly grey around the temples. He was writing art-criticism, and the kind of highbrow-pastoral poetry they used to call Georgian. His book on William Beckford had just come out and made quite a sensation.

I hated Strines because I was specially jealous of him. He visited you much more often than the others, and I knew that you went to see him, too. Also, you quoted his remarks to me from time to time; prefacing them with 'according to Strines——' or 'Strines has a most extraordinary theory that——' Your ironical tone didn't hide the fact that you thought them clever. You always addressed him as 'Strines'. And he called you 'Rydal', a bit of affection I loathed.

I became gradually possessed by the suspicion that you were having an affair with him. The idea seemed to me horrible and yet entirely natural; trying to look at him through your eyes, I magnified his attractiveness until he appeared as irresistible as a Byron. I watched your face intently when you spoke of him. And I used to watch his arrival at our house, from my bedroom window. I fancied I could detect in his manner the self-assurance of an accepted lover. 'He's going to kiss her,' I thought. 'He's going to touch her. He's going to go to bed with her.' I trembled with hate. In my slightly crazy fantasies, he always ended by leaving you for another woman, and this gave me a reason to pick a fight with him and kill him and get hanged, with you in tears outside the prison gates waiting for them to post the notice of my execution.

I'd been forced to meet Strines two or three times, when he looked in to see you unexpectedly, as he did now and then. I'd always found an excuse to leave you alone together within a few minutes. But at last, on that historic afternoon, the first of January, I was properly trapped. You'd invited me to tea, and we'd hardly sat down when he appeared. I was all the more disgusted because we'd just started a conversation which promised to become intimate. You'd asked me if I had any New Year resolutions for 1927, and I was excited and confused, wondering how to find a subtle way of saying 'I'm going to get to know you better'. And then, while I was hesitating over my answer, there he stood, smiling that thin teasing smile which narrowed his lips and eyes and was really a joyless grimace. 'Hullo, Rydal,' he said. 'Do I rush in where Forster fears to tread?' 'Certainly not,' you said, laughing. 'Though I wouldn't be surprised if he does. Last time he was here he tripped over that hole in the carpet, poor man, and hurt his knee. Sit down. I'll get another cup.' While you were out in the kitchen, Strines condescended to notice my presence, with a mock-courtly bow. 'I see I've caught you this time, Mr. Monk,' he said. 'This is a rare privilege. You've been somewhat elusive, you know.' I didn't answer.

'We were just talking about New Year resolutions,' you said, coming back into the sitting-room. 'Have you made any, Strines?'

'Certainly I have. I've resolved to ignore the new Epsteins.'

'Oh, you haven't seen them, then? I was longing to know what you thought of them.'

'Well, I confess I did lurk for an instant in the farthest possible corner of the gallery and venture one glance. They have a curiously obscene air of deflation, don't you know; like those rubber carnival figures, when the carnival's over and they're beginning to wrinkle and wilt. Tellement funeste!'

He went on like that, about Paul Nash and the Sitwells and Delius and Arnold Bennett, making all of them seem silly and little. And you enjoyed it. That was what I minded. Because, I said to myself, if *I'd* talked that way you'd have pulled me up at once. In your eyes, obviously, he could do no wrong. I felt you were in league with him against me.

Then he began to talk about a literary and political weekly that was about to be launched, called the *New Athenian*. 'It appears,' he said, 'that we're in for another classical revival, of the most dismally provincial kind. Shaw will have to do for our Socrates, I suppose. Who do you fancy for Alcibiades? I'm very much afraid one's reduced to Noel Coward. Unless, of course, we import one of those excessively dental American cinema stars.' You were delighted with this game; and the two of you played it until tea was over, making the most ridiculous suggestions you could think of, including Sir Edwin Lutyens for Phidias. If Strines hadn't been there, I'd probably have thought it all very funny. But I was in a state of scowling sulks. Whenever you asked me for my opinion—Strines didn't, once—I merely growled, 'I don't know.'

'But the most embarrassing part of it all is,' he finally told you, 'that they want me to do something for the first number.'

'Oh, Strines, what about?'

'My dear, you'd never guess. The workings of their minds are positively inscrutable. I'm to write on Milton.'

'*Milton?*' you exclaimed, laughing. By this time, you were laughing at everything he said.

'Yes—Milton! Isn't that peculiarly depressing? One read him at School, of course. . . . Why, this is providential! I'm sure Mr. Monk can help us. Mr. Monk, didn't they make you learn Milton, for your sins?'

'He's one of my favourite poets,' I lied, looking Strines coldly in the eye.

It didn't abash him in the least. 'But how splendid!' he said. 'Then I'll tell you my idea. I thought it might be vaguely amusing if one compared *Paradise Lost* and *Paradise Regained*; maintaining —with an air of deadly earnestness, of course—that *Paradise Regained* is infinitely superior. How does that strike you, Rydal?'

'Oh, what fun!' you said.

'The only trouble is, that one will have to make one's case in the most convincing detail. And I must confess that the prospect of studying *Paradise Regained* fills me with acute aversion. Mr. Monk, I appeal to you. Do give me some hints. Where shall I base my defence? What are your favourite passages?'

I felt myself getting hot in the face. 'It's a long time since I read it,' I mumbled.

Strines looked at me mockingly, with one eyebrow slightly raised. I knew he knew I was lying. 'Oh, come now,' he said. 'Really, Mr. Monk, it can't have been such a *very* long time, can it?'

Suddenly, I lost my head. I was wild with humiliation and

rage. 'And anyhow,' I said, 'it's the stupidest idea I ever heard of What's so clever about writing things you don't believe? They do that every day, in the newspapers. I'm sorry, Elizabeth, I have to be going.' I got up and walked out of the room.

That was the worst moment I'd ever experienced. Every step I took down those stairs was like a step out of your life. I knew I could never go back up them again. And yet I couldn't stop myself. I didn't even want to. I felt dizzy and, in a strange way, exhilarated, as if I was drunk. My hand shook so much that I could hardly turn the doorknob to get into our flat. Sarah was out, thank Goodness. I went into my bedroom and lay down on the bed, without switching on the lights. I decided to leave London the next day, for ever.

Then I heard footsteps coming down, and the front door opened and closed. I raised myself on my elbows and peeped through the window, in time to see Strines as he passed under the street-lamp, walking away. He looked pleased with himself, I thought. No doubt he was glad to have gotten rid of me so easily.

After a minute or two, there were more footsteps and a knock on our door. I didn't move. I lay tense, holding my breath. 'Stephen,' you called. I didn't answer. I heard you try the handle. 'Stephen, are you there?' The door opened. You came into the sitting-room, crossed to my bedroom door. It was ajar, and you saw me. 'May I come in, Stephen?' When I didn't answer, you came in and sat down on the foot of my bed.

'Please tell me what's the matter,' you said.

'Nothing's the matter,' I told you. 'Leave me alone.'

'Please tell me. I know you're hurt, somehow. Was it my fault? If it was, forgive me.'

I sat up. It was too dark to see your face, but your silhouette showed against the window. 'I was very rude,' I said. 'I apologize. You can tell Strines I'm sorry—if that'll make it less embarrassing for you.'

'Oh, Stephen,' you said, taking my hand. 'Don't be so formal,

and hostile! You *must* explain. This is terribly important—to
me, at any rate.'

'I don't see why,' I said, pulling my hand away.

'Poor Strines was quite bewildered. He felt he must have
offended you, in some way. It certainly wasn't intentional.'

'I don't care if it was or not. And I know it's none of my
business—how you feel about him.'

'Stephen, what on earth do you mean?'

'You know damn' well what I mean. I've seen how you look
at him, when you're together.'

'You think Strines and I——? Oh, my Goodness!' You began
to laugh, and then stopped yourself abruptly. 'But you can't
really believe that? It just isn't possible. Not if he were the last
person in the world. . . . Stephen, this is too utterly absurd.'

'I dare say it is—to you.'

'But, my dear—what do you want me to say?'

'You don't have to say anything. After tonight, you won't ever
see me again.'

'You can't be serious!'

'I don't know why you pretend to be so surprised,' I said.
'This must keep happening to you all the time. You meet someone like me, and he amuses you as long as he behaves himself.
Then he falls in love with you and gets jealous and tiresome, and
has to be thrown out.'

'Stephen,' you asked, very quietly, 'Do you honestly mean that?'

'What?'

'That you're in love with me?'

'I know, in your eyes, I'm practically a schoolboy. You think
I'm too young to have any feelings——'

'I don't. Of course I don't think that. . . . But there's such a
thing as, well, infatuation. It can happen very easily. Just because
I'm older, and seem to you—oh, something I'm really not. . . .
No, don't misunderstand me. Even if it's only that, I do respect
it. I think it's beautiful——'

'Yes. I suppose it tickles your vanity.'

'Stephen! How can you be so cruel? You sound as if you hated me.'

'Oh, what the hell do you care if I hate you!' I couldn't help it. I started to cry like a baby. I threw myself down and buried my face in the pillow, sobbing.

Then I felt your hand stroking my hair. You were bending over me. 'Darling,' you said, 'Hasn't it ever occurred to you that perhaps I might——'

Something in the tone of your voice stopped me at once. It was different, and shaky. I couldn't be sure if you were laughing, or about to cry, yourself.

'That I might be in love with you, too?'

My heart began to beat so hard that I could barely hear what you were saying.

'Well, darling, I am. In the most desperate, idiotic, old-fashioned sort of way. I'd firmly made up my mind never to tell you. If you must know, *I* thought I'd better go away somewhere—because it all seemed so unsuitable and impossible. Only, I found I couldn't. I just didn't have the courage. I had to keep on seeing you——'

'Elizabeth!' I sat right up again. I was almost more astounded than happy. 'Oh, God, it isn't true! It can't be!'

'I'm afraid it is.'

'I don't believe it!' I grabbed you in my arms as though you were about to vanish.

'Do you believe it now?' you whispered, after a minute.

'I'm beginning to.'

'So am I. . . . Oh, Stephen, Stephen, whatever is going to happen to us?'

'Does it matter?'

'No. Not yet.'

'But, Elizabeth—— Do you mean you'll actually——'

'Actually what, darling?'

'Marry me?'

You gave a kind of gasp. 'Stephen! You really are the most amazing angelic person I've ever met! You *want* to?'

'Then you don't?'

'Of course—of course I want to. More than anything else in the world. Only—it seems such madness.'

'What's mad about it?'

'Listen, darling. We *must* be sensible. I'll go off with you, tomorrow, anywhere you like. And we can try it for a while, until we're quite, quite sure.'

'Aren't you sure now?'

'*I* am. . . . But—suppose you got tired of me?'

'Oh, Elizabeth darling. I'm scared to death that you'll get tired of *me*! That's why I'm going to marry you now, at once.'

'Let's not talk about it now,' you said, kissing me. 'Another time. . . . Oh, my darling, we shall have to be very patient and gentle with each other. Much more than most people. Do you realize that——?'

It was then that we heard the sound of a key in the front door.

'My God,' I said, 'that's Sarah!'

'Oh, *no*!'

'I'll put the light on.' I jumped off the bed.

'Don't look at me!'

By the time I'd turned the switch, you were at the mirror, ready to tidy your hair. 'This is worse than *Lady Windermere's Fan*,' you said. We were both giggling. I dashed across the sitting-room and got the light on there, too, half a second before Sarah opened the door from the hallway.

'Why, Stephen dear,' Sarah exclaimed, 'How you startled me! That's strange—I fancied there was nobody home.'

Then you came out of the bedroom, as calm as Mrs. Erlynne. 'Good evening, Sarah,' you said. 'I just looked in to find out if Stephen——'

'Aunt Sarah,' I interrupted, taking your hand. 'I've asked

Elizabeth to marry me. And she's accepted. Haven't you, Elizabeth?'

'Well—yes. Apparently——' you said, beginning to laugh.

That was one of Sarah's greatest moments. Pale and tired after her long day at the dockside settlement in the East End, and burdened with her heavy shopping-basket, she stood looking from the one to the other of us. I shall never know what she was thinking. But then her face lighted up. She put the basket down, came over and clasped you in her arms, and kissed you on the cheek.

'Why, that's wonderful, my dear,' she said. 'My lands, I am surprised! But it's wonderful. Oh, I'm so glad for you both! I know you two children are going to be very happy.'

THREE

B Y the time Gerda came in to get me ready for breakfast, I'd usually been awake so long that her arrival seemed like the end of Act One of the morning, rather than the beginning of the day.

When I woke up, the first thing I knew was the cast. Sometimes it had appeared in my dreams, disguised as a heavy garment, or the walls of a very small closet, or a vague feeling that I was forbidden to leave the place I was in. But when I woke, it was simply itself, and there. At that time of day, I didn't hate it at all. My body had somehow become reconciled to it while I was asleep. It was part of my condition, and I accepted it as completely as I accepted my nose and ears.

Lying there, in the almost mindless calm of first waking, I felt as if I could remember everything I'd ever done or said or thought since I was a baby. Only this wasn't exactly remembering. Memory pieces things together gradually, making a chain; this was total, instantaneous awareness. The thousands of bits of my life seemed to be scattered around me, like the furniture of the room, all simultaneously present. I wasn't young, I wasn't old; I wasn't any particular age or any particular I. Everything particular was on the outside; and what was aware of this was a simple consciousness that had no name, no face, no identity of any kind. Consciousness lay here, anonymous, and looked at the accumulated clutter of half a lifetime. If there was a Purgatory, or some kind of lucid post-mortem interval, it would probably be like this. You'd be set face to face, inescapably, with what you'd made of yourself, and you wouldn't be able to ignore it or turn away. That evening at the Novotnys'. Those trips to London with Warren. The time I hit Sarah, when I was a boy. The scene with Elizabeth, in Orotava. The way I'd behaved to Michael Drummond. Cowardly, vile, disgusting, idiotic. And I could never wipe any of it out. I could never atone for it. I could never be sufficiently ashamed. But consciousness wasn't ashamed, because consciousness wasn't I. It refused to accept the least responsibility for what I'd done or been. It felt no relation to my acts. It knew no feelings, except the feelings of being itself; and that was the deepest, quietest, most mysterious kind of happiness.

Within this happiness were absolute safety, entire peace. But the safety and peace never lasted for more than a few seconds or, at most, a minute at a time. Because, as soon as you said to yourself 'if only this could go on for ever!', as soon as you began to will them to continue, you automatically became I, Stephen. You identified yourself with what was outside, with the surrounding mess of your life. And, immediately, they were gone.

(Once, I'd had the same sort of experience in connection with another person. There was a night during the summer of 1937, at St. Luc, when I'd woken from heavy dreamless sleep after making love with Jane, and hadn't known who or where I was. I'd seemed to be looking down, from some impersonal no-place, at our two bodies lying in each other's arms on the bed. I could swear that I'd actually hesitated, then, like a guest at the end of a party who looks at two overcoats, not sure for a moment which is which, before I'd decided 'that one's mine'.)

As I slipped back into being my individual self, Time was re-established. The light that paled the shadows on my bedroom ceiling was now the light of a particular, dated day; unlike all other days that had ever been or would be. I became aware of its first, unique sounds; of its special brand-new breeze stirring the window-curtains and filling the room with a smell of fruit-blossom that had the powerful, almost menacing richness of the oncoming summer. The house was carrying us, its three passengers, into the unknown future, at an enormous speed. Some mornings, my sense of the speed of Time was so acute that it became actually exhilarating. I lay there in a state of strange excitement, wondering where Sarah and Gerda and I were going.

This was happiness of a different kind. I was no longer calm or safe, but I felt unreasoningly optimistic. I wasn't afraid to look at the past. Yes, it was a filthy mess; and I had made it. I took full responsibility. Everything would have to be paid for. All right, I'd pay. But now this was a new day a new start, and somehow or other—I felt certain of it—I was going to avoid the old mistakes and do better.

Once, when I was in this mood, Gerda came in and found me grinning to myself.

'You are happy?' she said.

'Am I? Yes, I guess I am.'

'Why are you happy?'

'No idea.' I started to laugh. 'Isn't that stupid?'

'No. Not stupid at all. It is good. It is best when one does not know.'

'Does that happen to you sometimes, Gerda?'

'Me? Oh, yes. Rather often. I think it is the only way one can be happy nowadays, perhaps.'

When Gerda said things of this kind—she seldom did—I found myself up against that barrier which always separated us. Peter had become a real person to me, now. Gerda had shown me a lot of photographs of him: a fattish, nearly bald young man who got thinner in the later pictures but continued to look cheerful and gentle and amiably simple. (A peculiarly modern type of hero, I thought, who could jolly you through a battle by making danger seem funny. Quite the opposite of Michael, whom I imagined scowling furiously as the fascist bullets had whizzed around his head on the Madrid front, and muttering,

'God damn the bloody idiots!' Michael would make you brave by getting you to share his indignation that anyone should have the impudence to shoot at him.) Gerda and I talked about Peter every day, but it was an unnaturally cautious, restricted sort of conversation. I was consciously careful of my tenses, remembering always when to say 'does' and not 'did'. 'Does Peter like music?' 'What does Peter think of Thomas Mann?' I was sure Gerda felt the unnaturalness too, and longed to relieve it; but we couldn't. We didn't dare. Sometimes, when I looked right into her eyes, the questions I really wanted to ask her seemed about to burst out of my mouth with the brutal frankness of pity. You don't honestly think he's still alive, do you? For God's sake, admit it—admit you're losing hope. How can you stand this? Wouldn't anything be better? Wouldn't you rather know he was dead?

Gerda was always so neat and fresh-looking, at every hour of the day. After what she'd told me about washing at the internment-camp, I knew this was part of her self-discipline; and it made me so sorry for her that I found it almost exasperating. I used to wish she'd break down and pity herself, and come in with red eyes and her hair untidy. This neatness was part of the barrier between us. I couldn't get through it and reach her. I couldn't do anything for her at all.

Before I ate my breakfast, she'd help me to wash. I disliked this. The parts of me that were inside the cast were starting to smell sweaty and sour. I didn't like Gerda to come too close.

'Do I smell very bad?' I asked her.

'No. Of course not.'

'You know I do. I stink like a pig.'

'I do not mind.'

'Oh, don't be so damned polite! Why not say so?'

'You smell like a man, not a pig.'

'That's probably worse.'

'Listen, Stephen. I am not an elegant young lady. I have lived with a man. I do not mind how men smell. I like it.'

'You mean, Peter never washes?'

'Idiot! You know I do not mean that. But, in the camp, there were many of us women who did not wash. Pfui! I can tell you, I would rather smell the most unwashed man than an unwashed woman. . . . And now, do not be foolish, please. You cannot clean your back. I shall do it.'

When Sarah came in to say Good Morning, I would have finished breakfast and be lying propped up on the pillows, washed and shaved and combed; the model aseptic invalid. I used to splash my face and neck with the strongest after-shave lotion Gerda had been able to find at the drugstore. It was advertised as 'virile, tangy, bracing as an ocean breeze, masculine as a briar pipe'. The tang didn't last very long; but, at its height, it would have killed the smell of a skunk.

Sarah brought the newspapers with her and read me the head-lines, adding her own comments. Lindbergh's isolationist speech in New York: 'Such an earnest, troubled boy; I'm sure he never does anything but what he feels is right.' Churchill, after the fall of Greece, describing Mussolini as 'this whipped jackal': 'Oh, Stephen, if only our testimony for peace had half his eloquence!' Mr. Matsuoka visiting Stalin: 'I'm afraid it can't bode anything good; oh dear, we must pray they'll somehow be guided.' The President's illness: 'Poor Eleanor Roosevelt—to have this on top of all her other concerns! It's fortunate that she has such great spiritual strength.' Hess's flight to England: 'Whatever his motives were, I do think that was rather fine.'

Then Sarah would pass on to the local news and her personal problems. Everybody at 20 South 12th Street was talking about Hugh Pomeroy's denunciation of the Philadelphia slums. The Campus was buzzing over the resignation of Dr. Hotson and Dr. Reitzel from Haverford College. The plans for the community centre were running into snags, and the committee had settled down to a series of meetings that might well drag on through the summer, with members of the opposition rising to announce gravely: 'I have a stop in my mind about this' or 'Friends, I am not easy for this to go forward'. There were quilting-parties to be organized for the marriage of George Leeds and Margaret Partland. The Negro boys' clubhouse needed a ping-pong table. The tent-caterpillars were stripping the leaves from the trees in the orchard, and Sarah was afraid she'd have to get their nests burned out with kerosene torches, much as she hated to do it.

I used to listen to all this inattentively but with growing uneasiness and depression. In the past, the newspapers had never seemed to me quite as horrible and meaningless as they did now. I must have taken them more or less for granted; just as I'd taken for granted the whole outside world of people and events that didn't directly concern me. Now I felt astonished and ashamed that I'd been so insensitive. Out there, in the world around my bed, Churchill was a real old man blinking through his spectacles as he signed papers. Hitler was actually eating his vegetarian lunch, Stalin was alive and smoking his pipe and speaking Russian in the Kremlin, thousands of men were really firing guns or groaning with pain in hospitals, housewives were talking about matter-of-fact air-raids as they stood in line to buy food. The newspapers 'covered' all these circumstances but nevertheless missed the whole point; their despatches were like those reviews of Elizabeth's novels, in which you could scarcely recognize the novels themselves. The reviews were meaningless because they showed no understanding of why Elizabeth had written her books; and the news-items in the papers were meaningless in exactly the same way. Even if they were about you, you wouldn't be able to recognize yourself or your life in them. Indeed, they were far more horrible than life itself. They could never tell you anything good, because the one fact that outweighs all others—that life is bearable to most of us, most of the time, in spite of everything—is not news. Life is bearable because we know, or think we know, that it has a meaning; but the newspapers blandly presented a world without any meaning whatsoever. The meaning they pretended to impose upon it in their editorials was no meaning; just a bunch of heartless, tinny phrases about democracy, freedom, fascism, patriotism and so forth. Sarah was instinctively protesting against this when she pinned the headlines down to the reality of live human beings, but she was too deep in her own activities to have time to get indignant. Elizabeth had once said to me 'any news is bad news', and I'd laughed, taking it as a mild Oscar Wildean joke. Now it seemed to me that I understood what she'd really meant.

Throughout Sarah's morning visit, I was impatient to escape from the world of the newspapers into the world of Elizabeth. I fidgeted with eagerness to get back to the letters. The morning was the best time for them, because Sarah would be away in Philadelphia or the village and Gerda had the housework, and I would be left alone. The moment that Sarah had gone out of the room I would reach down for the file, which stood on the lower shelf of the table beside my bed, but I wouldn't open it at once. First, I had to get into the right mood. Sometimes I'd lie quite still with my eyes closed for as much as half an hour, letting myself sink slowly into a state of reverie that was almost a trance. I found that if I did this before I began to read the letters, I could remember things more easily. As the days passed, I became able to induce this reverie fairly quickly; just as a good medium can go into a trance at will.

The heavy drowsy spring weather helped me by deadening the sights and sounds of the present moment, making them dreamlike and vague. I seemed to be drowning in memory; it was like being drowsy-drunk or half-asleep. Only the remembering part of my mind stayed sharply clear, and all my senses were awake in the past. When Elizabeth mentioned the Schwar-zsee, I could literally smell the wet lilac-bushes; when she described our trip to Khalkis, I felt a sudden intense hunger for fried squid. Now and then, these sense-impressions were so vivid that I wondered if this wasn't something more than memory; if I wasn't, in some way, actually reliving the original event. That day we had lunch with Rose Macaulay in Carcassone —did I merely remember a bright green snail crawling up the table-leg or was I noticing it now for the first time?

When the mood was strongly upon me, it persisted through all the incidents of my daily routine. Gerda bringing in my lunch didn't interrupt it in the least. And, as my reverie-technique improved, I could even receive visitors without coming out of it altogether. Martha Chance dropped by to see me often, and there were the Harpers, and other Dolgelly neighbours. They chattered away and were quite lifelike, but no more so than Dorothea and Mr. Casaubon out of *Middlemarch*, which Sarah read aloud to me in the afternoons. I think I was perfectly rational and answered their questions sensibly; at any rate, they never seemed to suspect that I wasn't entirely with them. But Elizabeth remained with me throughout their visits and was much more substantially present than they were, although she'd withdrawn, as it were, to a far corner of the room.

During the first week of my bed-life I did have one visitor, however, who startled me right out of the reverie because he was unexpected. Both Gerda and Sarah were away that morning, and I was alone in the house. I heard steps on the stairs and along the corridor, where they seemed to hesitate, and then there was a sudden impatient knock at the door. It opened before I could answer. Bob Wood came slouching into the room.

'Hello,' he said.

'Hello, there.'

'What are you doing?' There was a kind of reproachful surprise in his tone.

'Just lying here on my ass. Did you expect to find me tap-dancing?'

Bob grinned. Then he seemed to lose all interest in me. He wandered restlessly around the room, picking up books and putting them down again immediately, as though he were hunting for something. I watched him, remembering how Michael Drummond used to do this too.

'Aren't you bored?' he asked abruptly. He sounded just like Charles Kennedy.

'No. That's a funny thing—I keep expecting I will be, but I'm not.'

'What do you think about, all day?'

'Oh—everything.'

'I'll bet you do.' Bob looked at me with sympathetic curiosity. 'You know, I kind of envy you? That's just what I need, right now; to be shut up some place where I don't have anything to do but think.' There was a pause. 'Charles says you were raised as a Quaker. Like me.'

'Yes. I was.'

'Do you believe any of that, now?'

'Well—it rather depends what you mean by——'

'Oh, for Pete's sake, Steve,' Bob interrupted impatiently, 'you don't have to be cagey. You know perfectly well what I mean. To begin with, do you believe in God?' He scowled angrily as he brought the word out, and his mouth pulled down sideways into a deprecatory grimace.

'Well, yes. Yes, I guess so. Only——'

'I do,' Bob told me aggressively, as if my answer had been No. 'But the trouble is, I just can't stand the sort of people who do.'

'Thanks,' I said. We both laughed.

'Oh, I'm not including you, Steve. You're different. At least, I think you are. . . . That's why I went to Meeting the other day. I hadn't been in years. I wanted to see if it was still the way I remembered.'

'And was it?'

'Pretty much. It was still there, this thing I used to feel—whatever it is. And I still couldn't stand the people.'

'They bothered me, too.'

'They did? Good, I'm glad of that. Then you do know what I mean. . . . Jesus, you'd think the Inner Light was something they owned! And they hate like hell to admit that anyone can get any of it without joining their club and keeping all their rules. I felt like a gatecrasher.'

'No, Bob! That's not true. I'm certain it isn't. I used to think that, myself. But I know I was wrong.'

'Well, maybe I'm exaggerating. I get a bit carried away, whenever I talk about them. . . . How did you feel about the Meeting itself?'

'The same way you did, more or less. The thing was still there.'

'Isn't it amazing, how it takes hold of you again?'

'I know. I kept fighting it, though. I didn't want it to.'

'Neither did I. . . . Charles couldn't possibly understand any of that. You couldn't expect him to, I guess. He doesn't have our background. . . . You know, Steve, you and I are kind of in the same boat?'

'Yes, I suppose we are.'

'That's why I had to come and talk to you. You see, I've got to do an awful lot of thinking. And quick. I might be going back in the Navy, soon.'

'Sarah told me.'

'When I enlisted before, I was just a kid. I did it because I wanted to make a big gesture, and show the Friends what a hell of a rebel I was. Whatever they believed in, I was against, automatically. As a matter of fact, my gesture fell flat. Nobody gave a damn, either way, what I did. And I had lots of fun. But everything's different, now. . . . Are you a pacifist, Steve?'

'Kind of. I haven't ever thought about it properly.'

'I hadn't, until quite lately. And I'm still all mixed up. Of course, I loathe all this wishy-washy brotherly-love talk. Just the same, you know, the Friends really have got something there. If you read what Christ said—not all those alibis and double-talk about what He's supposed to have meant—there aren't any two ways about it. . . . I suppose we'll get into this War, won't we, sooner or later?'

'Yes, I'm afraid we will.'

'It isn't so much that I'm scared of that. Though I am, of course. But I'd be even more scared of being a conchie.'

'So would I.'

'What did you tell them when you registered for the draft?'

'I haven't had to, yet. I'm just over age.'

'You are? You don't look it. . . . If I don't go back in the Navy, I'll be drafted. I didn't register as a C.O. I couldn't make up my mind to. Now I'd just have to refuse, and go to jail. . . . Would you go to jail, Steve?'

'I'd have to be awfully sure I was right, first. And, even then, I'd try to find some excuse to wriggle out of it.'

'You probably don't feel quite the same way about the Law as I do. That's natural. After all,' Bob's mouth pulled down sideways again, '*you're* not a professional criminal.'

'What do you mean by that?'

'Exactly what did Sarah tell you about Charles and me?'

'Not very much. Why?'

'Look, you don't have to play naïve. You're not like those old biddies in Dolgelly who keep trying to marry Charles off to their daughters. You've been around. When two guys live together, you know what that means?'

I smiled. 'Not necessarily.'

'Well, in our case it does.' Bob looked at me with a certain hostility. 'Charles said you'd know that without being told. Only I don't like leaving things vague.'

'And what am I supposed to do now? Ask you to get out of the house?'

Bob grinned uncertainly. 'That's up to you.'

'Sure, I understand all about that, Bob. And I'm glad you told me. I mean, I appreciate your wanting to. I kind of guessed, but I wasn't sure——' I tried hard, but I couldn't quite keep the embarrassment out of my voice. 'Naturally, I don't think it's wrong, or anything. Certainly not for people like you and Charles. You're not children. You both know what you're doing.'

'You're pretty broad-minded, aren't you?'

'Oh, Bob, don't be stuffy about this, please!'

'That's what you heterosexuals always say. We'll run you out of town. We'll send you to jail. We'll stop you ever getting another job. But please don't you be stuffy about it.'

'I only mean don't be so aggressive. That's what puts people against you.'

'Maybe we ought to put people against us. Maybe we're too damned tactful. People just ignore us, most of the time, and we let them. We encourage them to. So this whole business never gets discussed, and the laws never get changed. There's a few people right here in the village who really know what the score is with Charles and me, but they won't admit it, not even to themselves. We're such *nice* boys, they say. So wholesome. They just refuse to imagine how nice boys like us could be arrested and locked up as crooks. They're afraid to think about it, for fear it'd trouble their tender consciences. Next thing you know, they might get a *concern*'—Bob's mouth was twitching ferociously—'and then they'd have to *do* something. Jesus, I'd like to take them and rub their noses in it!'

'That wouldn't help Charles much, in his position.'

'Do you suppose I don't realize that? If it wasn't for Charles, I'd be out of this dump in five minutes, anyway.'

'Let me tell you something, Bob. There was a guy *I* liked, once. In that way, I mean——'

'Sure, I know.' Bob grinned ironically. 'Some kid in school. And afterwards you hated yourselves. And now he's married and got ten children.'

'No. This wasn't in school——'

'Well then, it was in some low bar in Port Said, and you were drunk, and you got picked up, and it was horrible——'

'It wasn't in Port Said, and it wasn't in the least horrible. It didn't just happen once, either. I told you, I liked this guy. He's one of the best people I've ever known. . . . And now, will you stop treating me like a public meeting?'

'Okay, okay,' said Bob, laughing. 'I'm sorry. You're all right, Steve. If everyone was like you, I wouldn't get so mad.'

'But you rather enjoy getting mad, don't you?'

'I do not. It makes me sick to my stomach. It's the only way I seem to be able to let off steam, though. In the Service, I was always getting into fist-fights, for no reason at all. I lost a couple of teeth that way, but at least there were no hard feelings afterward. It was a lot better than saying rotten things you don't mean and hurting someone you really care about. I do that to Charles, sometimes. I act like the filthiest little bitch. It's a wonder he doesn't throw me out. . . . Jesus, it's a bore being neurotic! Look, I'd better be going.'

'Do you have to?'

'You don't want to listen to any more of this dreary crap.'

'I'm in the mood for crap, today. The drearier the better.'

'Well, I'm not.'

'No, seriously, Bob, I just wish I could help you somehow. I mean, say something constructive.'

'You don't have to. It does me good just to talk to someone who isn't sick in the head.'

'How do you know I'm not?'

'Well, if you are, I don't want to hear about it. Don't

you ever lose your wig while I'm around. I won't stand for it.'

'I'll keep it glued on tight. . . . Come and see me soon again, won't you? How about tomorrow?'

'All right. If you really want me to. I'm not much of a sick-bed visitor.'

'You're the kind I like best. You haven't once said you were sorry for me.'

'I'm not. I'm too busy being sorry for myself.'

'That's the spirit!'

'Well—take it easy.'

'You too.'

Bob was already moving toward the door. He turned for a moment and gave me a quick smile that was both humorous and unhappy. 'I sure wish I could,' he said. Then he went out.

When Charles Kennedy looked in to see me, which he did two or three times a week, it would usually be around six o'clock in the evening. The day after Bob's visit, he appeared, bringing with him a contraption which he called a monkey-bar. It was a kind of miniature trapeze hanging from a metal arm which was made to screw on to a bedstead. I could take hold of it and pull myself up in bed, whenever I'd slipped down too far.

'You know Bob was in to see me yesterday?' I asked, while he was installing it.

'Yes. He told me.' Charles spoke in his briefest staccato. He was standing at the back of the bed where I couldn't see his face, but I knew at once that something was wrong.

'As a matter of fact,' I went on, 'I was expecting him to come again this morning. He promised to.'

Charles was silent.

'Is there any special reason,' I persisted, 'why he didn't?'

Charles didn't answer at once. He shook the metal arm to

make sure that it was firmly attached. Then he came around the bed and sat down on the end of it, facing me.

'It was probably my fault,' he said. 'Bob and I had a big argument, last night. One of the biggest we ever had since we've been together.'

'What about?'

'Well, it started about you.' Charles grinned at me painfully. He was obviously embarrassed. 'In fact, I suppose it was a rather ordinary kind of domestic jealousy scene. As far as I was concerned.'

'Jealousy? You surely don't mean that Bob——?'

'No—it wasn't quite as ordinary as that. But he came home and raved about you. How wonderful and sympathetic and understanding you were. Meaning that I wasn't.'

'But, Charles, that's ridiculous! If Bob does feel that about me, it's only because I'm a complete stranger. Strangers always seem to understand everything—until you get to know them.'

'That's exactly what I told him.' Charles smiled in a more relaxed manner. 'No offence to you, Stephen! I think you *are* an understanding person. And I think you might be very good for Bob. It was idiotic of me to get mad about it. Ordinarily, I wouldn't have. Only I happen to be under quite a bit of pressure, myself, right now.'

'Well, yes, I can imagine. With all your work.'

'It isn't the work that I mind. That's good for me. It keeps me from thinking. You see, the trouble is, Stephen, I don't really enjoy being a doctor. I'm not a bad one. As a matter of fact, I'm a lot better than average. I've got the talent for it, but no vocation. This isn't what I wanted to do in life.'

'What did you want?'

'I wanted to be a writer. Isn't that a laugh?'

'Why is it a laugh?'

'Because I can't write. Vocation but no talent.'

'Are you sure?'

'Absolutely sure. I found that out years ago. Oh, don't worry, I'm not about to ask you to read my stuff. There isn't any. It's all burned.'

'That's too bad.'

'Look, I'm not telling you this to get sympathy. I just want you to understand the situation. That's my personal problem, and ordinarily I can handle it. It's only when Bob needs help that I find I'm not on such firm ground myself. So then we're both in trouble. And when I can't help him and he turns to someone else, I get silly and jealous. . . . Bob's been going through a bad time lately. He told you all that, didn't he?'

'About being a conscientious objector?'

'That's only part of it. There's this whole thing of having been brought up as a Quaker. You see, Bob adored his Father and Mother. They do seem to have been pretty wonderful people, in their own way. When he was a kid, he believed everything they believed, on trust. Then they died, and he was put into a Friends' school, where the teachers weren't quite as wonderful as his parents; so he despised them for not being, the way teenagers do sometimes, and it all went sour on him.'

'He didn't tell me any of that.'

'No. I suppose he wouldn't. He hardly ever mentions his parents, because they're at the root of everything. . . . Anyhow, he decided that Quakerdom stank. And he's been trying to kid himself, ever since, that it never really meant anything to him. It's been working inside him all these years and now it's starting to act up. Just like with a lapsed Catholic. . . . The difficulty is, we get into a violent fight whenever we discuss this because he resents what he thinks is my attitude towards the Quakes. Actually, he'd resent *any* attitude I took toward them. He doesn't think I've got the right to have one.'

'You don't like them, do you, Charles?'

'That's what Bob thinks. He accuses me of sneering at them. But he's quite wrong. I respect them. And I admire them in a lot of ways. They don't sit nursing guilty consciences; they go right out and work their guilt off, helping people. They've got the courage of their convictions, and they mean exactly what they say, and they've found their own answers to everything without resorting to any trick theology. What I do hate about the Quakes, though, is their lack of style. They don't know how to do things with an air. They're hopelessly tacky. They've no notion of elegance.'

'But that's their great point, surely? They believe in plainness.'

'Plainness doesn't exclude elegance; it only makes it all the more necessary. Anyhow, "elegance" isn't quite what I mean. . . . In any of your voyages au bout de la nuit, did you ever run across the word "camp"?'

'I've heard people use it in bars. But I thought——'

'You thought it meant a swishy little boy with peroxided hair, dressed in a picture hat and a feather boa, pretending to be Marlene Dietrich? Yes, in queer circles, they call *that* camping. It's all very well in its place, but it's an utterly debased form——' Charles' eyes shone delightedly. He seemed to be in the best of spirits, now, and thoroughly enjoying this exposition. 'What *I* mean by camp is something much more fundamental. You can call the other Low Camp, if you like; then what I'm talking about is High Camp. High Camp is the whole emotional basis of the Ballet, for example, and of course of Baroque art. You see, true High Camp always has an underlying seriousness. You can't camp about something you don't take seriously. You're not making fun of it; you're making fun out of it. You're expressing what's basically serious to you in terms of fun and artifice and elegance. Baroque art is largely camp about religion. The Ballet is camp about love. . . . Do you see at all what I'm getting at?'

'I'm not sure. Give me some instances. What about Mozart?'

'Mozart's definitely a camp. Beethoven, on the other hand, isn't.'

'Is Flaubert?'

'God, no!'

'And neither is Rembrandt?'

'No. Definitely not.'

'But El Greco is?'

'Certainly.'

'And so is Dostoevsky?'

'Of course he is! In fact, he's the founder of the whole school of modern Psycho-Camp which was later developed by Freud.' Charles had a sudden spasm of laughter. 'Splendid, Stephen! You've really gotten the idea.'

'I don't know if I have or not. It seems such an elastic expression.'

'Actually, it isn't at all. But I admit it's terribly hard to define. You have to meditate on it and feel it intuitively, like Lao-tze's *Tao*. Once you've done that, you'll find yourself wanting to use the word whenever you discuss aesthetics or philosophy or almost anything. I never can understand how critics manage to do without it.'

'I must say, I can hardly see how the Friends would apply it.'

'Naturally you can't. Neither can I. That's because Quaker Camp doesn't exist, yet. Some tremendous genius will have to arise and create it. Until that happens, it's as unimaginable as Rimbaud's prose poems would have been to Keats.'

'Does Bob think the Quakers need High Camp?'

'He does in his heart, but he won't admit it. He can't criticize them or discuss them objectively, at all; he can only love them or hate them. He's in a classically schizoid predicament. His conscience is split right down the middle. You know, I really believe he's unable to think about anything except in relation to a conflict of loyalties. He has to do everything on principle. . . . It's only on principle that he stays with me, really.'

'You must know that isn't true, Charles.'

'Yes, I do. Of course. I'm starting to talk nonsense. Sorry.'

'Bob loves you very much. Even I can see that.'

'Oh, I know. And I love him very much.' Charles sighed. 'But it isn't that simple. . . . The trouble is, I can't seem to take Bob for granted. I'm always trying to understand him. And, of course, I'm the one person who can't, ever. If I did, that'd be another kind of relationship. We wouldn't feel the way we do about each other.'

'Does Bob try to understand you?'

'Gracious, no! He only tries to make me into what he wants me to be. All this respectability of mine drives him frantic. Medical etiquette. The bedside manner. Horse and buggy humour. Talking to the Dolgelly ladies about the weather. Sometimes he makes an effort to play along with it for a while, and then he gets furious with himself and me too. He'd like for us to march down the street with a banner, singing 'we're queer because we're queer because we're queer because we're queer'. That's really what we keep fighting about. And the idiotic part of it is, I'm actually on his side, and he knows it.'

'He's quite a crusader, isn't he?'

'That's just it. He needs an heroic setting. The best part of him just isn't functioning here, at all. He ought to be involved in some political movement, or storming barricades. Then he'd be completely alive.'

'You don't call the Navy an heroic setting, do you?'

'The Navy's a very old-fashioned and occasionally very dangerous kindergarten. If Bob goes back into it, it'll do its best to turn him into a loyal anti-crusading five-year-old moron.'

'Then you think he'd be better off in prison, as an objector?'

'Of course he would. But there, my attitude's completely selfish, I admit. I'm so deathly afraid of losing him for keeps. After an experience like that, he probably wouldn't need me any more. I can't see him coming back here and settling down again.'

Charles walked over to the window and stood there, looking

out. 'All that dogwood!' he muttered. 'Horrible sickly stuff. Like whipped cream.' He turned back toward the room. 'I don't know what I'd do if I lost Bob. Before I knew him, I was such a mess. . . . *I'm* no crusader. I'm sick of belonging to these whining militant minorities. Everybody hates them, and pretends not to. And they hate themselves like poison. You know something funny? My Father's name was Klatnik. He changed it. I used to tell myself that I'd change it back when I grew up. But I never did, of course. I found excuses not to. I didn't have the guts.'

'Well, for that matter,' I said, trying to get Charles out of this mood, 'I belong to a minority, myself. One of the most unpopular.'

'What's that?'

'I'm rich.'

Charles gave a sort of scornful grunt.

'You think that's nothing?' I said. 'Till you've had a lot of money, you just don't know what guilt is.'

'I dare say that's absolutely true.' Charles became more cheerful at once. 'You must tell me all about it, some time. I had an uncle who was rich. He spent his whole life explaining why he couldn't give us more money. He actually shed tears while he was doing it, too. He died of a broken heart.'

'I bet you were horrible to him.'

'We certainly were! We didn't regard him as a human being, at all. We treated him as a sort of golden monster. So he turned into one. All ghoul and a yard wide. . . . Look, I must go. I've got another patient to see.' Charles tapped the cast with his finger. 'How's this whited sepulchre?'

'Not too bad. Except for the stink.'

'Stink?' Charles bent down and sniffed at it. 'My poor friend, you call *that* stinking? Wait till you've been in it another two months. Nobody will be able to come near the house. Loathsome worms and beetles will crawl out of it. Buzzards and vultures will assemble and sharpen their beaks. And then, one morning, it'll crack wide open and the most gorgeous butterfly, all dazzling white, will emerge and spread its wings and flutter away over the treetops.'

'And that'll be me?'

'That'll be you, Brother. Never fear.' Charles laughed and patted me on the shoulder. Then, as he walked over to the door, he added: 'Don't get any wrong ideas about Bob and me and that argument. If I made it sound like a big drama, I didn't mean to. It's like what they used to say about Austria: the situation's desperate but not serious. The whole thing'll simmer down in a day or two, you'll see. Actually, Stephen, if we do have any more fights, it's you who's going to bear the brunt of them, from now on. We've been needing someone to act as umpire. And you're the heaven-sent victim. You can't run out on us. I'm certainly glad you threw yourself under that truck.'

'It was a pleasure,' I said. 'For you, I'd break one of my necks, any time.'

Bob reappeared two days later, bringing with him a pile of records and a box of radio valves, tools, wire and mechanical parts. 'Just another service of your friendly neighbourhood Dog People,' he told me, grinning. He worked all morning, installing a record-player and a radio beside my bed and a loud-speaker in a corner of the room. I couldn't help suspecting that this was his way of showing me that he didn't want any renewal of our previous conversation. During this visit he talked very little. As he worked, he whistled softly to himself as though he were alone, and only broke off now and then to explain briefly to me what he was doing, in a gruff matter-of-fact voice.

After this, he came to see me fairly often. Sometimes he seemed to have nothing to say at all. He was capable of vast but

vaguely expectant silences, during which he would sit looking
at me with his mouth slightly open until I got embarrassed and
started to chatter about anything that came into my head.
Sometimes—especially after he had been playing tennis or getting
a work-out at the College gym—he would be as noisy and silly
as a teen-age boy, walking around the room on his hands or
hiding under the bed and grabbing at Gerda's ankles, as if the
exercise had released him for a while from his tensions. And
there were other times when he would talk freely and naturally,
telling me funny stories of his life in the Navy or asking me
questions about places I'd been to. But our talk never again got
really intimate. Charles had been wrong there, apparently.
Bob didn't seem to want to confide in me any more; or maybe
his quarrel with Charles had somehow made that impossible for
him.

What struck me chiefly about him, always, was his quality
of loneliness; and this was even more apparent when he and
Charles came to visit me together. When, for example, Bob
was fixing our cocktails, his slim figure with its big shoulders
bending over the bottles would look strangely weary and
solitary, and he seemed suddenly miles away from either of us.
He was like a prospector preparing a meal in the midst of the
wilderness.

The cocktails gave me an added reason to look forward to
their visits, for these were the only times I ever got a drink.
Charles and Bob would come on evenings when Sarah and
Gerda were away in Philadelphia, and they always arrived with
a bag of ice-cubes, a shaker and several bottles of liquor. Once,
they also brought a load of Bob's paintings and held what
Charles described as 'Bob's first one-dog show'. The paintings
certainly weren't primitives, as Charles had called them; but
Bob had told the truth when he said that he painted in various
styles. Some of them were severe abstractions made up of
rectangles in pure colour, like Mondrian's. Others suggested a

gloomy disorganized impressionism; they were muddy and
scratchy. And there were a few gay, surprisingly humorous
landscapes which owed a lot to Dufy and Matisse. None of
them were very distinguished, but, as revelations of Bob's
mental condition, they were most interesting. I thought I could
see in them the conflict between Bob's birthright Quakerism
and Charles' 'High Camp'. Perhaps the creation of 'Quaker
Camp' would be the only possible solution to Bob's problems,
both as a human being and a painter.

It was probably the difficulty of making suitable and tactful
comments on the pictures that caused me to drink more than
usual, that night. Anyhow, I passed out cold. I woke, a couple
of hours later, to find that Charles and Bob had left, taking the
paintings with them. The lights were still burning. On the table
beside my bed, there was a note from Charles, in very unsteady,
straggling handwriting:

'So sad we had to lose our favourite patient. Here's the
latest X-ray photograph of you. Things don't seem to be working out too well. Frankly, I'm alarmed. Suggest you see a
specialist.'

This puzzled me, until I looked down at the cast. Bob had
drawn all over it in charcoal, continuing the lines of my body
and turning them into a kind of hermaphroditic mermaid, with
fantastic sexual organs.

A short while later, Sarah and Gerda arrived back home and
came up to say Goodnight.

'There's quite a chill in the air,' Sarah told me. 'Most un-
seasonable. Be sure to keep yourself very carefully covered,
Stephen dear.' In my still drunken state, this advice struck me as
so funny that I had a hard time fighting back the giggles. As
soon as Sarah had left the room, I pushed down the bedclothes
and showed Gerda the drawing.

'Pfui!' she exclaimed, laughing. 'So eine Schweinerei! But
this is clever, no? It is something like Picasso, I find.'

We agreed, regretfully, that it had to go, however. So Gerda wiped the cast clean with a wet face-cloth.

It was at this time of night that Gerda and I had our longest talks. One night, that same week, I had told her the whole story of my meeting with Elizabeth. 'And that reminds me,' I added, when I'd finished. 'I keep forgetting to order you that copy of *The World in the Evening*. I'll ask Sarah to get one, first thing tomorrow.'

'Thank you, Stephen'—Gerda was obviously embarrassed—'but this is not necessary. Already I get one. From a library in Philadelphia.'

'You have? Have you started it yet?'

'Oh, yes. Since a long time. Now I have read all.'

'But you never told me.'

'No. . . . I want, several times, to speak of this. But then I hesitate. You see, Stephen, I must be very sincere——'

'Of course. You mean, you didn't like it?'

Gerda shook her head unwillingly but firmly. 'I am sorry.'

'There's no need to be sorry.'

'It is very well written, I am sure. In a foreign language, one cannot judge about such things——'

'I quite realize that. That wasn't why I wanted you to read it. But can't you tell me what it was you didn't like?'

Gerda, I could see, was really distressed. 'I think it is better when we do not speak more about this,' she said.

'That's ridiculous.' In spite of myself, I couldn't help feeling slightly irritated. 'Why in the world shouldn't we?'

'Because I hurt your feeling. I cannot talk coldly, as a critic. Not to you. You love Elizabeth. To you, this is personal.'

'Now, really, Gerda! Do you honestly imagine that anything you, or anybody else could say would alter the way I feel about her?'

'No. I did not mean this. But you may be angry with me, perhaps. For this I should be very sorry.'

'You know that's nonsense. Go ahead and say whatever you want to. We've started this, now. We can't just stop and pretend it hasn't been mentioned.'

'Very well, Stephen——' Gerda hesitated, then continued with a kind of desperation. 'These people in the book—they are not like any people I have known. I do not understand them.'

'What don't you understand about them?'

'I do not understand how they can talk in this way. They talk always about their feeling, about love. But I do not think, really, that they have any feeling at all.'

'Why do you say that?'

'Because they seem not to care for what happens in the world outside. They are in this beautiful house, with these beautiful speeches and feelings. They make each other happy and unhappy. But it is like a game. Without heart, and so clever. They are quite safe, really. They are comfortable, in spite of all. They weep and are sad. But then the servants bring them tea.'

'But, Gerda, what do you expect them to do? Sit around discussing politics?'

'Politics!' Gerda's eyes flashed. I had never seen her so passionately indignant before. 'People are taken in concentration-camps and beaten and tortured and burned like the garbage in ovens—you call that politics?'

'Not in that sense, no. But all I meant was——'

'And why are such things possible? Because the rich and powerful ones who can stop it—all those in the other countries—what do they do? They sit in their beautiful houses and ignore, and talk of their beautiful private feelings. Until it is too late. This I find heartless, and without love——'

'But, Gerda, listen! You're being utterly unfair to Elizabeth,

when you bring that in. This book isn't about Hitler and the
Nazis—it doesn't pretend to be.'

'But it is published first in thirtyfour. I took specially notice
of the date. How could one write then, and not speak of the
Nazis? This I do not understand.'

'Well, for one thing, the story's supposed to take place at
least five years earlier. In the late twenties, and——'

'But that was more reason to speak! To show how such events
begin and are prepared. Already then, the Nazis were becoming
powerful. And you were in Germany and Austria, you tell me?
How could Elizabeth not know about them?'

'Of course she knew about them. And she certainly cared.
She cared terribly. She hated cruelty as much as anyone possibly
could. Far more than most people do. You must have realized
that, surely? It's all there in the book. That whole part about
Terence Storrs and Isabel—do you think that was written by
someone who was heartless? It's one of the most horrible descriptions of cruelty I've ever read.'

'It is well described, yes. But all this, what the young girl
suffers, it is in the feelings, only. It is just something mental——'

'And you think mental cruelty doesn't matter? You think
the only way people really suffer is when they're hurt physically?'

'You know I do not mean that, Stephen! This is not what I
try to say at all——'

'Now look, Gerda—*I* know what you're trying to say. I think
I understand your point of view, very well; in fact, I partly
agree with it. Only I want *you* to understand Elizabeth's. . . .
It's hard to put this clearly, but—well, you see, Elizabeth trans-
posed everything she wrote about into her own kind of micro-
cosm. She never dealt directly with world-situations or big-scale
tragedies. That wasn't her way. But she tried to reproduce them
in miniature, the essence of them. For instance, her reaction to
the news that a million people had been massacred might be to

tell a story about two children stoning a cat to death for fun. And she'd put into it all the pain and disgust and horror she felt about the things the Nazis do. . . . I think, instinctively, she was always protesting against the importance the newspapers give to numbers and size. She knew what most of us won't admit to ourselves, that numbers and size actually make tragedy less real to us. To kill a million people—can you grasp what that means? I can't. Elizabeth couldn't. She frankly admitted it, and so she kept to the kind of miniature, subtle effects she knew she could handle. I'm sure she was right, as far as her own talent was concerned. That was the sort of writer she was. . . . As a matter of fact, toward the end of her life, she found herself losing touch with most of the younger writers. Their attitude was very much the same as yours; and some of them wrote articles about it, attacking her work. They didn't have as much right to as you have, though, because they hadn't had your experiences. They were awfully priggish and theoretical. . . . Am I making this any clearer?'

'Oh, yes. Yes, I think so——' Gerda smiled at me hesitantly. 'I have been rather stupid, I find. . . . But you see, Stephen, I myself have lived in such a different condition. Peter and I, when we were young, we did not have this problem. For us, there was always only the fight against what was material— the bad food and houses, and the too small wages, and then the Nazis. And we could not look at these things distantly, or under- stand another meaning in them, because they were so very close to us. They were our life. . . . So how may I criticize what Elizabeth has written? It is not in my experience.'

'But I'm glad you have. I suppose I really expected you to. What I care about is that you should know the kind of person Elizabeth was. And you'd never do that if you'd been polite about this book. If you could have met, then I wouldn't even have asked you to read it. It wouldn't have been necessary. If you'd talked to her for ten minutes, you'd have known she cared about the same things as you do. In her own way. . . . You and Peter fight fascism, but you don't hold it against Sarah that she believes in non-violence, do you? You don't feel that you're on opposite sides?'

'I love Sarah very much.' Gerda smiled. 'And if the Nazis came to arrest her and I had a gun, I would first shoot as many as I could.'

'With her trying to stop you! Exactly! Well, then, you see what I mean.'

'Yes, Stephen. One cannot judge people in any other way, I think. Each must do what he thinks right. Or there cannot be true friendship.'

'I believe you do an awful lot of judging, don't you, Gerda? You know, it scares me, sometimes. I keep wondering when you're going to pass sentence on me.'

Gerda laughed. 'Oh, you I judge! Most severely. But now you are a poor invalid. I must be kind, until you are well.'

'That's right. You be kind to me. I need a lot of kindness.'

'Oh, you! People will always be kind to you, Stephen. You can make them feel sorry for you, with your look like a little boy. But that is bad, also. Because you know quite well what it is you are doing to them. I think perhaps it is you who are heartless.'

'You don't really, do you, Gerda?'

'I am not sure. I am not sure that I understand you at all. Sometimes you are too nice. It is not quite real. I would like to see you be mean and bad and not charming. Then I would understand better what you are.'

'I wish *I* knew what I was.'

'You do not?'

'Not exactly. Do you know what *you* are?'

'Me? Oh, I do not worry myself about such questions.'

'No—I guess you wouldn't. Any more than Sarah would. That's one of the things that make you such a wonderful person.'

Gerda blushed. 'Do not be silly, Stephen. I am not wonderful.

You think this only because you become tired to be so clever. And you like it in me, that I am quite stupid.'

There were nights when I felt very sorry for myself. Nights when it was hot, and my body itched in unscratchable places inside the cast or teased me with its little aches and pains. I hated the cast, then. It wasn't part of me and my condition. It was just an alien, senseless lump of plaster.

I used to try, selfishly, to delay Gerda's leaving me. I knew she had to get up early in the morning, but I didn't care. I coaxed her into telling and retelling me stories about her home and her parents in Hamburg, and her life as a little girl. Over and over again, I made her describe how she'd first met Peter at the youth rally, how they'd gone swimming and sailing on the Alster, and read books together and had long political discussions, and how he'd told her that he loved her, in a boat one summer evening, with accordions playing in the distance along the shore. In my maudlin mood, I gloated over their love like a movie fan, with tears in my eyes. While Gerda talked, I would reach out for her hand and hold it. She let me do this as though I were a child. And then, sometimes, she sang me to sleep with saccharine-sad German folksongs—*Kommt ein Vogel geflogen* and *Weisst Du wieviel Sternlein stehen?*—singing them in a small clear voice, very softly, so as not to disturb Sarah or start Saul (who loathed music) howling.

But more often she left me still awake. And then, when she'd gone, there was nothing but the night; the night that was like a long voyage on which you could feel the body labouring its way through life—the heart beating, the blood circulating, the lungs expanding and contracting—just as you are aware of the pounding of the engines and the straining of the hull of a ship at sea. A passenger isn't supposed to concern himself with the running of the ship; that is being taken care of by the crew, anonymous creatures down in the engine-room or up on deck, whom he never meets. But, in this case, I wasn't really a passenger. I was like a lazy or scared or drunken captain lying shut in his cabin when he ought to be on the bridge, giving orders. Sooner or later, I would have to come out and assume command and decide where we were going.

But not yet, I told the crew. You don't need me yet. Can't you see I'm sick? You're doing all right without me. Sure, I'll come, when we get near land. Just let me lie here a little longer. Leave me alone, can't you? Let me sleep.

FOUR

ELIZABETH and I were married early in February 1927 at a registrar's office in Chelsea, with Sarah and the registrar's clerk as the only witnesses. Sarah, I knew, would have loved a Quaker wedding; but that was out of the question. Even if I had been a Friend in good standing, I could hardly have subjected Elizabeth to the formalities required by the Discipline: the written announcement of 'intention' to the Monthly Meeting and the investigation by the committee of two which had to present it with a 'certificate of clearness'. We were in such a hurry to get the whole business settled.

'I'm sorry, darling,' Elizabeth had said, 'but I simply can't think of you as a fiancé'. I knew exactly what she meant. The very idea of our being 'engaged' to each other seemed ridiculous. And Sarah, in her innocence, made it more so by starting to treat Elizabeth as though she had suddenly become much younger and were a girl in need of a chaperone. If Sarah had ever been married herself, she would certainly have felt it her duty to have a private talk with Elizabeth on the facts of life; as it was, she confined herself to giving Elizabeth all kinds of information about my favourite dishes, my habits, and my likes and dislikes. Elizabeth took this wonderfully. She listened gravely to every-thing Sarah told her, admitted she couldn't darn socks, and submitted, in spite of my protests, to several sewing-lessons. 'But why ever shouldn't I, Stephen?' she said. 'I really want to learn. I want to be quite, quite different from now on. That's what makes this all so exciting. Don't you love fresh starts? Don't you want me to be a proper wife to you? I told you I'm being completely old-fashioned about us. Sarah understands me much better than you do.'

We reacted to the approaching ceremony in the same way, by developing a violent kind of 'flu which made our throats so sore that we could hardly swallow. On the morning of the wedding, we were so sick that Sarah begged us to postpone it. We refused, of course. 'Though it'll probably be the death of us,' Elizabeth said. 'Oh, darling—what a perfect announcement for *The Times*: Mr. and Mrs. Monk celebrated a *very* quiet Liebestod, with neither of them able to sing a note!' We drove to the registrar's office muffled up to the ears, and made the necessary statements, laughing at each other's croaky voices. We had arranged to leave that afternoon on the boat-train for France, and we did. The alternative, as Elizabeth said, was too embarrassing to be thought of. 'Imagine the two of us tucked up in the nuptial sickbed, with Sarah bringing us our medicine!' Twentyfour hours later, in Paris, we found ourselves mysteriously and entirely cured. But poor Sarah, left behind in London, caught our 'flu and was very sick with it for the next week; a fact she never mentioned in her letters, and which I only found out later from the charlady.

My own wish had been that we should have an enormously long honeymoon. I wanted to carry Elizabeth away with me like a stolen treasure, far out of reach of everybody—to take her to Africa, or India, or right around the world. Elizabeth smiled when I talked of these plans and seemed to consider them seriously. 'Do you know, darling, one of my childhood dreams was actually to *live* on an elephant? I wanted to have a howdah that was really a tiny house, all made of ivory and diamonds, with very rich crimson and gold silk window-curtains. Wouldn't you love that? Of course, it would have to be an awfully big elephant; and I don't quite know how one could manage about a bathroom——' But I soon realized that she was vetoing the idea by turning it into a fantasy. She didn't want to go far away, yet. This was only to be a holiday. The manuscript of her novel was waiting for her return.

I had talked to myself very sternly about that novel. I knew—
at least with the reasonable part of my mind—that I must never
let myself get jealous of Elizabeth's work. I could never own
that. I was lucky enough to have any of her at all. And so,
without further prompting, I decided that we should only be
away for a couple of weeks.

In Paris, we stayed at an hotel on the Quai Voltaire, in a room
overlooking the river with a sideways view of the towers of
Notre-Dame. 'This place is all gilt and red plush and speckled
mirrors,' Elizabeth wrote to Cecilia. 'An authentic shrine to the
Nineties—particularly, somehow, the English-in-Paris Nineties.
I'm sure Beardsley must have lived here, and Dowson and Theo
Marzials and Henry Harland; and I expect they still have unpaid
bills of Oscar Wilde's. And now—us! What a comedown! Not
one drop of absinthe have we ordered, not one puff of opium
have we smoked. And, horror of horrors, we're legally married.
The ghosts must be wringing their hands in despair. What have
English writers sunk to?'

Elizabeth spent quite a lot of time, during her stay, writing to
all her friends and acquaintances. She didn't show me any of
those letters and postcards then, and it was strange and painful to
be reading them now. In nearly all of them, I could detect a
note of apology. There were mock-formal announcements, in
which this apologetic attitude took the tone of strained, embarrassing facetiousness: 'E. Rydal, female authoress, begs to
declare her marriage with S. Monk, gent. No gifts or floral
tributes, by request.' There were announcements in the form of
postscripts to letters which spoke only of books, literary gossip
and the weather: 'PS. I'm here with my very first husband,
recently acquired. His name is Stephen Monk. You shall meet
him when we get back.' There was an exaggeratedly casual note
to the editor of one of the weekly magazines: 'Can you send me
the proofs of my story to the above address? Send them to Mrs.
Stephen Monk—that's my name now, and the only one the

hotel people know. We're here on our honeymoon, but I promise to find time to correct them and post them back to you by return.'

Only one letter seemed entirely frank and natural. It was written to Elizabeth's old friend Mary Scriven:

'Mary darling, I have some extraordinary news for you. I hardly know how to begin to tell it properly, so here it is, plumped right in your friendly lap. I am married—less than a week ago. My husband's name is Stephen Monk. You don't know him. He's twelve years younger than I am. We met last November. There!

I find I'm on the defensive already, as I tell you this. Why? Certainly not because I imagine you'll disapprove of *him*. Even if he were not the angel I increasingly suspect him of being, you just aren't the disapproving kind. But whatever will you think of this step I've taken? "Step", I call it! No, it's a great breathless jump from the highest of towers into empty air. I feel like some pioneer of aviation—perhaps that man who jumped with the wings Leonardo designed. Only *my* wings aren't going to collapse, I tell myself. I shall soar. I shall circle above the town, with all of you looking up at me and exclaiming "Who'd have thought the old girl could fly!"

Ah no, Mary dear, that's what's really worrying me. I don't want you to be a spectator, standing far below. I don't want to keep up aloft. I want to come down gently and safely to earth and share this with you and the very few others I truly love. That's where you must help me—you must help both of us.

How stupid and egotistical this sounds, as I write it. I talk as if nobody had ever been married before in the entire history of the world. I talk as if this were my problem alone, and not Stephen's too. (Well, in a sense, perhaps it is. Because he's so young and accepts all this so trustingly. And he hasn't been *out in the great woods*, as I have. Do you know what I mean by that? Once you've been out there, once you've been truly and utterly alone —oh, it's so hard to come back. Not that you pine for freedom. Not that this isn't a far greater happiness and peace. But it's hard to come back to this other life, the life of the human hearth. There's a chill in your blood which has to be warmed out of it, very very slowly.)

I realize, Mary, that I've never talked to you properly about your own marriage. I know it wasn't happy, but I've never felt that you were bitter about it, or regretted anything. So will you, when we get back to London, sit down with me and tell me all about it? I feel I have the right to ask you to do this for me, now. It isn't just curiosity. I do so need your wisdom.

One more thing. Perhaps I have no need to say this, but I'd better. Will you be, could you be hurt because I didn't tell you in advance about Stephen and myself? Believe me, I told nobody—not even Cecilia; though, in any case, the news wouldn't have reached her yet. And this wasn't because of a lack of trust or friendship on my part toward you. It was a lack of faith in myself, in my own star. Yes, I can smile and admit it now—but the truth is, I've been desperately afraid. Afraid the spell would break, the mirror crack from side to side. Afraid that Stephen would suddenly remember he was an angel, not a human being, and unfold his wings and vanish. (I haven't told *him* that, yet; and I doubt if I ever shall.)

Seriously, I feel a deep truth, now, in all those old fairy-tales and legends where the hero is forbidden to speak, on pain of losing the princess or the treasure. Silence is a tremendous magic. Well, I followed the wizard's instructions, and now I have my reward. I can breathe freely again, though I'm still shaken, thinking what I might so easily have lost. If I *had* lost it—but no, it's morbid to dwell on that. I only know this: I could *never* have gone back to the woods.

Don't wish me happiness, Mary darling. That I have already.
But do wish your silly Liz some sense.'

Elizabeth was quite right in telling Mary Scriven that I
accepted the situation 'so trustingly'. I would have been amazed
and bewildered if I had read that letter then. The idea that our
relationship would present any kind of a problem to Elizabeth
had never, as yet, occurred to me. I was convinced that she
always knew exactly what she was doing; that she had mastered
the whole art of living. I expected her to take complete charge.

I suppose I still regarded marriage as a kind of game. I thoroughly enjoyed my part of it, my role of husband. I loved it
when waiters would ask me if 'Madame' wanted this or that. I
used to get into conversations with the proprietress of the hotel,
simply for the pleasure of being able to say 'my Wife thinks——'
or 'when my Wife and I were out yesterday——' But it wasn't
quite real. I didn't entirely convince myself. And when Elizabeth
said 'my Husband has decided——', I wanted to laugh out
loud; it sounded so crazy and funny and wonderful. It was as
if the Monsieur-Madame front which we presented to the
outside world were just a protective device (perhaps what
Charles Kennedy would call 'a camp') to prevent anyone from
suspecting that we two had discovered a new, unnamed kind of
relationship.

For that was how it seemed to me. It wasn't merely that we
were quite different from what I thought of as 'ordinary' honeymoon couples. That was obvious. We were quite different, also,
from those much-advertised couples of 'great lovers' whose
high-pressure emotions intimidate mankind, generation after
generation. Paolo and Francesca, Romeo and Juliet, Mr. and
Mrs. Browning—why had they all made such a terrific fuss?
Because they were so busy churning up their sensations, so busy
being 'in love', that they could never relax. Love seemed to me,
then, like a huge wave pouring through the world, flooding

everything. The frantic, noisy lovers struggled and splashed about in it, half-drowned. Elizabeth and I, alone, had found the secret of riding it without the slightest effort. No—more than that. We didn't even have to ride the wave. We were part of it.

I didn't, of course, feel this all the time. But I had moments of feeling it—several of them—every day. There was that morning, for example, when we visited the Père La Chaise cemetery, and saw Wilde's tomb, and Chopin's, and the wall against which the Communards were executed. It was a grey day, with gusts of rain; but I wasn't depressed by the weather or awed by the dead. Elizabeth told me about the young Communard—a boy of fourteen—who asked permission to run home and give his watch to his mother, before he was shot. The officer in command was sorry for him and said Yes, thinking that of course he wouldn't come back. But the boy returned five minutes later, out of breath from running, thanked the officer politely, and took his place in front of the firing-squad. My eyes filled with tears, but I was trembling with joy. For the boy wasn't dead, Chopin and Wilde weren't dead; they were alive, like Elizabeth and I, within the wave of love. Within the wave, every action had its own sanction and beauty: Chopin writing the Nocturnes, Wilde waddling after the street-boys, even the officer giving the order to fire. As long as I myself was within the wave, I should always know this. And it seemed to me, then, that I should be able to re-enter it whenever I pleased, throughout the rest of my life.

What was Elizabeth feeling, that morning? I suppose my mood communicated itself to her, to some extent—I had described it to her as best I could—and she must have partly shared it. But for her it was different. In *A Garden with Animals*, the most autobiographical of her novels, she gave her version of the scene. Here, the lovers are in a museum in London. The story is told from the viewpoint of Laura, the heroine:

'Looking at Oliver, she thought: Yes, to him it's alive, all of it. He simply doesn't see what's dead, what's left—these sherds and broken implements and mummy-cases, these fossils and time-stained stones. He sees only what we all ought to see, and can't: the live hand that made them, the live brain that imagined them, the throbbing self that formed this covering shell and then slipped out of it, leaving it in our hands. And oh, said Laura to herself, if I could be like that! But I can't. I believe in museums because I've got one of my own. Sooner or later, we all start our dismal private collections. . . . There, right before her in her mind's eye, was the glass case containing the tiny horrible little dried relic which was all that Gurian had left for her.'

The character of 'Gurian' in *A Garden with Animals* is an easily recognizable portrait of Mariano Galdós, the 'cellist. Elizabeth had scarcely mentioned Galdós to me at that time—the subject must have still been too painful for her to speak of—but later she told me a great deal about him.

Elizabeth first met Galdós in Florence, in 1921. At that time, he had quite a reputation, and was on holiday after a successful series of concerts in France and Italy. The impression I later got from his photographs was of a rather undersized man in his late thirties, with a pale heavy pouchy face; scrubby and balding in a typically Latin manner. But I was prejudiced against him, naturally. To be fair, I would have to admit that the photographs were mostly snapshots or badly printed newspaper portraits, and that he must anyhow have had very compelling, vivid dark eyes.

In the novel, Elizabeth writes that 'Gurian' had 'the art of starting a friendship right in the middle—a friendship, that is to say, with a woman. It wasn't that he began by making love to her. Oh no, he was far subtler than that. He contrived to suggest that you and he had long since passed *that* point. Rather, he made you feel as if you were meeting an old lover again after an absence of months or years—made you wonder if, perhaps, the relationship might not be renewed.'

It was hard to say just what Elizabeth meant by this passage. Indeed, she was trying, in it, to describe something which is practically indescribable; something which could only be conveyed in glances and tones of voice. She did, however, tell me one thing about her meeting with Galdós which was curious, even if it wasn't subtle. They were eating at a restaurant with the friends who had introduced them to each other. They talked German, partly because the friends were Germans, partly because Elizabeth spoke German fluently and didn't know much Spanish. (Galdós could speak German because he had studied for some years in Dresden as a young man.) At the end of the meal, Elizabeth wanted to light a cigarette. Not wishing to interrupt the conversation by asking the others for matches, she half rose from her chair so as to reach over and take some from an unoccupied table nearby. At this, Galdós produced a lighter from his pocket, saying, as he did so: 'Bleiben Sie liegen', 'stay lying down', instead of 'Bleiben Sie sitzen', 'stay seated', which was obviously what he had meant. It was what the intellectuals of those days delighted in, 'a Freudian error', but the two Germans either failed to notice it or were too polite to make any comment. Elizabeth got the point at once, however. Galdós had involuntarily said 'Bleiben Sie liegen' because he had been imagining himself and Elizabeth lying side by side in bed together, after making love. She looked quickly at him, startled, amused and intrigued. He looked back at her without embarrassment, smiling slightly. And that was how it began.

Their relationship was unhappy, almost from the first. Galdós was a difficult, arrogant creature, vain and cowardly and given to hysterical self-pity. It was some time before Elizabeth knew that he was married, and that he took cocaine. Galdós was separated from his wife, but he would get maudlin fits of repentance in which he declared that she was the only woman who really mattered to him. The cocaine he managed to conceal from Elizabeth for a long while. When she found out about it, he got defiant and sniffed it publicly in a café, exclaiming against her English prudery. She left him, then. But abject telegrams and letters followed her, and she came back. Galdós got seriously sick. He broke his contracts and appeared less and less often in public. He begged her for money and she gave it to him. He became pitiful and shameless. In his rages, he would have liked to beat her, but he wasn't strong enough. Finally, at the beginning of 1926, he died of pneumonia in Rome. Elizabeth nursed him until the end.

If I had known all this at the time of our honeymoon I suppose I would have been terribly jealous—jealous of Galdós because he had made Elizabeth feel and suffer in a way which made my hold upon her seem slight and insecure by comparison. But I would also have understood her much better than I then did. I would have understood what I only learned to appreciate much later, her incredible capacity for loyalty. There was, no doubt, a good deal of masochism in Elizabeth's character. Perhaps she corrected her own kind of arrogance as a creative artist by abasing herself in her relationship with Galdós. But, over and above this, I think she wanted desperately to be needed. Galdós needed her, and that was sufficient.

When I realized that all this had happened so shortly before we met, I could see Elizabeth's consent to our marriage as a gesture of almost desperate optimism in the face of experience. And she admitted this frankly in *A Garden with Animals*. Laura, after her experiences with Gurian, feels that she has got to make Oliver 'come true', as she puts it. 'Because, if he didn't—if it was all a lie, a dream—then that proved something too terrible to contemplate. If Oliver wasn't true, then nothing was true. Then there was no God.'

I could never possibly have suspected any of this from Elizabeth's behaviour while we were in Paris. Indeed, she seemed to me to be so entirely relaxed, so completely in command of the situation, that I felt obscurely frustrated. I wanted to know her in some deeper way that I couldn't exactly define. Something eluded me. This, of course, was really what made being with her so continuously fascinating for me. I was watching her all the time, with the feeling that I daren't withhold my attention for an instant, lest I should miss some hint, some clue. It was as if I was waiting for a signal.

The last evening before we went back to London, while we were sitting at a café on the boulevard, I became suddenly aware that Elizabeth was watching *me*, with an unaccustomed kind of intentness. 'What are you looking at?' I asked her.

'Oh, nothing, darling——' She smiled vaguely. 'I was just wondering if you—— No——' She broke off, laughing. 'If I were to say it, it would sound too silly——'

'Elizabeth, that's not fair! Now you've *got* to tell me.'

'Very well, then. . . . I was wondering, darling, if you'd had a nice honeymoon.'

I fairly gaped at her. 'But—don't you *know* I have? *Nice*—my God, what a word!' Then, looking into her eyes as I tried to see behind what she had said, I added: 'Haven't *you*?'

'Of course, of course, darling. . . . But that isn't quite what I meant——' Elizabeth reached out and took my hand. 'What I mean is—well, you must so often have pictured to yourself— long, long before we ever met—when you were a boy at school —how, one day, you'd get married and have a honeymoon. Didn't you?'

'I don't know. I thought about sex and love, an awful lot, but——' I started to laugh. 'I suppose I thought of marriage as the end of everything. I thought that, by the time that happened, I'd be quite old. A lot older than I am, anyhow.'

'Yes—I suppose that's how men always feel. . . . Poor Stephen —you've aged quickly, haven't you? Your youth is over already.'

'But, Elizabeth, I don't think that now. You know I don't. How could I? I was just a silly kid——'

'You really don't, Stephen? You don't feel in the very least bit—trapped?'

'Elizabeth!' I was really alarmed. 'Is that how *you* feel?'

'I——?' She shook her head slowly. She was still smiling, but now she looked sad. 'Oh, Stephen——' she sighed, as though my question had made her aware of some enormous misunderstanding between us. Then, after a pause, she said: 'I think perhaps we're in too much of a hurry, darling. We want to know everything about each other, instantly; and it's so painful that we can't, isn't it? But we mustn't try so hard. We must be patient, mustn't we? We must just accept what we've got, and wait. . . . This *is* something worth waiting for, isn't it, Stephen?'

'Yes—oh my God, yes——' I said. 'It's wonderful—and the waiting's wonderful—I mean——'

Then the wave of love burst suddenly over us, sweeping away all my doubts and frustrations and anxieties and leaving me speechless. The traffic roared and tooted with love, the faces of the people on the sidewalk were transfigured, and the lights of the boulevard blazed with joy. This time, Elizabeth certainly felt it too. Her face shone with it. She looked so beautiful that my throat contracted until I was almost strangling, and I had to drink a glass of wine at a single gulp.

'I know, darling,' she said quietly, stroking my hand as if to soothe me. 'I know——'

And so we returned to London.

On the train, I started, for the first time, to feel badly about Sarah. I suppose I had been repressing this feeling throughout the past two weeks. Now I found that I was actually dreading our meeting. Perhaps Elizabeth was dreading it, too. I didn't want to ask her. I didn't want to face the situation until I was forced to.

We arrived back in the evening, after dark. Sarah met us at the station and kept up a bright chatter all the way to the house, in the cab. When we entered, there was a kind of Christmas banner inscribed with the word 'Welcome', hanging across the hallway. Then Sarah took us upstairs, to show us how she had made room for my clothes in Elizabeth's drawers and closets. 'And I had them bring up your favourite armchair,' she told me, 'so that you'd feel quite at home'.

It was all horribly touching and embarrassing. As soon as Elizabeth and I were left alone—Sarah had told us Goodnight very early, with a coy emphasis on our need for privacy—I said: 'You know, we shall have to get out of here as soon as possible.' Elizabeth couldn't disagree, but she asked: 'How on earth are we going to explain to Sarah? We can't hurt her, Stephen. I couldn't bear that.' 'Leave it to me,' I said. 'I'll think of some excuse.' But I had no idea how I was going to manage it.

I ought to have known that I wouldn't have to worry. Later, I felt ashamed that I hadn't known, because my anxiety showed a lack of faith in Sarah's understanding. The next morning, she called me down to our old flat. 'Stephen dearest,' she told me. 'I need your counsel.' She had a letter in her hand. 'This arrived a few days ago,' she continued, as she gave it to me. 'Perhaps it will be simplest if you read it.'

The letter was written from Philadelphia by an old friend of Sarah's named Hannah Duke; she had been to see us, some years earlier, during a visit to England. Hannah told Sarah that there was a position open for a Dean of Women at a small Quaker college in Ohio. Several of Sarah's friends had agreed that she would be just the right person to fill it, if she cared to do so; in fact, the job was hers for the asking. They would all be very happy to see her back in the States. There were a couple of English Quakers on the faculty as visiting professors, whom she already knew, so she wouldn't be entirely amongst strangers. Hannah finished her letter by asking Sarah to reply right away.

If she decided to accept the post, she would have to sail within the next month.

Sarah was watching my face, as I read this. 'Well, Stephen,' she asked, when I had finished, 'what do you think?'

'What do *you* think?' I asked, playing for time. I felt as guilty as if I had planned the whole thing myself, and I couldn't look Sarah in the eyes.

'I? Well—I hardly know what to say. I'm sure I don't know why they should want *me*. I've never done anything quite like this before. I couldn't imagine anyone less suitable——'

'Nonsense!' I interrupted, rather too heartily. 'You'd be splendid. Why, you could run America single-handed, let alone a bunch of girls! Of course you could. . . . But that's not the point. Do you really *want* to go?'

'Well—I should feel sad, leaving England. It's become a second home to me. . . . But this certainly seems like a splendid opening, doesn't it?'

'Aunt Sarah—it's no use if we aren't going to discuss this frankly. You wrote to Hannah Dukes, didn't you?'

'Yes, Stephen dear.' Sarah gave me a sly smile. 'Of course I wrote her. I write her quite often, you know.'

'And you just happened to mention that you were thinking of returning to the States, and did she know of a job for you?'

'Well, I didn't put it as directly as that. But I suppose I did speak of the possibility, yes——'

'And so Hannah made enquiries? That must have taken a good deal of time. In fact, you must have written to her quite soon after you knew that Elizabeth and I were getting married. The very next day, perhaps?'

'I don't remember the exact date.'

'Aunt Sarah,' I said, forcing myself to put my arm around her shoulders, though I felt quite physically sickened at the falseness of the gesture, 'what makes you think we don't want you here?'

'Stephen! I never said that! It's only that—well—we must be

realistic. Things are different now. You have your own life and
obligations to think of. I know you'd never be anything but
sweet and unselfish and kind to me. And Elizabeth too, bless her
heart. But my duty here is ended. Your darling Mother would
have been the first to admit that. . . . Besides, America is my
home. I've been very happy here, but I think I should like a
change. And we shall see each other from time to time, shan't
we? You'll be coming over, of course?'

'Yes—as a matter of fact, we've talked about it already.'
(This was a lie.)

'Then you see——? This won't be a real separation, will it?
Oh, I'm sure everything will work out beautifully. I feel as if it
was *meant* to happen. . . . I'd better send a cable to Hannah,
right away——'

That was the first stage of Sarah's leaving. The others that
followed it were progressively more and more painful. Sarah
was extra bright and brisk, as she made her preparations. I felt
as though I were watching her bravely getting ready to go to
hospital, to die of an incurable illness. I was miserably guilty
because I longed for the illness to be over. I longed for her to
leave. Elizabeth suffered nearly as badly as I did. 'Oh, Stephen,'
she said, 'why does everything have to have a price? Why does
Sarah have to pay for our being together? When she's such an
angel—I almost wish she was a fiendish old dragon of a mother-
in-law, so we could hate her and fight her.'

One of the worst moments was when Sarah came to me in an
acute distress of embarrassment and asked if I could lend her the
price of her steamship ticket. She promised faithfully to pay it
back out of her salary at the college. This brought me face to
face with a problem I had always avoided, the problem of my
money. In all the years I had lived with Sarah, we had scarcely
mentioned it. Through the family lawyers, she had been given
all the necessary authority to settle our bills and manage the

household; but she had practically no means of her own. My
Mother had died suddenly, still a young woman, without leaving
a will. So Sarah had never had the legacy she would otherwise
certainly have received.

I tried to get her to accept it now. I wanted to settle an income
on her. But she absolutely refused. I had never known her to be
so obstinate. 'It wouldn't be right,' she kept repeating. 'It
wouldn't be right.' And, one day, she spoke almost bitterly:
'I'm not a helpless old woman in need of a pension. As long as
I'm able to work, I won't be beholden to anyone—not even
you, Stephen.' Finally, I had to agree to her idea of the loan.
But I tricked her, later, by writing to the President of the college
and getting him to pretend to Sarah that there had been a misunderstanding; that her travelling-expenses had been included in
their original offer and that they had therefore repaid me themselves.

Elizabeth and I agreed that I should see Sarah off alone. I rode
down with her on the boat-train to Southampton. Right at the
last, we both started to cry—shedding the hopeless, painful tears
of two people who have gotten themselves into a situation they
can no longer control or understand. Now that the ship's siren
was blowing and the stewards were shouting, 'All visitors on
shore!', our parting suddenly became revealed as an altogether
meaningless, tragically unnecessary act. I could scarcely even
remember my impatience to get rid of Sarah. All I now knew
was that I was about to lose the one tremendous little symbol of
my childhood's security: the comforter, the provider, the storyteller, the listener, the tucker-up-in-bed—often rejected, dis-
obeyed, ignored, but relied on, always, to be available and there.
Why was she leaving me? Who was sending her away? I, myself. But that made no sense. If life was as crazy as this, then I
couldn't cope with it. I was as helpless as a child in the midst of
this mess I had created. And like a child I blurted out, between
my sobs: 'Oh, Aunt Sarah—you know I love you, don't you?'

She had to steer me, almost blind with blubbering, to the gangway. I was the last to leave the ship.

Going back on the train to London, after this violent emotional discharge, I felt limp and passive and pleasantly relaxed.
I had used up all the love in me, for the moment, and was capable
only of a cold-hearted, furtive relief. Sarah was gone. All right—
that was settled. I would miss her, certainly. But her going had
made my life much simpler. From now on, I would never have
to consider anybody except Elizabeth.

Soon after Sarah's departure, Elizabeth rather apologetically
mentioned Alexander Strines. 'You won't mind my seeing him
occasionally, will you, darling? Of course, he'll quite understand
that everything's different, now. He won't start dropping in on
us when we don't want him. In fact, there's no reason why you
two should meet——'

'But why shouldn't we?' I asked. 'I want to. I'd like to show
him I'm not such an idiot as he must think me. We'll probably
get along together very well.'

So Strines was invited to the flat, to tea. He arrived with
flowers, a wedding-present, and an obviously prepared speech.
The flowers were roses. 'I can now with perfect propriety offer
you red ones,' he told Elizabeth. 'In certain Latin countries, I'm
given to understand, red roses presented to a spinster are considered positively compromising.' The wedding-present was a
china inkwell, 'almost certainly used by Jane Austen while she
was living at Chawton': I felt sure Strines had hastily selected it
as being one of the least-wanted items in his own collection.
The speech began with a quotation from Doctor Johnson:
'you remember what he once said to a Newly-Married Lady?'
I forget what Doctor Johnson said, but it was something unpleasant and dogmatic, which Strines then proceeded to twist
into a long-winded compliment. There was no warmth anywhere in the whole proceedings. And I felt that Strines regarded

our marriage as a sophisticated kind of joke, of which Elizabeth would soon get tired. 'My dear Rydal,' he told her, 'you've always been so full of surprises.' Then, looking at me with his joyless smile, he added: 'I hope I have your permission to continue to call your Wife by the name she has made illustrious? It's a mark of respect, really, for your private rights in her, on which we wouldn't dream of infringing. Elizabeth Monk is entirely yours. Rydal belongs to all of us.' 'Really, Strines,' Elizabeth interrupted, laughing, but a little nervous, I could see, that I might take offence at his tone, 'you talk about me as if I were Hyde Park! Do I look as if the public had trampled me flat?'

Strines didn't succeed in making me angry: I could afford to tolerate him now, though I still didn't like him. But I felt immediately drawn to Mary Scriven, whom I met at about this same time. She was a middle-aged woman with a grown-up son and daughter, who lived in a tiny house in a mews and ran an art-gallery which was also used for concerts. She was an easy-going, charming person who seemed to have the secret of combining irony with good-nature and laziness with great activity. When Elizabeth and I went around to visit her, she was alternately cooking, answering telephone-calls and making a costume for some studio party, with a pleasant air of bohemian vagueness. Although Elizabeth and she were such old friends, I felt that she accepted us as a matter of course as an established couple, who might have been together for years. No one had treated me like this before, so I felt an extravagant gratitude to Mary and showed it by buying three blotchy landscapes by one of her 'discoveries', whose work she was currently exhibiting at her gallery.

'I'm afraid they're really quite ghastly,' Elizabeth said sadly, when we had brought the landscapes home to the flat and could examine them without politeness. 'They don't grow on you, do they?'

'They *shrink* on you.'

'Oh, Stephen, what on earth are we to do with them?'

'I don't know. We might give them to the poor.'

Elizabeth kissed me, laughing. 'That was one of your very sweetest acts,' she told me. 'Mary was delighted. I'm so happy that you like her.'

'I'm sure I'll always like your real friends.' The moment the words were out of my mouth, I realized how unkind they sounded. Elizabeth's face clouded at once.

'You mean, I haven't any others?' she asked quietly.

'No—Elizabeth! I never said that!'

'But perhaps it's true—almost. Yes, I believe it is. Stephen, this isn't a very pleasant revelation——'

Elizabeth brought the subject up again later. She had evidently been brooding over it.

'I suppose I've cultivated too many acquaintances,' she said. 'And they're like weeds; they grow up around the real friends and choke them off. Why do I bother with all these people, Stephen? Am I so empty and insecure that I need this fuss and noise around me?'

'I don't think it's that, at all. You go right away from everybody, deep into your work; and when you come up to the surface, you want distraction. That's very natural.'

'Oh, darling, how much better you make me sound than I really am! So you don't really disapprove of my acquaintances?'

'No—of course I don't disapprove; but——'

'But what?'

'I shouldn't think—I mean, I hope they won't be so necessary, now. Now you've got me.'

'But, darling—*you*! That's something utterly different. You're my whole life.'

'Except when you want to be distracted?'

'Stephen—I didn't mean to say anything unkind.'

'I know you didn't. And I quite understand, really. People

like—well, just for example, Strines—they talk your language. I can't. I probably won't ever be able to. You get something from them that I can't give you. There's nothing wrong in that. As long as it amuses you, that's all I care about. I'm not jealous, or anything. Not any more.'

Elizabeth took me in her arms and looked searchingly into my eyes.

'My darling,' she said, 'I hope you're being quite, quite frank with me?'

'Of course I am,' I assured her. 'Don't worry about it. Everything's quite all right.'

Elizabeth's intuition was correct, as usual. I wasn't being frank with her, or even with myself; for I resented the presence of her acquaintances even more than I was ready to admit. In the days before our marriage, I had been able to avoid most of them altogether; but now I had to meet them. Perhaps it would have been better if I had simply refused to go with her to their parties, but I couldn't bring myself to do this because, obviously, most of her pleasure consisted in taking me along. She wanted to go, she wanted me to go with her, and she wanted me to enjoy myself. That was asking a lot, I couldn't help feeling. So I usually started out in a mood of suppressed resentment.

There was no doubt that Elizabeth, who was ordinarily so considerate, had a blind spot here. She seemed unable to put herself in my place and know how I would be feeling. This wasn't very surprising. She was so completely at home in that world, she breathed its air so easily, that it was hard for her to realize I was gasping like a stranded fish. And, of course, she didn't altogether want to realize it, because that would destroy her own pleasure. She wanted this part of her life to stay the way it had been before we met, only with myself included in it.

When I recalled those parties now, I saw Elizabeth in the

extreme distance, right over at the other end of a room which memory had probably magnified to at least twice its actual size. A perverse pride or stubbornness would make me move away from her, as far as I could get, the moment the introductions were over. I wasn't going to ride through the party hanging on to her skirts, I told myself. But, actually, I was trying to punish Elizabeth, in my own mean little way, for having brought me. For I knew she would have liked me to stay near her. She'd keep glancing anxiously in my direction to see how I was getting along.

There she would stand, smiling and shining in her own un-questioned brilliance as one of the three or four first-magnitude stars around which the whole gathering was constellated; and I, in my sulky corner, might as well have been several light-years away. I couldn't hear what the big stars were talking about, and I almost convinced myself that I didn't want to. They were admirable people, no doubt, in their everyday lives; good to their families, bold against injustice, humble and earnest in their work, wearing their well-earned fame as simply as their clothes—but nothing they said in this atmosphere could be otherwise than trivial: surface-chatter no deeper than the lips and the front teeth. They weren't really enjoying themselves, I thought. All their animation was a trick of light flashing from the outer coat of their eyeballs. They weren't even bored; though their voices had the fashionable, graceful modulations of boredom. No—this was merely their way of relaxing and resting from the serious business of being themselves. Perhaps what actually separated and cut me off from these men and women was just that I had nothing to rest from: no vocation, no responsibility, no job. Being reminded of this made me feel guilty and inferior; and I think that was the chief reason why I hated those parties so much.

I would have preferred to be left alone in my corner, but I wasn't. Lots of people talked to me. The ones of my own age usually embarrassed me, sooner or later, by asking what I did, or by speaking about Elizabeth with the implication that being her husband was the one justification for my existence. A few didn't know who I was and said, 'I hear she's just got married. What's he like?' And then there were the older ones who came over to inspect me with smiling, half-malicious curiosity. Later they withdrew and gossiped, just out of earshot, nodding their heads and very carefully avoiding my eyes. Some of their verdicts, it seemed, were favourable. If I wasn't dismissed as a bore, I would be looked up and down appreciatively, by women and sometimes by men, as an attractive boy, Elizabeth's pickup.

Outwardly, I think I managed to take all this fairly well. I kept a smile of sorts on my face, most of the time, answered politely when spoken to, and even produced an occasional laugh. I used to drink a good deal: that helped. But it was dangerous, too; because I would be more than half drunk by the time the party was over, and then I had to be careful what I said to Elizabeth when we were alone together. I had resolved, over and over again, not to bring up the subject of parties or tell her how I felt about them, as long as she was working on her novel. I reserved the right to sulk a little, but I wasn't going to be as selfish as all that, I told myself.

However, the day came, as I suppose it was bound to, when I'd drunk a bit more than usual and was in a slightly worse humour; and suddenly—almost before I was aware of what was happening —the lid blew off my good resolutions, as we were driving home in a taxi.

'You don't know what these people are really like,' I told Elizabeth. 'They make a fuss of you, because they think you're Somebody. But they don't give a damn about you, or anyone else, as a human being. They can't. They haven't any feelings, except spite and bitchiness.'

'My darling,' said Elizabeth, taking my hand in hers, 'some-one's been horrid to you, haven't they? Tell me who it was——'

'Oh—what does that matter? Nobody special. They're all alike.'

'Stephen—I'm so terribly sorry. I'd no idea——'

'You needn't be sorry. I don't care.'

'But what did they say?'

'It isn't what they say. It's just that I get a bit tired, sometimes, of being treated like a gigolo.'

'Darling—you can't be serious!'

'A very respectable one, of course. A gigolo with money. What do you call a rich gigolo? A rigolo, perhaps?'

'But how horrible! Are you quite certain you aren't—imagining some of this?'

'Oh, I'm exaggerating, naturally. And, anyhow, this is only the way *I* feel. It's my own fault, really, for minding. I'll get used to it in time. I'll probably end up being just as bitchy as they are.'

'But that would be dreadful. I don't want you *ever* to change. Oh, Stephen—*you*, being bitchy——!' Elizabeth started to laugh.

'I suppose I am pretty funny,' I said crossly. She turned serious at once.

'Oh no, darling—forgive me. It's only that I'm a bit bewildered. I hadn't realized. You see, I'm so indecently proud of you. I love to show you off. It never occurred to me that that could hurt you. . . . How very selfish I've been, haven't I?'

'I don't think so, at all.'

'But it shan't happen again, darling. I promise you. Never.'

I didn't ask Elizabeth what she meant by that, because I didn't want to bring the whole question out into the open and share in the responsibility for settling it. I was the selfish one, not she. But I knew then, as she knew, that a decision had been made that would affect our entire future life. It was Elizabeth who had to make the sacrifice. I don't think she ever seriously regretted it; but, still, I let her make it alone. I didn't move an inch to help her.

The next morning, while we were having breakfast, she smiled at me and said: 'Stephen, did you know you were married to an Artistic Temperament?'

'What do you mean?' I asked.

'Well—I know this is tiresome of me; but, the last few days I've been feeling so terribly restless. Should you mind dreadfully if we went abroad somewhere, quite soon?'

'Of course I shouldn't. I'd love to. But what about your novel?'

'Oh, the novel's even more restless than I am. It wants a change of air. The wretched thing's so sickly. If it can't get out of this climate, it threatens to go into a decline.'

'We mustn't let that happen,' I said, grinning with joy.

'Darling, you're so wonderfully sweet and understanding. Are you quite sure you really want to go?'

'You know I do. . . . But, Elizabeth, are you sure *you* want to?'

'But, Stephen, it was I who suggested it——'

'I know. Only——'

'Only what, darling?'

'Nothing. . . . I mean—well then, that's settled. Where are we going to?'

'Let's look at the atlas, shall we? Oh, isn't this exciting?'

So I let it happen. Nothing whatever was said about acquaintances and parties. With Elizabeth's help, my cowardice avoided the issue completely. We left London a week later; and, except for two short visits, we never returned.

About the beginning of June, Elizabeth wrote to Mary Scriven:

'Well, Mary darling, here we are established at last. Looking back, it's hard to remember quite how we arrived. We stopped in Paris a day or two, took a sniff at Brussels and quite a deep breath of Nürnberg, nosed at Munich but somehow didn't altogether trust its smell, then caught an intoxicating whiff of Vienna on the east wind and followed it in full cry. Vienna was as lovely as ever, but so full of things to see that I couldn't settle to any work. Then a Dutch painter we'd made friends with told us about this place. It's a largish but little-known lake called the Schwarzsee, in the neighbourhood of Bad Ischl and Gmunden. We've taken a house here for the summer.

Can't you visit us? You would love it, I'm sure. There are high mountains with the snow still on them, so aloof and grand, shining like a whole arctic world, up there in the sky. Down on their lower slopes there are larch-woods, dark green, with the young green tips much lighter than last year's growth; they smell so heavenly in the hot sun. When it rains, there's a wonderful lush wooden wetness in the air, and you feel as refreshed as if you were the earth itself, drinking in the water. But I think I like the still grey days best, so uncannily still, when the lake is a great bright motionless looking-glass, with the mountains and the woods and the village and ourselves all upside down in it.

If you do come to see us, you'll arrive on the little puffing steamer which crosses the Schwarzsee from the other village, where the railway-station is, and we'll be standing on the pier to welcome you, along with all the rest of the population. (I wish I could promise you they'd be in leather shorts and starched petticoats, but these, alas, are getting rarer; worse still, being adopted by tourists with pillowy hips and pork-pie knees.) Then we'll show you the sights: the church, and the Post Hotel, and the beer-hall where they dance, stamping around to the music of the fiddle and concertina, and the Schloss, in its park among the lime-trees, which has been rented by a rich family from Bavaria, whose doings the villagers discuss from morning till night. And, finally, our own house, which I know you will love as much as we do, because it's really a woodland version of your house in London, only with a steep-pitched roof and a carved balcony along the upper floor. It's all wood, of course, with a delicious turpentiny smell that makes you sleep at night as though you were drugged. And you shall have flowers in your room; there are millions of them on the hillsides now, primulas mostly, mauve, red, violet, white and yellow. (I hate having to tread on them when we go out walking.) And you shall have trout from the mountain streams for supper.

Are you beginning to waver, as you read this? Oh, Mary, do, do come! You are the only human being I can imagine who would fit perfectly into the life we lead here. As far as I'm concerned, at any rate, it's perfect: I couldn't have dreamed of such peace and security, this side of the grave. For the first time, my work-life and my personal life seem to have joined, like two rivers mingling and running along the same bed. It's Stephen, of course, who's responsible for this truly miraculous feat of hydraulic engineering. What have I ever done, to deserve him? And yet, ungrateful as one is, I find myself continually thinking: why couldn't I have found him before it got so late—two o'clock, already, in my life's afternoon? Why couldn't we have met ten years ago? But then, I have to remember, he'd have been twelve! How strange and sad it is, this business of ages. Deep down, it doesn't matter, it has no significance at all: love, on that level, is so simple. It asks no questions. But up on the surface, where we spend so much of our time, there's a perpetual, tragic frustration. We have to wear masks, and keep pretending to be what we seem at that particular moment. And yet—if I had the magic power to make myself younger, or Stephen older, would I use it? No, of course not. That would be turning our relationship into something else; and I wouldn't dare. Who am I, to meddle with a masterpiece? I'd as soon alter one of Shakespeare's sonnets. But enough of this nonsense. . . . What I do dare to say is—as of this moment—that I really believe Stephen is happy.'

Yes, I was very happy at the Schwarzsee, that summer. In some ways, it was the best, or, at any rate, the most completely satisfying, part of all the time Elizabeth and I spent together. I was happy because I was beginning to believe in the day-to-day reality of our marriage. I was losing the feeling of inferiority I'd had at those parties in London; losing the fear that I was merely the junior partner in a love-affair. I was beginning to see that I could be necessary to Elizabeth the writer, as well as Elizabeth the woman. Far from having to stop myself being jealous of her work, I found I could actually share in it.

The resolutions Elizabeth had made before our marriage—to be 'a proper wife', to keep house for me and darn my socks— broke down almost immediately, when we were actually settled in our house. All the time we'd been travelling around, she had been fretting to get her novel restarted, and I saw her glancing rather furtively at the manuscript, several times, while we were still unpacking. I was delighted, of course; this gave me all kinds of opportunities to make myself useful. It was I who went down to the sawmill and bought planks to repair the bathroom wall, I who interviewed the carpenter, I who unskilfully re-painted the front door and the window shutters, I who found a woman to come in and cook for us. I'd never done such things before in my life—Sarah had always taken care of them—and I felt splendidly efficient.

When I showed Elizabeth my finished paint-work, she hugged me. 'Oh, darling, I'm so proud of you!'

'It isn't very good, I'm afraid. Look at that smear.'

'I think the smear's the most beautiful part of it. That gives it a kind of peasant touch. . . . I've just realized—none of the men I've known could even begin to do something like this. They'd pick up the paint-brush and then make some clever remark and put it down again.'

Elizabeth's praise made me ambitious. It showed me how to complete my triumph over Strines and all the rest of the London party-goers. I would become absolutely indispensable to her. I would be a real, masculine, all-providing husband.

I started by offering to type her manuscript. Elizabeth never did this herself, and often complained of the mistakes they made at the agencies to which she used to send her work. I went into Bad Ischl and bought a typewriter, pretending to her that I could type quite well, though, as a matter of fact, I was practically a beginner. She never knew how many copies I had to make, at first, before I got one that was perfect. But I learned quickly, and soon I was a fairly competent secretary. Then I began to look after her correspondence. Elizabeth hated writing business letters, and was completely vague about contracts, percentages and foreign rights. I discovered, to my own astonishment, that these matters weren't as complicated as I'd supposed. If I read a contract through carefully (which Elizabeth never did) I could understand it. Perhaps I had actually inherited some aptitude for business. After all, I was my Father's son. Elizabeth thought I was a financial wizard, and I was pretty pleased with myself.

Then there were letters from admirers of her work; not many of them, but enough to make her feel guilty. 'I do feel one ought to answer all of them—even the cranks and the autograph-collectors. But I'm always so embarrassed. It's like playing Father Christmas at an orphanage. One's expected to be so shamelessly genial.' So I answered those letters, too; amusing myself by trying to parody Elizabeth's style. This became an absorbing indoor game. Elizabeth roared with laughter when I wrote to a lady in Newcastle: 'Yes, indeed I'm married—how clever of you to guess! You ask what he's like. How does one describe a husband—if he's the right one? Do you ever do jigsaw puzzles? Then you know that piece which looks like a very wriggly island. After endless attempts, you realize that it's the key to everything. As soon as it's in place, the whole picture suddenly makes sense.' 'Stephen—you monster!' Elizabeth exclaimed, wiping the tears of laughter from her eyes. 'I feel almost afraid of you. I believe you'll end by writing my novels.'

Meanwhile, I developed my role of odd-job-man around the house. I learned, by experiment, how to fix the plumbing, how to build fires, saw wood, drive in nails properly, make doors and windows close or open, tack down carpets and keep the whole place clean. After carefully watching our cook, I decided to try the cooking myself, three nights a week; and soon began to produce casserole dishes which were much superior to hers, because they were prepared with love. Elizabeth over-praised them wildly, of course. She pretended to believe that I had special secret recipes, based on herbs I collected in the forest, and would detect new subtle flavours even in the eggs I simply fried for our breakfast.

Some of Elizabeth's enthusiasm was no doubt due to the fact that all this overt activity of mine put her on the defensive. 'I'm afraid I must seem terribly lazy to you, Stephen,' she said. 'I'm so glad you can't watch me when I'm alone in my work-room. You know, half the time I'll be turning over the pages of a book, or walking backwards and forwards muttering some nonsense or other, or just staring out of the window with my mouth open. And yet, I do promise you, something *is* going on inside, all the time. I wish I could learn better co-ordination, though. I'm like a leaky old engine with the driving-belt slipping and steam escaping from every joint: I only just manage to function. Don't get too impatient with me.' I assured her that I didn't. But, just the same, I was only now beginning to understand vaguely how Elizabeth worked. I suppose, like most other laymen, I had thought of literary composition as a self-contained activity like digging in the garden or sewing. You went to the desk, picked up the pen, started to make marks on the paper; and, when you'd finished, that was that. I now knew, what should have been obvious to me from the first, that Elizabeth composed not only during her working-hours but, on and off, throughout the rest of the day. Quite often, when we went for walks together, she would suddenly cease to be with me; her mind had gone back home to the manuscript. I could sense her departure and return almost immediately: while her mind was away, I kept silent, happy and proud that she should feel free to do this in my company without excuses. I felt even happier when she tried, sometimes quite incoherently, to say what she was thinking about: 'It's Adrian—I don't know—that scene with the policeman—it doesn't exactly—the way they *talk*, that's all right—only, somehow, it's too logical—too much to the point—— I ought to wander off, a little—— Wait a minute, though: how would it be if——? No—— But I do think I see a way——' She was talking to herself, mostly. I never interrupted.

'Darling,' she said to me, one day. 'I hope you know how much you're helping me. You're like a tuning-fork I keep striking, to hear if I'm still on pitch. . . . Oh, but I do wish——'

'What do you wish, Elizabeth?'

'That I could do the same thing for you. I wish you had something to tell *me*. I wish you'd go on and on about how you were making a fortune on the stock-exchange or how you'd designed a new kind of motor-bicycle. I wish you'd be terribly technical and abstruse. I think I'd really love it if you bored me to distraction.'

'You never bore me.'

'Don't I really, darling? I bore myself, quite often. Horribly, I'm only afraid I shall bore you too, in time. And not in the right way, either. That is, unless——'

'Unless what?'

Elizabeth smiled and kissed me. 'Oh, I have my plans. . . . Don't ask me about them, Stephen. Just be patient.'

The Schloss, as Elizabeth told Mary Scriven in her letter, had been rented by a rich family from Bavaria, intellectuals and great patrons of the arts. They filled the place with their guests: well-known poets, painters, musicians and theatrical designers.

One night, when the warm weather came, they had a magnificent dinner-party on a raft which had been towed out into the middle of the lake, bearing a dining-table, chairs, a silver centre-piece, and tall candles in glasses. Two motor-boats brought the guests, along with the food in big chafing-dishes. The village musicians played for them, sitting in a rowboat alongside. When they were ready for coffee, the butler sent up a rocket from the raft, and one of the motor-boats brought it, freshly brewed, from a portable stove on the shore.

'How charming of them to take all this trouble!' Elizabeth exclaimed. 'I'm sure they're doing it entirely to amuse us.' The villagers seemed to agree with her that this was a public spectacle put on for their benefit. Many of them had rowed out into the lake, as we had, to get a closer view. Our boats formed a wide spectator-circle in the darkness surrounding the brilliant stage of the raft, on which the actor-guests laughed and chattered. Perhaps the consciousness of being watched actually added to their enjoyment. Candle-light made every face dramatic; and it gave the hostess, who was a black-haired middle-aged woman, a kind of uncanny tragic beauty. 'What a marvellous first act for a play!' said Elizabeth. 'Only, you know, I have an unpleasant feeling that this isn't a comedy. Not even a satirical one. Don't you see something hovering over it all? It frightens me, somehow. I'm afraid it isn't by Shaw. It might even be Ibsen.'

The morning after the raft-party, there was a stranger on the lake. I first saw him as he passed our windows, quite near to the shore, in a collapsible rubber boat, bronzed like an Indian and naked except for a pair of very British-looking football shorts. His suntan made his blue eyes pale and vivid and his blond hair seem almost white. He was a strikingly handsome boy with a slim muscular body, and he paddled with ferocious concentration, as though he were a South Sea islander in a war-canoe, on his way to attack a hostile tribe.

That afternoon, I met him in the post-office. He was having difficulty explaining something about a money-order. When I rephrased his broken German so that the Postmaster could understand it, he frowned and blushed; but this was only shyness. Five minutes later, we were drinking beer together, and he was telling me all about himself. He talked rapidly and tensely, with frequent apologetic grins, as though he was afraid that what he'd said was silly.

He was eighteen years old, his name was Michael Drummond, and he had just left his public school. He planned to stay in Central Europe the whole summer, travelling around and studying, until it was time for him to go up to Oxford. Among other projects, he wanted to paddle right down the Danube in his rubber boat; as far as the Black Sea, if possible. 'But aren't there some very dangerous rapids?' I asked. 'Probably,' said Michael, in a vague impersonal tone, as if this could have nothing whatever to do with his trip. Then he looked at me, and we both began to laugh.

When I suggested he should come back with me to our house and meet Elizabeth and stay to supper, he hesitated, and then accepted with an eagerness he obviously tried to conceal. I guessed that he was lonely, as I'd so often been, myself, the year before in Paris. Like so many young people who go abroad by themselves, he'd probably imagined that he wanted to be alone—a solitary Byronic traveller—when, in fact, he didn't.

Elizabeth was at her very best, that evening: so beautiful and easy and lively. Her novel must have been going well. I saw her, in glimpses, as she must appear to Michael—the central figure in a legendary Evening With Elizabeth Rydal—and I found myself playing up to her, prompting her to tell her most amusing stories, being funny so that she could be even funnier. Michael's brilliant blue eyes flashed back and forth from her face to mine, never missing a word, and several times he laughed so much that he coughed and choked. He didn't leave us till midnight.

'What an adorable child!' Elizabeth exclaimed, after he had gone. 'Those eyes of his! Didn't they make you feel we were the most horrible old imposters? He's as embarrassing as a looking-glass.'

However, on closer acquaintance, Michael proved to be a looking-glass of the most flattering kind, and we both enjoyed his admiration, even though we made fun of ourselves for doing so. I myself had an additional reason for liking to have Michael around. He was young enough to accept me uncritically in my new role of the mature married man. With him, I felt I succeeded where I had failed so dismally in London. Elizabeth soon began to refer to him jokingly as 'our eldest son'.

With Michael I used to go fishing and rowing on the lake. Michael swam in it, too, but I couldn't stand the chill of the snow-water. We went on long hikes, high up into the mountains. At first, I urged Elizabeth to come with us, but she refused smilingly: 'I'm afraid I'm not very robust,' she said. 'I'd only be a drag on you.' I had noticed, already, that she tired easily and would get out of breath after any small exertion, and this worried me.

'It's nothing, really,' she assured me, when I asked her about it. 'I expect I'm over-cautious. A doctor once told me to be careful.'

'But, Elizabeth—you don't mean there's anything wrong with your heart?'

'No, of course not. Nothing dramatic. Just a little weakness. Please don't worry, Stephen darling.'

That was all I could get out of her.

Underneath his grins and laughter and tense gaiety, Michael was a very serious boy. He was an orphan, raised by a grim Scottish uncle, and he had been much alone as a child. He had thrown himself into the activities of his school life with Spartan fanaticism, become a fine athlete, won cups for track and boxing and captained the rugger fifteen; but he'd been too shy to make any close friends. When we were out together, we discussed all kinds of subjects. He was particularly interested in politics and economics, and certainly knew far more about them than I did. But we never mentioned Sex, except in the most indirect way. I felt, instinctively, that he could very easily be shocked, and I was quite sure that he had never had any experience.

When we were sitting in the boat on the lake, one morning, he said abruptly: 'When you and Elizabeth get tired of having me around, I hope you'll tell me.'

'Why, Michael,' I was genuinely surprised, 'what on earth makes you think——?'

'I know I'm a bloody nuisance, sometimes, trailing after you like a lost puppy.'

'Nonsense! Elizabeth loves seeing you. We both do.'

'I don't know why you should,' said Michael frowning. 'There's nothing particularly interesting about me.' He began to blush violently, and looked out over the lake, avoiding my eyes: 'If you want to know—after that first evening you had me to supper, I very nearly packed up and left this place. I felt I was beginning to like you both an awful lot, and I didn't want to. I didn't want to start being a bore. I decided to leave, and then I just couldn't.'

'Oh, Michael,' I said, touched, 'you mustn't ever feel like that. I mean, I understand how you could have—that's the way I might have felt myself, at your age. But you're quite, quite wrong.'

'I don't think you do understand,' Michael said, looking straight at me. 'And I'm glad you don't. But I won't talk like this any more. It's childish.'

It was about this time that Elizabeth suddenly announced that she would like to go to Salzburg for a couple of days. I was always pleased when she expressed a definite wish of this kind— she so seldom did—and I agreed immediately. To my slight surprise, she suggested taking Michael with us. 'I don't want to leave him here by himself,' she explained. 'It sounds silly, I know, but I just cannot bear to think of him being alone. He's such a painfully lonely person, isn't he? It wrings my heart.' Somehow, this didn't sound quite convincing; but I agreed, of course. So to Salzburg we all three went.

I'd supposed, naturally, that this was going to be a holiday for Elizabeth. But, the morning after our arrival, she said that she wanted to work and suggested that I should go sightseeing with Michael. I was disappointed and even a bit hurt by this, but I was careful not to show it. Afterwards, I was glad that I hadn't.

At lunch, that day, Elizabeth was in an extraordinary mood. She was gay to the point of silliness and kept making jokes which were quite idiotic. 'What's all the excitement about?' I asked her, as soon as we were alone together. 'Oh, Stephen darling— I've been wondering for the last three hours how I was going to tell you!' Elizabeth threw her arms around my neck and kissed me, laughing. 'And I still don't know! Perhaps I won't tell you. Perhaps I'll wait till you read it in the newspapers.'

'Read what, Elizabeth?' I asked, laughing too, though I didn't know why.

'Let me be the first to announce to you, Sir, that I propose to present Michael with a brother. He'd like a brother, wouldn't he, not a sister? Anyhow, I think I shall insist on a brother.'

'Elizabeth—Oh, my God!'

'Stephen, you look positively shattered!'

'I'm not. No, of course I'm not. I'm delighted. It's only— well, you know, this takes a bit of getting used to. . . . So that was why you wanted to come here? To see a doctor? And Michael was to get me out of the way while you did it? But why on earth didn't you tell me, darling? I'd have gone with you. Is he a good man?'

'One of the best specialists in Austria, I'm told.'

'What's his name?'

'Does that matter, darling?'

'I'd like to go and see him myself.'

'But, Stephen, whatever for?'

'I just feel I ought to. Doesn't one, usually?'

'Stephen darling, I'm going to ask you to do something for me. Will you promise?'

'What is it?'

'Promise first.' Elizabeth had become very much in earnest.

'All right, then. I promise.'

'I expect it's terribly female and psychological of me—but listen, Stephen, I want you to leave this whole business to me; having the baby. I promise faithfully to go to the doctor whenever it's necessary, and do all the things he tells me, and take every precaution. But somehow, I don't quite know how to explain it. I want to leave you out of this entirely. I suppose it's a kind of biological privacy. . . . You've promised, remember?'

'All right,' I said. 'I've promised.'

I had no reason, then, to suspect Elizabeth's truthfulness in saying all this, or her motives. But here was the note she wrote, that same afternoon, to Mary Scriven:

'You know what we discussed in London—the Great Possibility? Well, it has happened! I tell you this in the *deadliest* secrecy, and only because of that other confidence I made to you then. I almost wish, now, that I hadn't made it; because if no one knew, not even such a grave of secrets as yourself, then I could more easily pretend to myself that it was all nonsense and unfounded fear. Well—it isn't nonsense. I have to face that. There is the danger. But when it actually came to making the decision, I didn't hesitate for one instant—any more than any other woman in my position would have hesitated. The doctor advised me against it, of course; but then, that's what he *had*

to say, just as this is what I *had* to decide. Mary my dearest, I'm
telling you this so that, if anything *should* happen, you'll know
that I chose freely and gladly—and, one day, you'll tell Stephen.
But it sounds so absurdly melodramatic when I write this.
Nothing is going to happen. I know it. I'm determined to make
myself know it. I feel splendidly healthy, and so happy that I—
well, you'll know from your own experience. And now, please,
lock this away in the bottom of your mind, as I've locked it in
mine.'

Being back at the Schwarzsee seemed, after that day's excitement, rather anticlimactic. Life went on as usual. Elizabeth continued her novel and kept pretty well, with much less morning
sickness that we had expected. But often, when I woke up
beside her in bed, or at odd moments throughout the day, I
would remember that I was going to become a father. 'A father.
A father,' I repeated, trying to make the word relate to myself.
I couldn't, yet. 'Father' was still what the word 'Husband' had
been to me at the time of our honeymoon: a name for a wonderful new game. I was excited, of course, and proud and
pleased: but these feelings were all on the surface. Underneath,
I had really no idea how I felt, or how I might be going to feel.

Naturally, we talked about the baby a great deal. Elizabeth
said that we shouldn't worry too much about its sex—though
we both wanted a boy—lest it should feel unwelcome if it
turned out to be a girl. She suggested that, for the present, we
should call it by a name which would do for either; but neither
of us liked Evelyn, Dale or Lou, so, provisionally, we referred
to it as Mydal or Ronk. 'Mydal is more ambiguous,' said
Elizabeth, 'but if it *is* a boy, I think Ronk would be better—
such a manly name.'

We had told Michael, the evening of that day in Salzburg. I
had ordered champagne, we had drunk a toast, and he had con-
gratulated us with a formality which was unnatural to him,

almost middle-aged. I could see at once that the news had raised
a barrier between him and us. We hadn't been back at the
Schwarzsee more than three or four days when he told me
that he was leaving for Vienna.

'But, Michael,' I said, 'you don't know anybody there. Why
not stay here? The best weather is beginning.'

'No, Stephen.' Michael shook his head almost angrily. 'You
don't want me here any more. Don't pretend you do. You and
Elizabeth want to be alone together, now. Do you think I don't
understand that?' He turned away from me, biting his lip. He
was very near to crying. 'I've never met anyone like you two.
Most people are so rotten. Or else they're just fools. I think
you've discovered the way people ought to live. I wish everybody could know you like I have. I'll never forget you. Tell
Elizabeth that, too. I won't see her again. I loathe all this sickly
Goodbye business.'

I patted him awkwardly on the shoulder, embarrassed because
he was right. Since I'd known about Elizabeth's pregnancy, I
wanted to be near her all the time. Even when she was working,
I didn't care to leave the house. I would still have liked Michael
to be with us, now and then, but I wouldn't have gone off with
him on any more hikes. I felt restless, now, whenever Elizabeth
and I were separated for more than a few minutes.

'Good luck, Michael,' I said. 'And mind you write. We'll be
thinking about you often.'

Michael only wrote once; a postcard from Vienna. But we
talked about him every day for a long while. 'I do wonder
what'll happen to him,' Elizabeth said. 'I feel that almost anything might. That's what makes young men like him so mysterious and fascinating. You have no idea where they're going—
and neither have they.'

Toward the end of August, Elizabeth finished her novel, and
was eager for a change of scene. We had planned a visit to

Greece, allowing plenty of time to get back to England afterwards, before the baby was born.

Athens was terribly hot, and this worried me because it was an extra strain on Elizabeth: she got tired so easily. She made light of this, as usual; and she certainly loved the city as much as I did. Her letters and postcards home were full of descriptions —the Acropolis, the Lycabettus hill, Piraeus, the wandering evening crowds in the Zappeion gardens, the dark swarming Asiatic markets, the marble sidewalks, the resinated wine, the officers playing with strings of beads as they talked in the cafés, the smells, the dust, the cypresses, the beggars, the Turkish delight. I think she dealt with all these details so elaborately in order to avoid telling our one enormous piece of news. Except for Mary Scriven, she still hadn't told anyone in England about the expected baby.

During September and October we made several short trips— to Delphi, to Corinth and Patras, to Khalkis and the island of Euboea. It was Elizabeth who always suggested them. When I feared that she wouldn't be comfortable, and warned her of hot crowded trains, flies, dirty food and bumpy roads, she protested laughingly against my fussing. She assured me that she had never felt better.

Then came that night, early in November, when I woke from deep sleep to feel Elizabeth pulling at the sleeve of my pyjama jacket. 'Stephen, will you get a doctor? I'm bleeding. I don't think I'd better move.' Her voice was quiet and urgent. I knew she was frightened, but she kept perfectly calm. She had had a sudden violent haemorrhage. The sheets were soaked with her blood.

I roused the whole hotel and rushed her to hospital as quickly as I could; but there was much delay, because they discovered that my blood belonged to a different group from hers, and another donor had to be found for the transfusion. I went nearly crazy with fear and impatience. In a kind of nightmare daze, toward dawn, I listened to the doctor's medical explanations. I had to concentrate hard to understand his gabble of broken English and French. The word 'placenta' kept recurring: somehow, it seemed to me to express the very essence of this obscene horror. I didn't know exactly what it meant, but every time he said it, I felt sick. The placenta had become partly detached from the womb. The child was probably already dead. I was almost glad to hear that about the child; for some muddled superstition made me believe that its death would pay for Elizabeth's life.

That wasn't the worst, however. Three days later, she began to run a high fever and became delirious. An infection had set in. (Years later, an American surgeon told me that this was most likely due to the Greek doctor's carelessness: he must have examined Elizabeth without wearing rubber gloves. But, thank God, I didn't know that at the time.) By now, another doctor had been called in for consultation, a German specialist. He decided that Elizabeth's womb would have to be removed. It was the only way to save her.

The German evidently disliked me. He was a prim, thin, bitter man with a duelling-scar on his cheek. He muttered something to himself about 'criminal selfishness' and 'lack of all human feeling'. When I asked him what he meant, he glared at me scornfully. 'I think you know very well what I mean, my dear Sir. You deliberately gambled with your Wife's life, in order to have this child.' My look of utter bewilderment at this must have shaken him a little; for he went on in a milder tone, as if he'd suddenly realized that he was speaking to an idiot: 'Or, is it possible—can you not have known? Could any man in your position not have known? Well, perhaps. . . . Then let me tell you, Sir: your Wife suffers, since several years, from an extremely grave condition of the heart. You were ignorant of this? Incredible. . . . She should never, never, under any circumstances, have attempted to become a mother. As for this operation—it is a desperate measure. Please understand this: I promise nothing. Nothing. I accept no responsibility whatever.' He bowed to me coldly, and hurried off to get ready for the surgery. I think it was his harshness that helped me to pull myself together and sweat out the hours of waiting which followed.

At last, it was all over. And then there was hope, grudgingly admitted by the German: 'we are luckier than we deserve'. Then more hope, with caution: 'a relapse is always possible'. Then I was allowed to see Elizabeth.

I would never forget the shock of her appearance, that evening. She looked like a death-mask. Her skin was like alabaster. Her lips were absolutely white and bloodless. Even her finger-nails were white. She tried to smile at me, and that was worst of all. Forgetting the Doctor's warnings against upsetting her, and my own resolutions, I threw myself down on my knees beside her bed and burst into tears.

'Oh, my darling,' she said. 'I'm so sorry'. Her voice sounded as weak as she looked; and yet I'd never been as conscious of her inner strength as I was at that moment. It shamed me. I smeared the tears out of my eyes and blew my nose.

'My God,' I said, 'why should *you* be sorry?'

'Because I made such a mess of this.'

'Never mind that. Are you all right, Elizabeth? Are you going to be all right?'

'Of course I am.'

'But, darling, why didn't you ever tell me?'

'Tell you what?' she asked, with a smile that was almost teasing.

'About your heart.'

'You'd have worried.'

'*Worried!* My God, I'd never have let you have the baby.'

'But I wanted to have it—him, I mean. You know it was a him?'

'Yes. The doctor told me.'

'Ronk,' said Elizabeth softly.

'Ronk. Not Mydal. You were right about that.'

'And now there'll never be a Ronk. Or a Mydal, either. I won't ever be able to——'

'I know,' I interrupted quickly. 'But don't think about it, darling. Don't worry. It doesn't matter. I don't care a bit. As a matter of fact, I——'

At this moment, to my relief, the nurse came in to tell me that my visiting-time was up, and I must leave Elizabeth to get her sleep.

We avoided the subject, after that, for several weeks; until the time when Elizabeth was definitely convalescent. I'd begun to hope that she had somehow accepted her loss and put it out of her mind. And then, one day, I came in and found her crying quietly to herself. I didn't have to ask her what was the matter. I knew at once.

'I wanted to have him—so terribly badly,' she sobbed. 'I didn't care about anything else. I wanted to have him for you. . . . Oh, Stephen darling—you're so sweet—you'll never tell me— but I know how much you mind——'

'But I don't mind, darling. I swear I don't. Now that I know you'll get well. We've still got each other.'

'I thought—I hoped—if we'd had him, it would have been something we could share in—so you wouldn't ever—get tired of being—with me.'

'Elizabeth—that's just utter nonsense! You won't feel like this when you're well again. *Me* get tired! Why, I don't want anybody or anything but you. What do we need a child for? I'd tell you if I minded. Honestly. Don't you believe me?'

'You will mind—one day. Oh, I know you will—even if you never say so. Oh darling—I've failed you——'

I protested, over and over again. I held her in my arms. I tried to comfort her. In a little while, she calmed down and dried her eyes and said she was sorry for making this scene. 'I expect you're right, darling. I was just being tiresome and nervous. I shan't carry on like this when I've really recovered. I promise you, this won't happen any more.'

Elizabeth kept her promise. There were no more scenes. Nevertheless, for a long while, I felt a kind of thin shadow between us. I didn't see into her mind as clearly as before. I suppose the trouble was that I couldn't really understand how she had felt about the child. Perhaps I only fully understood it now, for the first time, as I lay in bed alone, with nothing left of her but these letters I held in my hands.

FIVE

*A*S BIRDS DO, MOTHER was published in the spring of
1928. Elizabeth and I were in Paris at the time; we had
travelled up there specially from Rome, so as to be able to talk
to her publisher more easily on the telephone and get the reviews
more quickly by airmail. 'You see,' Elizabeth wrote to Cecilia,
'I wanted to hover near the nest, but at a safe distance. I simply
couldn't face London and my own publisher's party. I've been
to too many of them already, for other people, and seen the
miserable author standing there like a garlanded victim amidst
all those hidden daggers. He may be somebody you know quite
well, but on that fatal afternoon he's the ritual victim, set apart,
ready for the knife. He's so utterly vulnerable that you can't
bear to look into his eyes. You know you've got to go up and
say something to him, and you rack your brains to think *what*,
because you probably hated his book or, even worse, found it
just completely ordinary and uninteresting. Finally you nerve
yourself to deliver your false flattering little stab, and the poor
creature thanks you and winces, ever so slightly. Towards the
end of the ceremony, he has usually drunk enough sherry to dull
the pain, and then he's like a wretched wounded animal, bleary
and stupid and helpless. No thank you. Je m'excuse beaucoup.
Let them find another scapegoat.'

As it turned out, the reviews of *As Birds Do, Mother* were
nearly all favourable. The critics decided that it showed a great
advance on Elizabeth's first novel, *The Faded Carpet* (which she
had written when she was twenty-three), and they treated it
most respectfully. 'Miss Rydal,' said one of them, 'is a writer in
a class by herself. She sets her own standards and defines her own

limitations, and she must be judged by them.' But this was exactly the sort of praise that Elizabeth didn't want. 'Oh yes,' she told Cecilia. 'I see I'm to be handled with kid gloves, from now on. I'm to have a "rare talent"—something exquisite and delicate. And if I behave myself and promise not to write too much—not more than six books at the most—then I'll be tolerated until the day I die, and perhaps five minutes after. Oh, Cecilia, is this why I became a writer? To be "in a class by myself", like one of those guaranteed genuine little treasures in a Bond Street shop-window that people look at and say: "Yes, I'm sure it's terribly *rare*, but who on earth would want it?" Ah, how I wish, I wish I could scribble off dozens of huge shapeless impulsive novels full of contradictory opinions and warmth and energy and silliness and *life*, like—yes, God forgive me—like Wells!'

During the next eighteen months, Elizabeth was at work on *A Garden with Animals*. She had begun planning it even before *As Birds Do, Mother* was published, and she sent long letters to Cecilia discussing the problems of its construction. On the whole, the writing went unexpectedly smoothly. 'Now that the end is in sight,' she told Cecilia in June 1929, 'I'm amazed and grateful that it has all been so easy. Do you know, I believe the reason I had so much trouble with *Birds* is that half of me was actually trying to write *Garden* at the same time? The two of them were lying interlocked in my mind, and as soon as I'd disentangled them from their incestuous embrace, the curse was lifted.'

Elizabeth had had a long convalescence, but now she seemed to have recovered entirely; at any rate, she was quite as well as she had been before the miscarriage. I noticed one change in her, however. Before, when she wasn't actually working, she had wanted mostly to be alone with me. Now, she seemed eager for company. I certainly didn't resent this, or take it personally.

My own position with Elizabeth was too secure for that, and I was only too glad to see her so happy and lively.

We spent those two summers back at the Schwarzsee, and the winter in Italy, with visits to France and England in between. There was a whole batch of postcards from Elizabeth—often with half a dozen other signatures squeezed into their corners—referring to parties, excursions, picnics, dances, charades in which she and I had taken part. 'Such a wonderful weekend at the Bertoluccis' villa, with Brian and Magdalena and Sandy and the Prescotts. How we all wished you'd been able to stay on for it!' 'Last night was unforgettable. Mary Scriven went as Queen Victoria, of course; Stephen and I were de Musset and George Sand—complete with cigar!' 'It rained in torrents, and a poor little French poet was attacked by bees in the wood. For some mysterious reason, this was one of the happiest days of my life.'

All kinds of people came out to stay with us; some of them the very same ones I'd thought of as malicious enemies in our early London days. I welcomed them now, and even got to like them. It was certainly much easier to be a host than a guest, and it seemed to me that their presence brought Elizabeth and myself closer together, instead of separating us. Especially at night, when we would lie discussing them and laughing about them in bed. Elizabeth was an extraordinary mimic. She could imitate Tarr to the life, saying, 'Picasso's a ruffian', and Mrs. Ockham appealing to her husband, 'I don't think we're *quite* as fond of Proust as we used to be, are we, darling?' and Propter raising his arms and dropping them despairingly into his lap as he sighed, 'As far as one can see, there's no prospect of anything but absolutely indefinite squalor.' While we were having fun like this, we might just as well have been children in a nursery. Our ages didn't have any significance at all.

In August 1929, Elizabeth finished *A Garden with Animals*.

And that autumn we finally went over to the States. Sarah had been begging us to come, in her letters, for the past two years.

The news of the stock-market crash reached us by radio in the middle of the Atlantic, during a gale, and made many of our fellow-passengers feel suicidal as well as seasick. I wondered vaguely if I was ruined, and had half-serious talks with Elizabeth about ways in which I might be able to earn a living. But I didn't worry much. I couldn't imagine myself poor because I'd never thought of myself as being rich. (Jane taught me to do that, later.) Our wandering bohemian kind of life was actually quite expensive, but it didn't seem so because it didn't include any big visible assets. Rich people, as I pictured them, had to have mansions and motor-cars and jewels and a staff of servants. 'I'm afraid we're something far more sinister,' Elizabeth agreed. 'We're the Invisible Rich. Even a communist couldn't detect us with the naked eye.'

As it later proved, I'd had no need to worry at all. The family business was perfectly sound. A cousin of mine on the board of directors explained to me, with a smile of discreet Puritanical smugness, that of course they hadn't risked any speculations; in fact, they had seen the whole thing coming, months ago. I got the impression that he regarded the crash with righteous approval as a sort of financial Judgment Day; and I felt relieved but a bit ashamed to find myself herded in with the prudent high-principled sheep instead of the reckless greedy goats. I hadn't done anything to earn my salvation, either, and it was obvious that my cousin disapproved of me and the dilettante life I was leading. Well, I disapproved of *his* life too, even if I had no right to. I wanted no part of it. I was glad to get out of Philadelphia again, that same day, and hurry back to Elizabeth in New York. And so I missed my only opportunity of revisiting Tawelfan that year.

We spent Christmas with Sarah at her college in Ohio. I was

so happy to be with her, and see how perfectly she fitted into her surroundings. ('Since she came into our midst,' the College President told me, 'we've been wondering how we ever got along without her.') But Sarah's surroundings were a bit too much for us. 'This little house is positively bursting at the seams,' Elizabeth wrote in one of her letters, 'and we're never alone with Sarah for an instant. I think she feels, bless her heart, that we're too precious to be kept to herself; it's her duty to share us with the entire neighbourhood. So we're being fed to the five thousand, in microscopic helpings. The first callers arrive for breakfast and the last ones leave long after midnight. And, oh dear, the introductions! It seems they have two sorts of names here; the sort that are too ordinary to remember, like Smith, Jones, Brown, and the sort that are too extra-ordinary, like Naddo, Hagenbuehler, Bachardy, Aufderheide. I repeat them over to myself in an anxiety-nightmare, trying to learn them; but I never can. They all know our name, however, *and* each others'. Americans must have a genius for this. Sarah certainly has. "I'm afraid you find it a little quiet here, now," she says apologetically, "but wait until the vacation's over! I can promise you plenty of company then." '
I made the excuse to Sarah that the mid-western winter was a strain on Elizabeth's health, and we left, early in January, for California.

In Hollywood, Elizabeth was fascinated by the movie world and we frequented it a good deal, watching its inhabitants at work in the studios and dining at their homes in the evenings. 'How Balzac would have loved them!' she wrote. 'But he should have come here a few years earlier in the great days of splendour, when they ate off gold plate in fake French châteaux hung with real Gobelin tapestry, and then went bankrupt over-night and committed suicide with sleeping-pills in their Jacobean beds. If Balzac had written a *Splendeurs et Misères des Vedettes*, he'd have made his Vautrin a film-producer whose terrible secret is that he's actually a runaway professor of literature from Christ Church. Vautrin's mortal enemy, a rival producer, would suspect this of course, and set a trap for him: at a magnificent banquet, he'd bribe a corrupt British novelist to misquote a line of Dryden in Vautrin's presence. Vautrin, very drunk, would forget his disguise and automatically correct the novelist— *with an Oxford accent*. Tableau!'

By April, we had moved on to San Francisco. 'What a fascinating, nostalgic city this is,' Elizabeth wrote, 'right out at the last edge of the earth. The gateway to the water-world. You watch the ships stealing off into the fog and the cold shadowy Pacific. Never in my life have I felt the "poetry of departure" as I do here. You long to take wing and fly, fly away westward to the uttermost islands.'

A few weeks after this, we had 'taken wing' ourselves, on a boat bound for Honolulu; and that was when our wanderings really began.

'It seems as if we can't stop travelling,' Elizabeth told Mary Scriven, nearly a year later. 'Tahiti, New Zealand, Australia, the Philippines, Japan, Shanghai, Hong Kong, Saigon, Bangkok, Singapore, Bali—when I make a list of the places we've been to, it sounds too utterly fantastic. If I could have seen it in advance, I think I'd have dropped dead from sheer exhaustion. But that's not how we do it, of course. We make no lists. We have no plans. We arrive somewhere, hate it and leave instantly, or fall in love with it and settle, perhaps for ever, we simply don't know. Only, if we do settle, there's a day when the call comes— the merest whisper it is, very often—and we're off again. The important thing is not to regard this as a journey, but as a way of life. Then it seems quite relaxed and restful.

If you're worried about my health, don't be. I'm wonderfully well, on the whole. Never any serious trouble with my heart. And the doctors I see from time to time seem quite pleased with me.

If any part of me feels tired, it's the organ of perception; that little sensitive animal one keeps pulling out of the unconscious by the scruff of its neck and exposing to each new collection of sights, sounds and smells. The creature has to be pampered and petted and protected from overstrain—for, without it, as a writer one is lost and blind. "Come on now, dear Guinea-Pig," I say to it coaxingly, "use your eyes and nose and whiskers. How does this place strike you? What's its essential quality? What am I to say about it?" Sometimes the Guinea-Pig is alert and astonishingly clever (it even surprises *me*) but more often it sulks and mutters "No comment" or "It looked better than this in the photographs" or "Why come all this distance when you could find exactly the same landscape in Surrey?" And then it has a maddening way of becoming interested in some irrelevant detail, something which doesn't "fit" into the milieu at all. In Singapore, for example, it would pay no attention to anything but an old family photograph-album belonging to a Brazilian priest! I just have to endure its humours, though, and be grateful for its help. And that reminds me, I wonder if the *New Statesman* has printed any of those travel-sketches I keep sending? I've done nearly enough, now, for a book.

Our mail seldom catches up with us, and so I find myself writing fewer and fewer letters; it requires so much faith to consign them to the unanswering void. Perhaps I'll simply put this one in a bottle and drop it into the Bay of Bengal, hoping it'll eventually float along the gutter of the mews to your doorstep. We're on our way to Calcutta—don't you envy us? Already I'm sniffing the land-breeze for the first whiff of curry.'

What brought us back to Europe, at the end of 1932, was chiefly Elizabeth's urge to begin another novel. 'I find I can write short stories almost anywhere,' she told Cecilia. 'I can sit down in a ship's cabin, or a hotel bedroom, or under a tree, and absorb myself in my little anecdote. But a novel—that's such an under-taking. For that I need elbow-room, a vast desk, familiar sur-roundings, regular meals, unlimited time; the illusion of im-mortality, in fact. No more trains and ships to catch. No more fuss about tickets and passports and Customs declarations. No distracting temples and pagodas, odd music, strange flowers. I need the dear friendly old Eiffel Tower rattling in the wind, and Notre Dame (looking smaller than ever, this morning) in the rain. We've taken a flat on the Quai de l'Horloge (note above address) at the top of a tall, tall house, right under the roof. The stairs are a real via dolorosa, so steep, but I climb them in easy stages with frequent rests, and it's worth it. My work-room has a window-box and I plan to grow wallflowers and daisies in it and muse over them wistfully like the consumptive girl in a Victorian novel who knows she'll never see the spring again. I have *every* intention of seeing the spring again myself, however. By then, I ought to have finished a rough draft of this book.

I told you all my plans for it in my last letter, so no more of that, now. But I've got a tentative title I'd like you to consider. I thought of it yesterday morning, when I woke up with those lines in my head from *The Progress of the Soul*:

> And the great world to his aged evening;
> From infant morn, through manly noon I draw.

The World to His Evening, how do you like that? Stephen says it sounds affected, precious, self-consciously quaint. Perhaps I agree with him. I don't know. It isn't *quite* right, and yet, it has the mood I want to convey. I can't make up my mind.'

Elizabeth had been too optimistic about the rough draft. 'Here we are, nearly at the end of May,' she wrote to Mary Scriven, 'and I'm still not more than three-quarters through the wood. I feel absolutely no interest, no enthusiasm. I only know that I have to go on. I drag myself to my desk. Opening my note-book is like forcing the door of a safe—a safe which turns out to be empty, anyhow!—and, psychologically speaking, my pen weighs at least a hundred pounds; I have to use all the muscles of my will to pick it up.

What a winter! What a spring! I scarcely stirred from the flat for weeks on end. I got ill, as I wrote to you, immediately after we returned here from our London visit. (Memories of those evenings at your house are almost the only gleams in this six-month gloom.) I must have picked up some particularly noxious kind of British 'flu-germ—specially bred for foreign tourists, no doubt—and it wouldn't leave me. I ached, I burned, I shivered, I coughed, I sneezed. And then, when the creature had finally exhausted its venom, my heart—which I'd begun to rely on again and not even think about—started being a nuisance, and the doctor sent me back to bed. Stephen has been such a *saint*, throughout all this. He must get dreadfully tired of his decrepit old wife, but he never shows it. His kindness and patience are past belief. I'm much better now. Only—"I have to be careful". Oh my God, how I've come to loathe that phrase! I want to scream, sometimes, with impotent rage, like the poor father in Turgenev: "I said I should rebel, and I rebel, I rebel!"

Forgive this self-pity. One's private aches and woes are nothing—less than nothing—nowadays. Oh, the ghastliness of these times! Mary, don't you smell *pest* in the air? It's spreading out of Germany all over Europe. It's carried from eye to eye, from voice to ear. The newspapers are rank with it. And the wireless, too. Merely to hear that hideous screaming voice of Hitler's is to be infected; you don't even have to understand a word of German. Everything is being tainted.

Some mornings, the vividness of the green leaves along the river-bank makes me absolutely sick with dread, as if I saw them against the black of an oncoming storm. How *can* people walk under them and say "il fait beau, ce matin"? But that's a stupid question, I know. Everyday life only goes on *because* of our utter insensitivity. Otherwise, we'd all fall down on our knees or into each other's arms on the spot, and the world would dissolve or turn into heaven, and the Nazis would be nowhere. And if I mind this more acutely than, say, our concierge—to whom the whole affair is perfectly normal; those pigs of Boches misbehaving themselves once again, according to their nature—it's not due to any spiritual superiority of mine, but simply because I've been so weak and ill and morbid.

At a period like this, it's hard to believe that art has any value, at all. My pen wavers in the middle of a sentence and I think: Oh, what's the *use*? What's the use of this game with words and shades of meaning and feeling? Oughtn't I to be *doing* something to try to stop the spread of this hate-disease? Oughtn't I to be attacking it directly? But, of course, this very feeling of guilt and inadequacy is really a symptom of the disease itself. The disease is trying to paralyse you into complete inaction, so it makes you drop your own work, and attempt to fight it in some apparently practical way, which is unpractical for you because you aren't equipped for it—and so you end frustrated and doing nothing. The only way I can fight the disease effectively is to go on with the work I understand. I know that's true, in my bones. Then at least I shan't be paralysed.

But, even as I tell myself this, I feel the constant wretched gnawing of fear. Suppose there's a war—and they take Stephen away, and your Maurice? No. We mustn't give way to such thoughts, even for an instant. Let's live from day to day, and meet things as they happen. Mary darling, we must keep in touch now, more than ever. We must help each other. Don't let go of my hand.

I believe Stephen and I will make a move soon. This flat will be too stuffy in the hot weather. So we're thinking of the mountains. I need a new air to give me strength.'

A month later, she wrote to Mary again:

'You see, we've returned to the Schwarzsee. You probably guessed that we would. The weather is glorious, and I feel my energy renewed. Another two months, and the rough draft will be finished. Very messy and tangled still—but finished!

This place has changed, though. The air is tainted here, too. How could I have imagined that it wouldn't be, since we've moved so much nearer to the source of the disease? The Third Reich is almost on our doorstep. And the villagers here are intensely aware of it. Stephen, who gets more opportunity of talking to them than I do, says there's a lot of covert sympathy for the Nazis. They think Hitler will take over Austria soon, and they're glad. It'll be a change. Something exciting. They see no further than that.

You know they've always had that charming custom of lighting bonfires on the hillside for Midsummer Eve? Well, the other night, Stephen saw the glow of a big one in the distance, so he walked up to get a closer view. And it was a huge swastika built of brushwood, blazing away all by itself with not a soul to be seen. By next morning, it had burned down to the embers and left an evil black scar on the grass. The local authorities condemn these demonstrations officially, of course, but they're careful not to make too many enquiries. No one in the village will admit to having the faintest idea who set the fire. They shake their heads vigorously—and then they smile.

You remember that family from Bavaria, the ones who rented the Schloss in 1927, and gave that wonderful party on the lake I told you about? They were Jews—and now we hear that the Nazis arrested the daughter at their home in Munich, and that she died "of pneumonia" in a concentration-camp. They've got the father too, somewhere, if he's still alive. The rest of the family is scattered in exile; with many of their guests, I imagine. And the villagers, who really enjoyed their being here and probably charged them triple for everything they bought, now talk about their tragedy with a loathsome, sly pleasure. "Ah, those Jews! Their money's no help to them now!" Oh, the envy, the terrible patient vindictiveness of under-dogs! My Goodness, how they can hate!'

When Elizabeth finally finished her rough draft, I felt enormously relieved. I knew she'd been overworking, in spite of all my warnings, and I kept fearing she would have another breakdown. I dreaded a winter like the last. We agreed to spend the next one further south, and in the autumn we moved to Spain. We were in Granada and Malaga, and then we went over to Tangier. It was there that *The World in the Evening* was revised. I hummed tunes to myself with joy as I typed up the last pages, made the typescript into a parcel and took it down to the post-office to be sent off to the publishers. That night, Elizabeth and I had a bottle of champagne with our supper.

In the spring of 1934, she wrote to Mary from Las Palmas in the Canary Islands:

'We're at a hotel on the beach. From our windows, we can see the fort—a white cube with one black window in the middle of it, like a dot on a die—and the rocks spread with drying laundry, and the funnels of steamers in the harbour behind the roof-tops on which people grow flowers and keep chickens and goats. A reef makes the bathing safe from our beach; but the sharks come in close to shore by the slaughter-house when offal is thrown into the sea, and there are said to be manta rays, too—great horrible creatures that wrap themselves round you like an overcoat and then vanish with you into the depths. (You know, I've just realized that I mentioned them for the same reason that one used, as a child, to wish wolves would howl around the house at Christmas-time—to add to the snugness of being indoors!) Away to the south, there's a huddle of brown hills around the extinct crater which forms the centre of this island. Today they're piled high with rain-clouds—such a towering topheavy stack of them—it looks ready to topple over and drench us. But, down here, the Playa is still basking in hot sunshine.

Since our arrival, I've felt happy, serene, almost secure. Not for any good reason. The news certainly isn't any less depressing, or Hitler any less frightening. Are you getting used to the Nazis; fatalistically indifferent to them? I'm afraid I'm beginning to feel like that, a little. And then, out here in the midst of the ocean, there's this vastness of water and sky all around: it seems to swallow your anxieties and fears. Fear flourishes in dark corners, gloomy hotel bedrooms, narrow streets; it simply cannot exist in this light.

We have our political excitements here, too; but they're strictly local. On May Day, the servants in this hotel were forbidden to work by their unions, which are very strong here. A couple of waiters did, nevertheless, but they were dreadfully frightened, and first drew every curtain in the lounge, lest some of their colleagues should see them from the street and throw stones. And, just a few days before we arrived here, one of the cooks, whom even the rest of the staff admitted to be quite incompetent, was dismissed. Encouraged by his union, he immediately sued the hotel for a thousand pesetas damages. The manager, in self-defence, had to collect the signatures of the guests to a written complaint about the food, so as to be able to prove in court that he'd been forced to get rid of the cook!

Did I ever mention a youth named Michael Drummond, whom Stephen and I rather adopted, that first summer at the Schwarzsee? He has unexpectedly reappeared after all these years, and is staying here. Talking about our labour problems reminds

me of him, because last night he infuriated a retired English
colonel by declaring that the servants had had a perfect right to
desert us on their holiday, and that we, the guests, should have
had the courtesy to cook for them and wait on them ourselves!
I secretly agreed with Michael but didn't have the courage to
say so. As for the colonel, who is rather a sweet old conservative
lobster, he became so indignant that he turned bright scarlet and
looked ready to be dished up and served with melted butter as
the entrée at a workers' banquet.'

The casual way in which Michael was introduced into this
letter didn't ring quite true. Elizabeth seemed to be trying to
suggest that his arrival was of no particular importance to either
of us, and that he was practically the same boy we had known
seven years earlier in Austria. And yet, when she wrote this to
Mary Scriven, Michael had been with us for more than a week
already; Elizabeth had remarked, several times, how much he
had altered, and she must have been quite well aware of the
new relationship which was developing between the three
of us.

I didn't even recognize him at once, that first evening. It
wasn't that he'd changed so much in appearance. It was his
manner that was altogether different. He walked into the hotel
with the air of a veteran traveller who is equally accustomed to
luxury and discomfort, and doesn't much care which he finds;
scarcely bothering to glance around him. On his back was a
bulky, heavy-looking rucksack; and a camera in a leather case
was slung around his shoulder. He appeared to have no other
luggage. As he crossed to the desk, his movements were so
purposeful and unself-conscious that he seemed, as it were, less
visible than the other arriving visitors, whose awkward newness,
loud foreign chatter and crude curiosity made them as obvious
as advertisements.

Just as I was going through the process of realizing who he

was—thinking No, it can't be but, yes, it is—he turned and saw me. He didn't seem at all surprised.

'Hello, Stephen,' he said, holding out his hand. 'You probably don't remember me, do you? I'm Michael Drummond.'

'My God,' I said, 'Michael! What are you doing here?'

'You haven't changed, you know.' Michael regarded me with a slightly amused curiosity. 'Or not nearly as much as I'd expected.'

'Well!' I grinned at him stupidly. 'This is amazing! Are you going to stay here long?'

'I don't know. That depends.' Again, I was aware of his amusement; and it puzzled me.

'I must run up and tell Elizabeth,' I said. I didn't know why, but I felt embarrassed. 'She'll be awfully pleased. We've talked about you so often and wondered what you were doing.'

'Have you?' I think he knew this was a lie, but he didn't seem to mind. His eyes were still on my face, but I got the impression that he hardly attended to what I was saying.

'No. It's really extraordinary,' he said, as if talking to himself. 'You've scarcely changed at all.'

When Elizabeth and Michael met, she threw her arms impulsively around his neck and kissed him. I saw Michael stiffen slightly as she did this. Then he smiled politely. But he didn't return her kiss.

At supper that night, we questioned him about his doings since our last meeting. The conversation went easily enough, but it wasn't intimate. Michael's tone was impersonal and extremely polite. He would tell us whatever we wanted to know, nothing more. Each piece of information had to be extracted from him separately, and it would be followed by a short silence, until our next question. He didn't ask us anything about ourselves.

Since leaving Oxford, we learnt, he had become a freelance

news-photographer, wandering around the world in search of
material. In 1932, he had taken pictures of the riots following
one of Gandhi's arrests, he had been in Manchukuo, and he had
covered the election of President Roosevelt. He had left the
States and arrived in Berlin in time for the Reichstag fire. Later,
he had been expelled from Germany by the Nazis for snooping
around their concentration-camps, imprisoned by the Czechs
while investigating the Nazi party in the Sudetenland, and had
his camera broken by a stray bullet during the bombardment of
the Karl Marx Hof in Vienna, that last February.

'My Goodness,' Elizabeth exclaimed, 'you were lucky!'

'As a matter of fact, I was. The film wasn't damaged, and I
had some quite good shots.'

'No, I meant you might have been killed.'

'Oh,' Michael looked vague. 'Yes. I suppose so.'

'And now you're working in Spain?' I asked.

Michael nodded.

'Do you expect trouble here, too?'

'There's sure to be, before long. Either Catalonia will break
away from the Republic or the anarchists and syndicalists will
start something, with or without the communists——'

'I'm dreadfully ignorant,' said Elizabeth. 'What, exactly, is the
difference?'

'To explain that,' Michael told her, smiling slightly, 'I'm
afraid I'd have to deliver a long political lecture.' He said this
pleasantly, without the least air of superiority; and then added,
as if to close the subject, 'Of course, there might also be a fascist
putsch.'

'But whatever happens,' I said, 'you'll be on the spot.'

'I hope so,' Michael agreed, impersonally; rather as if I'd
remarked that tomorrow would probably be fine.

Elizabeth asked if we couldn't see some of his pictures.

'I haven't got any with me that are worth showing. Actually,
you know, I'm a rotten photographer. I've never really learnt

how to use a camera properly.' Michael grinned, and suddenly, just for a moment, he was like the boy we'd known at the Schwarzsee. 'The magazines I sell my stuff to don't seem to mind that, as long as there's plenty of action. So all I do is to get right into the middle of things and blaze away. If it's out of focus, that only makes it look more dramatic.'

We both laughed at this, and the atmosphere seemed to have grown warmer. I suppose Elizabeth thought so too, for she tried a more personal line of approach.

'But, Michael,' she said, 'you haven't told us much about yourself, you know. You can't spend *all* your time, surely, amidst these scenes of violence and carnage? What do you do for relaxation?'

'Well, I'm kept pretty busy, of course.' Michael's face had instantly assumed its mask of well-bred politeness. He was on his guard, again. 'I play quite a lot of tennis.'

'And I suppose you have plenty of friends?'

'Naturally one meets a great many people,' he agreed, 'in this job.'

'That must be fascinating.'

'Some of them are quite interesting. Yes.'

At this, Elizabeth gave up. During the rest of supper she asked Michael no more questions; instead, she talked about our own travels, trying hard to put him at his ease. He appeared to listen carefully, and he smiled at the right places in her stories; but, after we had drunk four or five glasses of wine, I realized that he wasn't completely attending. In spite of themselves, as it seemed, his eyes kept leaving Elizabeth's face and turning to mine. And there was an expression in them which I couldn't interpret: it was some kind of a challenge or question, I thought. As though he were claiming a private understanding between the two of us, from which Elizabeth was excluded. His eyes made me feel vaguely uneasy, and I kept avoiding them; but I was also rather intrigued.

Elizabeth was watching Michael as she talked to him. I'd come to know that gravely thoughtful look of hers so well; it meant that she was deeply and sympathetically concerned about the person she was looking at. When she watched someone like that, she reminded one of a doctor making a diagnosis. Later, when we'd told Michael Goodnight and were upstairs in our room, she said: 'He's lonelier than ever, isn't he?'

'Yes. I suppose he is.'

'I'm worried about him, Stephen. He's under some terrible strain.'

'What kind of a strain?'

'I don't know. But he's been hurt, somehow—I'm sure of that. And he's gone deep inside himself. That handsome face and those nice manners—they're not him, at all.'

'He was always shy, you remember?'

'That's the whole point. He used to be. He isn't now. The shyness was only a thin crust, and he kept breaking through it. He was up near the surface, all the time. Now there's no crust on the surface. But somewhere, deep, deep down, there's a dark little cave of solid rock, and he's hidden inside it.'

'You make him sound like a mental case,' I said.

'Darling, you think I'm exaggerating, don't you?'

'Well—let's say, dramatizing.'

'Perhaps I am. I hope I am. It isn't that I expect him to have a nervous breakdown or anything. At least, not yet. But—did you notice his eyes?'

'What about his eyes?' For some reason which I didn't care to analyse, I was unwilling to tell Elizabeth how I'd felt at supper, when Michael had kept looking at me.

'That's where it shows—the strain he's under. Even though he tries so hard to hide it. . . . Promise me something, Stephen.'

'What's that?'

'If he should ever venture out of that cave of his, and try to

tell you what all this is about—promise you'll be very gentle
with him. He mustn't be hurt any more.'

'Why should I want to hurt him?'

'You wouldn't. Of course you wouldn't. But it'd be so easy,
without meaning to. He'd be bound to express himself awkwardly, because it would be so difficult for him to speak at all.
What he said might strike you as funny, or even shocking. And
you might show it——'

'Since when have I been so tactless?'

'Oh, darling, please don't misunderstand me! I only mean
that Michael has two or three skins less than the rest of us. You
see, he's still completely innocent.'

'What makes you so sure of that? He's certainly knocked
around as much as most people of his age. Or a good deal
more.'

'Oh, I don't mean innocent in a conventional sense. Yes,
he's had what's called experience, I'm sure; and it's hurt him.
But it hasn't made him cautious and calculating. Not yet.
He's still learning about life in the most painful way—like
a baby who thinks the fire in the grate is a beautiful new
kind of flower, and tries to pluck it. He's still pathetically
defenceless.'

'But, Elizabeth, how can you possibly know all this? We've
only been with him for a couple of hours, so far.'

'I don't know it. I feel it. And I do so hope I'm wrong.'

'But you're certain you're not.'

'Oh, darling,' said Elizabeth laughing, 'you always make such
fun of my intuitions. But they *have* been right quite often,
haven't they?'

'They have, indeed. . . . Well, then, assuming you're right
about Michael, I still don't see why he should come to *me* with
his troubles. I'd have thought he'd be much more likely to
confide in you.'

'He won't, Stephen. I know he won't.'

I grinned: 'You mean, you *feel* he won't? In that case, there's nothing more to discuss. We'll just have to wait and see.'

Michael was with us throughout the next day, and all day long I felt ill at ease with him. Elizabeth had certainly been right about one thing, I thought: he wasn't entirely present. The real Michael—whatever kind of a creature that was—stayed hidden in its deep cave. And the handsome body of the young man with whom we lay on the beach and splashed about in the water and ate lunch gave an air of unreality to everything we did. By not being a complete person himself, he made me feel as if Elizabeth and I were also puppets, going through an imitation of real human beings enjoying a seaside holiday. Even his eyes didn't betray him, now. They carefully avoided mine.

I knew, of course, that I would have to talk to him alone. I didn't particularly want to do this. I was mildly curious about his problem—if he really had one, as Elizabeth believed, and wasn't simply a thick-skinned bore—but I certainly didn't want to have to try to solve it for him. I didn't fancy myself as a father-confessor. These years of living with Elizabeth had made me ruthless in one respect. Much as I welcomed amusing visitors and casual acquaintances, I was always on guard to protect her and myself against the demands of the sick, the dependent and the sad. Michael's innocence had been charming at eighteen, but, if he hadn't gotten rid of it by now, that was just too bad. I refused to re-adopt him at twenty-five, especially as a problem-child.

The moment for being alone with him came after supper. I don't know if Elizabeth really wanted to correct the proofs of a short story, as she told us, or if she simply meant to leave us together. Anyhow, she went upstairs, and I suggested to Michael that we should take a walk on the beach.

It was quite dark by that time, and the sky was crowded with stars. Michael obviously wasn't going to start the conversation, and his silence quickly began to get on my nerves.

'Isn't it a wonderful night?' I said, for the sake of saying something.

'Yes. It is.'

'Have you ever seen the Southern Cross? The first time I did, I was terribly disappointed. It was so much smaller than I expected.'

'Actually, I've never been south of the Equator.'

There was a long pause. Well, that certainly hadn't been a brilliant opening, I thought. But he might have helped me out. He really is a bore.

I tried again: 'Do you expect to do any work, while you're here?'

'I don't imagine so. No.'

By this time I was getting rattled. 'It certainly was amazing,' I said, 'running into you again like this.'

Michael turned his head toward me. I couldn't be sure of his expression in the darkness, but he sounded angry and tense: 'Why do you keep on saying that?'

'Do I?' I was so taken aback that my tone was quite foolish. 'Well—it's true, isn't it?'

'I suppose,' said Michael, with a kind of angry sarcasm, 'that you won't be happy till you've made me admit it?'

'Admit what? Michael, what on earth do you mean?'

'You know exactly what I mean.' The way he was talking now made him seem like an altogether different person. 'You must know why I came here. You couldn't possibly not have guessed.'

'I thought you simply decided to take a holiday.'

'Why do you think I chose Las Palmas, of all places, and came straight to your hotel?'

'You mean, you came here specially to see us?'

'To see you.' Michael put a slight emphasis on the pronoun.

'But—but that's wonderful!' I said, in a false, hearty voice.

'Is it?' Again, Michael turned to look at me, and I was embarrassed.

'I still don't understand,' I said, to cover this up, 'how you knew we were here.'

'That was the only accidental part of it. Remember those friends of yours in Malaga, Dr. Vallejo and his wife? I went to see him two weeks ago, to get some facts for a story I was doing on Luis Companys. He happened to mention that he knew you. They showed me a postcard you'd just sent them, with this address.'

'And so you decided to come on over?'

'I suppose you think I was a bloody fool? Barging in, after all these years, and taking it for granted you'd be pleased to see me.'

'No, Michael. No—of course I don't. We *are* pleased. And I think that's the best way to do things: on the spur of the moment.'

'When they showed me that postcard, it seemed like a sign. . . . I've been wanting to come and see you for a long time. I kept finding out, in different ways, where you were. I hoped we'd meet in India, but I just missed you. And, last summer, I knew you were back at the Schwarzsee, but I was so busy, and then I got myself into that trouble in the Sudetenland, and it was too late.'

'Why didn't you ever write?'

'I did. I wrote several letters.'

'We never got them.'

'I always tore them up.'

'You should have let us know you were coming here,' I said —to avoid the question he probably wanted me to ask.

'So that you'd have had time to clear out?'

'Don't be an idiot. I only mean we might have missed you again.'

'Wouldn't that have been a disaster!'

'What's the matter with you, Michael? Why do you talk like that? You know how fond we both are of you.'

'Oh, for Christ's sake,' Michael exclaimed with abrupt violence, 'can't you at least be sincere? Stop pretending you don't understand.'

'What is there to understand?' I asked, and again I heard my voice ring false. I felt excited and just a little scared of what was coming next.

But Michael seemed suddenly to have lost his aggressiveness. 'Nothing,' he said wearily. 'I'm sorry. I was a fool to have come here. I'll leave tomorrow. Or as soon as I can get a boat.'

'Nonsense! We won't let you.' I put my hand on his shoulder for a moment, with a sickening, big-brotherly familiarity that was worthy of a professional scoutmaster. '*I* want you to stay,' I added.

'Do you mean that?'

'Of course I mean it.'

For the third time. Michael looked at me; trying vainly to search my face, as it seemed. But the darkness protected me, I knew. He wouldn't find anything there.

'I don't believe you do mean it,' he said, at length; and now he sounded beaten and rather pathetic. 'But it doesn't matter. I'll stay as long as I can, because I want to. I'm sorry I was such an idiot, just now. Let's talk about something else.'

'All right,' I said.

But, of course, there was nothing else to talk about. We walked most of the way back to the hotel in silence. Just as we reached it, Michael said: 'You won't tell Elizabeth anything about this, will you, Stephen?'

'You know I won't,' I said; and then added, rather too innocently: 'Anyway, what is there to tell?'

Michael didn't answer.

Three or four evenings later, Michael and I were sitting on

the hotel terrace after supper. Elizabeth had left us for a few minutes, to get a book from the bedroom. We were smoking in silence and watching the ghostly glowing line of phosphorus which the waves made, breaking out of the night along the shore.

After a little while, two of the other guests came out on to the terrace, a man and a woman. I had a glimpse of their faces in the light from the window of the dining-room: they were an American couple who had arrived the day before. They couldn't possibly have recognized us, sitting back in the darkness against the wall. They walked over to the corner of the terrace and stood looking at the sea, with their backs to us.

'Sure,' the man was saying, 'that's the one I mean. She's a writer, the manager told me. She's here with her husband.'

'Her husband?' The woman laughed incredulously. 'Not either one of those boys she runs around with, surely? They must be her sons.'

'The older one's her husband.'

'He couldn't be!'

'Want to bet?'

'Well, if he is, I think it's disgusting. He must be all of twenty-five years younger than she is.'

'I guess she has the money,' the man said.

Michael grabbed my arm and stood up, pulling me to my feet. 'Let's get out of here,' he muttered, in a hoarse angry voice. I followed him down the steps from the terrace on to the beach.

'The swine!' Michael exclaimed. 'If we'd stayed another second, I think I'd have knocked their heads together.'

'They didn't mean any harm,' I said. 'They were just talking.'

'You don't mind?' Michael sounded quite shocked.

'No, not really.'

'But you must mind.'

'I did at first, a little. You see, this has happened before—several times. I'd mind if Elizabeth had overheard it.'

'But she knows, surely?'

'Knows what?'

'Well'—Michael was embarrassed—'that people might think such things——'

'Listen,' I said; 'this isn't as tragic as you make it sound. Elizabeth's fortytwo. I'm nearly thirty. I dare say I do look younger than that. And perhaps she looks a bit older. She was terribly sick, you know, the winter before last. . . . But all that's pretty unimportant when two people have been together as long as we have. I'm sure it doesn't worry her.'

'I'm not thinking of Elizabeth,' said Michael, almost impatiently.

'Then I don't see—why all this fuss?'

'It's just that—no, you'll be angry if I say it——'

'Say what?'

'I'd better not.'

'Don't be stupid. Go on, tell me.'

'Stephen, I can't stand seeing you unhappy like this.'

'I don't know what on earth you're talking about,' I said sharply. 'Me unhappy? However did you get that idea?'

'I told you you'd be angry.'

'But, Michael, I'm not. It's too ridiculous.'

'I'm sorry I said it.'

'That doesn't matter. But it just isn't true at all. . . . Don't you believe me?'

'If it isn't true, I'm glad,' Michael said, in his formal everyday voice.

We had turned toward the hotel. And now I saw Elizabeth come out on to the terrace, and stand there, with the light behind her. Obviously, she couldn't see us. The two Americans were still there, watching.

'We're down here,' I shouted. 'We'll come up.'

As the three of us passed the Americans on our way into the house, Michael turned a scowl on them which made them lower their furtively inquisitive eyes. I wonder what you'd do, I thought, if I were to tell you *all* there is to know about us? And, thinking this, I gave them a broad grin.

SIX

ONE day at lunch, about a week after this, Elizabeth told us that she had been having a long talk with the Swiss woman who kept a small bookshop in the town. 'I went in there because she had some volumes of Tauchnitz in the window; and she was so interesting, I stayed nearly an hour. She was telling me about the middle of the island, down in the old crater. Very few tourists go there, it seems. And there are villages where they still practise witchcraft. They put spells on their enemies, and brew poisons for them—in case the spells don't work. . . . Oh, and there's an enormous rock called El Nublo—that means The Cloudy One, doesn't it?—which nobody had ever been able to climb, until last autumn, when a party of young Germans did it —they were Nazis, I'm sorry to say—and they planted a flag on the top. . . . Doesn't it all sound like a fairy-story?'

'The flag ought to have been a beautiful maiden,' I said. 'Then a prince could climb up and rescue her.'

Elizabeth laughed: 'Poor thing, she'd be rather weatherbeaten by this time, wouldn't she? But that's where the symbolism breaks down, I'm afraid—because, of course, this is an ugly wicked flag: a swastika.'

'You mean,' Michael asked, 'that it's still there?' He was obviously very much interested.

'It was, a fortnight ago. Frl. Etter saw it herself. She makes trips over there from time to time, to look for rare wildflowers.'

'I suppose the Nazis have left the island, by now?'

'Oh yes. They were only here on a holiday. Frl. Etter says they refused to tell anyone how they climbed El Nublo. They even claimed they'd been drunk when they did it, and didn't remember. . . . Why, Michael, of course—*you* ought to go there, and take pictures and write the story! Oh, why don't you?'

'I'm afraid it wouldn't be much of a story, if I can't talk to the climbers themselves, and photograph them.'

'Then why not go just for fun? I'd so love hearing all about it. And I know Stephen would enjoy going with you. He hasn't done anything like that for ages.'

'Stephen may not want to go,' Michael said, giving me one of his questioning looks. They didn't puzzle me now.

I grinned at him teasingly: 'Elizabeth's whim is my pleasure.'

Michael frowned slightly. 'Do you honestly want to go, Stephen?'

'Yes. Don't you?' We were talking to each other in the voices we used when Elizabeth wasn't present.

'You know I do. Only——'

'Only what?' I looked straight at him. Michael dropped his eyes.

'It might be quite a rough trip,' he said, lamely, after a moment.

'I'll survive it. If my corns hurt, you can carry me.'

'And you needn't hurry, you know,' Elizabeth put in, smiling. 'Stay away as long as you like. Frl. Etter says Maspalomas is beautiful. You ought to see that, too. I won't expect you back for three days at least.'

Michael looked at her uncertainly. 'Will you really be all right,' he asked, 'here by yourself?' It was as if he half hoped she'd say No.

'Of course I shall be all right,' Elizabeth told him gaily. 'And I shan't be by myself. There are lots of people in this hotel I want to get to know more about. I can smell at least two short stories.'

Michael still didn't seem quite satisfied, but 'All right,' he said, 'in that case, we may as well start tomorrow.'

Next afternoon, we took the post-bus to Tejeda. The village

lay at the bottom of the extinct volcano-crater; a deep thickly-wooded bowl, into which the bus descended by violent zigzags from the top of the pass. Michael and I were the only tourists on board, and we would have seemed absurdly typical to anyone who could have understood what we were talking about; for we stuck to the guarded British-intellectual 'Have you read——?', 'Did you ever see——?' kind of conversation which goes with pipes, heavy boots, rucksacks and hikes.

At the fonda, we were given a big dusty room which looked out on the back of the church. There was nothing in it but two ramshackle beds, one chair, and three ornamental wall-brackets. The toilet was overrun with chickens, and the food was luke-warm. We went to bed early. At intervals, the church bells would ring furiously for a few minutes and then stop abruptly. The bell-ringers must have gotten drunk and decided to practise.

In the silence after one of the bursts of bell-ringing, Michael said: 'Isn't this hell?'

'Utter and complete hell,' I laughed. Actually, for the first time since we had left Las Palmas, I was starting to enjoy myself. Throughout the bus-drive and supper I had felt bored, and vaguely apprehensive about what I had let myself in for: stodgy dullness or emotional tension. But now it seemed that perhaps, after all, we were going to have fun.

'You aren't sorry you came?' Michael asked, after a pause. In the darkness, he was nothing but a voice from the other bed, and I instantly noticed his change of tone. It was timid, hesitant, and yet, somehow, teasing. Here it comes, I thought. Oh, damn him. He's going to start something.

'Of course I'm not sorry,' I said firmly. 'I wasn't expecting the Ritz.'

'I didn't mean that. I just wondered how you were feeling— about Elizabeth not being here.'

'But, Michael, she couldn't possibly have come. You know how careful she has to be.'

There was a short silence. Then Michael said: 'I wonder what she's thinking about, at this moment.'

'She's sound asleep, probably.'

'I bet she isn't. She's lying awake and thinking about us.'

All right then, I said to myself: let's have it out now. Why not? It's got to come out, sooner or later.

'Michael,' I said into the darkness, 'why do you keep harping on what Elizabeth's feeling? What are you trying to make me say? This just doesn't ring true, somehow. Do you really care what she's feeling? I don't believe you do, one bit.'

There was a long pause. 'Of course I don't,' Michael said, at last: 'I don't care a damn about Elizabeth.'

'Well,' I said, 'at least that's honest.'

Michael didn't answer. But, just when I'd started to wonder what would come next, he got out of his bed, crossed over to mine, and sat down on the end of it. He felt for my hand, and gripped it hard.

'You hate me now, don't you, Stephen?'

'Don't be an idiot.' I pulled my hand away.

'It isn't that I've got anything against Elizabeth. And I didn't mean what I said just now. You know that. I'd be awfully fond of her—if it wasn't for you. That's how I really felt, even, at the Schwarzsee. Only I wouldn't admit it to myself then. I ran away from it. . . . Do you understand what I'm talking about?'

'Of course I do. I wish you'd stop it, though.'

'I was always jealous of her, underneath,' Michael continued, as though I hadn't spoken. 'I couldn't help thinking that perhaps, if you'd been there alone, you might have felt—differently, about me. It was because of her that you treated me as a kid. She wanted you to see me like that. So bloody pure and innocent. I'll bet she knew, all the time, what I really wanted. And she was afraid you'd start to want it, too.'

'Shut up, Michael,' I said. 'I've let you say all this, to get it off your chest. But that's enough about Elizabeth. I'm not going to listen to any more——'

'You're not going to listen?' His voice trembled with rage. 'You won't be able to help yourself. Because I'm going to tell you a lot of things—things you'd rather pretend you don't know——'

As he spoke, he made a violent forward movement and grasped my arm, as though he actually thought I might try to stop my ears with my fingers. But this was too much for the crazy old bedstead. Its back legs collapsed. In fact, the whole back part of the bed fell right off and hit the floor. And, exactly at that moment, deadening what would otherwise have been a crash sufficient to rouse the whole household, there was a tremendous clash of bells from the church tower.

Michael lay against me for a moment, where we had fallen. Then he began to laugh, explosively and rather hysterically. Still laughing, he picked himself up. 'Oh, Christ!' he exclaimed. I laughed too, partly to cover the situation.

'You'd better sleep in my bed,' he said, after the bells had stopped as abruptly as they'd started.

'No, thanks. I'll be all right on the floor.'

'Look here,' Michael's voice was getting tense again. 'It was my fault that it happened, and I'm damn' well going to be the one who'll sleep on the floor—if anybody does.' There was just a hint of a question in the last part of the sentence.

But I felt I was master of the situation, now. 'You can sleep on the floor if you want to,' I said. 'But I shall, too. I don't trust that other bed any more than this one.' Michael didn't move at once, so I added, in my scoutmaster voice: 'Now let's get some sleep.'

Later that night, I woke and heard Michael sobbing quietly to himself. I felt sorry, but I didn't say anything to him. I didn't want to start a new scene. Besides, the mattress was warm. I turned over and went to sleep again.

When I woke next morning, Michael wasn't in the room. I found him downstairs, morosely drinking a cup of coffee. The gloom was thick around him, and he barely reacted to my greeting. After we'd sat together in silence for some minutes, he said abruptly: 'I suppose you want to go back to Las Palmas?'

Just for an instant, I felt so irritated with him that I could have slapped his goodlooking, tiresomely tragic face. But I controlled myself, knowing that a quarrel was exactly what he wanted. 'Of course not,' I said. 'In fact, if you won't come, I'll go on alone.' Then, with a change of tone which I felt was even more revolting than my scoutmaster act, I added: 'Michael, we're supposed to be here to enjoy ourselves. Let's try to, shall we?'

It worked; I was a little ashamed to see how well. Michael flushed; and then, after a quick nervous scowl, his face brightened into the charming smile that was his best feature. It had always reminded me of a child being tickled under the chin. 'All right,' he said. Then, after a pause: 'Sorry. Vamos.'

The valley was still full of cool shadow. But high above us, on the edge of the crater-bowl, the great pillar of El Nublo stood in full sunlight, with the red speck of a flag, too small for the swastika to be visible, flapping from its summit against the blue sky. We made our way slowly uphill, through woods of laurel, full of waterfalls and streams that had roses growing wild along their banks. Men and women waved and shouted to us encouragingly from the doors of their farms. It was as if they all knew where we were going and wanted us to get there.

By midday, we had climbed out of the woods on to a naked slope of glaring, colourless rocks. Nublo was directly above us, towering several hundred feet into the air, as sheer as a slice of cheese. Its enormous mass gave me a kind of upward vertigo. I caught my breath when I looked up at it. As for Michael, he had become almost hysterically excited. He kept bounding on ahead and shouting back to me to hurry. Now and then, he yodelled. Everything was deathly still in the noon heat, and his voice, echoing around the crater, must have been audible for miles.

Presently, we scrambled up on to a huge platform of rock which was Nublo's base, and began to work our way around the pillar. This was awkward in places, and I began to feel really giddy. As we moved westward, the platform narrowed to a ledge, and then turned a corner where there was little more than a toe-hold. I hesitated. Michael edged himself round it and out of sight.

A moment later, I heard him shout: 'I've found it!'

'Found what?'

'The way the Germans started up. It must be. There's quite a promising crack.'

There was a long silence. 'Where are you?' I shouted. No answer. 'Michael!' I shouted.

For what was probably no more than a minute, I stood waiting. I was badly worried. I knew I'd have to make myself climb around that corner.

But, as I moved unwillingly towards it, I was startled by a laugh, coming out of the air, right above my head. I looked up. There was Michael—spread-eagled on the rock, about forty feet up the face of the precipice.

Even to look at him made me break out in a sweat of fear. 'Come down, you idiot!' I told him.

But he only grinned at me mischievously. 'I'm going up, first. I know I can do it. I'm going to show those damned Nazis. They probably used hook-ladders.'

'Michael, don't be such a bloody little idiot! You'll kill yourself.'

'What do you care?'

He looked really crazy and at the same time beautiful, laughing

so wildly, with his blond hair ruffled by the breeze and his lithe
body curved out over the awful sick drop below.

'Oh, for God's sake, come down!'

'What'll you give me if I do?'

'What do you want?' I asked, humouring him as if he were a
madman.

'Will you give me anything I want?'

'Anything I can—within reason.'

'Do you swear that?'

'All right. If you'll come down at once.'

'You've promised, remember!' Michael was gleeful with
triumph. He began the downward climb. The rock had an
overhang at that point, and he would certainly have missed my
ledge and killed himself, if he had fallen. Twice, he nearly did,
but this didn't seem to shake his nerve. He was completely
relaxed and fearless. Soon, he disappeared around the shoulder
of the cliff; and, a few moments later, he was standing beside
me.

'Why, Stephen,' he said, looking curiously into my face,
'you really got the wind up, didn't you? Were you so worried
about me?'

'Not a bit,' I grinned. 'That was just empathy. I was putting
myself in your place, like the audience does in the movies. It
was *my* neck I was worried about. Thanks for saving it.'

'All the same, I wish you had let me get to the top. I know
I could have. I've done quite a bit of rock-climbing since I saw
you last.'

We had planned to spend that night at a village called San
Bartolomé, which was down in one of the seaward valleys to
the south. This was quite a long hike. We had to cross a plateau
of tiny jagged stones which showed no trace of a path, and at
first it seemed that we would never find the way. But then
Michael had the bright idea of following the trail of droppings

left by the peasants' donkeys as they travelled between San Bartolomé and Tejeda. We laughed a lot over our detective-work, and this made the going easier. We got to San Bartolomé at dusk.

This fonda was no cleaner, but more cheerful; and the food was definitely better. We drank a lot of beer with it. An hour later, more than half drunk, I followed Michael upstairs and into a room. It had only one bed.

'Where's my room?' I asked.

'This is for both of us.'

'Why didn't you get two?'

'There aren't any more.'

'I don't believe it. I'll ask the landlord.'

Michael grinned. I knew he'd been lying. 'Is it so important?' he asked.

'No,' I said.

'I suppose you've forgotten what you promised?'

We stood smiling at each other across the bed, foxy-stupid with drink.

'Aha!' I said. 'The promise! I was waiting for that.'

'You said you'd give me anything—anything within reason.'

'You call that within reason?'

'I call it a very good reason.'

Suddenly, I didn't care any more. The problem had dissolved itself in the beer; and now there wasn't any problem at all, no drama, no tenseness. This was all clean fun, I told myself; and it didn't have to be anything more than that.

In the darkness I remembered the adolescent, half-angry pleasure of wrestling with boys at school. And then, later, there was a going even further back, into the nursery sleep of child-hood with its teddybear, or of puppies or kittens in a basket, wanting only the warmness of anybody.

There seemed nothing to be said about this, next morning,

and we said nothing. I felt animally cheerful and relaxed; and I thought Michael did, too. We walked downhill all morning, threading our way among the red rocks of the dry river-bed and pushing through rustling thickets of cane. Then, early in the afternoon, we came out into a region of sand-dunes which looked like African desert, with clumped oases of palm-trees, and the lighthouse of Maspalomas in the far distance, a slender white column against the dusky blue of the sea.

There was no fonda, but we got a room in a farmer's house. The room had a hole in the wall instead of a window; and its only furniture consisted of a double bed and a brand new sewing-machine.

'Well, you can't say I planned it this time,' Michael grinned, looking first at the bed and then at me.

We rode back to Las Palmas next day, on the bus. It wasn't until we were on the outskirts of town that Michael asked: 'Are you going to tell her?'

'Why should I?'

'Don't you tell her everything?'

'Usually. But we don't have a rule about it, if that's what you mean.'

'I expect she'll guess. People generally can, when they know each other well.'

'I shouldn't imagine,' I said, as crushingly as I could, 'that she'd think it was worth discussing.'

'Because it's happened so often?'

'No. Of course not.'

'Never?'

'Never.'

'You mean'—Michael giggled—'that I seduced you?'

I was too annoyed with him to answer. I looked out of the window, blushing in spite of myself, and feeling idiotic. Michael said: 'I suppose you're sorry it happened?'

'What is there to be sorry about?' I asked him coldly. 'It simply isn't important.'

Michael was silent for a while after this. Then he said sadly: 'I can't understand you at all, Stephen. First you made it seem important, and now you say it isn't. I feel as if I don't really know what's happened and what hasn't.'

'Did you have a nice time, darling?' Elizabeth asked me, when we were alone together.

'Oh, not bad.' I was very casual. 'We didn't see any witches, and no one tried to poison us. The scenery's rather like Hawaii. You didn't miss much.'

'I'm sorry. I hoped it was going to be really wonderful.'

'You wanted me to have a good time—away from you?'

Elizabeth smiled, but there was a look in her eyes which made me suddenly embarrassed. How often, I asked myself, had I said things to her like that? Was I developing a special tone when I spoke to her, a sort of bedside manner? If so, it was a shock to me to realize how completely she must be aware of it; she who so instantly detected the faintest note of falseness. She looked slightly disconcerted now, I thought, as though she had been addressed in a foreign language she didn't understand.

'Did Michael take many photographs?' she asked.

'No. No, he didn't,' I said; and this was the first time it occurred to me that he hadn't used his camera once, while we had been away.

At lunch, we related all the describable incidents of our trip in detail, making them sound so different from the reality that it was as if two other people had visited an altogether different country. Toward the end of the meal, I realized from Michael's face that he was getting into one of his difficult moods. And, as soon as Elizabeth had left us, he burst out: 'I can't stand any more of this! I've got to get out of here. You should have let me leave, last time I wanted to. Then none of this would have happened.'

'Oh, Michael, for Christ's sake, don't be so melodramatic! Nothing's happened—except in your imagination. How often do I have to tell you that?'

'Yes. I suppose it really *is* nothing—to you——'

'There's no earthly reason why you should go,' I went on, hurriedly. 'It'll look very odd if you do. As a matter of fact, just before lunch, Elizabeth suggested moving to Tenerife in a few days—the three of us. Wouldn't you like that?'

'Would you?'

'If you don't come,' I said cruelly, 'Elizabeth will be disappointed.'

Michael stood looking at me, and there were tears in his eyes. I knew he half hated me at that moment. I knew how he longed to be able to break away. But he couldn't, unless he could make me say the word that would release him. He simply didn't have the strength.

'All right,' he said, at length.

'You mean, you'll come?'

'You know I will,' he said, hopelessly, and turned to go out on to the beach alone.

At Orotava, on Tenerife, we stayed at a little hotel-café run by a German. 'Such an anxious creature,' wrote Elizabeth, describing him in one of her letters. 'He has a haunted, jumpy look, as if invisible alarm-clocks were going off throughout the day, to remind him of undone duties. His fat Spanish wife is just the opposite; as relaxed as a suet dumpling and such a marvellous cook. Although Herr Knauer has lived in the Islands for fifteen years and is a Spanish citizen, he has a large photograph of Hitler in his sitting-room. I noticed it the first time I went in there, on the day of our arrival. Then, a week later, we got the news of Roehm's arrest and the great purge. We could see that Herr Knauer was tremendously excited, though it was hard to tell

whether he was glad or unhappy about it. At any rate, the
Hitler photograph disappeared. And now that it's quite certain,
alas, that the Nazi Government isn't going to collapse, the
photograph is back again. Herr Knauer saw me glancing at it
this morning, shrugged his shoulders, and said apologetically:
"What am I to do? There are many Germans living on this
island. A man has to be careful. The Party has ways of keeping
discipline, even here." Hearing him say that, as we stood looking
out at this heavenly subtropical garden in the brilliant sunshine,
I got a feeling of sudden creepy horror. It was as if the flowers
of the trumpet vine might be microphones, listening.

Still, this place is perfect for work. I write out of doors,
mostly, under a big eucalyptus, with a wide view of the sea.
Stephen is very well. Michael Drummond is still with us.'

By this time, my relationship with Michael had become
acutely uneasy and guilty. Whenever we went out together—
to the beach to swim or down to the store for cigarettes—I was
careful, on our return, to account to Elizabeth for the time we
had spent. I found myself saying things like 'Señor Ortega
insisted on showing us his new boat—we simply couldn't get
away,' or 'It was so hot coming up the hill that we stopped for
a beer.' Elizabeth never commented on these unnecessary
apologies.

In the house, Michael and I were hardly ever alone together.
I only saw his bedroom once, for a moment, on the morning of
our arrival. That first evening, I had walked with him halfway
along the passage to it, and there we both stopped, with such a
sense of the taboo upon us that there was no need to say anything
except Goodnight.

I knew, of course, that this situation would come to a natural
end, sooner or later: Michael would have to go back to work.
If I hadn't known this, the situation would have become unbearable immediately after our return from the Tejeda trip. And

yet—such was the doubleness of my feelings toward him—I was sorry as well as relieved when he got a telegram one morning from an editor in Paris, asking him to go to the Asturias as quickly as possible. I think Michael felt the same way as I did: he hated to leave us and yet was thankful for an excuse to do so. And the prospect of this new assignment evidently excited him. 'I've been trying to get them to send me there for months,' he told us. 'It's the obvious place for the communists to start trouble; they're very strong among the miners. I ought to take off from here by the end of the week.' He hesitated, and then added: 'Stephen, there's something I'd like to do before I go, though. I'd been meaning to suggest it, anyway. Couldn't we go up the Pico? If we start tomorrow, we could be back again on Thursday afternoon.'

This time, it seemed to me, there were no hidden tensions or emotional overtones. Or, if there were, I chose to disregard them. Michael was certainly entitled to this trip, if he wanted it; and the least I could do was to go along with him. So I agreed at once—little as I relished the idea of hiking uphill for twelve thousand feet.

All next morning, Michael and I plodded up through steamy-hot banana-plantations, stripped to the waist and dripping with sweat. Above the bananas were open fields, and above the fields was the plateau called Las Cañadas which formed the roof of the island, a volcanically blasted region of grey lava-beds scattered with chunks of obsidian. The cone of the Pico stood in the middle of it.

The first part of the trip had been such hard work that we had made it mostly in silence; but, when we got on to the plateau, Michael began to talk. His talk was all about the future: how he planned to work for a while in a mine or a factory, learn Russian, and spend some time in the Soviet Union. He spoke excitedly, with an enthusiasm which seemed a bit forced.

He's trying to convince himself, I thought; and show me how dull and useless my life is, compared with his. Well, that was all right. I must just be careful not to lose my temper. I was afraid that I might, if I didn't watch out. The altitude was already beginning to make me feel nervous and tense, as well as short of breath. And I could see that it was having the same effect on him.

We had borrowed a key to the rest-hut which had been built about a third of the way up to the summit. It was made of piled rocks, and a cold wind whistled through the cracks between them: the temperature was dropping rapidly with nightfall. There was no chimney in the hut, but we started a fire in a brazier that stood in the corner, and let the place fill with smoke. By the time we had done this, it was quite dark. Our only light was from two bicycle-lamps which Herr Knauer had lent us. We ate some of our sandwiches and made a pot of coffee; drinking it tepid because, at that height, it would have taken so long to boil.

I was tired but not in the least sleepy. I hated to feel so wide awake. We were sitting together on one of the four bunks. Michael reached into his rucksack, produced a bottle of brandy, took a deep drink and handed it to me. I drank too, hoping it would relax me. It didn't seem to. I gave the bottle back to Michael. He took another drink immediately, as though he was in a desperate hurry to empty it, and held it out to me again.

'Come on,' he said impatiently. 'Drink up.'

'What's the rush?' I asked.

'Well, you needn't take all night about it.'

'I'm not ready for another one, yet.'

'Then give it here.' Michael almost grabbed the bottle from my hand, and took a third drink.

'You'd better be careful of that stuff,' I said. 'If you get drunk at this altitude, they say you have an awful hangover.'

Michael smiled at me nastily: 'Who says so? Elizabeth?'

'No.'

'Oh, Jesus Christ!' Michael exclaimed. He stood up off the bunk and began pacing the floor.

'What's the matter?'

'It's all wrong.'

'What's all wrong?'

'You are. My God, Stephen, I just wish you could hear your-self! Such an old auntie, fussing about the altitude and hangovers! What's been happening to you, all these years? I bet you don't even know how you've changed. It's pitiful. It makes me sick.'

'That's too bad,' I said, trying not to show how angry I was. Half of me was longing for the relief of a fight.

'At the Schwarzsee, you were quite different. Or I thought you were. If I hadn't been such an idiot, I'd have seen what you were going to turn into. It must have started, even then——'

'Michael, why don't you stop talking tripe?'

He gave an angry laugh. 'You don't like being told, do you, Stephen? I don't suppose anyone's ever talked to you like this before? Well, it was time somebody did. Because, if you don't realize what you are now, it'll be too late. Perhaps it's too late already. In another year, you'll be afraid to cross the road with-out Elizabeth holding your hand.'

'Have you quite finished?' I asked sarcastically.

'There's plenty more I could say.'

'I don't doubt it. But now you're going to listen to me. . . . I never asked you to come to Las Palmas, and run after me like this. Yes, I admit I may have encouraged you and given you some wrong ideas. But I'm not that way, and I won't ever be. If you are, I'm sorry for you. I'm sorry for anybody who's twisted and warped. But I'm not going to let you spoil my life. You don't understand the kind of life I have with Elizabeth. You don't understand any kind of real happiness. You know

that, inside; and all this talk about being sorry for me is just a
defence. You're the one who's pitiful. I'm sure Elizabeth's sorry
for you, too. That's why she's been so kind to you, and let you
hang around——'

Michael had stopped in front of me. I could literally feel his
rage; it was as infectious as fear. It made his face look quite
horrible in the dim smoky light.

'Well, listen to the big he-man! For Christ's sake, Stephen,
who do you think you're fooling with that kind of talk? Your
happiness! Your beautiful life with Elizabeth! You can tell that
to strangers, people you meet in hotels. Don't try it on me.
I've got nothing against her. It's not her fault that she's sick.
Only, for Christ's sake, don't pretend. I know you two don't
have a real marriage, any more. I'll bet the doctor won't even
allow her to——'

He didn't get any further, because I'd jumped up and hit him
in the face. I saw the blood spurt from the corner of his mouth;
and then he hit back at me with all his strength, catching me on
the eyebrow. We grappled and rolled on the floor, punching at
each other with short jabs. Within a few moments, in that thin
air, we were gasping for breath. We let go of each other and
scrambled slowly to our feet, panting.

I sat down on the bunk. My eye hurt, but not much; Michael's
blow hadn't landed squarely. Now he was mopping with his
handkerchief at his bleeding mouth. He looked so hurt and
young that I felt suddenly, keenly touched. I held out my hand
to him, as you do to a child or a dog. 'I'm sorry,' I said.

Michael looked quickly at me and evidently saw that I meant
it. He came over to me; and, all at once, his body folded as if
with exhaustion and he fell on his knees, burying his head in
my lap. It was such a childlike movement that I didn't pull
away or feel embarrassed. And when his shoulders started to
shake with crying, I found myself quite naturally stroking his
hair.

'Oh, Stephen——' I could barely understand what Michael was saying in the intervals between his attacks of sobbing: 'I love you—never mind anything I said just now—I do love you so much——'

I kept silent. Gradually, I felt him calming down; and presently he looked up at me. 'Aren't I a bloody idiot?' he said.

'No.'

'Will you forget I said those things?'

'I've forgotten already.'

'You know why I said them, don't you?'

'Yes. I think I do.'

'Because I love you. Do you believe that?'

'Yes, Michael. I do believe it.'

'Oh, Stephen,' Michael smiled at me with a kind of childlike sadness, 'why can't I make you love *me*? I still believe I could, if I got the chance. You know, we could have such marvellous times together. We could go to places you'll never go to with Elizabeth. When two men stick together, they can do anything. And I'd stick by you all my life. With a woman, you're never really free. They always tie you down, in one way or another. . . . And Elizabeth doesn't even need you as much as I do. She can get herself another secretary. That's all you are to her, now, isn't it? No, Stephen—no, don't be angry with me. Let me say it once, won't you, when it's the truth? You ought to be with me. I deserve you. She doesn't. She doesn't appreciate you. No woman would. I don't believe a woman ever looks at a man, properly. Elizabeth doesn't see how beautiful you are. Don't laugh—you *are* beautiful. I think you're the most beautiful person I ever met——'

'Michael, stop! You're just talking nonsense, now. I know you mean it—or, at least, you think you do. And I'm not pretending that I'm not glad that you feel this way about me. I am. Whatever names people may call it, it's still love—and any kind of love is wonderful. I believe I love you, too; in quite a different sort of way. And I certainly think *you're* beautiful. Anyone would have to admit that. . . . Only, Michael, you must understand this: as far as you and I are concerned, anything more is absolutely out of the question——'

Michael was sitting back on his heels, now, and looking at me with a smile that was radiant and sweet and slightly silly. I realized that he wasn't listening, any more, to anything I said—only to the tones of my voice. After all this emotional excitement, he seemed to have passed into a kind of euphoric daze.

'Come on,' I said, gently but firmly, as one talks to a friend who is drunk, 'Let's go to bed. We don't want to miss that much-advertised sunrise, do we?'

Later, when we'd extinguished the bicycle-lamps and climbed into our separate bunks, we lay silent for a long time. I was still wide awake, I found. But now I felt a different kind of tension. My heart was pounding as I admitted to myself what it was that I wanted to do. And I was going to do it. My brain was working quickly, like a crooked lawyer preparing a case in advance for his criminal client. I rationalized my shameless physical itch, transforming it into a big noble generous gesture, a gift of princely charity from myself, who had everything, to Michael, who had nothing at all.

At last, when the case was prepared, I cleared my throat and said softly: 'Michael, are you awake?'

'Yes——' Michael answered at once, and I could hear the eagerness in his voice. 'What is it?'

'Don't you feel sleepy?'

'Not a bit.'

'Neither do I. . . . We may as well stop trying.'

'You mean, you want to talk?' Michael's tone was excited and questioning.

'Don't you?'

'Of course.' He laughed, a little. I was certain, now, that he understood.

Just before dawn, we climbed up to the summit of the cone. It was a rough but easy climb, over the huge mess of broken stones. Sulphur vapour was fuming out of their crevices; the air reeked of it. If you turned a stone over, the earth was so hot that you couldn't touch it with your hand. Herr Knauer had told us to try holding a lighted match to one of the vapour-holes. When you did so, all the others began to steam more violently. There was one place where we could hear, or thought we could hear, the underground roaring of fire.

The sun was coming up out of Africa, which lay behind a long cloud-bank on the horizon, and dawn was breaking over the vast ring of the ocean. The other island peaks rose up, pink-lit, above a thick layer of grey cloud which looked like ruffled feathers on a bird's breast. Far away down below, we could see a few lights sparkling in the houses of Orotava. They still lay deep in darkness.

Looking down into the crater was a disappointment. I'd expected something more than this not very deep hollow, with less vapour coming out of it than was leaking from the sides of the peak.

'Herr Knauer says it hasn't erupted properly for hundreds of years,' I told Michael. 'A few of the smaller craters on the plateau have blown up, that's all.'

'Don't you wish it would, now at this moment?'

'No. Of course I don't.'

'I do. I think it would be wonderful.' Michael laughed excitedly. 'Imagine the whole mountain bursting wide open, and a great blast of fire shooting straight up into the air for thousands of feet, like you see in the old prints of volcanoes——'

'But *we* shouldn't see it.'

'I know, but'—Michael looked at me with shining eyes—'it'd be such a perfect ending.'

'An ending? Why do you want one?'

'Oh, I don't, really. I was just talking a lot of nonsense, because I'm so happy. I only meant, I wanted to stop Time from going on, somehow—that's all.' Michael caught hold of my arm and gave it a squeeze. 'Don't pretend you don't feel the same way, Stephen. Because I know you do. I was afraid you didn't, until—what happened last night. But now I'm sure. You don't even have to tell me——'

I didn't answer. I couldn't bear to look at his face, shining with beautiful silly joy in the sunrise. I felt horribly trapped; and for the first time I fully realized just what it was that I'd done to Michael. It was as if I'd written him a cheque for a thousand pounds and been caught without one penny in the bank. I almost wished that the Pico *would* blow up with the two of us.

He seemed not to notice anything wrong, however. The sheer stupidity of his happiness dismayed and irritated me; for it was really a kind of selfishness that made him so unaware of what I was actually feeling. When he had taken his photographs and we were ready to leave the summit, he started to glissade down a steep slope of loose shale, digging his heels into it as if it were snow and slithering downhill in a cloud of black dust and flying pebbles. He was shouting and laughing like a schoolboy, and the noise he made seemed a violation of the silent morning. Or so I felt as I watched him, in my guilt.

We got back to Orotava late that afternoon. We were tired and footsore of course, and we took hot baths and had drinks before supper. In my bath, I played half-heartedly with the idea of getting to Elizabeth first and giving her some more or less expurgated account of the situation. But I couldn't bring myself to face that: I had delayed doing it too long, already, and now it was too late. Whatever was going to happen, must happen. I couldn't prevent it.

The meal began with Elizabeth's telling us how the dog belonging to the gardener's boy had been killed that morning by a truck, and how the boy, in his fury against all automobiles, had started to scatter broken glass over the road outside the house. Elizabeth and Herr Knauer had talked him out of doing this. Although she didn't say so, I knew that it was Elizabeth who had really persuaded the boy, for he adored her.

Then I began to describe our trip, making a lot of the view from the top of the Pico and the sunrise. In the midst of this, Michael, who had been drawing hard on his cigarette and nervously working his jaw muscles, suddenly exclaimed: 'Oh, for God's sake, Stephen—Elizabeth doesn't want to hear all that! Why don't you tell her what's happened?'

Perhaps Elizabeth had been expecting some such outburst. At any rate, she didn't seem surprised. But I saw her eyebrows draw together for an instant in the quick sympathetic way they always did when she sensed pain. She was extraordinarily sensitive to it, and I had often made her wince by joking about an injury or an illness, simply because I didn't have enough imagination to feel the suffering involved, as she did. Then, after a moment, she asked quietly: 'What's happened, Michael?'

'Stephen knows what I'm talking about,' Michael said. He ground out his cigarette in the ashtray. 'He'll tell you.'

Elizabeth looked at me, and I knew now for certain that she wasn't surprised. She wasn't afraid, either, of what might be be going to happen. 'Yes, Stephen,' she said, 'I think you *had* better explain.'

'It's nothing, Elizabeth. Really. Just a lot of nonsense.'

'So you won't tell her?' Michael challenged me.

'No, I won't. There's nothing to tell. And I won't have Elizabeth upset like this——'

'You're an awful coward, aren't you, Stephen? But I don't

care—I can speak for both of us. . . . Elizabeth, this is going to be hard for you to understand. But it's the truth, and you've got to believe it. I'm in love with Stephen. And he's in love with me.'

'No, Elizabeth!' I exclaimed in a panic. 'It's a lie. Don't listen to him.'

'But I must listen to him, Stephen,' Elizabeth told me gravely, 'since you wouldn't tell me any of this yourself. Let him say whatever he has to. Let's be frank with each other. We're all friends, or have been.'

'I don't want to hurt you, Elizabeth,' Michael said. 'I hope you believe that?'

'Of course I believe it, Michael. And love ought not to hurt anybody—if it really *is* love.'

Michael looked at her suspiciously. 'I don't think I trust you,' he said. 'You're still pretending not to understand. Listen—I want Stephen to come away with me. To leave you, for good. Isn't that plain enough? How can you sit there and talk about love? You ought to hate me. You know you *do* hate me, underneath all this talk. I'm your enemy.'

'Oh, Michael dear,' said Elizabeth, impulsively reaching across the table and taking his hand, 'I'm sorry——'

Michael pulled it quickly away from her: 'What do you mean, you're sorry?'

'It must hurt you so, having to say all this.'

'I don't want your pity,' said Michael angrily. 'You feel very secure and superior, don't you? I suppose you think this is just a silly schoolboy crush? Quite different from your wonderful mature marriage—which isn't a marriage at all——'

'Michael,' I said, jumping to my feet, 'any more of that, and I'll throw you out of the house——'

'Before you do any more pitying,' Michael told Elizabeth, 'you'd better know this: Stephen and I have been to bed together.'

'Elizabeth——' I gasped. 'It isn't——'

'Do you deny it?' Michael shouted at me. 'Go on—deny it! Let's hear you. You see, Elizabeth, he can't! He can't, because it's true——'

'Elizabeth,' I said imploringly, 'Listen to me. He's building this up into something completely different. It isn't true. At least—not in the way you think——'

Elizabeth looked at me. 'How do you know what I think, Stephen?' she asked, very quietly. Then she turned to Michael. 'Do please believe me,' she told him gently, 'I didn't mean to sound superior. And I wasn't being insincere, when I said I was sorry. I am. I am, truly. You're the only one whose feelings matter, just now. What Stephen or I may feel isn't important. Because, you see, Michael, I'm afraid it's you who has to face the truth. . . . Stephen isn't going away with you.'

'I suppose you think you can stop him?'

'No, Michael. I didn't mean that. I wouldn't try. And I couldn't do it, anyway, if he really wanted to go. It isn't a question of whether he loves you or not. Perhaps he does, in his own way. But he won't go away with you. I can tell you that'

'You're very sure of yourself, aren't you?' said Michael, defiantly.

'Oh, Michael—that isn't it, at all. Do I really seem so arrogant, to you? No—it's just that I know him so well. The reasons why Stephen wouldn't leave me for you—or anybody else—certainly aren't ones that I can be proud of. They're actually quite humiliating—or would be, if I hadn't lived with them for so long. . . . No, Stephen, don't interrupt me: I haven't finished yet. There's one more thing I must tell you, Michael. It may help later, though you won't believe it now. Even if Stephen did go away with you, you two would never be happy together. I know that, too.'

Michael looked slowly from her face to mine. The violence was going out of him, together with his confidence. 'Stephen,' he said at last, 'is all this true—what she says?'

'Yes, Michael,' I said, avoiding his eyes.

'You won't come with me?'

'But, Michael—I never said I would. We never even discussed it. You know that. You must have worked the whole thing up in your imagination, until you believed it. But I never gave you any reason to think——'

'You don't really love me at all, do you, Stephen? No—you needn't answer. It's pretty obvious.'

There was an awful, empty pause.

'I see——' Michael's voice trembled a little, though he tried hard to control it. 'You were right, Elizabeth. I wish I hadn't said all those things to you. But I expect you'll forgive me. You seem to be good at forgiving people——'

I didn't hear any more, because I couldn't bear to listen. I felt I couldn't stay in that room with them another moment. Mumbling some excuse or other, I left them and ran out of the house, across the garden, and through the doorway on to the road. Running at first and then walking, I pushed through the darkness, blindly following the unlighted lanes that wound up and down the hillside. I must have walked for nearly three hours, until I was so tired that I was ready to go back, even though it meant facing Michael and Elizabeth again.

I found Elizabeth still up, and reading in the sitting-room. Some people, when they're worried about your absence and waiting for your return, will pace the floor fidgeting and smoking and then, when at last they hear you outside, will grab up a book and pretend to have been reading all the while, just to show that they didn't care. But Elizabeth was quite incapable of such play-acting. I knew that she'd been making herself really read and attend to what she was reading. That was part of her extraordinary self-control.

'Oh, there you are, Stephen,' she said. 'I'm so glad. I was beginning to get anxious.'

'Where is he?' I asked.

'He's gone.'

'You mean, he went out, too?'

'No. He's gone away. Herr Knauer phoned for a taxi, and he drove down to the port. He was in plenty of time to catch the midnight steamer.'

'He left—just like that?' I asked, stupidly.

Elizabeth looked at me, with a faintly ironical expression. 'What else did you expect?'

I came over and knelt down beside her chair, putting my arms around her. 'Oh, darling,' I said. 'Will you ever be able to forgive me?'

Elizabeth kissed me on the cheek. Her tone was thoughtful and sad: 'It isn't very difficult for me to do that, Stephen. I'm not even sure that there's anything for me to forgive—or only in the most conventional, French kind of way. How idiotic their use of the word "deceived" is, isn't it? As if anybody ever really was——'

'Don't, Elizabeth!' I exclaimed. 'Please don't talk like that! I'm so terribly ashamed.'

'Are you, Stephen?'

There was something in her voice that pulled me sharply out of my wallowing, confessional mood. 'You know I am,' I said, reproachfully. Elizabeth smiled at my tone, but she didn't seem really amused.

'You're ashamed because you've been caught out, and made to look silly. You're ashamed of the way Michael behaved this evening. Be honest, Stephen—isn't that it? Are you really ashamed of how you behaved to Michael? Do you know what he said to me, just before he left? He said: "I'm not sure I'll ever be able to believe in anyone again." That's a dreadful thing to make somebody say—even if it isn't true.'

'My God—isn't there anything I can do to make it up to him for this?'

'No, I don't think there is. Not directly. Certainly not now.'

'What's the matter with me, Elizabeth? What makes me behave like this? Am I so completely rotten?'

'Don't be silly, Stephen. Don't talk like that. Now you're just enjoying feeling wicked.'

'If only I could see where all this started. What did I do wrong? I ought to have come straight to you, of course—as soon as I knew how Michael felt. You certainly warned me. Did you guess, right from the start?'

'I wasn't sure.'

'Of course, I encouraged him. I know that. I admitted it to him, myself. I suppose, really, I was flattered——'

'Stephen, you know the Shakespeare sonnet that begins: "They that have power to hurt and will do none——"? Well, darling, you have the power to hurt. Oh, don't pretend you don't know it! Of course you do. . . . What I'm trying to say is that it would be so much better if you'd realize that and be frankly vain about it—even ridiculously vain. At present, you're not nearly vain enough—you still feel in some mysterious way inferior—and that makes you cruel. You can't resist using your power. You have to keep proving to yourself that you're attractive.'

'Elizabeth, how can you say that? This has never happened before——'

'Oh, darling, please let's be open with each other, now! This may be the first time that it's actually "happened", as you call it. But it's certainly been on your mind before. You've wanted it. You've played all round it. Won't you even admit that?'

'Well, yes, perhaps—in a way—only, I promise you——'

'If we can't be frank about this, Stephen, we're lost. Then our whole life together has failed, anyhow—just because this physical thing has ended. And you don't believe that's true—do you?'

'Of course I don't. And besides——'

'Then why shouldn't we face the simplest facts of Nature?
Are they really so terrible? That you're still young and strong
and healthy. And that I'm—not.'

'But, Elizabeth darling—you're making it all sound so much
more important than it is.'

'No, Stephen! Don't you see—it's *you* who make it important?
By being sentimental about it. By refusing to speak of it.
After all, this isn't something new. We've both known it for
some while, now. I've wanted to talk to you about it, many
times. But you've always made me feel that I couldn't.'

'How did I do that?'

'Oh—by the way you looked and behaved, whenever we
came anywhere near the subject.'

'How did I look?'

'Defensive. And rather frightened.'

'I must say, I don't remember any of those times.'

'You really don't?'

'No. Not a single one.' The tension between us seemed greatly
eased, now, and I found myself on the verge of smiling.

'Well—if I must refresh your memory'—Elizabeth actually did
smile at this point—'we had a very good reason to discuss this a
year ago, that last month in Paris.'

'A reason? Elizabeth—you can't mean——?'

'That charming little Madeleine Jouffroy.'

'But she—that was nothing at all!'

'It was a reason.'

'I suppose so. Just barely.'

'And then there was the Danish engineer's wife—what was
her name? I never liked her—at the Schwarzsee. And that nice
Irish girl—Cathleen somebody—in Tangier——'

'Stop!' I exclaimed, laughing. 'You make me sound like
Casanova. Darling, I swear to you——'

'That nothing ever actually happened? I'm sure it didn't, if
you say so. But, Stephen, that's exactly where you keep dodging

the point. And I don't mean that I used to sit at home gnawing my nails with suspicion. But those were times when there was enough of a situation to make it worth discussing. And you never would, however much I encouraged you to. We could have done it so easily, then. When Michael came along, that was far more difficult. I mean, it would have been ever so much more embarrassing, if I'd been wrong.'

'When you found out, weren't you at all—disgusted?'

'Because it was a man? What difference does that make? You know, I had a friend, once, whose husband used to have affairs with men. I asked her if she minded that more than if it had been with women. And she said: "Neither more nor less. What I grudge is the time he spends away from me. And that's the same, in either case." '

'Oh, Elizabeth!' I laughed. 'Doesn't anything ever shock you?'

'Yes, Stephen,' she had become serious again, at once. 'Unkindness shocks me. Terribly. And, next time this happens, I want——'

'There'll never be a next time.'

'Next time this happens,' Elizabeth repeated, laying her hand on mine, 'I want you to promise that you won't let the other person believe all kinds of things that are impossible and untrue——'

'But I told you, there won't be——'

'Will you promise?'

'All right. I promise. . . . But, darling, you do at least realize, don't you, that I couldn't ever be serious about anybody else?'

'That's the whole point. I do realize it.'

'I'm glad.'

'Only, you see, knowing that doesn't make me altogether happy. Because this being "serious" is only partly love—a great deal of it is nothing but dependence. That's what I was trying to tell Michael. . . . Darling, have you ever thought what would happen to you if *I* were ever to leave *you*?'

'Leave me? You mean, with somebody else?'

'No. Alone.'

'You mean you might go off by yourself? You might get so sick of me that——?'

'No, silly. I only meant I might die.'

'Oh. . . . I wish you wouldn't say things like that.'

'But, Stephen, I fully intend to die some day. Don't you?'

'Yes, of course. But——'

'Well then, I want you to love me—oh, as much as ever you can—but try to need me less. Let's stand side by side—not cling to each other.'

'You don't really need *me*, do you? Not in the wrong way, I mean.'

Elizabeth smiled at me, rather sadly. 'How I wish that were true! But I do—desperately, sometimes. I hope you'll never know how much.'

'You just say that, to make me feel better.'

'You don't believe me?'

'How can I? I think you're about the strongest person in the whole world.'

'Oh, Stephen darling!' Elizabeth shook her head with a kind of amused bewilderment. 'Is that really how I seem to you—after seven long years?' She passed her hand over her eyes, as if brushing something away. And now I became aware that she was utterly exhausted. This evening must have used up almost the last reserves of her energy. I took her arm, gently helping her to her feet, and we walked together into the bedroom without saying another word.

A few days after this, a parcel arrived for me from Las Palmas. From the feel of it, I thought at first that it must be some piece of laundry we'd left behind at the hotel. But when I'd undone the wrappings and unfolded what appeared to be a large red cotton tablecloth, I found myself looking at a faded Nazi flag.

One of its edges was ravelled and tattered, as if it had been flapping for a long time in the wind. There was nothing else in the parcel.

I was too ashamed to show the flag to Elizabeth. I kept it hidden for a couple of days, wondering guiltily what on earth I should do with it. Then I burned it secretly in the garden incinerator, after cutting off a small corner, the size of a postage stamp. This I carried around with me in my wallet for a long time; until, finally, I lost it.

After this, I heard nothing more of Michael for the next three years.

It was early in the summer of 1937, and I was back at St. Luc. I was sitting alone, one morning, in the little café on the corner of the waterfront, looking at the gulls and the patched sails of the fishing-boats in the harbour and dully wondering, as usual, why I was there and what was going to happen to me next. Whenever I was alone, at that time, I had more or less the same mixture of feelings: a basic wish never to go back to the villa, or see Jane or any of the rest of them again; and a nagging anxiety about what they—and especially Jane—might have been doing while I was gone. There was the harbour, and there was I, and there was the situation. It was all as usual.

Until I saw Michael. He appeared—as all authentic ghosts are supposed to—without any dramatic portents; just another figure among the ordinary figures of the waterfront, which only caught my notice because it carried its arm in a sling. He was passing the café with his eyes on the cobble-stones before him, seemingly deep in thought, and I'm sure he wouldn't have seen me if I hadn't called his name.

When I did so, he looked up. He seemed to recognize me without much surprise but quite slowly, as people do when they're drunk. 'Oh—hello, Stephen,' he said.

I saw how thin he was. The bones of his body made hard

outlines inside his shabby sports-coat and threadbare flannel trousers, and his cheeks were hollow. Underneath his dark suntan, he looked tired and ill. His blue eyes were extraordinarily bright, so bright that I thought he must be running a fever.

'Where in the world have you sprung from?' I asked, when he'd sat down at my table.

'Spain. Madrid, actually.' He put his free hand into his pocket, extracted a pack of cigarettes and jerked one out of it, bending to take it between his lips. I lit it for him.

'So you're still on the same job—taking pictures?'

'No. Not the last few months. I was in the International Brigade.'

'Gosh!' I nodded toward the sling. 'Is that how you got this?'

'It isn't much.' Michael glanced down at it indifferently. 'But they made a mess of it somehow, at the hospital. The bone didn't set right. Now I've got to have a skin graft.'

'And so you're out of it, now?'

'I'm no use to them like this.'

'Are you going back to England?'

'I'm on my way there. I'll be leaving tonight. There was a Frenchman in my company who got killed. His mother lives here. I have to go and see her. That's why I came.'

'I see.' We'd been talking to each other in the dry, bored tones of two upper-class Englishmen discussing cricket. Michael's terseness was infectious. Now we were silent. I sat watching him. He kept his eyes on the table.

'I heard about Elizabeth,' he said at length, with an obvious effort. 'I'm sorry.'

'Thanks,' I said mechanically. The mention of her name only seemed to make the gap between us wider. Suddenly I knew that, as I couldn't get rid of Michael immediately, I wanted to stop being alone with him. If we stayed there any longer, we would either have nothing to say to each other—or far too much.

'Look here,' I said, 'how about coming up to my place and having a drink? I've got a villa here, you know. It's quite nice—right on the beach. And there's some people I'd like you to meet. That is, if you don't mind meeting people?'

'No. I don't mind,' Michael told me; and I could see that he didn't. He simply didn't care. To him, these weren't going to be real people, because this wasn't a real place. I knew, from his whole manner, that that was how he felt.

When we got back to the house, they were all of them there. They were always all of them there. Lee and Dale and Ben and Jo and the girl Lee had brought back from Toulon, and Martin and Joyce and Shirley and Glen, and the two silly Belgian girls and Pierre, the show-off muscle-boy, and the nice tall vague girl with huge feet whom for some reason we called Donald. And, in the midst of them all, as always, Jane. She was lying in a chair on the terrace—this was one of her lazy days—and she didn't get up. But she looked Michael over appreciatively, as I didn't fail to notice. I couldn't help myself: I always watched her, pretending not to, whenever she met a new man.

The gang made a huge fuss over Michael. They were more than ready to welcome any stranger—and this one was handsome, and a wounded hero. Just why he had been fighting at all, and what the Civil War was all about, were matters beyond their understanding. One of them even asked 'Which side were you on?' Michael answered, 'The Government's,' politely and without a trace of surprise or annoyance; while two other members of the party, who were a little better informed, were embarrassed and tried to shut the questioner up. The girls wanted to know what kind of a uniform you wore in the Brigade, and whether it was true about the Moors raping women of seventy. And poor old Mr. Willoughby, our neighbour from up the hill, fuddled with drink and anxious to impress, rambled on about the Boer War and trotted out his vocabulary of military terms.

Michael was quite polite and gentle with him, too. 'You probably hate talking about all of this,' said Jane, who was often more sensitive than the others to the way people felt. 'Don't let them heckle you.' Michael smiled at her and answered: 'No, really, I don't mind.' And, watching him as he sat there with the tall gin drink in his hand, I remembered what Elizabeth had said in Las Palmas about the dark little cave.

Michael went off during the afternoon to see the mother of the dead Frenchman, and then came back to the villa to eat supper with us before his train left. In the meanwhile, we had had one of our typical domestic dramas. Pierre and Shirley and the Belgian girls had been flying a kite on the cliffs near the highway, along which there were power-lines. They had made this kite themselves, and tied a lot of tinsel Christmas stars to its tail. Without any warning, the kite had suddenly dipped in an air-current and fallen on the power-lines, where the tinsel must have caused a short-circuit, for there was a blinding flash, and the lines had burned through and broken and fallen across the road, spitting sparks, and Pierre and the girls had run away. Now they were all working themselves up into a state of panic, lest they should be traced, arrested and thrown into prison. (They probably wouldn't have been, anyhow; but, to calm their fears, I went down to see the Chief of Police next day and used some money in a discreet manner. That year, I had to take care of several similar situations.)

While this story was being retold for the tenth time, and the gang's attention thereby diverted from Michael, I kept wondering what he was thinking of us all. I was determined to find out. After the daily overdose of Martinis, I was in a thoroughly nasty mood, half maudlin, half aggressive. Michael's presence made me more than usually ashamed of the life I was living here, and I wanted to punish him for that. To make some kind of a scene, I didn't care what. I only knew I had to break through and touch the raw of his feelings, and try to hurt him.

'Let's go into the other room,' I said to him. 'You must have had about enough of this circus, haven't you?'

Michael didn't answer. He merely gave me a faint smile. I took him by the elbow of his good arm and steered him out through the doorway into the dining-room, shutting the door behind us to cut out the noise.

'It's like this all the time,' I continued. 'I expect you think we're crazy?'

Again Michael smiled but said nothing. I realized that I wouldn't get anywhere with this approach.

'You saw your friend's mother?' I asked.

'Yes. I saw her.'

'I suppose she was terribly upset?'

'At first, she was.'

'What on earth do you say to people in a situation like that?'

'I forget exactly what I said.' Obviously, Michael didn't want to talk about it.

'I suppose you told her he was killed instantly?'

Michael looked quickly at me, and I saw that I'd startled him. 'How did you know?' he asked.

'That's what one always tells the relatives, isn't it? I've heard they used to, in the Great War.'

'No, I mean how did you know it wasn't true, about Henri?'

'I didn't. How could I have?'

'Of course you couldn't, actually. It just seemed strange, your saying that——' Michael appeared to be speaking more to himself than to me. There was a silence.

'Henri——' I said, to start him off again. 'That was his name?' Michael nodded absently.

'He was a special friend of yours?'

'He was my best friend.' Michael glanced uneasily around the room, and then down at his watch. 'I say—it's getting late. I'd better be going.'

'You've got lots of time.'

'I think I'd better, just the same.'

'What you mean is,' I said aggressively, 'that you refuse to tell me any more about your wonderful Henri. Isn't that it?'

'It's not just Henri. You wouldn't understand.'

'What wouldn't I understand?'

'Anything I said about the war, or the Brigade, or how Spain is, nowadays. Your friends didn't understand, either. It's not your fault. You haven't been there.'

'Nobody understands, except you. You've been feeling very superior, haven't you, watching us getting drunk and screaming about a kite? We must seem to you like a bunch of shirkers. Don't you think we ought to be out in those trenches?'

'No,' Michael grinned at me, quite at his ease now. 'Not necessarily. I wish you'd give us some money, though. The ambulance units need it so badly.'

'All right,' I said. 'I'll give you some money, you wounded hero. I'll give you lots of money, to ease my conscience. Then I won't feel so guilty about you.'

'As for my being a wounded hero—if you want to know,' Michael laughed quietly, 'I got hit by a stray bullet while I was playing cards. It was my own silly fault. . . . And I don't know what you mean about feeling guilty. Surely you aren't still harping on that business in Orotava? I got that out of my system, ages ago.'

'Because of Henri, you mean?'

'Yes, partly. He helped a lot.'

'You want me to be jealous of him, don't you? You want me to wish I'd been with you, over there, instead of him? Just imagine—I might have been! If I'd gone away with you that night——'

"I'm glad you didn't, Stephen. That was a crazy idea of mine. It'd never have worked.'

'Why not?'

'Because it wouldn't have.'

'You think I'm a coward? You think I'd have disgraced you and your wonderful war? I'm not even worthy to be told about Henri.'

Michael didn't answer. He stood looking straight into my face, and I believe he saw with compassion something of the miserable mess I was in.

'My God,' I said, 'you despise me, don't you?'

'You know quite well that's a lot of rot.' Michael put his free hand on my arm, as if to steady me. 'You wouldn't say it if you weren't drunk. . . . I don't know what makes you talk like this, Stephen; but I can see you aren't happy. I wish there was something I could do about it. But there isn't. I've found that out. You have to work your way out of these things by yourself. I hope you'll manage to, before long. . . . Look, do you mind if I push off now, without saying Goodbye to your friends? I've got this train to catch.'

I sent Michael his cheque to an address in London he gave me, and he thanked me for it in a brief formal note. That was the last I'd heard of him, to this day.

SEVEN

WE didn't stay long in Orotava, after Michael had gone. It seemed as if he had left something of himself behind him; something that confronted and reproached me at every turn and every hour of the day. Although I never discussed this with Elizabeth, I know she must have felt as I did, because of an otherwise cryptic passage in a letter she wrote at that time: 'Oh yes, believe me, the living have their ghosts, too. And they're much more intimate, much more boldly aggressive, than the other kind. They don't appear palely behind window-panes or in the distance, on the edges of battlements. They come right into the room and push you out of the chair you meant to sit down in. I met one of them myself, only the other morning. It was raining, and I thought I'd like to try how one of the unoccupied bedrooms in this hotel would do for a workroom; it has a view of the sea and lots of light. But, as soon as I'd opened the door, there he was, the possessive phantom. I couldn't *see* him, but his presence was as solid as a human body. "You keep out of here," he told me. And I did! I think we'd better move from this place soon. I only hope he won't follow us!'

After we left the Islands, we stayed for a while in Lisbon, where it was too hot; and at Funchal on Madeira, where it was cloudy. Then we returned to Paris. In September, *The World in the Evening* was published. Its reviews were much as I'd expected—plenty of admiration, a few outbursts of personal spite, and some of the condescension which is usually shown toward the successful by the young—but both I and Elizabeth were astonished by its sales. So were her publishers, and one member of the firm wrote her a not very tactfully worded letter to say so. 'You'd think,' she told Cecilia, 'that they were actually a little shocked to find I'm acceptable to the vulgar palate. I'm no longer caviare to the general, it seems; so perhaps, horrible thought, I'm not caviare at all but some cheap imitation dish!' The book sold very well in the States, too; and, in due course, Sarah sent us a favourable notice clipped from her local newspaper. 'Everybody on the campus is talking about it,' she wrote, 'and I'm afraid I let myself bask a little in your reflected glory. I'm terribly ashamed to say that I haven't read it yet, myself, because I've been so beset with activities and concerns, but I'm planning to do so during the Christmas vacation. I know that will be a real treat for me and a richly rewarding experience.'

'Oh dear, I do wish she *wouldn't* read it!' Elizabeth said to me. 'It isn't that I'm ashamed of it, exactly. With all its faults, it's the best I can do. And I don't suppose Sarah will be shocked. But, somehow, when I think of her taking it up to her little room, and polishing those plain honest spectacles of hers, ready for the rewarding experience—Oh, Stephen, I feel so small and artificial! What will she think of Terence and Isabel? What will she make of my subtleties and clever complicated sensations? And yet—I have to be what I am. If one's going to abase oneself before the simplicity of people like Sarah—beautiful and wonderful as it is—then one just has to stop writing altogether. Or else be a Tolstoy. And I'm not sure I'd want to be like him, even if I could.'

The excitement of getting the novel published, and the interviews and correspondence it involved, tired Elizabeth very much. She seemed almost always to be tired, that autumn. The doctor told her to rest, and do as little travelling as possible. But neither of us wanted to stay in Paris for the winter; and so, in November, we moved down to St. Luc.

'I've never cared especially for the South of France,' Elizabeth wrote to Mary Scriven, 'but it seemed to be the only place we could go to, now. The walls of my life are steadily closing in around me. I daren't venture too far from civilization. In my present state, I must resign myself to staying within reach of competent doctors, ambulances, drugs, hospitals, and all those other dreary medical conveniences.

And this little town in certainly charming. I like it much better than St. Tropez or St. Raphael, and it isn't too primitive, as the smaller places are. I love the steep terra-cotta hills (Oh, if only I could climb them!) and the silvery light in the olive trees, and the crowding yellow houses of the port, which look as if they were being herded down the narrow valley to the sea, and the boats and the fishing-nets and the fishy-winey-garlic smells, and the rock-pools full of magic treasures, under the cliffs. But you know this country, of course. You can picture it for yourself.

Our villa is in the newer part of St. Luc, to the east, on the big bay. It's quite comfortable, modernish, with hideous sten-cilled designs on the walls—Stephen is painting them over—a large cheerful living-room opening on to a terrace from which there are steps down to the beach, a dining-room, two bedrooms, a small absolutely useless entrance-hall, which we've crammed with extra chairs and fussy tables belonging to the former owners, and an adequate bathroom and kitchen. Along with the kitchen, we've inherited a cook named Virginie, a pious horse-faced dolorous woman who rolls up her eyes like one of the mourners around the dead Christ in an El Greco paint-ing. Her bouillabaisse and her omelettes are delicious beyond belief.

And, just think, the villa actually *is* ours—the very first house we've ever owned! It was amazingly cheap, and Stephen insisted on buying it, saying that it was really time we established a base. I feel that, too. In these days, it's good to have one, as a symbol of security. Let me never forget, though, that it's *only* a symbol. It's built, quite literally, on sand. And I must prepare firmer foundations inside myself, against the night of the great tide——'

(This was the last in the series of letters that Mary Scriven sent me, when I wrote her after Elizabeth's death. It wasn't until later—the spring of 1936, when I visited England and saw Mary in person—that she gave me the three others that followed it. 'I hadn't the heart to send them to you,' she told me, 'so soon after it had happened. At first, I thought I'd better burn them, but then it seemed to me I hadn't the right to do that. After all, they do really belong to you. I know they'll hurt you, Stephen, but I'm sure you ought to read them.')

The first of these three letters was headed 'Our eighth wedding anniversary', which fixed its date at February 6, 1935:

'Mary, I feel I must write this to you at once. I don't want to lose a moment. Because, you see, this morning, the realization came to me, not in a vague apprehensive way but vividly and with a kind of terrible prosaic matter-of-factness, that I may quite possibly, even probably, die this year. Millions of people are going to die this year, all over the world, and I shall probably be one of them. There are no words which can convey to you how horribly strange this seems. I thought I had faced and accepted the probability, long before this. But it seems that I hadn't.

Yes, it's my heart, of course. The old village pump. The noise in my ear is getting steadily worse. If I'm in a crowded street, or if, for any reason, I get excited, it becomes really loud— louder than the loudest drum-beat in a symphony orchestra. I feel as though my head, and sometimes my whole body, were throbbing in time with my heart-beats. If I stand up too long, I turn giddy; and, once or twice, I've actually lost consciousness. Not, thank God, when Stephen was in the room, and anyhow only for a few moments. Sometimes I can feel my heart battering

against my breast, as if it were fighting to get out. Ah, that's
horrible!

But much worse than this is the *fear*. I've had attacks of that,
and it's almost unbearable, even when you're prepared for it and
remind yourself that it's just a symptom of the disease. With me,
it takes the form of fearing to be alone. It's completely illogical
and unreasonable. I haven't found any way to overcome it, yet.
But I shall. I must.

Nevertheless, I'm working a good deal, nowadays—in short
spurts, so as to conserve my energy. There are several stories I
want to get finished; I daren't plan anything longer. I've had to
invent a whole new method of working—rather like those
techniques for reducing the number of physical movements
made by an operative in a factory. I have to race along at top
speed and yet remain perfectly calm.

Oh, Mary darling, every instinct urges me to destroy this
shameless letter. But I shan't. I shall send it to you. As I can't
tell any of this to Stephen—that would be unforgivable, since he
has to live with me, poor darling—I turn to you, as I know you'd
wish me to. Between you and me, there should be no pretences.
And, please remember, this is only a description of a state of
mind. Another day, another mood.'

The second letter must have been written more than two
months later, toward the end of April:

'What you wrote—that long wonderful letter—made me
ashamed of myself. That's why I've been such an eternity,
answering it. You didn't mean to make me feel ashamed, I
know, quite the opposite. But you did. In my selfishness, I
hadn't realized that what I wrote would give you so much pain.
And then your offer to leave everything and come out here to
be with me—that made me cry with gratitude. I nearly, nearly
said Yes. But it would have been utterly wrong, Mary darling,
I know that now. If you were here, you couldn't help me in the

way you do at present. And there'd be secrets between us and doleful womanly weepings in corners, and Stephen would have to be told. I simply couldn't bear that. We'd turn this place into a hell of gloom within twenty-four hours.

That's why I sent you that telegram, saying No. Did it sound cold and distant and ungrateful? I fear it may have.

Since I wrote last, I've had more ups and downs than there are in the Alps. The most extraordinary thing—and my doctor confirms this—is the way in which my whole outlook on life is transformed when the heartbeats get slower. He says that the change probably occurs somewhere between forty and thirty-five beats to the minute. When the heart is functioning fairly regularly, around forty, I'm quite my usual self. I'm absorbed in my work and in Stephen, and I stop worrying about the future. But then, when I drop to thirty-five, I'm immediately reduced to a bitter venomous invalid, cursing Fate.

When I'm in this mood and Stephen is with me, I have to keep biting my lips to stop myself from complaining to him. And, Mary, there are moments when I almost hate him, just because he's well. No—that's an exaggeration. The worst I ever feel, with him, is envy. But I do sometimes hate the young vital people I see on the beach. I shouldn't grudge them their little hour of health and strength, I tell myself—and yet I want to spoil it, like some evil old witch. I want to make them aware, just for one instant, of their latter end. I want them to suffer fear, and smell the smell of death. Yes, God forgive me, I do. There are some girls here, Americans, who seem to be the most perfect imaginable examples of insensitive, unthinking, grabbing youth. And I hate them, I hate them, I hate them!

Don't let this disgust or horrify you, Mary. I wouldn't dare to describe such feelings if I didn't have them under strict control, even when I'm at my lowest. And, today, they're as unthinkable as a cloud would be, in this stainless sky. The sun is shining as warm as summer, the sea is sparkling like joy itself, and we're going to picnic at our favourite rock-pool. Yes, at this particular moment I can honestly say that I'm perfectly, utterly happy.'

One of those American girls was Jane.

Her name was Jane Armstrong, then. The Armstrongs were a wealthy Pittsburgh family, and Jane had inherited some money of her own; just enough to make her even more independent than she was by nature. This was the second year she'd come to Europe, with no chaperone but a friend called Shirley, of her own age. These two had gathered around themselves a group of men and girls, Americans mostly, who were their playmates and hangers-on. They had rented a villa near ours, and all crowded into it somehow; and their housekeeping disturbed the whole neighbourhood. They went from house to house, borrowing glasses for their parties; they burned their food so that you could smell it a quarter of a mile down the beach; and the night would resound with their yells of dismay and roars of laughter when the water-heater flooded or the plumbing got stopped. They had a phonograph which played Sophie Tucker and Rudy Vallee and the Blues; and they sang while they danced. Then you would see them tearing out across the sand to the water and swimming for the diving-raft as if they were being pursued by sharks. After these frantic spasms of activity, they'd lie oiled in the sun for hours, or drink cocktails on their terrace under a big red umbrella.

It was Jane's friend Shirley who approached me first. I was lying alone on the sand at the bottom of our steps; resting after several hours of carpentry and painting—for our villa still needed a lot of fixing up. Shirley came straight over to me with the air of a girl who never feels the least embarrassment about accosting males and asking them for anything she wants. Her self-assurance was explained and excused by the cuteness of her nose, the blueness of her eyes and the fluffiness of her hair. Probably she didn't often attract anyone very violently, but she would attract almost any man just a little bit, and that was all that was necessary for her everyday purposes. 'We need a fourth for tennis,' she said, not wriggling or grinning too much, but doing a good deal with her eyes, 'and I thought you looked like you could play. Can you?' I was mildly flattered, and took note of the fact that she was interested in me. I wasn't going to get off to a bad start by playing tennis with them, however. If I did, I should only make a fool of myself: these beach tramps all played like professionals. Instead, I resolved to show off my diving, next time they were all in swimming. And I did. And that was how I got to meet Jane herself.

I think she would have stood out in any kind of a group—and, in fact, she proved to me that she could, under all sorts of circumstances, later. This wasn't because of her appearance, although that was pretty sensational; or because of her brilliance, although she could be quite startlingly funny; or because of any indefinable quality like charm or warmth. If she had been an actress, you could have said that she had perfect timing; but that would imply a deliberately created effect—and, in all the years of knowing Jane, I never once suspected her of trying to create one. No, the timing was instinctive. It was just that she had, so to speak, a rhythm that was different from other people's. Her remarks and actions came in, as it were, between the beats, so that she was continually causing little diversions: making you wait an instant to see how she'd react. Thus, she didn't usually lead the group. She was much more likely to go off alone in the opposite direction. When, for example, everybody else had decided to swim, she'd take a walk in the town or simply stay on the shore. And this wasn't bitchiness or obstinacy: she merely couldn't help being different. The others liked that; it fascinated them. I believe all of them sincerely liked Jane—except, maybe, some of the girls when they were temporarily suffering from sexual jealousy. She was so independent, and so good-humoured, and she seemed to be having such a fine time without any particular assistance from anybody.

Needless to say, I didn't make these observations right away. At first, I couldn't think of anything but the way she looked; I thought I'd never met anyone who was so physically attractive. It was her skin, chiefly. There was a kind of golden bloom on it which you almost never see except on the bodies of idealized nudes on semi-pornographic wall-calendars put out by business firms. Jane's skin had an all-over richness, so that any one bit of it made you feel as if you could imagine her whole body naked. And this meant that the more clothes she wore, the more exciting she became.

I don't remember much about our first three or four meetings. We were never alone together during any of them, and yet the other people seemed quite shadowy. The one who stood out most clearly was Shirley. She actually talked to me a lot more than Jane did; in fact, she made quite a play for me. But it would seem to me as though she were really speaking for Jane. Shirley would tell me that my accent was cute, or that my crawl-stroke was dandy, or that she just loved tall men—and, meanwhile, Jane would be looking at me with lazy amusement in her eyes, as if she thought these compliments were as corny as all hell and yet, at the same time, somehow approved of them. As for me, I flirted with Shirley, every bit as cornily, and kept right on looking at Jane. We understood each other perfectly, I felt. I think I knew from the very first what was going to happen between us.

We didn't even have to make a date. An evening came—it can't have been more than a week from our first meeting—when Elizabeth was extra tired and had supper in bed. I told her I was going for a walk on the beach, to make me sleepy.

The villa where Jane lived showed no lights; and yet I walked straight toward it, instead of passing it along the edge of the water. It was as if I already knew that I'd find her there. Jane was sitting in a steamer chair on the terrace. 'Hello,' I said, 'what are you doing here, all by yourself?'

'The others went to a movie. Garbo in *Queen Christina*. I saw it years ago, back home.'

'Want to come for a walk?'

'Sure. Why not?'

'Good,' Jane said. This was about an hour later, while we were lying together on the sand, still naked, on the leeward side of the remains of an old rowboat which sheltered us from the very slight night breeze. We had walked a mile or so along the shore, to where there were no more houses; and ours was the only chain of footsteps, trailing off into the distance, inky-black in the moonlight.

'What do you mean—good?' I asked her.

'Well, wasn't it?'

'Gosh, yes. Marvellous.'

'I really meant, it was good the way it happened. Don't you think it was?'

'Of course I do.' I wasn't sure just what she wanted me to say. 'It was all so—simple.'

Jane laughed out loud. 'Because I'm such a pushover?'

'Jane—you know I didn't mean that! After you've been so sweet to me——'

'You're very polite, aren't you, Stephen? It's kind of misleading. . . . When I first met you, I—well, I'd never have thought you had it in you——'

'What?'

'Oh—this last half-hour.'

'Neither would I!' I started to laugh, and then spat, discovering some sand in my mouth. 'But then, nobody's ever made me feel quite the way I do with you.'

'Honestly, Stephen? You know, it really sets a girl up, to hear that——' Jane kissed my shoulder and then pulled a little away from me. 'Ouch! My arm had gone to sleep. That's better. . . . No—the reason I said "Good" was because I made up my mind, quite some while ago, that if I met another boy and liked him enough, I'd be frank about it and not stall around and go into a virginal hesitation act. It's so corny, and kind of dirty, too—like French postcards. That's why I feel good about tonight.'

'Have there been many other boys?'

'That's none of your Goddamn business!'

'I'm sorry.'

'Okay. No—not many. A few. More than I wanted. They weren't always the right ones.'

'Am I a right one?'

'What do *you* think? But we don't have to get smug about that, either of us. It was just a bit of luck, our running across each other.'

'It certainly was!'

Jane smiled, and stretched herself lazily. Her arched body looked so exciting in the moonlight that I grabbed her in my arms again. She kissed me hard for a few moments, but then she began to push gently away from me.

'Listen, Stephen. I don't want to, any more than you do, but —don't you think we ought to be getting back home? I mean—won't your Wife be wondering——?'

'Well—no, not really. You see, with Elizabeth, it's different. It's a bit hard to explain——'

'Then don't. I don't want to hear. And let's get this straight—I'm no home-wrecker. Couldn't be, even if I tried. I'm just not the type.'

'Were any of the others married?'

'Oh, the hell with the others! You're not going to fuss about the others, all the time, are you? If you are, I give up. It's too tiresome.'

'All right. No others.'

'That's the spirit!' Jane laughed and jumped to her feet.

'And when am I going to see you again?' I asked, after we'd finished putting on our clothes.

'Oh, any time. We're always around.'

'I meant—us two alone.'

'Well—whenever we're both feeling like it.'

'Is that apt to be soon?'

'I expect so, as far as I'm concerned.'

'As far as I'm concerned, it can be any time at all.'

Jane looked up at me and smiled. 'Why, Stephen Monk,' she exclaimed, with a mock Southern accent, 'you say the sweetest things, I declare!'

I had a flash-lamp which I kept just inside the door of our villa, so that, on evenings when Elizabeth had gone to bed earlier than I, I could find my way around without turning on lights or making a noise, falling over things in the dark. But this evening, as I came into the bedroom, Elizabeth startled me by switching on the table-lamp which stood between our two beds.

'Why aren't you asleep?' I asked.

My tone must have sounded rather accusing; for Elizabeth smiled at it and said: 'I'm sorry. I ought to be, oughtn't I? I was just lying here thinking.'

'What about?'

'Oh—a story I may start writing tomorrow.'

'Is that the one you haven't told me about yet?'

'Don't say that so reproachfully, darling.' Elizabeth was still smiling. 'I always tell you about them as soon as I know they're going to hatch. It's only the failures you never hear of. You don't mind my having *some* secrets from you, do you, Stephen?'

I wondered if she meant anything by that. I thought not. But, when I'd kissed her Goodnight and gotten into my bed, I realized that she'd never asked me if I'd enjoyed my walk.

After this, I began going out a great deal to join Jane and her friends on the beach. I managed to spend hours with Jane every day, but, as I always returned to our villa for meals, the pattern of my life with Elizabeth was scarcely disturbed. Elizabeth must have known, of course, what was going on. Even a stupid woman would have known. When I was away from Jane, I probably acted like a dog which is being kept from a bitch on heat. I was frantically restless. And I couldn't come within five yards of her without wanting to touch her body. I had to keep doing it, even while the others were around. This certainly didn't shock Jane's friends. I don't think they were even particularly interested; for they were young themselves and preoccupied with their own affairs. I was often struck by their lack of curiosity. They were like a pack of young animals, playing together and sometimes squabbling, but without any strong individual relationships. If a member of the group left suddenly to go back to Paris or the States, there would be noisy Goodbyes, and then, an hour later, he or she would be completely forgotten.

Sometimes Jane and I made love on the beach at night, after supper; sometimes we did it during the afternoon, in her bedroom, which had only a plywood partition to separate it from the room where Shirley slept. Often, as we lay there in the afternoon heat, with the drawn shade making an orange dusk that hid nothing of our nakedness, we could hear Shirley moving around next door. 'What's the matter with her?' I once asked Jane, whispering right into her ear so that Shirley shouldn't hear me. 'Why does she have to keep messing about in there?'

'She's jealous,' Jane whispered back, giggling. 'She thinks you're cute. Why don't you give her a break, Steve? Glen says she's terrific.'

'Do you want me to?'

'Do I want you to? What have I got to do with it?' Jane smiled at me teasingly. 'I don't care. If you're interested, go ahead.'

This indifference drove me wild, because it showed that Jane felt free to do what she liked; and I knew, only too well, that our physical obsession with each other was far too hot to last.

If only I could be cured of it before she was! The pain of wanting Jane so badly made me cruel, and I punished Shirley for it by making love as loudly as I could whenever I knew that she was listening on the other side of the partition—grunting and panting and making the bed creak, with a shameless exhibitionism which added enormously to the excitement of the act. And if I met Shirley in the passage as I was coming out of Jane's room, I'd look straight into her eyes and grin at her shamelessly. I felt as if I could have had any girl in the world, just then. I wasn't entirely sane.

In this condition, I had to keep passing back and forth between the two utterly dissimilar halves of my life, which were only separated by the three-minutes' walk from our villa to Jane's. I remembered coming home one afternoon and entering the sitting-room, where Elizabeth was resting on the couch. I was naked except for my trunks, and darkly sunburned. As I stood before her, I caught sight of myself in the big mirror. My teeth were very white in my dark face, and I was grinning down at her without any human expression, like an animal baring its fangs. I remembered how Elizabeth looked up at me then and gently took my hand. 'You're having fun, aren't you, darling?' she said; but her tone had so much compassion in it that it was as if she'd meant: 'You're suffering terribly, aren't you?' I knew now that, at that moment, she saw all life as pain—attachment as pain, gratification as pain, possession as pain—and, in the midst of this realization, found some kind of clarity and peace. But I couldn't have understood that, then. 'Sure I am,' I said (already I was catching some of Jane's Americanisms); and, avoiding Elizabeth's beautiful searching eyes, I turned from her to leave the room.

It was about this time that Elizabeth wrote what was to be her last letter to Mary Scriven:

'Mary darling—something marvellous has happened. It gives

me hope that perhaps the fear is conquered, for good and all.

The other evening, I was out by myself for a short walk. (Stephen *very* seldom leaves me—he is so sweet and patient about that, and you must never dream that anything I write to you about my being alone implies the slightest criticism of him. Most husbands in his position would have contrived to get rid of me long before this—as the Esquimaux turn out their old people to die on the ice.) Well—as I was walking back towards the villa, the thought came to me—it was like a small quiet mocking voice: "You're going to die in there. This evening. All by yourself." It was so silly and yet so horrible. I found myself trembling all over. My legs went weak and my hands shook so that I could hardly turn the door handle. It was like entering my own tomb. I made a prodigious effort, opened the door, went in and collapsed on the nearest chair. "Very well," I said to myself, "perhaps you *are* going to die now. What does it matter? Everybody dies alone, even if it's in a hospital ward or the middle of a battlefield. No one can really help. Why should Stephen be present? Do you want to torture him? Or are you, by any chance, planning a farewell speech? What's behind all this?"

But it was useless, talking to myself in that way, because, as I then realized, I had inside me a terrified animal, a creature absolutely blind and deaf and senseless with fear. No use arguing with it or getting angry. No use trying to beat it into submission. Violence would never make it budge.

It was then, Mary, that I suddenly knew what to do. I gathered the creature up into my arms, as it were, ever so gently, and nursed it, and soothed it. I don't really quite know what I mean by this, because I don't know exactly who the "I" was, who did the nursing. But it *was* done somehow, and that's the only way I can describe it. And the doing of it made me feel, to an intense degree, the distinction between the physical part of me and the—

Oh dear, how I *hate* that word "spiritual"!—let's call it the higher, or deeper will. I was two quite distinct people at that moment—that much I know—and one of them tended the weakness of its animal sister and carried it into the bathroom, where it vomited. And then—utter, utter relief! The creature wasn't frightened any more; it was far too busy relieving itself. And I felt touched by its weakness, and amused. I actually began to laugh, between the spasms, and I said to myself, "How I wish Mary were here, so that we could laugh over this together!" I'm sure you *would* have laughed, Mary, if you'd been with me. I'm only afraid that reading about it in this letter may harrow you. That's the last thing I want. And yet I have to write this to you. It's really important to me. And perhaps it'll seem so to you—one day, if not now.

Darling, your letters have been so wonderful. I live by them—by what they express of your strength—and I shall die by them, I hope. I could never make very much out of church-religion. They seem to me to have turned their God into such a very constitutional monarch. They've smothered Him in deference and bowed Him practically out of existence. But still I do believe in Him—or in my version of Him, which I prefer to call "It". At least, I'm sure now (I used not to be) that there's a source of life within me—and that It can't be destroyed. I shall not live on, but It will. And by that I don't mean any of that sickly humanist stuff about being remembered by and living in one's books or one's friends' minds, or anywhere else. That would anyhow be a short, a very short extension. Because the friends and the books will die, and the very language wear out and change. No. No. There are so many of us—so very many everywhere—that nobody, not even God, could be concerned with all of us individually. I simply cannot believe that His eye is on the sparrow—at least, not on sparrow 789443 as distinct from sparrow 789444. But every sparrow, and everything that ever was born, is part of It.

I, like everything else, am much more essentially in It than
in I.

Yes—I know all this. I know that Stephen is essentially in It.
But what really hurts me, in my ignorance, is my attachment to
Stephen as an individual, and the thought that I must leave him.
I keep telling myself that we shall still be together as part of It.
But that's no comfort at the moment; it's horribly painful. I
suppose it won't be when it happens, because then I shall under-
stand that what I think of as "Stephen" has been changing and
dying a little, every hour of every day, just as "Elizabeth" has.

Isn't that, perhaps, the Original Sin of novelists—that they've
tried to persuade their readers, and themselves, to see human
beings as "characters"; beautifully complete three-dimensional
wholes? Oh yes, the novelists pay lip-service to the idea of the
fourth dimension, which is time and change. They often let their
characters "grow old". But it's only a masquerade; as if a make-
up man were to powder an actor's wig and draw a few wrinkles
on his face. Novelists daren't really accept the fourth dimension
with all its implications, because, if they did, their characters
would blur and dissolve, and the whole novel would disintegrate.
Characters have to have characteristics; they have to be "well-
rounded", as the reviewers say. But human beings can be
anything and everything. They're full of contradictions; and
they have no shape, rounded or otherwise, only a general
direction. This lie of the novelists is a sin because it encourages
the belief that you can treat human beings as characters; that
you can know them fully, and possess them—in the same
way that one can know and possess Emma Bovary or Alyosha
Karamazov.

I see you smiling, Mary, and saying to yourself: "Why, how
philosophical she's getting, in her old age! Will all this wisdom
prevent her from writing any more novels?" No—of course it
won't. Even now, I must confess to you, I'm toying with an
idea——.

Oh, if I could only know—will there be *time*? But I must stop thinking about that.'

Meanwhile, the day was rapidly approaching when Jane and her friends would leave. Jane was going to join her parents in Paris and then travel back with them to the States. I looked forward to her leaving: there was no question in my mind about that. My obsession had become so painful to me by now that I honestly longed for it to end. But it made a last, rather strange demand. I felt that I absolutely must be together with Jane for one whole night.

As I got this idea fixed in my head, I also thought of a way to carry it out. Jane would be travelling to Paris alone; and it would be very simple for her to stop off the train for a night in Marseille, without anyone at either end of her journey knowing that she'd done it.

Jane agreed to my plan at once, with her usual air of slight indifference. 'All right, why not——' she said, 'if you want to.' However, she made up for this by proving unexpectedly practical about the arrangements; so I suspected that she was more interested in the project than she'd admit.

Dealing with Elizabeth was a much more serious problem. It was so unheard of for me to suggest going away anywhere, ever for one night, that I hardly knew how to approach the subject. After racking my brains for two days, I finally came up with an involved and peculiarly unconvincing tale. It was a terrible nuisance, I told her, but a French painter I'd met on the beach with those Americans (I always affected a vagueness about their names when speaking to Elizabeth) had trapped me into agreeing to spend a night with him and his family at their home in Marseille. 'I really don't see,' I concluded, 'how I can possibly get out of it.'

'But surely, darling,' said Elizabeth with a smile, 'that wouldn't be so difficult—I mean, if you hate the idea so much?'

'What do you mean?' I asked, speaking rather sharply because of my guilt.

'Only that you're lucky enough, always, to have a ready-made excuse.' Elizabeth laughed gaily and ironically. 'Your poor tiresome sick wife.'

'But, Elizabeth,' I said hastily, 'you know that would never work. He just wouldn't believe it. I mean—you couldn't be ill *all* the time. This is a standing invitation.'

'I could be ill each time that you tried to go.' (I began to suspect, now, that Elizabeth was teasing me.) 'Quite a lot of chronic invalid wives do it. He'd understand, I'm sure—Frenchmen always seem to understand those things—so he wouldn't be offended; he'd only feel sorry for you. Because he'd know that women who behave like that are just pathologically jealous.'

'But, darling, you can't want him to think that about you! I certainly don't. Besides, it's too ridiculous for words.'

'I can hardly care what he thinks about me, Stephen, when I've never even set eyes on him. And, anyway, we were only discussing how you could wriggle out of this invitation you dislike so much. I'm quite ready to sacrifice my reputation if I can save you from being bored.'

'Oh, perhaps I shan't be as bored as all that,' I said, rising to my feet with the air of having made an unwilling decision. 'And it's really too tiresome, having to invent all these lies; when, in any case, I'll only be away for twentyfour hours, at the most. . . . I'd better go.'

I thought that had settled the matter; but it hadn't. The day that I was due to go to Marseille, Elizabeth suddenly spoke to me at breakfast. I could tell from her manner that she'd been preparing herself to do this ever since she'd sat down at the table.

'I wonder, darling,' her tone was almost humble, 'if you'd do me a very great favour?'

'Of course,' I answered; quite easy in my mind, and not in the least expecting what was to come. Probably, I thought, she was going to ask me to get something for her at one of the Marseille shops.

'I wonder if you'd mind putting off your visit—just for a few days?'

'But, why on earth——?' I began; growling a little, already, like a dog who sees his bone threatened.

'Well'—Elizabeth sounded more and more hesitant as she went on—'it's only that I haven't been feeling quite up to the mark—nothing serious, of course—and—I know this sounds dreadfully silly—but, when I'm like this, I do rather hate being left alone.'

'I think you might have told me this a bit earlier,' I said, my voice getting hard with resentment.

'I'm so sorry, darling, but, you see, I didn't *want* to say anything about it. I kept putting it off. And then, this morning——'

'I'd better go for the doctor.'

'Oh, no—that's not necessary. There isn't anything he could tell me that he hasn't said a hundred times already.'

'He could tell you you ought to be lying down,' I said coldly. 'If you're sick.'

'Very well,' said Elizabeth submissively. 'You're quite right. I will.'

'And you really want me to cancel this trip? They'll think it awfully rude—at the last moment, like this.'

'You *did* say it was a standing invitation. So I thought——'

'Of course I won't go,' I said harshly, 'if you're really sick. But you said yourself it wasn't serious?'

'Oh, it isn't.' Elizabeth sighed faintly. 'It isn't really important. I'm sorry I spoke about it. I thought this trip didn't matter to you particularly, either way. Otherwise, I'd never have suggested——'

'I haven't said it mattered to me, have I? I only think it's rude to change one's plans, for no particular reason.'

'You're perfectly right, darling. It is. Of course it is——'

'But if you insist——'

'Oh, Stephen,' Elizabeth cried, with a kind of despair, 'you *know* I don't insist! When have you ever known me to insist on anything?' She forced a smile, and reached out to touch my hand. But even this didn't soften me.

'Just tell me,' I pursued, like an inquisitor in a torture-chamber who was hungry, and eager to get the signed statement before his supper, 'do you want me to stay, or don't you?'

'Oh, go—go! Please go! Never mind what I said. I'm sorry I was so silly——' Elizabeth turned her head quickly away and I knew, with shame and annoyance, that she was hiding tears. 'I'd hate it—if you didn't go, after this. I shall be all right.'

'Very well, then. Then that's settled.' I gave her a quick formal kiss on the side of her averted face: a model patient husband with a petulant wife. 'Au revoir, darling.' I walked toward the door.

But, just as I reached it, Elizabeth exclaimed with a gasp: 'Stephen, wait——'

She turned her face to me, now; and it shocked me—or came as near to shocking me as anything could, in my stupefied state of unfeeling. It was naked with fear. She reached out her hand. I gave her mine unwillingly, and she squeezed it with a sudden nervous spasm. 'Promise me——'

'What?' I asked, suspicious again.

'When will you be back?'

'Tomorrow, before lunch. The train gets in here about eleven fifty I think.'

'And you won't miss it, will you?'

'Of course I won't. Why should I?'

'You *will* come back?' Elizabeth had dropped all pretence, now. But I couldn't possibly admit that I knew what she meant.

A certain softening of kindness must have come into my face, however, for I saw it eagerly caught and reflected in her eyes.

'I'll be back,' I assured her. 'Don't worry about that.'

'Shall you miss me?' I asked Jane, next morning, as we lay in bed in our room at the Marseille hotel.

'Oh, Steve! What a corny question!'

'You mean, you won't?'

'Sure, I will. But you don't have to make it into a big drama, for either of us. I'll probably meet a boy in the States and marry him. And then I'll *have* to forget about you, and the others, and be a prominent young society matron.'

'You really want to get married?'

'Not particularly. But I guess I will, sooner or later. What else is there?'

'I can't see you married, somehow.'

'Can't you? Well, I expect your friends couldn't see *you* married, either. But you got.'

'That's different.'

'Why is it different?'

'It just is.'

There was a silence. Jane must have sensed that she had better not ask me any more questions. As for me, it was as if I'd been suddenly startled awake and made aware of the insanity of this situation. I saw myself—as if in one of those mirrors that are hung over the beds in whorehouses—lying naked with this girl who now meant nothing to me; sprawling on the crumpled sheets, with the smell of her flesh all over my body. It was a picture that all my self-love, all my faculty for self-deception couldn't make flattering. I had to shut the eyes of my mind tightly, not to see it. And I succeeded. I didn't immediately jump out of bed; though I knew that I had to leave as soon as possible. Our Goodbyes to each other were of the most casual kind. And the parting kiss I gave her was as full of relief as any kiss given by any weary husband to a wife he's grown tired of.

I don't think I travelled back to St. Luc with any actual fore-boding. What I felt was more like the sudden anxiety of a child on finding that it has wandered a long way from home. I made the ten-minute walk from the station to our villa into a five-minute run.

Virginie met me at the door. She cried out on seeing me. Thank God that Monsieur had returned. Several times, they had feared that it was all over. Madame had seemed to be no longer breathing. The doctor had almost despaired——

I pushed past her and ran into the bedroom. I found Elizabeth lying in bed, propped on some pillows, smiling at me.

I'd been prepared for something near to a corpse; and the shock made me exclaim, with an almost indignant relief: 'My God! But I thought you were——'

'I know, darling. I heard Virginie telling you. I tried to call out and stop her from frightening you so, but my voice wasn't strong enough.'

It was only then that I realized how deathly pale she was looking. 'But, Elizabeth, it's true, isn't it? You've had one of your attacks?'

'Well—yes.'

'A bad one?'

Elizabeth looked at me gently, as if deciding how much to tell me. Then she said: 'Quite a bad one.'

'And I wasn't with you!'

'Oh, please don't feel badly about that, Stephen! Why, it might just as easily have happened when you'd only gone out for five minutes, to buy a newspaper.'

'But Virginie was here?'

'No—and that was because of my own silliness. You see, she offered to stay with me, when she heard that you were going to be away for the night. And, like a goose, I said it wasn't necessary. That was very unfair to *you*—I see that now. I've made you feel somehow guilty and responsible, all through my own thoughtlessness.'

'But I still don't understand—how did you get help?'

'Well, you see, as it got later in the evening, I changed my mind. I suddenly felt I didn't want to be alone, after all. There you have the typical spoiled female, I'm afraid; and if you have *any* responsibility whatever for this, darling, it's only that it was you who did the spoiling. . . . I decided to walk round to Virginie's house and ask her to come back with me.'

'You walked—all that way! Couldn't you have found some-one to send?'

'Yes, it was silly of me, I know. But I thought it would be all right if I took it very slowly. Well, that's where I was wrong——'

'My God—you mean you had the attack right in the street?'

'It was really rather a good place for it, as it turned out. I didn't fall, or bump my head, or anything. I just sank down gracefully on to a doorstep. At least, I *hope* I was graceful. Pavlova would have done it exquisitely. . . . And then that nice boy who's the nephew of our butcher happened to be passing, and he took charge of everything—got help, fetched Virginie and the doctor, and brought me back here. . . . You know, I think he'd appreciate it very much if you were to go round to the shop and thank him personally. You wouldn't mind doing that, would you?'

'Mind? I wish I could give him a medal!' I kissed Elizabeth. Then I drew a long breath and said: 'There's something I want to tell you. I'll never go away again. Not even for a single night.'

'Darling,' Elizabeth smiled at me, 'please don't let's have any more promises.'

'This isn't a promise, exactly. It's just something I know for certain. Something I want you to believe and be sure of.'

'Very well, Stephen.' Elizabeth's tone was soothing, as though it were I who had to be reassured.

'That's all over,' I said; knowing that, now, we needn't pretend any more not to understand each other. 'Listen, Elizabeth: this time, I'm not going to *say* I'm sorry, like a naughty little boy running to his mother. I've behaved like a child, but I'm not one; and that's not good enough. I know I hurt you terribly; and I know you've forgiven me. But the point is, now, what am I going to do about it? You say you don't want any more promises. No wonder you don't. You needn't remind me what I promised in Orotava—that this wouldn't happen again. I said that then and meant it, because I didn't know I could go completely crazy, the way I have been, these last weeks. I'm almost glad I did, though—in spite of it hurting you—because now I've got it out of my system. I know that. But I don't ask you to believe it now. I'm going to prove it to you.'

'Oh, Stephen darling,' said Elizabeth, 'you don't know how happy that makes me—for both of us! Only, don't let's talk about it any more. Not now. Not for a long, long time.'

The doctor told me that Elizabeth's attack had been very serious. He refused to make any predictions: there might be more attacks soon, and, again, there might not. He urged me to get a night-nurse, but I knew already that Elizabeth would never agree to this; we had discussed it several times.

Yet, even now, I somehow wasn't really alarmed. This was partly due to the awful scare I had had, all those years ago in Athens, at the time of Elizabeth's miscarriage. She had come through that, and I had an illogical faith that she would be all right now, too. Even less logical, and indeed purely superstitious, was my feeling that I'd paid for Elizabeth's recovery by giving up Jane, and any intention of looking for another Jane, in the future. As long as there was never another Jane, Elizabeth would be all right: that was what I wanted to believe.

The weather, those next few days, was beautiful. We sat out on the terrace, talking, or reading aloud to each other. I felt pleasantly tired and relaxed. It was as if I, not Elizabeth, were convalescent. After the strain of the past weeks, I was glad to be resting. Virginie waited on us both.

After supper, on the fourth evening, I read to her from Turgenev's *First Love*. It moved both of us, very much. 'That's how I've always wanted to write,' Elizabeth said. 'Like water running. I wonder if I ever could? One day, perhaps, if—— Oh, Stephen, isn't it absurd? I'm so full of plans and hopes, as if life were just beginning——'

'What's absurd about that?' I asked—and immediately wished that I hadn't. Elizabeth didn't answer. It was obvious what she'd meant. But that was only a momentary shadow on our evening. Presently she began to talk, with increasing animation.

'You know, darling, I sometimes feel such a longing to go back to the States. Perhaps we really ought to. After all, it is your real home, isn't it—even though you know it as little as I do.'

'Where would you like to go?'

'Oh, certainly not New York or Hollywood. Not to any of those places we actually visited. That's the odd thing about it, I'm homesick for somewhere I've never seen—unless it was in a photograph or a painting. . . . There's an old white wooden ranch-house under two cottonwood trees. Big crimson rocks behind it, shaped like clenched fists. And a long sloping view down to an almost dry river, with more trees, some of them green and some of them that marvellous flaring yellow. And, in the distance, great quiet snow-mountains. . . . Do you suppose there's a place like that?'

'Hundreds of them, probably.'

'And we could actually find one of them, and buy it, and live there. How extraordinary that seems!'

'What's extraordinary about it?'

'That life has such millions of alternatives. And yet one so seldom seems to make any conscious choice. One just lets oneself be pushed this way and that. I'd like to have made my life so much more, well, intentional.'

'But, Elizabeth, you have, surely? What about your writing?'

'That's just the trouble. I feel as if I'd put all my will into deciding what to call a character, or whether to use a semi-colon instead of a comma. In life itself, I've drifted. And I've dragged you along with me. I've been terribly selfish, I'm afraid.'

'What nonsense! Even if I have drifted with you, I've certainly wanted to. It isn't your fault.'

'Oh, Stephen, what a very strange thing a marriage is!'

'I suppose they all are—the ones that last.'

'Has it been at all like you expected, being married to me?'

'I forget what I expected.'

Elizabeth laughed: 'You know, I used to keep dreading the most awful difficulties?'

'What kind of difficulties?'

'Well—I suppose, really, about our ages.'

'Oh, Elizabeth! That might have mattered at the beginning. It doesn't now. You know that. Why, very often, I feel——' I hesitated for an instant, because I'd been about to say 'quite middle-aged, myself,' and then substituted 'a lot older than you are'. But this didn't sound right, either; so I added: 'In fact, I never think about it.'

Elizabeth nodded, thoughtfully: 'And how that teaches one, doesn't it, that there's really nothing in the world to be afraid of?'

'I don't see how one can help being afraid, sometimes.'

'Oh, no, Stephen!' She spoke as if this were something for which she could answer without hesitation; and her face was quite radiant. 'I've been afraid, darling—terribly afraid—and I can promise you, it isn't necessary. We only get afraid because we cling to things in the past or the future. If you stay in the present moment, you're never afraid, and you're safe—because that's always.'

'I don't trust that kind of mysticism,' I said, rather impatiently. 'It seems to me awfully over-simplified.' I didn't like the turn our conversation was taking. I didn't like Elizabeth's tone. It was beginning to make me feel uneasy about her.

'It may be simple, darling. But it's true. One day, you'll know——' Then, as if she realized that I didn't want to hear her talk like this, she went on: 'Speaking of the present moment, did I ever tell you about that weird young Welsh poet I used to know, in the early twenties? He believed that art could only be truly enjoyed at moments of crisis. He'd made that discovery during the War, in the trenches. And, to prove it to us, he insisted on reading sonnets aloud while we were riding the switchback at the Wembley Exhibition. We were supposed to concentrate on them, and ignore the dips.'

'And could you?'

'Well, not altogether. But I think he proved his point, in a way. It really was an astonishing sensation. That feeling of apprehension, as we were climbing to the top of the track, *did* give a kind of new, quite unintended meaning to lines like ". . . in mounting higher, the angels would press on us"; and then, when we started to plunge downhill, the young man had to shout, of course, at the top of his voice—I can hear him now, yelling "I shall never look upon thee more," and then losing his breath, so that the recitation died away with a gasp in the tunnel. . . . The rest of us laughed so much that we nearly fell out of the car. And of course the other passengers simply thought we were insane——'

'Who else was with you?'

'Oh, Ethel, and Clive and his wife, and that woman who ran the bookshop in Buckingham Street—what *was* her name? Don't you remember? She always wore that hair-ornament which looked like some kind of device for detecting enemy aircraft——'

We talked like that for nearly an hour, recalling all sorts of people and situations. And then Elizabeth went into the house, still laughing, to get ready for bed.

I stayed out on the terrace for a while, smoking and looking at the stars, and feeling a sort of calm thankfulness. Yes, I had gotten away with murder; but I wasn't going to be like the other husbands who did that. I was going to take it as a warning and second chance. No Jane in the world was worth one instant of my incredible good luck in having Elizabeth; and I would never forget that again. I would be quite different to her, from now on. I'd make her see that I'd changed and matured, and was fit to be her companion.

I wanted to tell her about my new resolutions at once. But when I came into the bedroom, she was already asleep, and resting so quietly and deeply that there was no question of disturbing her. I undressed and got into my own bed and fell asleep almost instantly, like a child, with a complete childlike confidence that everything was going to be all right from now on, for ever and ever.

That was the night Elizabeth died—at about three o'clock, the doctor said. She died only a few feet away from me, and I never woke; so she couldn't have cried out, or made any loud noise. The doctor thought that she'd felt nothing whatsoever. At any rate, there was no trace of pain on the smooth waxen face of the thing she had left.

EIGHT

ONE morning, when I had been at Tawelfan about a month, Gerda came into my room after breakfast with an air of teasing excitement.

'Today,' she said, 'I bring you a big surprise. Something you never had before.'

'Something to eat?'

'Oh, no! Much more surprising! Your first letter——' Gerda handed it to me; she had been hiding it behind her back. 'I am so glad for you,' she added. 'I begin to think none of your friends know how to write.'

I looked at the letter. It was from Mr. Frosch, the Los Angeles lawyer. As soon as I began to open it, Gerda discreetly left the room.

'Dear Mr. Monk,

I carried out the instructions contained in your last letter with regard to Mrs. Monk, and since then I have remained in touch with her. It now appears that Mrs. Monk is anxious to obtain a divorce from you as soon as possible. According to the laws of this State, a year would have to elapse before the divorce became final, and it would therefore be better if the suit was filed in Reno, since, as you probably know, the laws of the State of Nevada are considerably more expeditious. Desertion and mental cruelty would be the grounds urged, I imagine.

However, as I have pointed out to Mrs. Monk, this situation is most irregular, since I cannot act for both of you in this matter. So I would like to have a clear expression of your wishes. I do not even know that you will be in favour of letting Mrs.

Monk file suit for a divorce uncontested. There are many points to be straightened out here, and I would suggest that, at this stage in the proceedings before any official action has been taken, you should write to Mrs. Monk herself and discuss this matter fully, in order that there may be no misunderstandings later. Once the suit has been filed, it will be most inadvisable for you to do this, lest you should be charged with collusion. If you will write in care of this office, I will see that the letter reaches her, as she is no longer in California right now.

Mrs. Monk wishes me to tell you definitely that under no circumstances will she accept any alimony that may be awarded her by the court. I cautioned her against making such a statement, but she asked me to pass this on in my private capacity as a friend of both parties. This does not of course bind her legally to maintain her intention; but I may tell you unofficially, and as a private friend, that I think she means what she says. She is a very determined little lady in all respects, as you no doubt have discovered by this time!

May I say in conclusion that I greatly regret what has taken place, although I know from my own experience that with human beings you never can tell, and some of the greatest guys and the swellest gals I have known couldn't seem to hit it off together, even though individually so popular with all who met them. If you are both resolved to go through with this thing, then we will try to get it through for you without any undue formalities, because "least said soonest mended" may be a truism but holds good in such matters, as always.

> With sincere regards, and write me soon, willya?
> Your friend and legal adviser,
> Morton Frosch.'

I was still holding this letter in my hand when Gerda came back into the room. My first instinct was to slip it under the covers, out of sight. (I seemed to be becoming more and more secretive as my bed-life progressed: my habit of keeping Elizabeth's letters hidden had affected the whole of my conduct.) But, instead, I smiled at Gerda and said brightly: 'Well, I'm getting divorced.'

'Please?'

'I'm getting divorced. From my wife. Jane.'

'Oh. . . . I am sorry.'

'No need to be sorry. I'm not.'

'You are not?'

'No. It's the best thing, for both of us. We ought never to have married, in the first place.'

Gerda said nothing. She went on tidying the room.

'Why didn't you ever ask me about Jane?' I said.

'Because I do not think you like to talk about her.'

'Oh, you noticed that?'

'Certainly I notice it.' Gerda smiled. 'You speak of all things in the world, except that you never say anything of your wife. Is that natural? Do you think I am complete idiot?'

'I think you're very discreet. . . . But now I *do* want to talk about Jane. I'll tell you anything you like.'

'Very well. . . . You say you should never have married. Why did you marry?'

'I told you about the villa Elizabeth and I had, didn't I—at St. Luc? Well, in 1937—that was nearly two years after she died—I finally went back there. I hadn't felt like going before, as you can imagine, and I didn't want to, then. But the villa had to be sold, and I couldn't get any action just by writing to the agent. And there I met Jane again. She'd been living almost next-door to us, when Elizabeth was still alive. And she'd come back for another visit, too. So I knew her already, you see.'

'And you married her because she was a friend of Elizabeth?'

'That's a strange thing. Actually, she and Elizabeth never even met. And yet, if it hadn't been for Elizabeth, I'm sure I wouldn't have married Jane. There was some sort of connection between them, in my mind.'

'How—a connection? I do not understand.'

'I'm afraid I can't explain it any better than that. It's too complicated, and, besides, I——

'It does not matter. And when did you and Jane get married?'

'That same year. In July.'

'And then you started not to agree together?'

'Just as soon as she got the ring on.'

'About what did you not agree?'

'Oh, all sorts of things—it could be a party I didn't want to go to, or an argument about something in the newspapers, or a movie we'd seen——'

'These are no reasons.'

'No, they were just excuses.'

'You know, Stephen, there is only one true reason why two people will make a divorce. That they do not love each other.'

'You're a wise girl, Gerda.'

Gerda smiled. 'As I am so wise, I will tell you something else. I do not believe that you wish really to talk about Jane. There are many things hidden—things you cannot tell me. Isn't it so?'

'I guess it is.'

'Good—then we say no more. One should not discuss such things with another. But if this makes you sad, I am sorry.'

'It doesn't.'

'Then I am not sorry.'

We both laughed. 'Look, Gerda,' I said. 'Please don't tell Sarah anything about this. I would hate for her to know.'

'I think Sarah knows already.'

'Good God, how can she?'

'She says to me, quite soon after your accident: do not ever speak to Stephen of Jane unless he speaks first to you. That was all. But she knows, I am sure.'

'Do you suppose Jane can have written her? No, that's impossible——'

'Sometimes, Stephen, you are very simple.' Gerda smiled. 'Why should Sarah not guess, as I have? You men think women are stupid. We are not so stupid. And Sarah, she is least stupid of all. She sees much in me, that you do not see.'

'What does she see?'

'Never mind! She sees. Do not underestimate Sarah.'

That night, after Sarah and Gerda had gone to bed, I settled myself to write to Jane:

'I've just heard from Frosch that you want a divorce. He suggests that I write you, so I'm doing it at once. I'd have written you anyway, before long, as I've had a lot on my mind I wanted to say. This looks like being a lengthy letter, so let me tell you right away that it isn't a plea for reconciliation, or any such thing. I most certainly shan't try to get you to change your mind. I entirely agree with you, it's high time we were divorced, and I'll do everything necessary to help it along. If Frosch doesn't handle it himself, he'll get you an attorney. I agree in advance to anything you decide.

He says you don't want any alimony. I won't kick if you change your mind about this later—though I doubt if you will. You're not one of those gold-digging whores. And if I've ever suggested, or thought to myself, that you were, I take it back now, with a humble apology. Yes—that's a sincere bouquet; but, believe me, as I said above, I'm not throwing it with any sinister reconciliation motives. In this letter, I'm going to tell you the truth about certain things, as well as I can, simply in order to straighten out the record. I think it should be straightened out, because there's no reason why we shouldn't end up friends, whatever we may do with our lives in the future.

I don't know if the news will have leaked through to you that I had an accident and broke my thigh. If this is the first you hear of it, don't be alarmed; I'm well on the way to getting better. I only mention it because I want you to know that I've had a lot of

time to think things over, lying here in bed, and this has resulted
in a different attitude, not only toward what happened that night
at the Novotnys', but toward our whole marriage.

After that night, I came straight on out here to Tawelfan and
Aunt Sarah. I suppose it was a somewhat hysterical move. A lot
of people would say that I ought to have stayed and had things
out with you. But I'm glad, now, that I made a clean break; and
I'm sure you are, too. There were things I did that night that I'm
still bitterly ashamed of, though. I only hope you have enough
humour to forgive them.

The first thing I want to get said is this: I'm quite well aware
that I made you do what you did, at the Novotnys'. Underneath,
I was hoping you'd do it. I'd been trying to provoke you to
something of the sort, for months; even though I didn't admit it
to myself. I was such a coward that I had to make you take the
decisive step. Maybe you realized that, and that's why you did it.
But even if you didn't realize, I'm grateful to you anyway, just
because you didn't give a damn. One of those gold-diggers
would have been too careful ever to get caught. She'd have
cheated on me every night and still hung on to me for the rest
of my life.

When I try to understand what went wrong between us, I
have to go back to the very beginning. Well, no, not quite the
beginning—not the first year at St. Luc—there was nothing
wrong with that, as far as it concerned you and me. It's one of
the most exciting things that ever happened to me, and I'd have
felt wonderful about it, if Elizabeth hadn't been there in the
background. Which wasn't your problem. And you were much
more honest about the whole thing than I was, that's certain.

But when I met you again, in 1937, that was all wrong, every
bit of it, from the start.

To do you justice, you knew it. You knew we oughtn't to
begin our affair again. You saw the awful morbid state I was in,
miserably lonely, and bitter and aggressive. Like lots of unhappy

people, I was really shopping around for a victim to vent my misery on. And you were the ideal one, because I could punish you for what I'd done to Elizabeth by sleeping with you in 1935. You smelt all that sickness in me, and it disgusted you, because you're healthy. You tried to shake me off. I remember how you actually said, "What you need, Steve, is a mother or a nurse. Why don't you go look for one? I can't help you." But I was obstinate and quite shameless. I was determined to get you, and I used every trick in the book to do it. I suppose you finally gave in because you felt sorry for me, and because it wasn't that important to you, either way.

I think that second stay at St. Luc was the purest period of hell on earth I can imagine. For me, I mean. I guess you enjoyed it. That house was always swarming with people and cocktails and hangovers; and the laziness and the drifting drove me nearly frantic with guilt. You see, I was raised with a Puritan conscience about work, and I'd lived almost all of my life with people who really did it; first Sarah, and then Elizabeth. I'd got to feeling that Elizabeth's writing was something I had a share in—and I had, too, in a way. That salved my own conscience. Now that she was gone, I had nothing whatever to do. I felt horribly guilty because I was doing nothing, and I hated all of you because you didn't encourage me to do anything. That was completely unfair of me, as I see now. Why in hell *should* you and your friends have done anything? You didn't have Puritan consciences, and I was paying for the drinks. (That's so typical of Puritan ghouls, like me; they pay for other people to get drunk and then sit around with long faces, disapproving of it.) Anyhow, the kind of life you all led was much more genuine and innocent, really, than a lot of people's. At least you didn't pretend it mattered. Like those millionaire hunters and fishermen who spend their time killing every living thing within miles, and being so deadly serious and holy about it. Or those businessmen like your Father, who are actually the most unbusinesslike men in the world, and waste eight hours a day flapping around the office and barking into electric boxes, while their employees quietly go on running the firm in spite of them. What utter fakes they all are!

But it wasn't only the laziness and the drifting that made St. Luc so hellish for me. Much worse than that was my feeling of not belonging. I could never tell you about that, of course. I was ashamed to, and anyway you wouldn't have understood. I used to feel as if the whole lot of you were in league against me. When some newcomer would arrive and be given a drink, for instance, Lee was fond of saying, "You don't have to sip it— it's on the house," and then he'd glance at me quickly, to see how I'd take it. It was like a game you all played: seeing just how much I *would* take. And then the atmosphere of mock deference when I made a remark. And the winks behind my back when my accent was particularly British, or I used some unfamiliar, literary word. Oh, yes, I know I imagined a great deal of that—but it wasn't entirely imagination.

When I started sleeping with you, that only made it worse. It was as if I'd forfeited all claim to you in the daytime, by having you in bed at night. I knew they kidded you about me and you laughed, in that off-hand way which never showed if you were on my side or on theirs.

Sometimes I tried desperately hard to belong; sometimes I stopped trying, and sulked. When I tried, I never could do it right. If I made up my mind to get drunk with the rest of you, I'd get too drunk and pass out. Remember the time I suggested we should swim back to the shore after lunch on that rich Texan's yacht, when we were anchored way outside the harbour —and the water was so rough, and Donald nearly got drowned? I only did it to impress you, of course; but afterwards you acted bored and told me I was an idiot.

Deep inside, I was longing to get away. And I suppose, in the normal course of events, that's what would have happened.

I'd have simply disappeared one morning, leaving a note and a cheque to cover expenses. I often played with the idea. I remember sitting watching you all dancing at the Casino, and thinking: I could do it now, before they come back to the table. It was my secret joke. I imagined myself like a whale which a party of people have mistaken for an island. They're living on its back and really having a ball; but that old whale is just biding its time. Suddenly, it'll sound, diving away down to the deepest depths of the sea, and leave them all floundering in the water. And there isn't a thing, I said to myself, that any of them could do about it.

That's where I was mistaken.

Let's get one thing straight, here. That night you told me you were pregnant, you said, "I suppose you think I did this on purpose?" Well, I never thought that. And I certainly don't think it now. You'd never stoop to that kind of bitchery. And anyhow, if you'd simply wanted me to marry you, you could have had me any time. I definitely hinted at it more than once, but you shut me up. You wouldn't even discuss it.

It's very important that you should understand this, because of what I'm going to tell you in a minute. I didn't object to marrying you one bit; it was I who insisted on doing it right away, remember, as soon as I knew about the baby. I didn't even feel trapped. I didn't feel anything. It just didn't seem particularly important. Maybe it's not very charming of me to say this, but it's the truth. Marrying you seemed like paying some unexpected income-tax, that's all. It was a shock, but I obviously had to do it, and I could afford it. I was too completely bogged down in the present to worry about what would happen later to the two of us. It didn't make the situation any worse, and certainly not any better.

But what I *did* mind about was the baby itself.

I didn't want to have a child with you. The very thought that I'd made you pregnant filled me with disgust. There—I've said it. I could never have told you this to your face, and I could never be writing it to you now, if we weren't about to split up. Even so, I'm resisting an impulse to crumple up this sheet of paper, and rewrite the whole thing in a more tactful way. But I know I mustn't. I must try to tell you the exact truth.

I know how you hate psychology—all those pat little explanations. But I'm afraid you're going to have to put up with some of it here. At least, it's home-made and quite unscientific.

I can think of three separate reasons why I didn't want that baby. The truth is never in reasons, but it's somewhere in between them or around them. Reasons are the nearest I can get to it.

First, a good old-fashioned one: I wasn't in love with you and you weren't in love with me. There's a lot in that.

Second: I still thought of our affair as a triangle, with Elizabeth. If you'd gotten pregnant that first summer, while she was alive, I'd have felt ever so much guiltier. But the feeling carried over; and when you did get pregnant, it was as if I were still cheating on Elizabeth. That's partly true, too—only it's a bit too subtle. If I'd been in love with you, I don't believe I'd have felt that way.

Third, and maybe nearest to the truth: I didn't want a child at all—not yours or anybody else's. In fact, I had a horror of having children. (I say "had", because I believe I would want them now, with the right person.) Why? Well, when Elizabeth's baby died, I felt guilty. This sounds crazy, because her miscarriage certainly hadn't anything to do with me. But the truth is, I was jealous—although I never admitted it to myself at the time. I was afraid the baby would come between us. And when it died, I was glad and guilty; and I hated the poor thing, because it had nearly killed Elizabeth and ruined her health for the rest of her life.

All right—we've cleared that hurdle. Now we come to the big water-jump. I wish you were in the room now; because maybe you've guessed what I'm going to tell you, and if I knew that, I wouldn't have to write this down. Do you know, my hand is actually beginning to shake, at the thought of doing it? Isn't that stupid?!'

This was perfectly true. My hand was trembling so much that I had a hard time holding the pen. I'd avoided thinking about that whole business for such a long time that it came back to me with an extra vividness of shame.

It happened three days after Jane and I had gotten married. This we did very quietly, because Jane didn't want any rumours leaking out to her parents. She was afraid that her Mother, who was in Europe somewhere, might come swooping down on us and find out more than it was good for her to know. So we were married by the American Consul in Marseille, and stayed on for a few days at a hotel there. (Not the same one we'd stayed at in 1935: Jane had seemed to understand, without our discussing it, that I would want to avoid that.) We hadn't told any of the gang about the wedding. We were going to break the news when we got back to St. Luc.

It was late in the evening—we'd been out to a restaurant and then danced—and Jane was sitting brushing her hair in front of the mirror in our room. I stood behind her, with my eyes on her reflected face in the glass. (For some reason, I'd always thought of that as being the classic pose of the jealous husband—to stand in a shadowy background and question the back of your wife's head and her reflection.)

'I wonder what Martin Gates is doing now,' I began.

'Who knows?' said Jane. 'He's probably as high as a kite, wherever he is.'

'He's in Paris, isn't he?'

'Is he?'

'Didn't he say he was going to Paris?'

'Did he?' Jane yawned. 'I forget.'

'You don't seem very interested,' I said.

'I'm not. Should I be?'

'You used to be interested in Martin. Quite a bit.'

'I liked him all right, if that's what you mean. I still do.'

'I mean, you used to sleep with him.'

At this, Jane turned around on her stool and faced me. 'Sure I slept with him, Steve. I told you that, right away. I slept with him a couple of times this spring, before you showed up. I thought he was kind of attractive, but I wouldn't have done it if I hadn't been loaded. It didn't mean anything special. We've stayed good friends, just *because* it didn't mean anything. . . . What are you getting at?'

'Nothing.'

'You aren't getting jealous of Martin, surely? It's a little late in the day for that.'

'I never said I was. I just find this sudden lack of interest rather curious, that's all.'

'Steve—you *are* getting at something. Tell me. You know how I hate hints and mysteries. What are you thinking?'

'Martin left here rather suddenly, didn't he?'

'Did he?'

'Yes, he did.'

'So what? All the people we know are like that. They're all apt to pull up stakes without warning. There's nothing strange about that.'

'No, I guess there isn't—except the time he chose to leave.'

'The time? What do you mean?'

'You know what I mean.'

'Now see here, Steve: either you tell me what you're getting at, or quit beating around the bush. You make me nervous with all this crap.'

'Do I?'

'Yes, you do. What's the matter with you tonight?'

'Okay, I'll tell you. If you're quite sure you don't know——'

'Oh, for Christ's sake——'

'Very well—why did Martin leave exactly one day before you told me you were pregnant?'

That hit her, though she made a tremendous effort not to show it. She turned back to the glass and went on brushing her hair.

'So that's it?' she said, finally.

'That's it,' I said.

I was expecting an explosion. I didn't like the way she smiled at herself in the mirror. 'What am I supposed to do now,' she asked quietly, 'drag out a Bible and swear on it that you're the child's father?'

'I don't care what you do.'

'You mean, you wouldn't believe me anyway?'

'I didn't say that.'

'Oh, go to hell,' Jane said. 'Get out of here.'

'All right. I'm going.'

I went down to the Old Port, found a congenial bar, and got drunk—exactly as jealous husbands are supposed to. I didn't return to the hotel until very late, and I half expected to find our room empty. But when I opened the door, there was Jane, sound asleep in our bed. That was just like her. She always surprised you.

'Well, whether you've guessed it or not,' I wrote, continuing my letter to Jane, 'the truth is that I never really for one moment thought that Martin Gates was, or could have been, the child's father. That's a terrible thing to have to confess, considering the way I acted, and what happened as the result. But at least I do ask you to believe that this wasn't a deep-laid plot of mine. I didn't plan any of this consciously. I just let myself drift into the situation. Does that sound incredible? It does, I guess. But it's the truth as far as I can discover. And, as a matter of fact, I suspect that lots of people just drift, like that, into the worst actions of their lives—including murder.

I don't think I even knew, when we came back to our room at the hotel, that night, that I was going to mention Martin. I only knew that I was miserable and trapped and resentful, because of the kid. I wanted to get at you somehow and hurt you. And I started probing and feeling my way toward a fight. Martin's name came into my mind—God knows why—and so I started using Martin. I'm sure I'd never thought it strange that he left St. Luc when he did. Not until the moment when I said it was—and then it suddenly *seemed* strange. It was a kind of inspiration, on my part. It astonished me, probably just as much as it did you.

Of course, if you'd cared to, you could have talked me out of that fantastic accusation and back to my senses—by kidding me a little and making me see how absurd and crazy I was being. I'd have dropped the nonsense about Martin in two minutes, if you'd argued with me. But, after all, why should you have? You were innocent. I was behaving like a heel. And, anyhow, it wouldn't have done any good. Because Martin wasn't what I was really getting at. It was the existence of the kid.

You'll probably be wondering just what I *did* expect would come out of that scene about Martin. Did I hope you'd run out and leave me then and there? Perhaps. I doubt it, though. I don't think I knew clearly *what* I wanted. I was simply sulking, like a baby who feels uncomfortable. The baby doesn't bother its head about what Nanny should do to make it comfortable again. It just sulks.

Maybe, too, because you always acted so indifferent and self-controlled, I imagined you were thick-skinned. I hadn't any idea what an effect my saying that about Martin would have on you. I supposed I'd have to keep needling you for weeks, before I made any impression.

Believe it or not, that's the truth. And Jane, I do most solemnly swear to you—and you know I've no reason for lying, now—

that no one could have been more surprised and horrified than I was, by what happened next——'

I didn't sleep much, that night, and I don't think Jane did either. Several times, I was aware that she was awake, too. I spoke her name but she didn't answer. I tried edging up close to her and sliding my arm over her body as though I were doing it in my sleep. But her body didn't respond to mine; and there was a curious physical hostility between them.

In the morning, it was Jane who rang for the coffee. Her voice was quiet and very self-contained. She wasn't sulking. She answered two or three matter-of-fact questions, and we were quite polite with each other. I was watching her face all the time She managed to avoid my eyes without seeming to do so. Once, while she was passing me my plate with the rolls and butter, I took hold of her free hand and squeezed it a little. She let me do this without the least sign of distaste but quite passively, and she held the plate in mid-air, waiting coldly and politely until I'd finished. I let go of her hand, feeling baffled and completely idiotic.

After we had had our coffee and bathed and dressed, she turned to me. It was as if she were now giving me her full attention for the first time.

'Stephen,' she said quietly, 'did you mean what you said last night?'

This was just exactly the sort of question I didn't want to be asked, right then. I didn't want to be asked it because it challenged my whole behaviour, and the secret intentions behind it. So I was on the defensive at once.

'I didn't "mean" anything,' I said obstinately, avoiding her eyes, 'I merely asked you——'

'Oh, for Christ's sake,' Jane interrupted, getting visibly rattled for the first time, 'don't let's start any more of this double talk! You know perfectly well what I'm getting at——'

'Last night,' I said, forcing back a sly smile which I felt coming to my lips, in spite of myself, 'I asked you a simple question about Martin Gates. You immediately flew into a rage. You refused in advance to answer another question which, as a matter of fact, I've never asked at all——'

'And so you decided that Martin's the father?'

'I didn't say that.'

'I know you didn't. You never have the guts to say anything. But that's what you think.'

'It's what a lot of people might think, under the circumstances.'

'But is it what *you* think?'

'You seem to want me to think it.'

'Do you know, Steve,' Jane said, looking at me intently and with a kind of dismay that almost touched me because it was so truthful, amidst all these lies I was spinning, 'I don't believe you give one damn about any of this—not about me, or Martin, or the kid? I don't believe you've got any feelings at all.'

'Don't you?' I asked, poker-faced, but having difficulty with that smile, again.

'I don't know,' Jane sighed; there was a note of despair in her voice. 'I just don't know if you're a human being, or what——' She moved toward the door.

'Where are you going?' I asked.

'I'll be back.'

'When'll you be back?' I felt suddenly alarmed. I didn't like her to go off like this, leaving everything up in the air. I felt somehow unsatisfied. It was like making love without an orgasm.

Jane smiled bitterly. 'I'm not running out on you, if that's what you think. Though I don't suppose you'd give a damn if I did. . . . But I'm not. Not yet. I'll be back by suppertime, I expect.'

After she'd gone, I went out too and wandered around the

town most of the day. I felt anxious and uneasy, wondering what Jane was up to. But, at the same time, I was excited. There was something exhilarating about the situation. We couldn't go back to where we'd been, twentyfour hours earlier, and I was glad we couldn't. I welcomed almost any kind of a change.

Toward the end of the afternoon, I returned to our hotel, found that Jane wasn't back yet, and sat down at a table out in front on the sidewalk, to wait for her. I hadn't been waiting more than a couple of drinks when a taxi drove up and Jane got out of it. I followed her into the hotel and we went up together in the elevator. Neither of us said anything.

I followed her along the passage to our room. As we reached the door she faltered, and swayed a little. I thought she was going to faint. She was very pale. I caught her by the arm.

'Don't,' she said, shaking me off as if she hated to have me touch her. 'I'm all right.'

'What's the matter? Are you sick? Shall I get a doctor?'

'Open the door,' Jane told me, between her teeth.

I let her into the room. Jane went over to the bed, sat down on it, and then lay back. I got the impression that she'd made it only just in time. As I shut the door, she closed her eyes for a moment and her face looked very sick. But the weakness passed almost immediately. By the time I'd crossed over to the bed, she was in control of herself again,

'Do you want some water?' I asked.

Jane looked at me. Then she said, in a tone of intense, quiet hatred: 'You dirty sonofabitch.'

'Jane, what's the matter with you, for God's sake?'

'I've done it,' Jane told me, in the same tone. 'I've gotten rid of it. That's one child that won't grow up to be called a bastard, you bastard.'

'Jane! You—— Oh, my God—you didn't——?'

'Sure. I got rid of it. Remember that girl, two years ago—the one Pierre brought with him? It happened to her, too. I never

told you that, did I? She went to this same doctor. He's a good
man. He did a good job. I'll be all right.'

'But, my God, this is awful!'

'Sure. Just the same as murder—that's what the Catholics say.
How does it feel to be a murderer, Steve? Or have you done it
before? I'll bet you have.'

'Jane, I—I just don't know what to say——'

'It's what you wanted me to do, isn't it? Why couldn't you
have come right out and told me to? But you'd never do that,
would you? You'd never have the guts——'

'I swear I never even imagined——'

'If you'd told me to, maybe I could respect you a little. But
you're too smart to do anything like that, aren't you? And now
you've got it the way you want it. Are you satisfied now, you
sonofabitch?'

'Jane, don't talk like that! Listen to me—I swear I——'

'Now that the kid's out of the way, you don't have a thing to
worry about. No scandal. Nothing. We can just call it quits. Too
bad there's all the bother of getting divorced. But what do you
care? You can afford it——'

'Jane, please don't talk like that——!' I tried to put my arm
around her. She shook herself free violently.

'Don't touch me, you filthy lying bastard!'

I grabbed her again, more firmly this time, so that she couldn't
escape. She struggled for a moment. Then she burst into tears.

'Jane darling,' I said, very gently, 'you've got to listen to me. I
won't try to excuse anything I said. It was horrible. I don't know
what got into me. If you want to know the truth——' Here I
checked myself hastily, on the verge of confessing everything:
how I'd felt about the baby, and how Martin had been nothing
but an excuse. I didn't dare tell her that, then. She could never
have forgiven me; right after what I'd driven her to. So, to
cover up my hesitation, I went on: 'The truth is—I've always
been jealous of Martin. I couldn't bear it, having him around and

knowing that he'd been with you those other times. So I got the
idea in my head that he might have—— Oh, I know I was all
wrong, now—I was crazy ever to have thought it——'

'I don't give a damn what you think—any more——' Jane
sobbed. 'I'm through——'

'But you can't be!' I exclaimed, in a panic. 'You can't leave me
now! I need you so terribly, Jane darling. I'm not fit to be
around by myself. I'm such a mess. No one else would even
bother with me. I know I've no right to ask you to stay, after
what I've done. I don't suppose you'll ever be able to forgive me.
But won't you—won't you let me have one more chance?'

By this time, I was crying, myself. After a moment or two,
Jane began to cling to me. 'Oh, Steve——' she sobbed. We
went on crying together for at least five minutes, without speaking; and it was awful and shameless and wonderfully soothing.

'Well, I won't say any more,' I wrote, 'about that part of it. It
was a horrible business. All we can do is try to forget it. But,
looking back over our whole married life, I see how it might
quite easily have had a happy ending. I mean, if we'd been two
other people. Or maybe even if one of us had been another
person. Let's face it, Jane: we just weren't made for each other,
except in bed. I ought to have had the guts to recognize this and
let you go, right after that night in Marseille. It was only my
weakness that wanted you. I can't blame you for not leaving *me*,
considering all the fuss I made; but I do think there was a good
deal of weakness in your attitude, too. Laziness, in fact. After a
certain point, you just couldn't be bothered to go on being firm.
I can imagine you saying to yourself, "Well, if that's the way he
wants it——" and then settling down to live your own life in
your own way, letting me string along if I cared to. So what
if you were extravagant? You always looked marvellous in the
clothes you bought. And what if you did go to parties and run
around with people who bored me? I never offered you any

real alternative, and you enjoyed yourself, and I hadn't any important work you were disturbing. If you'd offered to do exactly what I wanted, I wouldn't have known what to tell you. I really only wanted you to be as dreary as I was.

You remember how, at first, I kept hinting that I wanted another child? Quite naturally, you refused, and I'm glad you did, because I didn't honestly want one—as I've already explained. I was only kidding myself that I did, because I felt so guilty about what happened in Marseille. Later on, I think, *you* wanted one—am I right about that? But you were much too proud to say so, right out; and I pretended not to realize it. By then, I had my excuses for refusing—I mean Roy Griffin's predecessors—don't be offended—I'm not about to bring all *that* up!—and excuses were all I needed.

There are things about the last year of our marriage that I don't want you ever to know. There's no reason why you, or anyone else, should know them. They're too filthy and squalid, and best forgotten. When you have nothing else to do, hating is a way of keeping busy. It becomes a kind of game, and I suppose it has the same sort of appeal as collecting evidence has for a district attorney. You keep building up your case and rehearsing the speech for the prosecution, dwelling with relish on all the damning facts and filling in the weak spots with rhetoric. By the time I was through with you, you were all ready to be sent up to Alcatraz for life.

It *is* a game, though, because you never really believe in your own indignation: hating is always, ultimately, just for the sake of hating. And it's a dangerous game, too. One night, while we were living in Beverly Hills, I had an amazing experience: I can only describe it as a hate-nightmare. I saw my hatred as something objective: it was a kind of black stinking bog. And I realized, just for a moment, that it had an existence all of its own. It had nothing to do with evidence or reasons, and nothing whatsoever to do with you. I had developed it myself, and even if you were to disappear out of my life, I knew, it would still be inside of me. Unless I got rid of it, I would have to use it. I would have to hate somebody else, or a whole lot of people; and in the end it would spread through my body right out to my finger-tips and the hairs on my head, and then I would go mad or grow a cancer or burst out into boils and running sores. It was so utterly loathsome, that filthy bog, that it scared me sick. I woke up scared, and I was scared all morning. I wanted to tell you about it, but I couldn't. I was ashamed to. I knew I had got to do something to be rid of it before it destroyed me. I don't know if I would ever have done anything, though. Thank God, you took the decision out of my hands. You see, it was less than a week later that we went to the Novotnys' party.

And since then? Somehow or other—in some way that I don't in the least understand—the bog is being drained. I feel this. In fact, I know it. I don't try to explain to myself what is happening to me, yet. I'm just thankful. It's a sort of miracle.

That's why I can sincerely say I hope you're happy, wherever you are. (I imagine you've gone back home?) Because I'm happy, and in a way I don't think I've ever been before, in my whole life. It's quite different from the way I was happy with Elizabeth. All I can say about it is: I feel free. Of course I'm not physically free right now; lying in this sweaty bed and smelling like a garbage-dump inside this cast and reading till my eyes ache. But I know that everything's going to be all right. And I'm not miserable and dreary and scared, any more.

I would like to prove this to you. I wish I could see you again, even if it's only for an hour or two. Would you consider it— I mean, of course, after we've been respectably divorced and don't need a chaperone? Maybe you'd rather not; but I doubt that, because you were never one to bear grudges. I'm quite certain, at least, that you don't hate *me*. You're not the hating kind.

It's very late now, and my hand has gotten tired writing all this stuff. I do hope you don't tear this letter up as soon as you see who it's from. I'll just have to rely on that proverbial female curiosity. Which reminds me that my male curiosity has a couple of dozen questions it would like to ask you, some day.

Remember, if there's anything you want that I can give you, you've only to name it.

Eagerly looking forward to being able to sign myself

your ex-husband

Stephen.'

PART THREE

A BEGINNING

ONE

AS Charles Kennedy had predicted, I got out of the cast in ten weeks, almost to the day. After that, I had a brace on my leg and walked with crutches for nearly three months. From the crutches and the brace, I graduated to a stick and a limp. I was still limping slightly at the time of Pearl Harbour.

I was in New York by then, having moved up there in the middle of October, and I didn't return to Dolgelly until late in January, 1942. The immediate reasons for my visit were two postcards, one from Sarah and the other from Charles. Charles' card told me that Bob was coming home on what was almost certainly his last leave before being sent overseas. Sarah wrote: 'Gerda has some wonderful news. Won't you come down and share it with us? And, as usual, your tiresome old Aunt has a concern which needs your guidance.'

Sarah met me at the station. 'Why, I declare,' she exclaimed, when she had looked me up and down after our greetings, 'you've put on a little weight, I do believe! And the leg doesn't pain you any more, I hope?'

'Not a bit. It's better than new. . . . But, Aunt Sarah, what's all this about Gerda?'

'Why, Stephen—can't you guess?' Sarah smiled teasingly up at me. I remembered how, when I was a boy, she used to love making me drag some piece of news out of her, little by little.

'It's something to do with Peter?'

Sarah nodded delightedly.

'She's had news of him?'

'She's had news *from* him!'

'And he's all right?'

'Very much so!'

'You mean it wasn't true what Gerda feared—they never did send him to Germany?'

'Oh yes, they sent him. He wasn't spared that. And I'm afraid it must have been a terrible experience.'

'But the Nazis haven't discovered who he is?'

'Indeed they discovered! And they put him into a camp—one of the worst ones—under sentence of death——'

'But in that case, how can he—— Oh, you mean he's escaped?'

'Yes! Wasn't it marvellous of him? He must be a most resourceful young man, mustn't he? We don't know exactly how he did it, yet. His letter doesn't go into details—out of prudence, no doubt. Gerda thinks it's probably because there may be others who hope to use the same means.'

'But, if he's back in France, won't he have to hide? He must be in great danger still.'

'Ah, but he isn't in France! He writes from Switzerland.'

'Switzerland? Goodness—that's wonderful! Then he's really safe. Gerda must be very happy.'

'Stephen dearest, I can tell you, she's like a changed person! Lately, you know, I'd been greatly worried about her. She was brave as always, but she seemed to be losing faith. I really began to fear that she'd give way to some wasting sickness. And now —you should see her! Well, you will, of course, in the morning. Not tonight, because she's gone into Philadelphia——' By this time, we had descended the station steps and gotten into a taxi. As we drove off, Sarah switched to another subject without even pausing to draw breath, the way she often did when she was happy and excited. 'I never come by here without thinking of your dreadful accident. I've warned everybody I know to be careful on that crossing. And we've been petitioning the authorities to put up a traffic light. I very much doubt if they'll do it now, though, in spite of their promises. I'm afraid this War is going to be used as an excuse for all kinds of procrastination and penny-pinching.'

Sarah then went on to tell me about the effects of the War on Dolgelly. At the time of that false report of the bombing of San Francisco which was spread around soon after the news of Pearl Harbour, she had overheard a lady in the drugstore remark comfortably: 'Well, I guess we can take it, if the British can.' 'I felt sorely tempted to remind her,' said Sarah, 'that England is not three thousand miles wide.' Old Mrs. Yale had been afraid to let the young Japanese student who lodged with her go out to his classes in Philadelphia or even leave the house at all before dark, for fear he would be lynched. 'She was getting all ready to defend him with her life,' Sarah told me, gaily. 'Poor dear silly woman! So much courage at her age, and not one particle of sense!' At length, after Mrs. Yale had kept up her precautions for a couple of weeks, the driver of the bus on which the Japanese had ridden into town every morning had asked her where he was, saying, 'I kind of miss that smile of his. He's always got a smile for everyone. He hasn't been sick, I hope?'

And then, only a short while ago, Sarah told me, the District Attorney's office had issued a new set of regulations for enemy aliens. These regulations, literally applied, would have confined Gerda to a tiny area around Tawelfan which didn't even include the post-office, the movie theatre or the nearest store, not to mention the Meeting House. 'As soon as ever we got word of this,' said Sarah, 'Emily Bradbury and I put on our war-bonnets and were off to Philadelphia on the next train. We made such a clamour that the D.A. saw us himself, and I have to admit that he was just as charming as he could be. Poor man, I really believe he was somewhat afraid of us! He lifted nearly all of the restrictions at once, and apologized for our trouble. So I told him: 'Never mind. If we sometimes make a mess of bureaucracy in this country, it's only because we're not used to it, thank Goodness.' That made him laugh. And what do you think, Stephen, he actually invited us to lunch with him!'

'So now Gerda can go where she likes?' I asked.

'Yes; anywhere within the Philadelphia area. And even to New York, if she just calls the office and tells them in advance. But, of course, we weren't only thinking of her when we went to see the D.A. There are many others in the same situation. And this was really more a question of principle, as far as Gerda was concerned. You see, she'll most likely be leaving us soon, anyway. She naturally wants to join Peter as soon as she can.'

'Where would they meet?'

'Well, that would depend on circumstances, of course. She might be able to get through to Switzerland, legally or otherwise. Or Peter might be able to get out. I've begged her to do nothing rash and she's promised, but I'm sure she'll forget all about that when the time comes, bless her heart. . . . In any case, she feels she should go to Portugal for a start, and then consider the next step to be taken from there.'

'But that's impossible these days, surely?'

'Not *quite* impossible, no. There's someone in the State Department who is willing to consider her case on what they called "compassionate grounds"—I always think that's such a beautiful phrase——'

'But how in the world did you get this person interested?'

Sarah smiled slyly. 'Well, you see, I was once able to do a little favour to an old servant of his, whom he valued because of family associations. It was nothing at all, really, but as somebody—it couldn't have been Emerson, could it?—once said, it's the truly distinguished who are most capable of gratitude. And this particular person—I don't think I ought to mention his name, even to you—is very distinguished indeed. If he says Gerda may go, she will go.'

'Well, that's fine. Tell me, how long did you have to twist his arm before he started feeling so grateful?'

'Oh Stephen,' exclaimed Sarah, laughing, 'you always make me out to be such a terrible bully! And sometimes I'm afraid I

am. But, you know there's so many people in this life who just
refuse to admit to their own goodness of heart. It's as if they were
positively ashamed of it. They get quite angry with you, sometimes, if you show them you know how kind and helpful they
really are. So then you just have to be firm with them. They're
usually glad that you were, in the end.'

Bob Wood came around to Tawelfan with the car to pick me
up, shortly before supper. He was in his Navy uniform. He
grinned at me with the embarrassment almost any serviceman
feels on first meeting a friend who has known him only in
civilian clothes.

'Man, it's real sharp!' I said.

'*This* old thing?' Bob shrugged his shoulders, putting on a
mock-blasé voice. 'It's just something I slip into to be comfortable, around the house. I'm almost ashamed to go out on the
street in it. One sees such dreadful common people wearing
them, nowadays.' He laughed and punched my arm. 'Christ,
I'm glad to see you, you bastard! Charles is tickled to death, too.
He's been cooking all afternoon. He says his patients can rot,
tonight. He's staying home.'

I had been to their house often, during my convalescence. It
was on the opposite side of the valley, just below the woods; a
dramatically angled modern building of redwood and glass. The
living-room was cantilevered out from the hillside so that one
end of it looked like the bridge of a ship, with an outside gallery
that was at least thirty feet above the ground. Bob used to do
handstands on the rail of this gallery when he had had a few
drinks.

Charles came out of the kitchen to welcome me, wearing a
woman's apron over his trousers. On his huge body, it looked
almost as small as a fig-leaf. 'Make yourself at home,' he said,
'while I put the finishing touches to the ragoût d'agneau Navarin.
Bob—the Martinis.'

While Bob fixed the drinks, I walked over to the big book-case. I had gotten into the habit of doing this on previous visits, and I knew the arrangement of one particular shelf by heart, now; if anything so haphazard could be called an arrangement. Chandler's *Introduction to Parasitology*, Robin's *La Pensée Grecque*, *Tender is the Night*, Wolcott's *Animal Biology*, Bloch's *Le Marquis de Sade*, Benedict's *Patterns of Culture*, *Der Zauberberg*, *The World in the Evening*, *The Collected Stories of Elizabeth Rydal*, *A Garden with Animals*, *As Birds Do*, *Mother*, *Letters in a Bottle*, and *The Faded Carpet* in the rare British first edition.

I had spotted them the very first time I came to the house, and asked: 'I'd no idea you were a Rydal fan, Charles?'

'Oh, indeed I was!' (I noticed the tense.) 'A raging fan. . . . And, talking of that, when are you going to publish the letters?'

'Letters?' I had very nearly been caught, but managed to look blank. 'What letters?'

'Elizabeth's letters,' Charles had said, looking me straight in the eye. 'She wrote letters, didn't she? Most people do.'

'But how did you know I was thinking of publishing them?'

'Aren't you?'

'Well, maybe.'

Charles had grinned. 'I told you I was an inquisitive bastard.'

'You certainly keep your eyes open,' I'd said, remembering the evening of Bob's picture-show when I'd passed out, and wondering uneasily what Charles had been doing in the room after I lost consciousness.

'That's our Charles,' Bob had put in, as if to confirm my suspicions, 'The one-man F.B.I.'

'Well,' I'd told Charles, 'I don't know if I'll publish them or not. Not yet, at any rate. I might get them all sorted out and leave them some place, in some library. I couldn't publish all of them, anyhow.'

'You know,' Charles had said, 'you and Elizabeth were great

figures in my young life. When I went to Europe in 1936, I actually made a pilgrimage to the Schwarzsee and saw the house you used to live in.'

'You didn't!'

'I most certainly did! I even discovered three people who remembered you quite well. Your cook, and the hotel manager, and a man at the post-office. Your cook adored you both. She said it was so cute, the way the young gentleman used to try to fix meals and kept burning his fingers.'

'But, Charles, why in the world haven't you ever told me this before?'

'I thought you'd probably hate talking about it. . . . Besides, I only talk about something when I want to ask questions. And I only ask questions when I don't know.'

At supper, which we ate late after at least six Martinis, we drank Bob's health.

'Do you know, Steve,' said Bob, 'this is nearly our fourth anniversary? Charles never remembers things like that.'

'I do too,' said Charles. 'But it wasn't till March.'

'It was February,' said Bob, 'and I can prove it. By March we were in Baltimore.'

'Maybe you're right. Okay—so it was February.'

'Did I ever tell you, Steve, how Charles and I met?'

'No, you didn't.'

'Bob,' said Charles, 'that's a very intimate confidence.'

'So what? Steve's a very intimate friend—aren't you, Steve? Well, it was like this. Charles was down in Florida, at Miami, on vacation. And he went into a restaurant and proceeded to get drunk at the bar—really plastered. In fact, I've never seen him so drunk since. And who do you think was in that bar? Little old me.'

'Ogling me,' said Charles.

'That's a Goddam lie. I was ignoring you with well-bred

disgust, and wondering what made a nice guy like you turn yourself into such a slob.'

'Be that as it may——' said Charles. 'He somehow slithered and crawled along that bar, which was full of people, until he popped up right under my elbow.'

'Whereupon,' said Bob, 'he grabbed my arm and informed me that we were going to drink together until I was as stinking as he was.'

'And did you object?'

'I did not. Because, being well brought up, I didn't wish to create a public scene.'

'There was a scene, however. Quite a considerable scene.'

'And who started it?'

'I started it. I freely admit that.' Charles and Bob had their eyes on me, their audience, throughout this dialogue, like comedians in an act. 'I started it by asking a very simple question. I asked, "Can you swim?" That's a simple question, isn't it, Stephen?'

'It's simple, all right,' I said; 'but whatever made you ask it?'

'You see, Steve,' Bob interrupted, 'it was like this. I was wearing civvies—I was still in the Service—it was my last month—but I had a pass, and that was okay. So when Charles asked me what I did, I told him the truth. I said, "I'm in the Navy." And he asked "Can you swim?" And I said, "Yes." And he said, "I don't believe it." And I said, "Well, don't." And he said, "I'm going to find out if you can swim or not." '

'You're missing the whole point of the story,' Charles interrupted. 'You see, Stephen, this restaurant was built around a patio, and in the middle of the patio was a swimming-pool. And this swimming-pool was floodlit. . . . I hear they have a lot of those floodlit pools in California. You must have seen one, haven't you?'

'I have indeed,' I said.

'What's the joke, Steve?' Bob asked. 'Why are you grinning?'

'Never mind,' I said. 'Go on with the story.'

'You've seen them on a fine night,' said Charles, 'when there's a little chill in the air, and the water's been warmed, and it steams? Then you know exactly how I felt. That pool looked so inviting, but—what do you think?—those bastards had put up a sign saying "No swimming allowed after sunset". It was then, Stephen, that I decided to conduct a small experiment, with Bob as its guinea-pig.'

'If that pool looked so good to you,' said Bob. 'why didn't you just up and jump into it yourself?'

'Ah,' said Charles, 'that's where you fail to follow the extraordinary subtleties of the intoxicated mind. I knew I could swim. But I still hoped that maybe you were bluffing, and couldn't. Because, don't you see, if you hadn't been able to swim, it would have been all right to throw you in the pool? They'd forgotten to include that on their lousy sign. It was only the swimming that was forbidden.'

'That was a good point,' I said. 'You could have argued that in court.'

'I meant to. I'd have taken it to the Supreme Court, if necessary.'

'So what happened next?' I asked.

'Why,' said Bob, 'this big ape picks me up in his arms and starts out of the bar, making for the pool, so he could dunk me. Then, of course, all hell broke loose. The bartender vaulted clear over the bar with some kind of a Stone Age club—which surprised me, because I'd thought this was a real refined place— and a couple of other guys grabbed Charles' arms and tried to get me away from him. Only, Charles can be awful strong when he's in an obstinate mood——'

'But it was Bob who stopped them,' Charles broke in. 'Do you know what he said to them, Stephen? He looked them all up and down very coldly, and he said, "This gentleman is not annoying me." Wasn't that terrific? "This gentleman is not annoying me." Just like that. They were so surprised, they stood there gaping at us. They'd never heard that kind of talk before. It was truly regal.'

'But what did they finally do?' I asked.

'Well,' said Bob, 'that was sort of an anti-climax. Because Charles was just as surprised as any of them. He put me down, and seemed rather dazed. So I felt I had to see him safely home.'

'And the anti-climax,' said Charles, 'has continued ever since.'

Bob hit him in the ribs. 'Thanks a million,' he said, 'You dreary ungrateful unromantic hog.'

'Since we're being so personal,' said Charles, grinning, 'I'd like to ask you a question, Stephen.'

'Go ahead.'

'It's a *very* personal question. I've been wanting to ask you for a long time, but somehow I never could——'

'What is it?'

'Don't you tell him anything, Steve,' Bob said. 'He'll only use it against you, later. He's such an utter fiend.'

'Ask me anything you want to,' I told Charles. 'I don't care.'

'I wouldn't ask this if I wasn't drunk. Remember that time you wanted to know why I'd never talked to you about Elizabeth? Well, the real reason I hadn't was because I was afraid this question would come up, and I wasn't sure how you'd take it. Look, all kidding aside, you don't have to answer this if you'd rather not——'

'All right. I won't.'

'Good. . . . Then, to begin with, have you read any of Elizabeth's books lately?'

'Not right through. But I've looked at them. Why?'

'How do they seem to you, now?'

'Well—you see, I know them so thoroughly. And I got to know them so gradually—I mean, because she used to talk to me about them while she was writing them. I know so well what she *wanted* to say, that——'

'That you can't be sure if she actually managed to say it?'

I nodded. 'There's some things I'm sure about. Several of the stories. . . . You remember *Afternoon of a Gargoyle?*'

'About the old woman gambling at the Estoril Casino? Yes, that's one of my favourites.'

'And then there's *As Birds Do, Mother.* You know, I really like that the best of her novels?'

'I absolutely agree with you.'

'As for *The World in the Evening*—I'm not so sure about that. Bits of it are wonderful, of course——'

'Bob hadn't ever read it. Not until this summer, when I made him. I wanted to see how he'd react. He thought it was awfully sentimental.'

'Oh, you bastard!' exclaimed Bob. 'I didn't, Steve—I mean, not just like that. And anyhow, what do I know about writing?'

'For Pete's sake, don't go apologizing to me,' I said. 'Honestly, Bob, I don't mind. I'm not living on Elizabeth's reputation, I hope. Though, perhaps, in a way, I *have* been pretending——'

'Ah,' said Charles, 'that's exactly what I wanted to get at! What have you been pretending, Stephen?'

'Well—naturally, when I did that introduction to her stories, and when I've discussed her work with admirers, I had to talk as if I thought everything she wrote was perfect——'

'And you don't?'

'No, of course not. Not everything. Not even very much, I'm afraid.'

'You never told her how you felt?'

'I never even knew I felt it, until I reread her, the year after she died.'

'Did she know it, about herself?'

'I think so. Yes.'

'And did she mind?'

'She probably did when she was young. Not so much, later. She knew she'd always done her best. She never made any compromises, and she never stopped trying. She may not have been first-class, but she was a real writer: a serious writer. It's something to know you're that.'

'It certainly is,' Charles agreed. 'And it's a whole lot more than most of these whores can say of themselves, nowadays.'

When it was time for Bob to drive me home, Charles didn't offer to come with us. I realized that this was because Bob must have told him that he wanted to talk to me some more, alone.

'Well,' Bob began, with the familiar ironical twist of his mouth, 'I did it, you see. I got myself into this'—he glanced down at his uniform—'bandwagon suit. After all my big soul-searchings——'

'About being a conscientious objector, you mean?'

'You and I never talked any more about any of that, did we? Not after that first time.'

'You never seemed to want to. I used to lead up to it, but you always changed the subject.'

'I wanted to, all right. Often. I used to come and see you, just to do that, and then I couldn't. I was ashamed to.'

'Why were you ashamed?'

'Because I knew darn' well what would happen in the end.'

'But that isn't anything to be ashamed of, Bob. You simply made up your mind. Like thousands of others.'

'I didn't. Not properly. I just let myself be pushed. . . . You know one thing that did decide me not to be an objector, though? You'll laugh.'

'Not if it isn't funny.'

'I thought to myself: I can't be a C.O. because, if they declared war on the queers—tried to round us up and liquidate us, or something—I'd fight. I'd fight till I dropped. I know that. I'd be so mad, I wouldn't even feel scared. . . . So how can I say I'm a pacifist?'

'You can't, I guess.'

'Steve, you sonofabitch, you *are* laughing!'

'Not at you, Bob. I'm just picturing the battle. Your side would be pretty ferocious. You'd quite probably win.'

Bob laughed, too. 'Don't think I wouldn't shoot you down with the rest of them.'

'You would not! *I'd* be a C.O., then. Or else one of your spies.'

'Of course, I could have gotten out of this whole thing. I could have told the psychiatrist, when I had my medical examination. All you have to do is to tell them you're queer, and you're out. I couldn't do that, though. Because what they're claiming is that us queers are unfit for their beautiful pure Army and Navy—when they ought to be glad to have us. The girly ones make wonderful pharmacist's mates, and the rest are just as good fighting men as anybody else. My God, look at all the big heroes in history who—sorry, Steve! I'm starting that lecture again——'

'That's okay, if you want to let off some more steam.'

'No. Not really. But I'll tell you something I do honestly feel. Compared with this business of being queer, and the laws against us, and the way we're pushed around even in peacetime—this War hardly seems to concern me at all.'

'Well, I can understand that, I guess.'

We drove the rest of the way back to Tawelfan in silence. When Bob had stopped the car in front of the house, I didn't get out. I sat there beside him in the darkness, not wanting to say Goodbye.

'This kind of feels like the end of everything, doesn't it?' Bob said, at length.

'I know it does, Bob. But I don't believe it is.'

'I don't, either. You know, maybe, when this is over, things won't have changed so much, after all. Maybe we'll have another evening, just like this one, and I'll be driving you home, like tonight.'

'We'll have lots of evenings.'

'Yes, we probably will. It's funny to think that, now, when there's so much that's got to happen, first. The hell of it is, you can't be sure, either way. I almost wish I could know for certain, even if—— No, I don't though——' Bob hesitated for a moment; then he added: 'Take care of yourself, you old bastard.' Throwing an arm around my neck, he drew me toward him and we kissed each other on the cheek. I got out of the car. Bob turned it, waved his hand to me through the window, and drove away.

TWO

NEXT morning when I came down to breakfast, I found Gerda alone in the kitchen. I took her in my arms and we hugged each other hard. 'I'm so glad,' I told her.

'Stephen—Oh, I too! You do not know how much!'

'It must have been hard to believe at first, wasn't it?'

'At first, I did not dare. When the letter came, I imagined—all kind of stupidness——' Gerda hesitated and gave me an embarrassed smile. 'I think, perhaps this is some delusion: I am become insane in the head. Perhaps I only imagine this letter is from Peter. So I take it to Sarah, without one word, and say only, "Read." . . . And then, when I know I do not imagine the letter, I become afraid and think: This is some cruel trick of the Nazis. Perhaps they make Peter's handwriting falsely—so I will not know he is dead. . . . Is that not crazy of me? But then another letter comes, from the office of the Red Cross in Zuerich, that Peter is there. You see, Peter himself has asked them to write me this, because he knows I will be unsure. Always, Peter understands everything what I am thinking——'

'So now you really believe it?'

'Now I believe.' Gerda quickly brushed a tear from her eye and smiled at me radiantly. 'I believe more and more, every day!'

I had invited Gerda and Sarah to have dinner with me that evening, in town. Sarah said she couldn't come; she was too busy. This may have been true, but I suspected that she wanted Gerda and me to spend the evening alone together.

Philadelphia had become a wartime city, with a partial blackout. Stripped of its neon lights, it seemed grimmer than ever, and the tall downtown buildings were like up-ended coffins in the clammy midwinter fog. The streets were crowded with naval and military drunks; hundreds of dazed, displaced boys killing time, waiting to be taken away to the War. They were a new, anonymous race which was growing and spreading enormously all over the land. And one of them, somewhere, was Bob.

But the fish-restaurant to which I took Gerda still seemed as bright and snug as in peacetime. We sat in a booth, eating lobster and drinking white wine.

'This is so nice, I find,' she said. 'After the War, I shall bring Peter here.'

I looked into her shining eyes. 'You never used to say things like that.'

'I did not dare, Stephen. . . . You know, now I feel almost ashamed? I have not the right to be so happy. But I cannot help it. Just now, when the War comes to this country, and so many more people will begin to suffer, it is as if for me the War is almost over.'

'You've had your share, don't worry. You've had more than enough War for one person.'

'Oh, Stephen—I have been so much afraid!'

'I think I guessed that.'

'You helped me. Very, very much. You and Sarah. I do not know any more how I shall repay what I owe. But Peter and I, we shall find a way.'

'Take it easy! Get yourselves back here, first.'

'Oh, to get back—that is nothing! Now nothing seems difficult. We shall come back. I know it.'

'Tell me something, Gerda—that is, if you can. What really kept you going, all the time Peter was in Germany and you had no news?'

Gerda thought a little. 'Can anyone tell such a thing? It is not to explain. You go on because life goes on—and what else shall you do? For me, there was my daily work. That was very good. Most especially, that I had you to be looking after.'

'I'm glad that helped.'

'Oh, a lot!' Gerda laughed. 'It was so kind of you to have this accident! You know, every time I am unhappy because of Peter, I think to myself: this what I feel is in the mind only, but poor Stephen has the pain in his leg.'

'I wouldn't have traded with you, believe me.'

'And then there was Sarah. Stephen—never, never in the whole of my life have I met anyone like her. Only now I first begin to understand this.'

'Sure, Sarah's wonderful.'

'You say that, Stephen. But I think you too, you do not understand her. You think you know her, because you have lived together with her so long, when you are a child. I think nobody knows her.'

'Just what do you mean, exactly?'

'You know, Stephen, that I do not believe in this what the Quakers believe?'

'Yes. You told me that.'

'It is good, I am sure. I would like to believe it. But I cannot—not in my deep feeling. . . . But now I tell you something strange: what Sarah believes, I believe in that.'

'But you just said you didn't——'

'I know. It does not make any sense. I know only this: what Sarah believes, this is true.'

'You mean, true for *her*?'

'No. True for all. Because it is *she* who believes, and not another. That what she believes, *must* be true. When I am with her, I know this. When I am not with her, as now, that is different. I do not know. I remember, only. . . . You yourself, did you not ever feel this with Sarah? Tell me truthfully.'

'No, Gerda. I'm afraid I never did.'

'Then perhaps she was not always like this. Perhaps she is changing.'

'I wish you could tell me more about it.'

'I do not know what to tell. . . . No, wait, there is one thing. You know, this last time, since you left, has been for me very bad? I can speak of this, now it is passed. I began to feel, what is the use to hope? Peter is dead, I think.'

'You'd never thought that before?'

'I would not think it. I made my will not to. But at last it was no use. One night, Sarah and I are sitting together, and I begin crying. This I never did before. We are sewing to make clothes for a Negro family who are Sarah's friends. And, suddenly, I cannot go on. I stop. I am crying so much that I cannot see the needle. . . . And, Stephen, do you know what was so strange? All the time that I am crying, Sarah is sitting there, and still sewing, and she says nothing.'

'That certainly *is* strange,' I said, picturing the scene, and the Sarah I knew; the Sarah who ran to pick up children who had fallen in the street, and who would shed tears—rather too easily, I used to think—when she heard of the misfortunes of complete strangers. The picture of this different Sarah was so odd that it seemed even a little spooky. I felt my skin rising into goose-pimples.

'She is sitting there, sewing,' Gerda continued, 'and at first I think that she has not noticed. But that is impossible. And then I know that she knows—all what I am feeling, everything. She is with me, so close, although she has not moved. It is as if she holds my hand. I want to speak to her, but I cannot. And then I do not want. It is not necessary. The room gets very still. I cannot describe—but it is like when you are in a place with deep snow all around—so still. You feel only the stillness. . . . And it was then that I knew——'

Gerda paused. 'You knew what?' I prompted.

'I knew that it is all right.'

'You mean, that Peter was safe?'

'Oh no. Much more than this. It is all right—even if Peter is *not* safe—even if the worst happens, to him and to me. Suddenly, I knew that. Sarah made me know it. . . . I cannot explain more.'

'And didn't Sarah say anything at all?'

'Not for a long, long while. Or it seemed long. Perhaps really only two, three minutes. Then she looks up and says—you will never guess——' Gerda laughed quietly. 'She says, "I think I will make us some hot chocolate." That was all. Then she puts down her sewing, and gets up and goes into the kitchen.'

After Gerda had finished speaking, neither of us said anything for some time. Gerda sat looking down at her plate on the table. Probably she was thinking of what she'd just told me. Then, at length, she raised her eyes and saw that I was watching her.

'What is?' she asked, smiling.

'I was wishing Peter could see you now,' I said.

'Why now, especially?'

'Because you're beautiful.'

'I?' Gerda laughed and shook her head, but I could see she was pleased. 'I am not beautiful. Not ever. Only now perhaps I look a little bit nicer, because I am happy.'

'And you're going to be, always, from now on. I'm sure of that. Peter is damned lucky.'

'I think I am very, very lucky to have Peter.'

'Well, I guess you deserved each other. . . . You know, Gerda, all last summer I was kind of in love with you?'

Gerda smiled. 'Perhaps I liked you also, a little.'

'You did? Honestly?'

'Why not? Why should I not say the truth? I found you quite attractive. Also, you were sick. I am your nurse. That is normal.'

'No—it wasn't just that. Not with me. Because I still feel the same way; only, now, it isn't so personal. I just wish I could find myself someone exactly like you.'

Gerda laughed again. '*Exactly* like? You say this as if I am an automobile! Except that you prefer a more new model, I suppose? 1942, with all latest improvements? No, Stephen— you do not want a copy. Of me, or of anybody. But, believe me, what you really want—that you will find. Those who only think they want—they never get.'

'Tell me some more. I love it when you give me advice.'

'So you can make fun?'

'I'm deadly serious.'

'Oh, I believe! But I tell you one thing more, and *I* am serious. . . . Be alone, first, for a time. You have never been enough alone, I think. I do not mean, to go in the desert, in a hole. You may have many people all around you. But in your personal life be alone, until you know that you can live without the support of others. That is not pleasant, always, but it is good. So do not hurry to find someone. Be patient and wait. She will come, the one you want; and when she comes, you will know. Only, first, it is better for you to be alone.'

'I'm awfully glad you say that, Gerda. Because, as a matter of fact, I'm planning to be.'

Next morning, when breakfast was over and Gerda had left the dining-room, Sarah asked: 'Do you really have to go back to New York today, Stephen dearest?'

'I'm afraid I do, Aunt Sarah.'

'But you'll come down here again soon, won't you?'

I was expecting the question, of course. Indeed, I'd lain awake for more than an hour, this morning, wondering how much to tell her. And yet, I didn't know for certain how I would answer until I heard myself saying: 'Sure. Very soon.'

'You won't stay away another three months?'

'Why, no—of course not.' Then, to cover my embarrassment and take Sarah's mind off the subject, I went on: 'You said on your postcard there was something you wanted to discuss with me?'

'Well, yes, Stephen, there is. I've hesitated to mention it, because it's a very great favour I wished to ask of you. It isn't for myself——'

'Not for *you*, Aunt Sarah?' I pretended utter amazement. 'I thought for sure you needed another pair of diamond clips. You mean, you haven't lost the ones I gave you last year?'

'Why, Stephen, I declare—you're teasing me again! Not that I don't know you'd give me anything for myself I cared to ask for. . . . I must admit, I don't quite understand you, though. Do you mean clips for holding papers together? Why in the world should anyone want them made of diamonds?'

'No, Aunt Sarah—they're to wear.'

'Oh, how stupid of me! I might have guessed that, mightn't I? . . . Well now, what I wanted to ask you is this. You know that our community centre never did get built? And now all kinds of building materials are being frozen—such an odd expression, isn't it? Imagine keeping doorknobs in the icebox with the butter!—and I don't suppose the centre can possibly be completed until this War is over. And so I wondered if you'd consent to our using Tawelfan? Just temporarily, I mean——'

'Why, of course. Go ahead as soon as you want to.'

'You'd always have your room when you wanted it, naturally. We shouldn't be using the upstairs bedrooms. I'd put all the good furniture in storage, and we'd make every effort to prevent any damage. Just the same,' Sarah sighed, 'it does seem a kind of desecration. . . . You know, I'd always hoped that you and Jane would live here, some day——' She laid a hand on my arm. 'You don't mind my speaking of that now, do you, Stephen dearest?'

'Of course I don't. It's practically ancient history, by this time.'

'I know how deeply you must have felt it, though. And Jane, too. . . . She's a fine, sensitive person, Stephen.'

'Yes. I think I understand her a lot better, now.'

'Of course, I know you'd never bear any ill-will. Don't you feel how this terrible War seems to make personal unkindness even worse than it usually is? Surely, we ought to be extra considerate of each other, nowadays? At least we can do that, even though we can't stop what's happening on the battle-fields. . . . You know, I met Charles Kennedy in the village, yesterday morning? He had just seen Bob off on the train. I wanted so to say something to him, but I couldn't find the words——'

'What did you want to say?' I asked, feeling my curiosity suddenly aroused.

'I wanted to tell him—Oh, it's hard to express it without sounding presumptuous—not to mind too much if we haven't understood him as we should have. I mean, I'm afraid we're all of us apt to be very cruel and stupid, in the presence of what we're not accustomed to. I fear that Charles feels cut off from us now, and bitterly lonely; and we refuse him any word of comfort. We refuse to recognize what it was that he and Bob shared together. Oh dear, we're so dreadfully smug and arro-gant, most of us; so very sure we know what's right and what's wrong. Sometimes, Stephen, this lack of charity—even among those of us who call ourselves Friends—it horrifies me!'

'Oh, Aunt Sarah,' I said, putting my arm around her shoulder and giving her a squeeze, 'bless your heart!'

Sarah looked up at me innocently. 'Am I being silly again, Stephen? I know you think me terribly sentimental, sometimes.'

'I think it's wonderful, that you feel this way. And it would mean a lot to Charles, to know that you do.'

'Couldn't you tell him? You're so much closer to him than I am.'

'No. You must tell him. It'd mean more, coming from you.'

'Well,' Sarah smiled shyly, 'One day perhaps, I'll try. . . . All these last weeks, with so many young men going off to the wars, I've been reminded so often of those lines from William

Penn: "They that love beyond the world——" You know them of course, Stephen?'

'Only vaguely. Say them to me.'

'Oh dear, my memory! I know I've forgotten part of it, in the middle, but—"They that love beyond the world cannot be separated by it. Death cannot kill what never dies. . . . If absence be not death, neither is theirs. Death is but crossing the world, as friends do the seas; they live in one another still——" How I wish I could remember all of it! I must look it up again. . . . And do you know who first showed me that? Your Father.'

There was a long pause, as we both looked up at the painting. Something very strange was happening to me, I found; a kind of hypnotic effect. For the first time, I seemed to be seeing it through Sarah's eyes. Was she willing this? The face on the canvas didn't exactly change, but it presented a different expression. As I examined it, feature by feature, the mouth looked to me more flexible, the eyes deepened. Wasn't there, after all, a certain humour in them, as Sarah had claimed?

'I think,' said Sarah reflectively, 'that that's a much better picture than most people realize. It may seem a little cold and official, at first glance. But the painter caught something, underneath. . . . You know, sometimes, when I look at it for a long while, it seems to me as if the real man were hidden inside it? It's as if he didn't wish everybody to see behind the outward appearance. Only those who loved him——'

'You loved him, didn't you, Aunt Sarah?' I had said it without thinking. There was such a sense of rapport between us at this moment that the question didn't even seem particularly personal. But it startled me, after I'd asked it. And I added, awkwardly and apologetically: 'It's funny—I've never asked you that before.'

'Yes, I loved him, Stephen,' Sarah answered simply. 'Very much. I never loved anyone else.'

'I always knew that, I guess. . . . Did he know?'

'Yes, I think so. We never spoke of it, of course.' Sarah

hesitated a moment, then she continued: 'Stephen dearest, since we are talking of this, there is one thing I want you to be quite sure of. Never was there any doubt in his own mind that your dear Mother was the one he loved—I am certain of that. And, even if he had never met her, I am sure that he would never have felt otherwise than he did——'

Sarah didn't add 'about me'; but it was obvious what she meant. There was something so touchingly young and innocent about her at this moment that it made my eyes fill with tears.

'You can't be sure of that, Aunt Sarah. And, who knows? He might have been a lot happier, if——'

'Hush, Stephen! We must never think that. Never once did he give me the smallest reason to imagine—— And then, your darling Mother was like a sister to me. There couldn't possibly have been any question of jealousy between us. I put the thought completely out of my mind——'

'And my Mother? Did she know?'

'No. Oh no, I'm sure she didn't. She was a very dear, trustful person. She thought of me always as her friend, with absolute faith. Even if she had been told—I mean, if there *had* been anything to tell—she simply wouldn't have believed it.'

'But, all those years you were together—— It must have been terribly hard for you?'

'It wasn't. Not after the first. When one really loves, these situations have a way of solving themselves, I think.'

'I guess I've never really loved anybody. Not like that. I don't believe I have it in me.'

'Oh, but you will, Stephen dearest! I'm sure you will, one day. And then you'll know what I mean. There's no question of asking more than the other person is able to give. One's so grateful for what one has.'

'You know, Aunt Sarah, as long as I've known you, I've never once heard you complain about anything to do with yourself?'

'But why in the world should I complain, Stephen? I have such an enviable life. I often wonder if it isn't downright selfish of me to be so happy with all my interests and concerns, seeing that most of them arise out of other people's troubles. But I can't help it. There's so much to do and see and know, and people are so good to me. You, above all——'

'I wish you could teach me to live like that.'

'I don't think it's something that one person can teach another. Each of us has such different problems. But you'll find your own way, Stephen. Whatever you do, wherever you go—in the end it'll be all right.'

'That's what I've often noticed. You worry about all kinds of things, but you never seem to, about me. Why don't you?'

'Why should I worry, Stephen? Whatever you do, you'll be guided. I know that.'

'I don't understand. How do you know?'

'I just know,' Sarah told me, smiling. 'Believe me.'

'But *how* do you know?' I insisted.

'I'm afraid I can't tell you that, exactly, Stephen dear. It isn't the kind of thing one can explain in so many words. But I'm quite, quite sure.'

It was then, suddenly and for the merest fraction of an instant, that I saw, or thought I saw, what Gerda had seen. There was something about the smiling little woman, at that moment; something that wasn't the Sarah I'd known. That wasn't Sarah at all. The look in her eyes wasn't hers. I had an uncanny feeling —it was very close to fear—that I was somehow 'in the presence' —but of what? The whatever-it-was behind Sarah's eyes looked out at me through them, as if through the eyeholes in a mask. And its look meant: Yes, I am always here.

I wanted to ask, 'What are you?' but I couldn't. I didn't dare admit that I had seen what I'd seen. That would be getting in too deep. The whatever-it-was was so vast that I daren't let myself go toward it. And, already, the instant had passed—

before the clock could tick or the dust-motes move in the shaft of sunlight from the window. Sarah was just Sarah again, and everything was as usual. From the kitchen, we could hear Saul barking. 'My lands,' Sarah exclaimed, 'that must be the plumber!'

'I'd better go up and pack my bag,' I said. 'It's getting late.'

When the taxi arrived, Saul got so furiously excited that Sarah had to hold him. This gave me a moment alone with Gerda, the only one I'd had that morning. She came close to the taxi window and took my hand in both of hers. Her eyes were full of tears. 'Goodbye, my dear friend,' she whispered.

'Goodbye, Gerda. Come safe to Peter.'

As we drove away, I found that I was crying, too. I looked back and saw the house, and Gerda waving, and Sarah doing her best to wave, with Saul barking in her arms.

'Maybe this is the last time——' I said to myself. But that was just a lot of melodramatic nonsense. I didn't really believe it for a moment. And, by the time we got to the station, I was feeling fine.

THREE

'SO Sarah doesn't know yet?' Jane asked.
This was the next day, in New York. Jane and I had met
—for the first time since our divorce—to have cocktails and
lunch at a hotel on Central Park; and I had just finished
telling her about the civilian ambulance unit in which I'd
enlisted as a driver, to go to North Africa.

'I simply couldn't tell Sarah,' I said. 'I meant to, while I was
down at Tawelfan. I told Gerda—the German girl. But Sarah
would have gotten so upset. I couldn't face that. I'll write her
about it just before I leave.'

'When'll that be?'

'Quite soon, I guess. It depends on convoys, or something.
We have to be ready all the time. We only get twenty-four
hours' notice.'

'How thrilling that sounds! Only I wish it wasn't you that was
going. Oh, damn this War! I did hope you'd be sticking around
for a while. I want to see you in your uniform.'

'It's just a uniform.'

'I'm sure you look cute in it.'

'Well, thanks,' I grinned. 'You aren't looking any too repulsive
yourself, right now.'

Jane smiled vaguely, as she always did when she had been
flattered. She was a shade plumper—in a few years, she would
have to watch her figure—but, at present, it suited her. In
California she had gotten a tense, even, at times, an almost hag-
gard expression. Now her face had smoothed out. That wonderful skin of hers was in full bloom; and, of course, she was
dressed exactly right, as usual.

'How does Roger look in *his* uniform?' I asked.

'Fine,' Jane said. Then she added quickly and rather defensively: 'But they won't let him go overseas. There's something lined up for him in Washington. Pretty important.'

'Intelligence?'

'Well—no. It's something to do with Army supplies. Clothing and equipment and so forth. Roger understands all that, because of his business. He's awfully good at organizing things.' Jane gave a nervous little laugh. 'I suppose somebody has to.'

'Of course. And that means you'll be able to be with him. That's swell. When are you two getting married?'

'Oh, soon.' Jane gave me a quick look. 'Does it make you jealous, talking about him?'

'Maybe just a little,' I said politely, feeling so wonderfully thankful that it didn't.

'I think that's sweet of you.' Jane squeezed up her nose. 'I want Roger to be jealous of you, too. In moderation, of course. No knives. Nothing Latin.'

'And how does your family feel about Roger?'

'Wildly in favour. Dad'll probably take him into the firm, after the War. Make him a partner. You know, we've known each other ever since we were six? I told you that, didn't I? Childhood sweethearts find each other at long last, is how they see it.'

'And how do *you* see it Jane?' I asked, in a tone inviting confidences.

Jane looked down at her hand, and its engagement-ring. 'I'm all set to make a go of it this time, Steve. I've just got to.'

'I want you to. You know that, don't you?'

'Sure, I know that.'

'And I'm certain Roger's going to be a lot less difficult than I was.'

'Oh, I wouldn't say that. He's got a will of his own. I found that out when we were teen-agers.'

'Did you and he ever——?'

'Mercy, no! Nothing more than kisses at proms. Roger was a good boy. He had principles. He was always accusing me of being too wild. We fought, mostly. But the point is, I've learned an awful lot. He's never going to know how much he owes to you.'

'No—don't you ever tell him. If you want it to stick.'

'I won't.' Jane finished her drink, and sat looking at me. Her eyes were shining, the way they did when she was starting to get high. 'Oh, Steve,' she said, 'why did you and I have to make such a mess of it?'

'You got my letter? I went into all that—or as much as I can understand.'

'It was a beautiful letter. And I agreed with most of it. Only— you don't know everything. . . . There's one bit I think I ought to tell you.'

'What's that?'

Jane giggled. 'It's—kind of embarrassing. I couldn't write it. That's why I never answered yours. I'm no good at writing things, like you are. I could only tell you to your face. . . . These cocktails are good, aren't they?'

'I'll say!'

'How many of them have we had?'

'Four, I think. Or is it five?'

'Well, let's have another. I need support, if I'm going to tell you this. I wish I could do it in the dark.'

'Shut your eyes, why don't you?'

I ordered the cocktails. When the waiter had brought them, Jane continued: 'I know I'm going to be sorry I told you this. But I don't care. Only, don't look at me until I've finished. Look out the window——' She took a big gulp of her cocktail. 'You see, when I read that letter of yours, I realized, more than ever, that you'd never understood how I was feeling. All that time we were at St. Luc, I mean. You never understood the one thing that stuck out a mile You don't even realize it now.'

'What don't I realize?'

'That I was in love with you, you dope.'

'Oh, Jane—no!'

'I *was*. . . . Steve, I told you not to look at me! That's better. . . . Anyone but you would have known it. All the others did.'

'But you always acted so uninterested. I mean—beyond a certain point.'

'Wouldn't you have, in my place? Look—I liked *you*. And you actually wanted to marry *me*—only it was all for the wrong reasons. I didn't want you to want me just because you were lonely. I hoped, if I waited, you'd feel differently. So naturally I had to play hard to get. And the fact that we were sleeping together made it just that much more difficult. . . . Well, then I found I was pregnant. I'll never know how that happened. I thought I was being so careful. And it looked so damn' much like a trap I'd set for you—a real lousy bitch trick. At first I thought I wouldn't tell you at all. Just clear out and get rid of the baby. And then I thought, "Hell, no, I'll see how he takes it." And you were so terribly sweet about it. When you said, "Can't we get married tonight?" I *really* loved you—and, what's more, like an idiot, I began to think maybe you'd started to like me, too. I mean, in the way I wanted——'

'Oh, Jesus! I certainly fouled things up.'

'No, Steve! Please don't think that. I'm not telling you this to make you feel like a heel. You were right, in your letter. It would never have worked, anyhow. You were never in love with me, properly. And I—well, that was just a kind of crush——'

'You mean, it didn't last long?'

Jane smiled at me teasingly: 'Would you like me to be carrying a torch, Steve? I'll bet you would! You're a pretty conceited bastard. Well, even if I was, I wouldn't tell you. So you'll never know.'

'I'll never know,' I said. 'That suits me. I can imagine things.'

'You *are* sweet, you know. To look at you, no one would ever think you could be so mean. Well, that goes for me too, I guess. . . . What made us be so mean to each other? Was it obstinacy, or vanity, or both?'

'Both.'

'Yes, I suppose so. Did you think I was the biggest tramp in creation?'

'No, Jane. Not the biggest.'

Jane laughed loud enough to make the people at the next table turn their heads in our direction. 'Steve, you bastard! Don't you dare talk to me like that! No—seriously, though, how much did you know about me?'

'It depends what you mean by "know." I didn't have you followed by any detectives. But I got a kind of rough idea.'

'Oh, I knew *all* about you! Let's see—there was Gloria, and Lois, and Yvette—you certainly picked them with the cutest names.'

'Jane! How in the world did you——?'

'Well, you see, some of the boys I ran around with knew them, too. And they thought that if they told me I'd be—grateful.'

'And I took all that trouble, being so discreet!'

'I know—always in the afternoons. You told me you were going to steam-baths.'

'I actually did, sometimes.'

'Well, as far as I was concerned, I'd like you to know that it happened much less often than you probably imagined. A lot of times, I just let you *think* it was happening. . . . And as for that evening at the Novotny's——'

'Do we have to dig that up?'

'Yes, Steve. Because I want to tell you something. You were more or less right—what you wrote in your letter about my general attitude. I guess I did want to bring things to a climax, like you said. I wasn't enjoying our marriage any more than you were. But I didn't up and create a scandal deliberately. It didn't happen that way, at all.'

'Then what did happen?'

'Well, Roy Griffin and I were both fairly high, and we walked out into the garden to get some air. And then we were standing by the doll's house and Roy said, "Let's try if we can get inside." You know how I am about any kind of a dare? And, of course, Roy *is* attractive—though I wasn't specially interested in that. When we did get in, it was terribly uncomfortable. I immediately wanted out. But then Roy started to make love —to coin a phrase. I told him to stop but he wouldn't, so I let him, because I didn't want my clothes torn to shreds—yes, Stephen Monk, you may well hang your guilty head! You know, Roy was trying to prove something. That's what made him so rough——'

'What was he trying to prove?'

'Oh, what a big he-man he was. Because, actually, he's half and half. You must have realized that, didn't you?'

'I'll say I did! In fact, one of the things that made me so mad was that he'd practically made a pass at *me*, only a couple of evenings before.'

'He *did*? You know, somehow I kind of suspected that? But you weren't interested?'

'No—of course not.'

'What do you mean, *of course*? Listen, Steve, you don't have to pretend, with me. I've seen you look at fellows in that certain way, now and then——'

'Well, if I did, it was only sort of theoretical.'

'You know, maybe you should have tried being one. You might have been a whole lot happier, that way.'

'I doubt it. It takes so much character—much more than I've got—to be a good one. And I can't stand the other kind.'

'Well, you know your own business best. . . . But, let me tell you, when you banged on that doll's house roof, little Roy very nearly had a heart attack.'

'Ha, ha, did he?'

'I don't know if he thought it was the Vice Squad, or Sid Novotny, or what. *I* knew it was you, at once. And I told him so. I told him you'd probably come around to his house and tear him apart. I told him you once fought a duel with a man in Greece and shot him down dead like a dog.'

'Oh, Jane, you didn't!'

'I most certainly did! I don't believe he slept at his place for a month, after that. He kept staying around with friends. Or so I heard.'

'You never saw him again?'

Jane shook her head. 'Never saw any of them again. Never wrote any of them, either, after I left. . . . All of that time seems awfully far away, now. And it'll seem even farther, when I'm married to Roger.'

'Are you going to miss it?'

'No—not really. Not too much. You know, Steve, I got an awful scare, when you and I split up? I saw how I'd very nearly turned into a real tramp. Remember Shirley, at St. Luc? She's a tramp now. She went off with some band-leader, and he ditched her. She had a terrible fight with her folks. They won't even talk about her. I never, never want to be like that. I'm playing it safe, from now on. As far as I'm concerned, those days are over for good.'

'You'd better just forget they ever happened.'

'Oh, but I don't want to. Not altogether. The worst of it is, I can't talk about them to Roger. And I can't have him meet people who knew me then. I can't trust them. All except for you, Steve.'

'You can trust me.'

'Sure. I know I can. That's why we've got to be great friends— so we can talk about the old days, sometimes. . . . I'll tell you a very strange thing. Do you know who I keep thinking about so often, now? Elizabeth.'

'Elizabeth? But you never even met her!'

'I know. But I feel almost as if I had. I feel as if I met her in you, somehow. I got all of her books from the library and read them, last year, trying to get to know her better. I didn't understand parts of them, but I think they're just terrific. Why didn't you ever tell me more about her?'

'You never seemed to want me to.'

'Maybe I didn't, then. I was jealous of her, I guess. . . . You know, Steve, there was something about you I never could quite understand. Something glamorous and kind of strange. Perhaps it was really what made me fall for you. And that came from Elizabeth, didn't it? You got it from being with her.'

'I suppose I must have.'

'Well—this'll make you laugh—but I *know* Roger feels the same thing about me. I got it from you. Elizabeth gave it to you, and you gave it to me. It's a sort of background. . . . Of course, Roger doesn't care much about books, or any of that. But he likes it that I have this thing. He kind of thinks of me as an authority. He thinks you and I talked about those things, and that now I know. . . . Oh, he's sweet, Steve! You must be awfully nice to him. He does so love it when people are what he calls unusual. It's his kind of romance. So I want us all to be friends.'

'I hope we will be.'

'Oh, if only you weren't going off to this War! We'll keep in touch, won't we? I'll worry about you a lot. But you're not going to get killed. I know that. I refuse to allow any of my friends to get killed. . . . What'll you do when it's over?'

'All sorts of things. I'm not making any plans, though.'

'You know, Steve, I have the most wonderful feeling about you? That you're starting a new sort of life. And now everything's going to be fun and exciting for you. And you won't ever get dreary and scared any more, like you used to.'

'That's what I think too, Jane.'

'Even if it's bad for you, sometimes, in the War, it won't be the same kind of bad. It'll be wonderful, too. I really envy you. . . . Oh, Steve darling, I do feel so very good about you and me and Roger and everything!'

'It's these cocktails.'

'I know it! They're just loaded with faith, hope and charity. I think the bartender must be a saint in disguise. Another one of these, and I'll even forgive Hitler.'

'I'll even forgive myself. As a matter of fact, I just have. Do you know something, Jane,' I said, as I emptied my glass, 'I really do forgive myself, from the bottom of my heart?'